A wave of terror has swept through the Empire and Chaos is on the move. Mutations are increasing and strange creatures roam the streets at night. Some say it is the end of the world whilst others say it is the beginning of a new order! Against this backdrop of terror, battlefield looter Angelika Fleischer meets up with a group of pilgrims heading for a remote abbey in the dangerous Blackfire Pass. Dogged by goblin attacks and an unknown killer in their midst, they journey together to see a renowned priestess of Shallya, whose touch is said to cure all ills. But with Empire forces and the hordes of Chaos converging on their destination, Angelika uncovers a dark secret that could cost her her life.

A WARHAMMER NOVEL

# SACRED FLESH

## ROBIN D LAWS

*To Frank Mansfield*

**A BLACK LIBRARY PUBLICATION**

First published in Great Britain in 2004 by
BL Publishing,
Games Workshop Ltd.,
Willow Road, Nottingham,
NG7 2WS, UK

10 9 8 7 6 5 4 3 2 1

Cover illustration by Geoff Taylor.
Map by Nuala Kennedy.

A CIP record for this book is available from the British Library

ISBN 1 84416 091 2

Distributed in the US by Simon & Schuster
1230 Avenue of the Americas, New York, NY 10020, US.

Printed and bound in Great Britain by
Bookmarque, Surrey, UK.

See the Black Library on the Internet at
**www.blacklibrary.com**

Find out more about Games Workshop
and the world of Warhammer at
**www.games-workshop.com**

THIS IS A DARK age, a bloody age, an age of daemons and of sorcery. It is an age of battle and death, and of the world's ending. Amidst all of the fire, flame and fury it is a time, too, of mighty heroes, of bold deeds and great courage.

AT THE HEART of the Old World sprawls the Empire, the largest and most powerful of the human realms. Known for its engineers, sorcerers, traders and soldiers, it is a land of great mountains, mighty rivers, dark forests and vast cities. And from his throne in Altdorf reigns the Emperor Karl-Franz, sacred descendent of the founder of these lands, Sigmar, and wielder of his magical warhammer.

BUT THESE ARE far from civilised times. Across the length and breadth of the Old World, from the knightly palaces of Bretonnia to ice-bound Kislev in the far north, come rumblings of war. In the towering World's Edge Mountains, the orc tribes are gathering for another assault. Bandits and renegades harry the wild southern lands of the Border Princes. There are rumours of rat-things, the skaven, emerging from the sewers and swamps across the land. And from the northern wilder-nesses there is the ever-present threat of Chaos, of daemons and beastmen corrupted by the foul powers of the Dark Gods. As the time of battle draws ever near, the Empire needs heroes like never before.

# CHAPTER ONE

THE ORC'S LANCE, its head jagged and rusty, ripped through the man's golden-breasted tunic, searching for his kidneys. It found the gap between the front and back plates of his cuirass. Grunting in surprise and alarm, the man stepped back, hoping to slip free. The orc twisted the weapon, digging the toothy notches of his spearhead into his victim's flesh. The man groaned; his left ankle twisted beneath him. The orc withdrew the spear, now freshly crimsoned.

Exertion had reddened the flesh of the man's face. Middle age had taken its toll on him: the beginnings of a double chin hung from his once-handsome jawline. His grey hair was flattened to his temples with sweat. A bony brow hooded his dark and intelligent eyes. His outfit, now marked with dark Blackfire soil and a spreading patch of his own blood, proclaimed his identity as a former officer in the army of Nuln. The breast of his sleeveless over-tunic was the colour of the summer sun, slashed to reveal the jet-black fabric of a second shirt beneath it. Looping braids of scarlet silk decorated the cuffs of the man's sleeves – an affectation common among proud ex-officers. He regained his footing and slashed wide with his sabre. It landed on the orc's shoulder, hitting the crudely quilted pauldron and slashing open its leather outer layer. Straw and feathers showered into the cold morning air.

The orc was actually six and a half feet tall, but it stood in the crouching posture typical of a rampaging greenskin, and thus seemed to have only a head's worth of height advantage on its opponent. Its face alone had to be two feet long, most of it misshapen, osseous jaw. Yellow, uneven tusks lined its mouth. Its eyes were beady red pinpricks. Taut, rocky muscles shifted under tight, shiny skin, mottled in a range of hues from olive to emerald. It wore piecemeal armour: a layer of loose chain cocooned its chest, with bits of scavenged, hammered-out human armour attached to it with loops of wire. Leather guards covered its arms and its left leg. The right was bare, except for a thick, mouldering bandage swaddled around the creature's knee.

The orc pulled its spear back for another thrust, but the old campaigner spanked it easily aside with the flat of his sabre blade. The orc bellowed out a thwarted groan and dropped its spear. From

a scabbard at each hip, it jerked loose a pair of serrated, crescent-shaped daggers. It lunged.

Its target – the old campaigner – fought on,
defending a knot of terrified fellow humans. They
huddled together, wedged between a large wooden
cart, sprung from its axle, and an outcrop of sharp-
edged, barren rock.

Others fought alongside the man of Nuln. To his
left, a short, slim man with a round, bald face
waited in a defensive stance. He traded ineffective,
testing swipes with an orc opponent of his own. To
the campaigner's right, a pudgy man perspired
through a face padded in baby fat. He thrusted a
hayfork at a one-eyed greenskin that had a human
femur stuck in its belt. The fourth defender was tall
and gnarled. His head was topped with a flat brush
of hair and he held the handle of an oaken cudgel
in his knobbly fist. He poked it confidently out at a
runtish orc, keeping up a constant patter of salty
taunts. The orc, uncomprehending, darted at him.
The gnarled man jerked back, his display of bravado
spoiled.

The grunts of the defenders and the expectant,
sibilant hisses of the foamy-lipped orcs found echoing surfaces amid rocky slopes to the east and west.
They were battling in one of the narrower points of
the Blackfire Pass, the strategic fissure inside the
Black Mountain range, which separated the Empire
of men from the wild and hostile lands to the south.
Dark peaks imposed themselves all around the battling figures, their lower reaches strangled by twisted
pines, their frozen pinnacles hooded in ice and

snow. Rain and dew dampened the ground beneath the skirmishers' feet before they turned to frost. When they stepped, the battlers slid in frigid mud.

The smallest of the orcs, the one who fought the gnarled man, slipped in the muck. The runt bleated as he fell on the flat of his long, needle-like blade. The gnarled man took swift advantage, leaping forward to bash repeatedly at the orc's head. The creature's face bounced up and down as the cudgel smacked into its helmet, building a dent in it.

Across the narrow flat of the pass, two figures, sprawled out on their stomachs, surveyed the scene. They were concealed from both sides by the rotting trunk of a fallen pine.

'See?' said Angelika Fleischer. 'No altruism's required here. They've got things well in hand.'

'Only the smallest of the orcs is down,' observed her companion, Franziskus.

Angelika Fleischer was a long, scrawny woman of young but indeterminate age. Her cheekbones were high, her nose slim and narrow, her chin a little pointed. A dark mop of ragged hair covered her head. A cracked leather coat clung close to her lithe frame, drawing tight across her shoulder blades, yielding to each protruding vertebra. Below it she wore a sooty tunic that extended below her belt, forming a bit of a skirt. That added a second layer of fabric to her meatless buttocks. Black leggings and long leather boots completed her field attire. A long dagger waited for her in its home at her belt; its twin did the same hidden in the cuff of her boot.

She kept her glittering eyes fixed on the unfolding skirmish. The black pools of her irises were indistinguishable from the depths of her pupils.

In an expression already familiar to her, Franziskus furrowed down the fine lines of his aristocratic face, pressing his blond, scarcely visible eyebrows near to one another. At the same time he formed a pout with his pale lips. Blue morning light heightened the azure of his eyes. His mane of flaxen hair had not seen water in many days, so it hung sullenly around his head and shoulders, deprived of its full glory. He had carefully arranged himself so that he was entirely covered by his elk-hide cloak, a recent and extravagant purchase. It was collared in soft and rusty fox-fur. Beneath the cloak he wore a nondescript white cotton shift and brown cotton trousers. Flat-soled, low-cut boots shod his narrow feet.

'That may be so,' said Angelika. 'But you know my policy. I don't intervene in a fight till it's over – and then I only do so to profit from its leavings.'

The small orc bounced up from the sodden ground and, apparently unfazed by the dozen or so vicious cudgel blows its cranium had sustained, lunged at the gnarled man, hissing phlegm at him. The orc chewed the man's ankle as the man waved frantic arms, working to maintain his balance. Arse-first, the man went down. The orc crawled up his leg. The man kicked it in the face.

Meanwhile, the other three men traded blows with the other three orcs, clanging sword against sword or landing ineffectual blows against armour.

'We must act. Virtue commands it,' said Franziskus, wriggling forward to improve his viewing angle. 'There are women, there, among the pilgrims.'

'There is a woman here,' replied Angelika, hiking a thumb at herself, 'and she's fought more than enough orcs for one lifetime.' She positioned herself for a better look. 'What makes you say they're pilgrims?'

'Why else would ordinary folk come so far down the pass?'

Angelika saw a flash of silver on the ample bosom of one robed woman, but could not identify her jewellery with any precision. 'Silver?' she said, unable to suppress a note of rising interest.

'If they are pilgrims, we have a religious duty to assist them,' said Franziskus.

'To hell with gods, and those who follow them.'

Franziskus's hand fidgeted on the scabbard of his sabre.

The small orc gnawed on the gnarled man's knee. The man slammed the burl of his cudgel into the left side of its skull. The orc's eye popped from its socket. With the heel of his kicking boot, the man ground it to paste. The stunted orc screamed. The man deftly flipped his cudgel, so that the handle pointed outwards, and jammed it into the orc's mouth, breaking through a wall of tusky teeth. He rammed the handle down deeper, navigating it into the orc's gullet. He was choking the creature. Arms twitching, hands flailing, the orc helplessly slapped wet ground. The man persisted. The orc quivered.

Gore erupted from its mouth, coating the cudgel and the knotty hands that held it. The man pushed it further in. The orc went limp. The man slid his weapon free of his suffocated enemy. The orc flopped onto the ground.

'As I said,' said Angelika. 'Well in hand.'

Whip-quick, the big orc snaked out its hand, grabbed the ex-officer by the wrist and, in a single quick and brutal motion, snapped it back. The dull crack of popping bones reverberated through the pass. The sabre fell uselessly from the campaigner's hand and splashed into a shallow puddle. The orc stabbed down with the curved dagger in its free hand, digging it into the flesh between his prey's neck and clavicle.

Franziskus said, 'This cannot be borne.'

He heaved himself out from behind the fallen log. Inarticulately hollering, he drew his sabre, waveing both it and his free arm over his head. At first, Angelika thought he had gone completely and utterly mad, but then understood his intent: he was trying to draw the attention of the orcs away from the pilgrims.

All heads, man and greenskin alike, swivelled toward the shrieking madman bounding at them. The short, bald man recovered first: he opened a gash on his opponent's knee with the edge of his sword. The rotund fellow with the hayfork was the slowest to regain his wits. His orc punished him with a helmeted head-butt to the forehead. He staggered back. The one-eyed orc swerved around him to get at the shaking, moaning huddle of pilgrims.

The pudgy man spun and launched himself at the orc. He wrapped himself around the marauder's waist, using his considerable weight to bring it down. He bounced on the small of its back, pinning it to the earth.

The big orc had the campaigner on his knees, pushing him off his blade. It raised its arm for another blow. The gnarled old man leapt into him, banging shoulders, before bouncing off and sliding into the mud. He grabbed at the orc's leg. The big orc stomped down at his head, but the old salt rolled from the path of the blow.

A man in an elaborately embroidered robe broke from the huddle of pilgrims to grab the campaigner's shoulders and drag him away from the big orc. The campaigner protested, blood bubbling from his mouth. The fancy-robed man dragged him anyway.

The big orc landed a kick to the gnarled pilgrim's gut. The man doubled up at its feet. The orc raised its curved knife, looked down at the man then seemed to reconsider. Instead it plunged into the mass of helpless pilgrims. It seized the nearest of them: a portly woman covering her hair with an intricately folded sister's wimple. Grabbing her habit by the neck and waist, the orc heaved her over its head, howling in sadistic triumph. She yowled her terror in a surprisingly deep contralto voice.

Franziskus arrived, circuiting around a maze of mostly-prone combatants. He grunted out a challenge to the big orc, demanding that it turn and fight. The orc dropped the woman; pilgrims surged up to break her fall. She fell into them, making a tangle of limbs and torsos.

Franziskus hacked up at the creature's neck, but it turned, and he hit only the shoulder piece of its armour. It dangled over the orc's chest, its strap severed. Franziskus slashed the orc again. The blade made a metallic banging noise as it made joint-wrenching contact with a solid chunk of breastplate.

'Someone help me!' Franziskus cried. 'It'll take more than one to put this monster down!'

The pudgy pilgrim bounced on top of his writhing orc and shrugged. The man in the embroidered robe looked abashedly away. The gnarled man staggered, crouching, looking for his dropped cudgel. The big orc sliced the air under Franziskus's nose with its crescent blade. Franziskus jogged backwards, slipping on slick grass. He aimed an ill-balanced blow at the orc and swung wide. He'd only recently switched from a duelling rapier to a heavier blade, and had yet to master the new weapon.

Angelika shook her head and rolled her eyes. Keeping her head low, she crept into the melee. She sidled up to the fat pilgrim sitting on the orc. She had her dagger out. 'Grab its head up,' she told the man. He stared at her uncomprehendingly. 'Grab its head up!' she repeated.

Franziskus ducked another of the big orc's blows.

The fat man grabbed his orc's head and pulled it up, exposing its neck to Angelika. With the point of her dagger, she sawed a long incision in the green-skin's throat, opening it up. Gore flooded out like water through a bursting dam.

Angelika pointed to the fallen campaigner's sabre, which lay in the muck a few yards from the fat man's sausage-shaped fingers. 'Take that and join the fight!' she commanded.

The pudgy pilgrim's mouth dropped open.

Angelika slapped him on the back of the head. 'Join the fight!' she repeated, louder.

Jowls jiggling, he stumbled over to the sabre, hefted it in his hand, and reluctantly edged to Franziskus's side. The orc pushed through them, heading away from the pilgrims and toward his spear. Franziskus rang his sabre on the greenskin's helmet. The orc seemed to totter for a moment, then it plucked up its spear and wheeled on them, charging.

'Trip him!' Angelika cried, climbing up the side of the cart, her nimble feet perched on one of its wheels.

Franziskus nodded and slid on his knees through the mud, hitting the greenskin's legs with his shoulder. The orc toppled onto him. The gnarled man, cudgel now ready, gripped it in both hands and bowled the helmet, croquet-style, from the big orc's head.

Now on the roof of the cart, Angelika got down on one knee and intently studied the fight between the small bald man and his orc. Each still danced around the other, with no sign of a serious blow on either side. Angelika held her dagger by the blade, between thumb and forefinger, waiting. She studied the slight man's movements. He anticipated the orc's feints skilfully, ducking under certain blows, sidestepping others.

Franziskus still lay beneath the big orc. It bit down at his face, blowing rancid breath at him. Franziskus tightened his gorge, suppressing the urge to vomit. It would be ignominious to die choking on his own puke, trapped beneath an orc.

Angelika finally saw what she'd been hoping to see: she'd discerned the pattern in the slight defender's manoeuvrings. She counted under her breath. She threw her dagger. On schedule, the man ducked under an aimlessly swung orcish sword. Angelika's dagger flew past him towards its intended target: the orc's eye socket. The man pivoted, squinted at her, and stepped back. The blow killed the orc instantly. Its body collapsed straight as a plank into soggy grass.

'Get that orc off him!' shouted Angelika, pointing at Franziskus. The gnarled man and the fat man stood to either side of the big orc, and exchanged helpless looks. The orc raised itself to its knees and shot its bandaged knee into Franziskus's crotch. Franziskus gave out an airless, choking groan.

The small man leapt over his slain greenskin, his sword raised over his head, and slid into the big orc. The pudgy man scrambled out of his way, but mud squirted out beneath his sandaled feet, and he thumped to earth. The small fellow chopped his sword down on the big orc's neck. It moved its shoulder to catch the brunt of the blow, its armour shedding broken links of chain. It pushed itself off Franziskus, kneeing him in the gut as a parting gesture, then stomped at the small man, wrapping muscular gloved fingers around his throat.

Franziskus found the grip of his sabre and rammed the weapon's razor tip into the gap between the orc's thigh and codpiece. He felt it find purchase and pushed. It screamed like a gored ox. Franziskus scrabbled to his knees, using the force of the move to push harder on the sabre. The orc reached down and grabbed the sabre blade, howling and yanking it free. It had turned its attention away from the slight man, who now stood with his arm levered back, searching for the best spot to plant a jab.

'You two!' Angelika shouted, waving at the pudgy man and the gnarled man. 'Get in there! Outflank it!' The gnarled man met her eyes, gripped his cudgel tighter, and waded in. The pudgy man reached down for the downed soldier's sword and did the same. The big orc now stood surrounded, an opponent at each of the four compass points. It snarled, allowing a gob of gluey sputum to escape from its toothy jaw, then caught the hefty man in the side of the head with the point of its elbow. The man collapsed to one knee; the big orc pushed past him, turned on its heels, and commenced to back away from the fray, swiping the air with its curved dagger.

The gnarled man took a step forward. 'No!' Angelika cried. 'It's leaving – let it go!'

The gnarled man took a step back. Its gargoyle features snarled up in purest hate, the big orc continued its withdrawal. It backed away for another hundred feet, then turned and trotted into the trackless pines. Soon it was gone from sight, though the sound of its crashing through the bush resounded for several minutes thereafter.

Angelika crawled down from the cart and made her way to the injured officer. She tore open the remains of his tunic and, with cold and delicate fingers, worked free the damp leather straps of his cuirass, teasing them from their buckles. She pulled the front breastplate free of the quilted padding beneath it. The quilting was soaked through with fresh, bright blood. Angelika pulled her second dagger from her boot and tore through the quilting. She winced, failing to contain her disgust: the orc's serrated spearhead had torn a sizeable hole in the man's side, churning skin, muscle, fat and organs into a glistening, gobbety mess.

Pilgrims gathered tight around her. She stretched out an arm and pushed them back. 'Give us room!' she demanded. She looked up at them. They were all slack-jawed to varying degrees, vacantly staring at their fallen defender. They showed all the intelligence of a flock of chickens. It was the shock of events, Angelika told herself. 'Can anyone here dress a wound?'

A young man dully blinked. 'I am a physic,' he said. He shook his head, as if to clear it of cobwebs, then straightened the set of his shoulders, adopting a demeanour of sudden authority. 'My name is Victor Rausch,' he said to Angelika, his eyes firmly on his patient. Atop his head roosted a pillbox hat, quilted in turquoise silk and chased with copper-coloured threads. He wore a curiously tailored robe of crushed blue velvet, which was cut like a doublet above the waist; it clung flatteringly to his well-developed pectorals. From the waist down, it flared out like a robe, pulling away from tawny leggings and a pair of pointy-toed boots, their leather dyed the colour of honey.

He knelt over the wounded man, arranging his handsome, open face into an expression of high concern. 'Someone please fetch my bag!' he cried.

Immediately the short, bald man with the nut-coloured complexion appeared, lowering the bag into his hand. Victor snapped open its brass clasps and gazed forlornly into its interior. He dropped his voice. 'Truth be told, in my home village I am more a dispenser of draughts and potions than a sawyer of bone and flesh. He is badly mangled. I am not sure what I can–'

The wounded man's eyes popped open. Victor started back. The pilgrims gasped. Victor stammered. 'Thomas! I did not realise…'

The ex-officer coughed up blood. 'You say I'm badly mangled?' He worked his lips silently, waiting to recoup his breath. 'No need to mince words, ' he gurgled. 'I myself am minced enough.'

Angelika touched the physic's arm. 'You must at least have bandages, and a draught to dull his pain.'

'Don't waste them on me,' the wounded man mumbled, his voice fading.

Victor planted a hand on his forehead. 'We've faced many hardships on our journey to this awful place. My supplies are now all but expended.'

Angelika's shoulders tightened. 'But you do have them, yes?'

Victor nodded.

'Then use them.'

The wounded man panted and looked up at Angelika. 'What's your name, girl? Mine is Thomas Krieger.'

Angelika decided to forgive the old officer his use of the word *girl*; he was, after all, already mortally wounded.

'I'm Angelika Fleischer. My companion here...' she glanced around for Franziskus, but he was hanging back from the herd. 'My companion is Franziskus. No surname, I'm afraid. He seems to have lost that shortly before I met him, and never recovered it.'

A sardonic smile began on Thomas's lips, but it pained him. He clenched his teeth and squinted, pressing solitary tears from the corner of each eye. 'Thank you for helping us.'

'It was his idea,' she said.

'I won't be going on from here. The young physic's right. The first aid must be spared for those who might be saved by it.'

'You don't want to be one of those supremely annoying self-sacrificing types, do you?' She turned to Rausch. 'Patch him up.'

The physic looked at Thomas; he looked at Angelika. He gulped. He reached into his bag and streamed out a length of cotton.

'It's a gut wound,' Angelika said, once more addressing the dying officer. 'You might linger a long time. It won't do these frightened souls any good to watch you suffer and squirm. So the physic's going to truss you tight and dispatch you off to dreamland. Unless you're so anxious to save on bandages that you're willing to let one of these people finish you…'

The pilgrims muttered and shifted.

'I would not ask it of them,' Thomas said.

'Then get to work,' she told the physic, thumping him on the back, and rising to her feet. She strode idly to the bodies of the three orcs and kicked at them. It was a first principle of her profession that orcs never had anything good on them, so she did not bother to remove their boots or open their rancid packs. She did, however, yank her dagger from the orcish skull where it had taken up temporary residence.

She bent to pick up a leaf, using it to wipe sticky clumps of brain from the blade. A more thorough cleaning could wait for later.

The matronly woman who'd been hoisted up by the big orc hung back until Angelika's gruesome task was done. Then she tugged at Angelika's coat. 'I must echo the words of our guardian, Thomas, and thank you, and your friend, for your intervention on our behalf. I shudder to contemplate what would have transpired had you not happened along. I am Prioress Heilwig, of the abbey at Gasseburg.' She was the one, Angelika noted, with the silver pendant.

'Please, stop introducing yourselves. There are too many of you to remember your names, and we'll soon be leaving at any rate. Soon as I see to it that your young physic hasn't butchered his task.'

Prioress Heilwig exchanged baffled glances with her fellow pilgrims. There was little of her to see; a habit of brown cotton covered her from head to toe, with only an oval of cloth for her fleshy face to poke out from. Though her garments were modest at first glance, Angelika looked into her cuffs and noted a lining of plush silk. Heilwig's headpiece folded in on itself elaborately, to form two large wings of stiffened fabric that flew out from each of her temples. At certain angles, it made her look as if she were wearing the prow of a ship. She was in her mid-forties, signs of bygone beauty still clung to her thickening features. 'Young woman, your brusqueness perplexes us,' she said. 'It is evident that you arrived in response to our fervent prayers. Yet now you not only announce an intention to depart, but do so in a fashion we cannot help but find impertinent.'

Angelika sauntered to the cart. At its head, she saw the deep hoof prints of an ox. 'Where did your beasts go?'

'We had only one ox left,' answered the pudgy man. 'It shirked its yoke and ran off when the orcs came. I never thought an ox capable of such speed.'

'Should we go off in search of it?' asked another of the male pilgrims.

'Why are you asking me?' Angelika demanded. She softened her tone: 'I see why you'd want to recover a thing so precious as an ox, but you'll likely just get yourselves lost. Most probably it's dinner for some orc or ogre by now. The Blackfire Pass swarms with dangers, as you may now realise.'

'Yes,' said the prioress. She clasped her hands and gazed up into the sky. 'This hostile place has been an even greater test of our faith than we anticipated.'

Franziskus, seeing an irreligious quip forming itself on the tip of Angelika's tongue, quickly interjected. 'You're far from civilised lands. Where have you come from?'

'We hail from various places, but assembled in Grenzstadt for the journey.' Franziskus knew Grenzstadt, it guarded the Empire's southern border. He figured hastily; it was about two weeks' journey from here.

'All of the guardians we hired to protect us have been slain,' Heilwig moaned. 'First we were attacked by goblins. Then by bandits. And now this. Thomas was never meant to take up arms for us – he was another penitent, no more and no less. And now it seems as if he, too, has fallen in the cause. Yet we shall pray to Shallya, and in her boundless mercy, I am certain we shall be delivered.'

Thomas groaned as the physic applied the first layer of bandaging to his wound.

'And what wondrous place do you pilgrimage to that justifies a trek through the Blackfire?'

'Surely we are not the first pilgrims you've encountered!'

'We've been down south for awhile, in the lands of the Border Princes.'

'But certainly you have heard of Heiligerberg, the Holy Mountain?'

'Can't say I have.'

The prioress indulged herself with a puzzled grimace. 'Several leagues south of here is Heiligerberg? Where two thousand years ago, the goddess herself manifested before the girl-child priestess, Pergunda?'

Angelika scratched an itch on her neck. 'No, none of this sounds familiar.'

'During the golden era, back when all of these lands were civilised, Shallya set herself down on the mountain and showed her beneficent visage to the faithful. The mountain flowed with rose petals, and all who gained audience with Pergunda were healed, both in body and in spirit.'

'This hell pit was once civilised? That must have been a long time ago.'

The prioress's face twitched in confused frustration. 'It is mildly understandable that you have not heard of the mountain, or its history. But surely you have heard of Mother Elsbeth?'

Angelika managed an indifferent shrug.

'Mother Elsbeth, the most famed and holy vessel of Shallya. Whose miraculous feats of healing are celebrated throughout the southern Empire. Who lifted the plague at Ruren? Who cured the grand theogonist of his congenital pleurisy?'

'I was unaware that the Theogonist was so afflicted.'

'Not the current Theogonist!' Heilwig's voice trebled. 'Nor even *his* predecessor – you truly know nothing of this?'

'It is a subject I find uninteresting.'

The prioress shook her wattles. Franziskus approached. 'Please pardon my companion, your grace. She is an iconoclast, and takes perverse joy in tweaking the pious.'

'But you have heard of her, surely,' the prioress pleaded, grabbing a good hank of Franziskus's sleeve.

Franziskus nodded. 'It is as she says, Angelika. Even the most impious wretches speak reverently of Mother Elsbeth's great feats of healing.' He turned to the prioress. 'But did they not occur decades ago? I was not even sure Mother Elsbeth still lived.'

'She must be quite elderly, now, but Shallya be praised, she has once more begun to grant audience to the faithful. No doubt the dire times we now face have inspired this fortuitous end to her long seclusion.'

'Your tale seems dubious,' Angelika said. 'The times are always dire.'

'Dubious?'

Like a crowd of menacing cows, the other pilgrims began to edge around Angelika. She sought out the pudgy man and levelled an icy stare at him. He moved back. The others did the same.

'Are you sure these are not baseless rumours?'

Prioress Heilwig huffed. 'I am quite well informed on these matters. Hundreds – no, thousands – of pilgrims now flock to Heiligerberg, to take advantage of this rare opportunity for grace. If it were false, we would see as many disappointed worshippers returning north as are swarming south.'

'I ask because I wonder if the rumours might be a trap, to lure gullible victims. Perhaps this Heiligerberg of yours has been occupied by bandits, and all the pilgrims who've come to bow and scrape before your Mother Elsbeth now rot in a common grave.'

A gasp escaped from the knot of pilgrims. They whispered and muttered.

'Now look here,' said one who had not spoken before: a grey-haired fellow in a grand brocaded coat, his head adorned with a plumed cap. He poked a finger at Angelika. 'I won't have you frightening these fine, devout people with gruesome speculations. They may be taken in, but as I am an expert in negotiation and argument, I can easily glean your motives.'

Angelika crossed her arms. 'And what motives might those be?'

'You aim to increase your fee, by exaggerating the dangers we face.'

'My fee?'

'Do not be disingenuous. You know very well the position we're in. We've lost our bodyguards, and now Thomas, the only experienced fighter among us, lies dying.'

This last comment aroused a series of dirty looks; the man's fellow pilgrims made a point of glancing over at Thomas, to indicate that he was still in earshot. The plumed man did not acknowledge them.

'Let me guess,' Angelika said. 'You're an advocate, aren't you?'

The man inflated his chest and extended the height of his neck, then gave Angelika a peremptory bow. 'Stefan Recht, advocate of Pfeildorf.' He proudly smiled. 'How did you know?'

'You claimed to be an expert in negotiation, though mostly it was your combination of arrogance and callousness.'

Recht deflated.

'As for a fee,' Angelika said. 'Your most recent brush with death has befuddled your senses, all of you. Fee or no fee, I no more intend to accompany you on your pilgrimage than a pig intends to sprout wings and buzz about the spires of Altdorf.'

The prioress flapped her jaw up and down. 'But you are needed!'

'Your needs are not my concern.' Angelika turned to leave.

Heilwig quickly seized both of Franziskus's pale hands in her own, squeezing tightly. 'It cannot be. I prayed for rescue, and she came.'

'In fact,' said Angelika, 'it is Franziskus who bolted from our position of safety to foolishly endanger himself on your behalf. If your goddess sent anyone to save your skins, it would be him, not me.'

She headed across the floor of the pass, toward their campsite. Franziskus followed her, trailing Heilwig, Recht, and several others behind him.

Walking quickly to keep the pilgrims out of earshot, Franziskus hissed into Angelika's ear. 'Trying to rid yourself of me?'

'You can't blame me if I persist in trying.'

'We've had this discussion countless times.'

'Yet somehow I never get through to you.'

'You saved my life, from orcs bent on sacrificing me. Honour dictates that I extend to you my undying allegiance.'

'That's why I've got to stop saving people from orcs. You can never get free of them afterwards.'

'Please, stop, I beg you!' It was the prioress, who was now standing behind them. Franziskus stopped. Angelika didn't.

Heilwig reached out for Franziskus's hands again. He surrendered them to her hesitantly. 'You are not an undutiful young man,' she said to him. 'We can see it in your eyes. Clearly, this... companion of yours is, ah, rough-hewn. But one would expect no less in a place like this. One might even say that it is a necessary trait for survival.'

'One might indeed say that, your grace.'

'Then you must intercede with her. You two must safely guide us the rest of the way to the Holy Mountain.' She directed a pre-emptive, silencing look at Recht, the advocate. 'We are willing to pay what is necessary.'

Franziskus checked Angelika's whereabouts; she was gathering their packs. 'Truly,' Franziskus said, 'the size of your purses is not at issue. My companion has, ah, a certain mode of, ah, securing income, and a great reluctance to hire herself out. She's been dragged into adventures before, you see, and their outcomes have been generally, ah, less than pleasant.'

'You must see to it that, in this instance, she changes her mind.'

Franziskus bit his lip. 'I must tell you...'

Franziskus beheld a pair of limpid blue eyes, regarding him frankly and neutrally. They shone at him from the soft, clear face of a young woman

standing a few paces behind the prioress. She wore
a habit like the prioress's, except that it was authen-
tically modest, devoid of gewgaws or silky linings. A
gently curling strand of auburn hair slipped out of
its place in her simple headpiece, draping itself
down on her perfect brow. She shyly batted at it,
stuffing it back up into her wimple. It fell back
down again.

'Devorah!' snapped the prioress. 'Do not stand in
the young man's field of view.'

'Franziskus. My name is Franziskus.'

'You're distracting Franziskus. Please step out of
his field of vision while we continue our important
discussion.' She squeezed his knuckles together,
somewhat painfully.

As gently as he could, Franziskus freed himself
from the prioress's steely claws. 'Tell me, Prioress
Heilwig,' he said. 'You say there are hundreds of pilgrims converging on this spot – this Holy
Mountain?'

'Nay – thousands.'

'And this mountain – is it truly a mountain, or is
that just a dramatic turn of phrase, as is sometimes
the case when legendary places are described?'

The advocate, Recht, broke in to answer the question. 'None of us have been there, but I have done
careful research, and my understanding is that it is
a mountain as jagged and treacherous as any in
this awful pass.' He looked around meaningfully at
the black crags rising all around them. 'I have pon-
dered the point, and at first it seems a peculiar
irony, that the goddess of mercy would enjoin her

most fervent devotees to clamber up a sharp and treacherous slope to receive her blessing. But then, on further reflection, any person of sense will realise that the difficulty of the climb is the very nub of the point – it is the profoundest test of faith and determination.'

Off in the woods, Angelika had her pack on, and now hefted Franziskus's in her arms.

Franziskus tugged at the lobe of his ear. 'So there are hundreds, even thousands, of pilgrims, scrabbling up the face of this – what was your word? – this treacherous mountain. Most of them like yourselves – ordinary persons of the Empire, unfamiliar with, and unsuited for, this sort of exertion?'

'It is a point we do not care to dwell on, but yes, I imagine it is as you say.'

'And, as Shallya grants not only spiritual solace but the healing of wounds, defects and sundry diseases – it might also be reasonable to guess that many of them are infirm to begin with.'

Recht waved his soft and uncalloused palms about. 'Yes, yes. Please get to the point, sir.'

Angelika approached, calling out to Franziskus, telling him to get his behind moving.

'Then, I must be blunt in order to be brief,' said Franziskus. 'Throughout their journey to the Holy Mountain, might one posit that large numbers of pilgrims will be dropping dead?'

Recht coughed. The prioress choked. Beautiful, auburn-haired Devorah blinked her liquid eyes.

'Ah, what you say is, I reckon, indelicate but true.'

Angelika clunked Franziskus's heavy pack at his feet, making sure that it landed on one of his toes. Franziskus did not flinch.

'You coming?' Angelika asked him.

'In a moment.' He turned his attention back to the prioress and the advocate. 'I have a possible solution. Not necessarily one I endorse, mind you. It requires a degree of, ah, moral compromise you'll likely want to avoid.'

Angelika raised an eyebrow, her interest piqued.

'I am unsure,' the prioress said.

'We are desperate,' the advocate replied.

Franziskus nodded. 'Very well. Excuse us while we discuss the matter.' He took Angelika by the elbow to lead her away. She picked up Franziskus's pack and dropped it into his arms. They walked out of earshot, back to the fallen log.

The pilgrims watched them. Franziskus meekly gesticulated. Angelika gave him an incredulous look. He ran his fingers through his heroic tangle of hair. She jolted forward, laughing.

The prioress placed her hand on the advocate's shoulder. 'How can we be sure that this is not an elaborate ruse, to lure us to a throat-slitting?'

'I'm open to any other suggestions you might be harbouring, Mother Heilwig.' As he said this, Recht leaned slightly forward in hopes of making out a word or two.

Young Devorah spoke. Her voice had a papery tremor in it. 'The young man, mother.'

'Yes?' said Heilwig, forbiddingly.

'Where do you think he is from? I cannot place the accent.'

'I could not think to guess,' harrumphed Heilwig.

'Stirland,' said the advocate. 'Rural nobility, I'd venture.'

Devorah sighed.

'But a scoundrel, to be sure, to be out here in this land of blackguards and exiles, instead of at his family estate, or serving in the army.'

Devorah cast her eyes toward the hem of her habit, which trailed all the way down to the mucky ground, her toes nowhere to be seen.

Angelika clapped her hands together and rapidly strode toward them, the glint of business in her eyes. Franziskus followed, looking slightly queasy.

'Very well,' said Angelika, addressing the prioress. 'I agree to your terms. But I won't put up with any carping – you must agree to this with open eyes.'

'Agree to what?' blenched the prioress.

'I haven't told them yet,' Franziskus explained.

'Told us what?' the prioress demanded.

'Ah,' Franziskus said. 'My friend here makes her living as a, ah, she recovers...'

'I loot battlefields,' Angelika said.

'Ah, yes,' said Franziskus. 'That is what she does. She steals, one might say, but only from those who have already lost their lives. I don't condone this, but am nonetheless sworn to her service. Normally, Angelika has occasion only to sift the pockets of men slain in war, who are plentiful in these parts. But, in exchange for your solemn agreement not to hinder her in any way, she – and I – will accompany you to Heiligerberg and do our best to get you up its slopes.'

The prioress squinted her left eye shut. 'Hinder her from doing what?'

'He is hoping not to have to spell it out,' said the advocate.

'Hinder me,' Angelika interjected, 'from looting the corpses of any expired pilgrims we may encounter during the trip.'

A silence descended, interrupted only by the distant cawing of crows. Crows were also plentiful in the Blackfire Pass.

'Including our own?' the prioress asked.

Angelika gravely nodded.

'And what is to stop you from hastening our demises, that you might relieve our mortal husks of worldly goods?' She fingered nervously at the silver dove dangling between her matronly breasts.

'If you don't trust me, I understand. As a rule, it isn't smart to trust people you happen to bump into in the Blackfire Pass.'

'I assure you,' Franziskus submitted, 'that Angelika does not mug, waylay, or otherwise rob the living. Her ethic forbids it.'

'Ethic?' Prioress Heilwig sputtered. 'You expect us to entrust our fates to the moral code of a corpse looter?'

Angelika shrugged. 'You'd sooner trust yourselves to the mercy of Shallya?'

# CHAPTER TWO

HANDS ON HIPS, Angelika studied the pilgrim's wrecked cart. She bent down to study its underside: it was one of the axle mounts, not the shaft itself, that had broken. Without oxen to pull it, it did not matter if the cart could be repaired. But Angelika could tell from the pleading faces of the milling pilgrims that they expected her to at least think about it. She did not relish the idea of leading anyone, much less a helpless throng of prayer-chanting incense-burners. Still, it would not be right to turn down the fee they'd offer – a hundred crowns justified a great deal of aggravation. Certainly, she could go to the mountain on her own, searching for deceased pilgrims in need of looting, but by gathering a swarm of penitents around her, she'd be giving herself cover against any still-breathing idolaters who might otherwise take offence at her activities.

Mostly she was looking at the cart to give herself time to think. She decided that she would wring the maximum possible obedience from them if she made herself hard to please. Her charges were eager to do so. She would be distant, stern, forbidding – just as she was with Franziskus. In fact, it was as if she'd now saddled herself with fifteen additional Franziskuses. Or worse – Franziskus, at least, could swing a sword with passable effectiveness.

She turned to face them. 'Enough lolly-gagging,' she called, as if she'd been the one waiting for them. 'We'll assign shifts to see who'll be first to pull the cart.'

Each of the fourteen gathered pilgrims – except Krieger, who lay unconscious on several layers of bedding over a flat bit of rock nearby – looked studiously away from her. Angelika had no intention of having anyone pull carts, but she wanted to get the arrangement off on the proper foot, by making them all feel they'd disappointed her.

'We won't be able to organise ourselves if you keep clucking around like geese,' she called, slapping her hands loudly together. 'Into a line, into a line!'

The more genteel pilgrims, such as the prioress, the advocate and the physic, stared up at her in offence and astonishment. Others, including the novitiate, Devorah and the pudgy-faced man who'd fought against the orcs with a hayfork, doddered unquestioningly into a ragged formation. 'That means all of you. Even those of you who are pri-oresses of abbeys at Gasseburg!' Heilwig bustled into line beside young Devorah, quacking her discontent.

Angelika marched stiff-legged along the line of pilgrims, as she had seen sergeants do when they reconnoitred the scenes of imminent battles. 'Your lives will depend on your quick and unthinking obedience to my commands,' she informed them. 'I've no desire to be your boon companion. But I must know who you are – or rather, what you can do to further the survival of this group. You'll answer the questions I put to you, and only those questions. Do you understand me?'

A mumbling ensued.

'Do you understand me?' Angelika cried. This was a question she had often heard shouted by sergeants. It was an unfair question – of course they understood, they were simply too cowed to answer – but unfairness seemed central to good discipline, and Angelika planned to dole it out in generous quantities.

Finally the group managed to gather its collective composure and nod to Angelika – yes, they understood. She stepped close to the fat man who'd fought the orc. Still mimicking the sergeants she'd seen, she stepped uncomfortably close to him, jutting her nose just an inch from his face. He smelled of berry wine and bacon grease.

'You there!' she shouted, sending him flinching backwards. 'Who do you think you are?'

'A-a-a-a-a,' he stammered.

'Who?'

'A-a-a-a-a,' he repeated.

She stomped on his foot.

'Altman Gericht!' he cried.

'And you are what?' Angelika asked.

'What?'

'Who are you?'

'I-I-I'm a bailiff.'

'You were reasonably brave against the orc.'

'Uh. Thank you.'

'Yet you're afraid of me.'

'A-a-a-a-a…'

'That shows good judgement.'

'Uh. Thank you.'

'What do bailiffs do?'

'I m-manage the lands of a lord named–'

'Don't interrupt me when I'm speaking to you. Bailiffs push people around and make sure minor tasks get accomplished. Is that correct?'

'A-a-a-a-a.'

'Well then you'll be useful to us. I anticipate giving you many orders.'

She approached the next pilgrim in line. He was a thin, hollow-chested man with curly black hair and wide eyes. Large, round ears framed his face. Eyes darting, he fidgeted with the collar of his plain penitent's robe. The garment was new, it gave away no hint of rank or status. Angelika looked at his hands: they were clean and soft. She checked his feet. From beneath his robe poked a pair of fine and well-worn boots, freshly re-soled. Angelika glanced down the line; all but a few of the pilgrims were wearing sandals, or flimsy shoes better suited for day-to-day wear. This one's boots, on the other hand, would stand him in good stead during a difficult mountain climb.

He swallowed. 'I won't be intimidated,' he said, the pitch of his voice uncontrolled and flutey. 'We are the ones hiring you. You should be snapping to our orders.'

He flinched, as if expecting Angelika to hit him.

Instead she lowered her voice. 'What is your name?'

'Kirchgeld. Ivo Kirchgeld. I am a man of some religious importance, as are many others here, and it defeats the purpose of a pilgrimage, which is to bind us closer to the world of holiness and virtue, if we are to be subjected to irreverence and disrespect on the–'

She stopped him. 'Do you want to get up the mountain alive, Ivo?'

'That's a rhetorical question!' he cried, his pitch wobbling up several notes. He added emphasis by pointing his forefinger into the sky. 'Naturally the entire point is to survive the pilgrimage. But surely this can be accomplished without bullying and insults.'

'Oh, shut your flapping mouth.' This was another of the pilgrims, clad in a grimy shift. He had stepped out from the line to gesticulate at Ivo. He was stooped and worn from a life of toil. His head was bare, except for a last vestige of flour-coloured hair that ran from ear to ear, along the back. 'Even if the putting on of airs was more important than getting us safely to Heiligerberg, you, Ivo Kirchgeld, have got the least reason to. Put on airs, that is to say. You're nowt but a cheat and a charlatan, and if anyone deserves a measure of irreverence and disrespect, it's you.'

Compressing his face into a mask of quivering outrage, Ivo took a darting step at the older man, who held his ground and his composure. Ivo checked his fellow pilgrims for signs of sympathy. Detecting none, he snorted like a horse and retreated. The careworn man laughed and threw up his hands.

'Tell me who you are,' Angelika said.

The old man responded with a quick, sardonic bow. 'Jurg Muller, and as my family name suggests, I'm a miller, from a long line of millers. An honest trade, not like his.' Again he pointed at Kirchgeld.

'Which is?'

The miller held his little patch of frostbitten grass as if it was a stage and he was a performer on festival day, declaiming the feats of Sigmar in the village morality play. 'He styles himself a pardoner. Says he's specially licensed by the gods to wash away offences, sins, even taints of Chaos.'

'Taints of Chaos I never claimed to cure!' Ivo howled, jumping out of line again. Angelika sidestepped, so that the two men had a clear path to one another, if they really wanted to fight.

'You strongly implied it!' scoffed the miller, turning showily away from him.

'No! No! No! You falsely inferred it!' The pardoner advanced and laid his hand on the miller's shoulder. The miller swatted it away. The pardoner turned to Angelika to plead his case. 'He styles me a charlatan, but I tell you the contrary is true! I trace my family line back further than any miller. Mine goes all the way back to Sigmar's time and it was that mighty deity himself who granted the first Kirchgelds the right to raise funds for the building of temples and the acquisition of ceremonial finery.'

'Tell her,' said the miller, 'how you raise these funds.'

'It is no secret,' Ivo said. 'It is a source of pride! It is by the selling of minor indulgences – forgiveness for acts of a minor nature which might otherwise stain one's soul in Sigmar's fiery eyes.'

'Blasphemy!' spat Prioress Heilwig.

'A false doctrine!' cried another of the pilgrims, crooking an objecting finger into the air.

'At worst, it is controversial.' Ivo inhaled a breath, ready to launch into a new speech.

'Quieten yourselves – all of you!' Angelika commanded. She shoved Ivo the pardoner back into line. Then she glowered at the miller until he too retook his place.

She paced down the line. 'If I'm going to lead this pilgrimage, you have to know that there are two things I won't tolerate.' She reconsidered for a moment. 'Actually, the list of things I won't tolerate is extremely lengthy. But at the top of that list are squabbling, and religious squabbling. I don't care if the selling of indulgences is doctrine or blasphemy. I don't care if your ancestor met Sigmar, or if Shallya herself appears to you on rainy autumn nights. Just because this is a pilgrimage, it doesn't mean I have to put up with a lot of god talk. Do you all understand?'

The prioress harrumphed and then nodded. The others nodded with her. Angelika was not sure where Franziskus had situated himself, but she could nonetheless sense his disapproval.

Having successfully cowed her new charges, she kept the rest of the introductions curt and businesslike. In addition to those she'd already met, she found among the pilgrims a friar, a widow, a merchant and a monk. The short, bald fellow with the nut-brown skin, who had held off one of the orcs, introduced himself as Richart Pfeffer. He made his living as the owner of a smallholding of land in the southern province of Averheim. The gnarled, salty-tongued old man who'd forced the hilt of his club down the runty orc's throat identified himself as Ludwig Seeman, a retired sailor.

Last man in line was Waldemar Silber, the fancy-robed man who'd briefly joined the fray to drag the wounded Thomas out of it. His long hair gave a dashing air to his hawkish face, which also boasted dark, deep-set eyes and a majestically pointed nose. Fetching streaks of silver ran through his hair and the neatly clipped little beard that adorned the mere tip of his sharp chin. In other circumstances, Angelika might have found him pleasing enough to bed, at least until Silber announced that he was a summoner. This seemed to be yet another minor position within the large and complicated hierarchy of the Sigmarite church.

Except for the obvious fact that the post called for the wearing of a lush peacock robe, Angelika was not sure precisely what a summoner did. And she didn't know whether summoners were fully ordained priests, or mere lay functionaries – not that she would have understood the distinction, anyway. She didn't give two figs. Doubtless she would have this explained to her in exhausting detail at some point during the journey.

'The cart can't be repaired,' she said, raising her voice to make sure everyone could hear. A wind was whipping up, that rustled the branches of the pines and spruces covering the slopes around them. A gust seized the lawyer's cap and sent it swirling; he bolted awkwardly after it. 'The cart can't be repaired,' Angelika repeated. 'So you'll be carrying your gear from now on. Go into the cart and get only what you absolutely need. Whatever you take, you'll have to carry on your own back – unless you can fool someone else into lugging it for you. And no matter what weight you think you can heft for hours at a time, I can promise you: you can truly only carry half that much.'

Their faces fell and Angelika was panged by secret sympathy. She thought of her own network of hiding places throughout the region, each of which contained little pouches of gold. Priests and their other piety-mouthing ilk were forever railing about material belongings, and how one ought to pretend that they were worse than worthless, but Angelika believed the opposite. Possessions were infinitely more dependable than people. To be forced to abandon one's hard-gathered goods was to suffer a genuine wound that no moralist could ever hope to understand. 'If orcs are coming back, we'll hear them long before they arrive. We can run then.'

The pilgrims went off to sort through their packs. Angelika sidled up to Franziskus. 'I never should have agreed to this. I allowed myself to be conned into it by someone much more subtle than he looks.'

She saw Ludwig carelessly toss a couple of new shovels from the cart, discarding them to get to items of greater interest. 'Someone take the shovels!' she called. 'We'll need those,' she added, under her breath, 'for the digging of graves.'

Franziskus worked up his best cheery expression. 'We can do it, Angelika. We just have to think very carefully before we give instructions.'

'We?' She snorted. 'It's not you they're all looking at, with their doe eyes.'

'You're the one who took charge, who slew those orcs. You're the one they want to trust.'

'I'd sooner have their fates on your conscience than mine.'

'You keep professing not to have one.'

'You keep reminding me how burdensome they can be.' She beckoned Franziskus to follow her as she strode over to the flat rock where Thomas, the former officer, was laid out. He opened his eyes as they approached. Angelika looked for Rausch, the physic; he was clambering around inside the cart, struggling with a large, unruly roll of Araby carpet. What on earth could have possessed anyone to take such a thing on a trip into the Blackfire?

'Did he bandage you up properly?' asked Angelika, lifting up Thomas's tunic. The blood flow seemed to have slowed.

'I've had worse medics,' Thomas coughed. 'I might be better off if he'd hastened my end. I've a couple of painful days of dying ahead of me.'

'We'll have to get a stretcher together,' Angelika thought, aloud.

'No, don't do that either,' said Thomas. 'Leave me.'

'I won't leave a man to die. And you're in no position to argue.'

Angelika marched over to the cart and grabbed the physic's rug from him. Franziskus pulled the axle from beneath the cart and began to smack at it with his sabre, to break it into lengths suitable for a stretcher.

It dawned on the physic that Angelika meant to commandeer his carpet. 'You can't just take that!' he said. 'It's worth twenty crowns!'

'We're making a stretcher for Krieger,' she said. 'You, of all people should be willing to donate to the cause. What use did you plan for it, anyway?'

Rausch shifted on slippered feet. 'A number of us brought goods, to sell along the way. To defray the expense of the pilgrimage.'

Angelika looked into the cart. She saw silver plate, candles, incense, prayer blankets, glass jars for holy water and a pile of spare robes. She shook her head in disbelief.

The widow woman, whose name was Kinge Kloster, bustled up to Angelika's side. Thick curls of rust-coloured hair covered her head and a pair of spectacles sat in the middle of her round, well-fed face. Her face was powdered, then rouged and a paste of particularly artificial crimson covered her lips. Her eyebrows had been plucked to non-existence and then recreated in grease pencil as thin, semi-circular arches. The effect would have been whorish, were it not for the widow's air of merry self-satisfaction, which made her exagger-ated appearance seem perfectly ordinary.

'I organised this,' she proudly declared. 'It is well known that many pilgrims come ill-equipped for their journeys, and others are robbed of their things or see them meet with mishaps along the way. I, and some of the others, thought we would assist those unfortunate souls, and virtuously enrich ourselves as an incidental part of the bargain.'

'Carpeting? Silver plate?'

'Wealthy pilgrims often undertake extended stays at their holy destinations. I would assume that Heiligerberg has many such guests; they might wel-come the chance to purchase a few bargain luxuries, from their fellow believers.'

'I'm sure the orcs and goblins will enjoy lining their lairs with them.'

The widow's jaw fell. 'What? '

'We can't certainly can't haul this with us, can we?'

'But the expense! No, no, no! You must allow us–'

'Take heart. Anyone following your trail will stop to root through the cart, and that'll buy us time.' She raised her voice. 'Now listen here everyone! Take only what you can carry – I want the lot of you ready to move by the time this stretcher's ready!'

Angelika and Franziskus got to work fashioning a stretcher. She took a length of heavy leather cord from her kit and quartered it with her dagger. Franziskus cut strips from the carpet and wrapped them around the axles of the cart. With a thick iron needle, also from her pack, Angelika threaded the cord through the rug, sewing loops of cut fabric onto it. Franziskus stuck the poles through the loops.

'We have to test this,' Angelika said. She ordered Ivo to approach. He pretended not to hear. Angelika picked up a fist-sized rock and strode toward him. He goggled his eyes at her.

'You weren't calling for me, were you?' he asked, feigning innocence.

'Get on,' she said.

'What?' he asked.

'We need to test the stretcher, to see if it holds, before we attempt to put Thomas on it. Get on the stretcher.'

He waggled his head like a beagle trying to get honey off his muzzle. 'Why me? Why not the miller, or the shipman? Surely you can find someone better suited to this indignity!'

'I can think of no such person. Get on the stretcher.'

Not without inarticulate sounds of protest, Ivo laid down on the rug. Angelika and Franziskus bent to heft the poles. The left front loop gave way, as the leather cord freed itself. The aft loop on the same side followed suit. Ivo rolled out onto the ground, yowling. He leapt up quickly, brushing bits of grass from his robe.

'I hope you're happy,' he said.

'Not as much as you'd think,' replied Angelika, looking into a wooded patch about a hundred yards away, where a low, red-leafed bush rustled. She knew the difference between a bush that rustled in the wind and one whose rustling was caused by something creeping behind it. This was not the wind. She snicked her dagger from its scabbard and ran toward the bush. She heard a hissing sound; a crouching figure retreated as she came at it. She caught only a flash of its fur-clad back and warty green skin, but that was enough. A sniff of the air confirmed it – the acrid tang of vinegar, wolf urine and sour ordure was unmistakable.

'A goblin,' she announced, returning to the others. 'A scout, most likely. We have to assume it'll be back, soon, with an entire horde, maybe on the backs of war-wolves. This place is crawling with greenskins, big and small. It must be all you pilgrims – they're flocking to take advantage of easy prey, like frogs in mayfly season. We've got to get moving.'

'Then leave me behind,' called Krieger, attempting to sit up.

'I'm fixing this stretcher,' Angelika told him, 'and then we're moving.' She re-sewed the stitching on the left side. Devorah, the pretty sister, hovered nearby and when Angelika had finished, she volun-

teered to test the stretcher. She was not heavy
enough for an ideal test, but Angelika let her do it
anyway. She lay down demurely on the rug, azure
eyes fixed on Franziskus. He and Angelika hefted it,
and this time it held. Franziskus stuck out his hand
for Devorah; she let him clasp her delicate wrist and
pull her chivalrously to her feet. Then he broke the
gaze, picked up the stretcher, and carried it to
Krieger's side.

'This'll hurt like hellfire,' Angelika warned Krieger,
as she and Franziskus stooped to heft him onto the
stretcher.

Krieger barely grunted as they laid him down. 'If
there are goblins coming, you'll have to leave me,'
he said, perspiration beading on his face and neck.

Angelika assured him, 'At the next sign of greenskins, we'll do just that.'

# CHAPTER THREE

ANGELIKA HAD FIRST thought that they would start out with herself and Franziskus ferrying Krieger through the woods. She would lead by example, showing up any potential complainers unhappy with the pace she expected them to keep. Then she counted the number of pilgrims who seemed capable of contributing to the group's defence, and saw that there were only four: Altman the bailiff, Ludwig the sailor, Waldemar the summoner and the landowner, Richart. The monk, Brother Lemoine, seemed robust enough, but he refused to bear arms, claiming to have taken a vow of pacifism. The physic, Victor Rausch, was also a healthy man, but Angelika did not want to risk his hide so early in the journey, as he'd be needed as the others began to sustain injuries.

She and Franziskus would be put to better use on point, Angelika concluded. The two of them knew the wilderness and its danger signs. She assigned the pacifist, Lemoine, and the miller, Muller, to haul the stretcher for the first leg of the hike. They'd make a slow tramp of it, but Angelika doubted that many of her charges could travel much faster anyway. She assigned Richart and Ludwig to bring up the rear, sternly warning them to whistle out at the slightest indication that they were being watched or followed. It was better to seem foolish and give a false alarm, she lectured, than to dismiss a strange noise or movement and get caught out by a squad of bandits or onrushing greenskins. She bunched the other pilgrims behind the stretcher, with Waldemar on the left flank and Recht, the lawyer, on the right. Recht did not seem the warrior type but at least he had a rapier on his belt.

Angelika gave the signal to move out, and immediately their marching fell into disarray: the pilgrims scattered like quacking ducklings. She moved them back into place, seizing some of them, such as Ivo, by the back of the neck. She threatened vivid bodily harm to the next person to break formation.

The pilgrims stayed in place for ten minutes, until they reached the first bit of sloping ground on their way into the hills. Then the formation once more dismantled itself, as some forged ahead, others slowed, still others stopped dead, as if they thought the slope would flatten out if they waited for a little while.

Angelika sighed deeply and bitterly. 'I can't keep this pack of fools alive,' she muttered.

'Have hope,' Franziskus told her.

'False hope's gotten many a throat slit,' Angelika replied.

They found a narrow trail, half overgrown, and Angelika wondered whether to take it or not. Greenskins could follow trails, too. On the other hand, her hapless pilgrims would find it difficult to navigate rockier ground, or through uncut under-brush. They might fall, or twist their ankles, or step on vipers, whose fangs might drip with poison. Angelika hated situations like this, where there was no right answer. She chose the trail. She'd stay roughly parallel to the pass, to keep herself oriented. Much of this land she knew well; it wouldn't be long before she found some landmarks she recognised.

The trail meandered up a hillside, wandering from one stand of leafy bushes to another. It had been made, Angelika realised, by deer and elk, as they moved from one good grazing spot to another. Though she might have liked a straighter route up into the mountains, a deer path was better than one favoured by goblins or other marauders.

The stretcher-bearers lasted for less than half an hour before they cried out, begging for rest. By barking out some choice threats, Angelika got another quarter of an hour out of them. Then they laid Krieger down and plopped their backsides in the underbrush, gasping for breath and mercy. Angelika stomped back to make new arrangements, but the prioress had taken charge, and had given the job to the physic and the merchant. Angelika returned to point position, gratified that at least one of the pilgrims had the wherewithal to shoulder on some of the burden.

The pilgrims puffed up a rocky incline. Brother Lemoine cried out when his sandaled foot was stabbed by a sharp stick protruding from the ground. The physic moved to check his wound, but Lemoine waved him off. Minor wounds, he explained, were to be borne with courage. They were a gift from Shallya; they taught you to inure yourself to pain, so that you could better withstand truly serious injuries, should you be unlucky enough to suffer them. Or so Lemoine had been taught, in his monastery in far-off Bretonnia.

'I said, no god talk!' Angelika yelled, from the front. The doctrine seemed convoluted, at any rate.

Next the entourage threaded up through a thick stand of straight young pines. The summoner, Waldemar, exclaimed in outrage and his deep-set eyes flashed when a scaly branch whip-lashed his dashing face. He accused Muller of holding the pine branch so it would do just that.

'Pish!' said Jurg. 'The summoner imagines things!' His eyes twinkled with a delight that seemed to contradict his denial.

'I imagine nothing! It was plainly intentional!'

Muller kept walking, moving closer to Angelika and Franziskus, and their point position. Rather than respond directly to his accuser, he addressed the group at large. 'As a great and lofty summoner, festooned in silk and jewelled rings, Waldemar here's learned to think of himself as the centre of the world, with all others merely in orbit about him. So it's little wonder he'd think the accident of a misplaced branch could be none other than a calculated assault upon his person!'

Waldemar stood still and fumed. 'Listen to him! Listen! He clearly pursues some motiveless grudge against me. Even as he denies it, he confirms it!'

'Pish,' Muller clucked.

'Shut up, the both of you,' suggested Angelika.

'I'll not be silenced,' declared the summoner. 'Not with such an obvious affront thrown in my face!' He spun on his heels, fixing young Devorah in his beady gaze. 'You saw it, did you not? You were right behind me. You saw him flick that branch at me!'

Devorah flushed. She fluttered her eyelids and bowed her head. 'I am not certain what I saw, father.'

Waldemar adopted a velvety tone and placed a paternal hand on each of the girl's shoulders. 'Now, young sister,' he said. 'You know as well as I do that the miller flicked that branch.'

Muller spun and headed back in the summoner's direction. 'She knows no such thing, because no such thing happened. If she says she didn't see it, you shouldn't be bullying her.'

The prioress stepped in Muller's path, before he could reach Devorah and forcibly remove Waldemar's hands from her shoulders, which seemed to be his intent. Waldemar still stepped back from her.

'Disgraceful!' Prioress Heilwig exclaimed, puffing herself up with a huge breath of air. She treated the miller to her most withering look then turned to give the same to the summoner. 'Are you not pious

men? On a holy pilgrimage, no less? What example
do you mean to set?'

Kinge, the widow, slapped her right haunch, thun-
dering out a mighty guffaw. 'Pious they may be, but
they're still men! That means they have the temper
of mules – and the sense, to boot!'

Others – the friar, the shipman and the pardoner
– joined in her mocking laughter. The procession
had now halted completely. The merchant took the
opportunity to let down the aft end of Krieger's
stretcher, and Rausch the physic, on its other end,
did the same. Angelika slapped a disgusted hand to
her forehead, but hung back, waiting for the right
moment to step in.

'My grievance is legitimate!' the summoner
lamented.

The pardoner's fluting voice joined the fray. Ivo
gesticulated into the air with his left hand as he
clapped his right on Waldemar's back. 'Indeed and
yes,' he exclaimed. 'I didn't see him lash you with
the branch, but I've no doubt he did, because that
miller is nothing but a slandering varlet!'

Muller guffawed. 'Varlet?'

Waldemar whirled on his defender. 'Your help is
no help at all – pardoner!' He spat the word as if it
was the vilest of insults. 'The day I need defence
from a – from a–' The summoner stammered, at a
loss for the right words of condemnation.

'From an unworthy peddler of sacrilege?' the friar
volunteered.

Waldemar vigorously nodded. 'Yes – that's it!
The only one here who's not fit to criticise this

flour-handed scoundrel is you, Ivo Kirchgeld, you cut-worm, you – you – heretic!'

Angelika rocked forward on her heels, ready to spring down and visit her unholy wrath upon them. Friar Gerhold spared her the trouble. He was a squat, doughy man, worn and rounded down by age. Wild, snowy hair cascaded down from his ball-shaped head, spilling all the way to his wrinkly, bouncing jowls. Sharp, black eyebrows accented his impish, clever eyes. The friar's brown robe was the colour and texture of a turnip sack, and was threadbare at the hems. Even the rope he used as a belt was grey with soot and soil. He stepped in, his voice quiet, his palms held out in a gesture of conciliation. 'Come, fellow pilgrims,' he said. 'Is there really any need to abuse one another so?'

Both Waldemar and Jurg eyed him ungratefully. Gerhold waited for an answer, but got none, and so continued, 'Do you not think the goddess watches us, even as we approach her holy shrine? Shallya is the very personification of mercy. How can we expect her blessing, if we do not show mercy to one another?'

Ivo drew in a great sniffing breath of vindication, his chest swelling out. 'Touchingly put, my brother,' he said to Gerhold.

Gerhold put his arm around Ivo. 'I am no theologian,' he said, still flashing his charming smile at the summoner and the pardoner. 'A mere country friar am I. Yet one of my duties is to settle disputes between the farmers of my humble parish. And I have learned that hardly any argument is ever truly

about the matter supposedly at hand. Often it is a
long forgotten slight, as the complainant is
remembering a grievous harm done to him by
some entirely different person. This Ivo Kirchgeld
has done nothing to you. You scarcely know him.
So on what honest grounds do you despise the fellow?'

Waldemar clucked his tongue as if carefully
weighing the friar's various points. He pinched his
thumb and forefinger reflectively through his silvery
beard. He nodded, having reached a conclusion.
'Because he is a pustule on the forehead of true
faith. He is a bowl full of urine, dashed in the faces
of the gods.'

The pardoner lunged at him.

Angelika got in the way. She grabbed both the
summoner and the pardoner by the collars of their
robes and pulled them close to her face. Muller
crossed his arms in profound satisfaction.

'What do you god-addled nitwits think you're
doing?' Angelika demanded.

'Well I–' stuttered Waldemar.

'Did you see how–' stammered Ivo.

'Listen to me and listen well.' Angelika released
her hold on the squabbling churchmen. 'I know
that there's nothing you pious types love more than
to call down anathemas on each other. It's the
whole point of being a churchman, from what I can
see. But to point out the obvious: your survival
depends on your ability to get along when trouble
finds us – and to stay quiet, so it won't! We will
move in silence till we find a camp for the night.

And that might be hours. The next person who talks gets a smack in the mouth. Understand?'

Ivo talked. 'But we can speak in general, yes? You mean only that arguments are forbidden.'

She smacked him in the mouth.

'Ow,' he said, touching his lips, looking for blood. There was none. The faintest of red spots could be seen where she'd struck him.

'If you see trouble,' elaborated Angelika, 'speak up. Otherwise, keep your traps shut, all of you, till I say otherwise.'

The cowed pilgrims kept quiet as they made their way through tall grass and up a steep incline. They indulged in muted whispers as they panted up the side of a brambly hill. They laughed and gossiped across an alpine meadow, tromping on periwinkles and flattening fields of queenslace.

By the time they trudged across a barren plateau, a purple sunset flared up behind them, and they returned to their full-throated chattering, as if they were drunken patrons in some cavernous Altdorf mutton house. Angelika shushed them, to only momentary avail. She found a patch of sod clinging tenaciously to the plateau's granite face, and decided that this was as good a place as any to camp for the night. It was out in the open, so they would be exposed to the view of hostile roamers – but her sentries would then have plenty of time to spot charging marauders and sound the alarm.

She ordered the group to a halt and told them to start pitching their tents. Complaints began. The prioress said she'd hoped to camp near water, so that her morning ablutions might be performed as usual. Ivo Kirchgeld clutched his hands to his upper arms, suggesting they find a place where the wind would not blow on them.

Thomas Krieger gasped from his stretcher, 'Do as she says. She works for your safety.'

The complainers seemed abashed for a moment, then set about fumbling with their tents and bedrolls. Angelika and Franziskus went among them, helping them pound in pegs and screw support poles together. Half of the tents were completely inadequate and impossible to erect even in a slight breeze; the other half were expensive and surprisingly elaborate. The tent of Stefan Recht, the advocate, took the form of a small chapel and had more floor space than any room Angelika had ever lived in and required half an hour to put in place. Recht sputtered briefly when Angelika ordered him to take in all of the pilgrims whose tents could not be put up. He gave in quickly after seeing the angry light in her eyes.

Without needing to be ordered, Richart and Brother Lemoine scaled down the side of the plateau into the wooded area below, in search of firewood. They came back with armfuls of dead branches. Caution dictated that Angelika let them build only a small fire that could be quickly extinguished. But the bedraggled pilgrims, damp with sweat and chilled by a steady mountain breeze, seemed to need a lift in spirits. As vexing as they might have been, they'd made it safely through a day of hard travelling. A good flame would be their reward.

Franziskus expertly piled the collected branches and set to work with his flint and tinder. Soon the group sat huddled and mesmerised around a reaching blaze. They watched the progress of the bluest licks of flame eating away at beech wood and pine bark. Franziskus circled the pilgrims, gazing abashedly at Devorah, whose lovely skin had turned ruddy in the damp, chill air. He looked down at the spot on the ground beside her. The prioress bustled her robe and settled in closer to the young sister, all the while flashing Franziskus a warning look. He cleared his throat and wandered off, as if to check on the tents. The prioress laid her head on Devorah's shoulder and was soon gently snoring, her lips periodically rippling, her eyes moving restlessly beneath their lids.

'Some pilgrimage this is,' said the widow, Kinge Kloster. She shook the rusty curls of her hair and attempted to settle her generous rump into a more comfortable position.

'What have you got to complain about?' asked Ivo Kirchgeld, his peevish voice fluting up. 'At least you don't have to withstand the constant abuse of ignorant, chattering magpies.' Angelika watched temptation flit across the faces of Ivo's adversaries, Waldemar and Jurg, but they refused the bait, contenting themselves with a few modest grumping noises.

The widow gesticulated enthusiastically, warming to her topic. 'Where are the sackbuts? Where are the cornets? Whenever you hear about pilgrimages, in all the epics and romances, you hear of the celebrations of the journey. The fine ales. The ripe cheeses. If I'd known it was all going to be damp ground and waiting for the next round of inhuman creatures to attack, I'd have selected a journey of some other sort.'

Brother Lemoine, scandalised, pursed his lips and raised his brows. 'Good lady, this is not a pleasure jaunt. It's a holy duty we here undertake.'

Widow Kloster leaned across Ludwig, the sailor, to tug at the hem of Lemoine's sleeve. 'But we perform it in the name of the goddess of mercy, don't we?'

'Certainly,' said Lemoine, gently unhooking his garment from her short-fingered paw. He spoke with the reluctant tone of a man well aware that he was being led into a metaphorical alleyway for a rhetorical mugging.

'Well,' continued the widow, 'if I wanted to show mercy on this wilted gang of sorry sojourners, I'd have music, dancing and wine. Surely Shallya wouldn't object to any of those things. She isn't forbidding old Sigmar, with his angry beard and his hauberk spotted with the blood of the unrighteous.'

'Milady!' gasped Lemoine.

'Good widow!' sputtered the friar.

'More blasphemy!' choked the summoner.

Widow Kloster rocked back on her haunches, pleased with herself. 'I bet she's laughing at your sorry sour faces right this minute. That's why faith should never be left to the clergy – all you want to do is squeeze all the joy out of living.'

'There'd be plenty more joy in my life if you'd shut your gob, you nattering old harpy.' It was Ludwig Seeman, the gnarled, white-haired sailor.

A feline smile flitting across her face, Kloster edged over, forcing the old salt to do the same. 'Harpy, is it? It figures that'd be the worst insult you could dredge up.'

'What are you saying?' Ludwig muttered.

'It's my womanly nature that gets up your nose. As a man who's spent his entire life out on the seas, in the company only of other men, you plainly fear the female species.'

'Fear?' Ludwig demonstrated his amazement at the idea by hocking a generous wad of spit into the flame, where it briefly fizzed. 'I no more fear women than I fear the buzzing gnat, or the crawling earth-worm.'

Kinge caught Angelika in her gaze. 'Are you going to let him impugn our sex in this way?'

Angelika threw up her hands. 'You started it.'

'I know what we can do to while away the time,' said Jurg, brightly. He paused for someone to ask him what this might be. His shivering companions peered at him distrustfully. When it became apparent that no one was prepared to pick up his cue, he said, 'We can discuss the provenance of the gewgaw that dangles from the bailiff's neck!'

'Oh shut up about that,' said the puffy-faced bailiff.

'We were interrupted as we discussed this before. Tell us again what that is around your neck.'

'Just ignore him,' Seeman said.

But Altman could not. He wobbled to his feet, fumbling under his tunic to produce a length of silver chain. Angelika's posture straightened, as it always did in the presence of jewellery. At the end of the chain swung a pendant, about the size of a baby's hand. It was comprised of a ring of rough, crudely worked silver, encircling a smooth chunk of dark, polished wood. Ancient engravings, perhaps runes, incised the setting's surface; they seemed as if they'd be too worn to read even on close inspection. Angelika frowned; it was merely a religious relic. These were difficult to sell. The settings were usually crude, like this one, rarely worth much for the metals or gems alone. Their value depended on their authenticity, which, in the case of a piece lifted from a corpse, could never be proven.

Angelika did not believe that even supposedly real divine relics had any miraculous powers, but even if they did, it was not a thing you could test, like the purity of a gold bracelet. If she were to take Altman's relic to her buyer, Max, he'd offer, at most, a handful of shillings for it.

'This is a true piece of Sigmar's hammer!' the bailiff cried, stepping around the fire to wave it in the miller's face.

'I've seen a thousand just like it!' the miller laughed.

'It was splintered off from the handle of the great hammer right here in the Blackfire Pass, at the decisive battle of the World's Edge Mountains. It was picked up by Sigmar's banner-bearer, Haug the drummer, who worked this silver with his own famous hands–'

'In all my surveys of the ancient texts, I've never seen any mention of a drummer called Haug,' Waldemar sniffed.

Altman shook the fist that held the pendant. 'He existed then as sure as you and I do now, summoner! Surer! Because it passed down through his family for generation upon generation, then to a noble family of Altdorf, who fell on hard times, whereupon it became collateral for a debt incurred at the gaming table. And then it fell to me, or rather my lord, in lieu of rent, and I paid a solid hundred crowns – a bargain for a thing so holy and potent as this. I paid out of my own pocket for it. And I am not a wealthy man, I assure you. Simply a devout one, who could not bear to see such an object pass into irreverent or ungrateful hands.'

The miller fell into a fit of laughter so severe he had to gasp for breath. 'And you did not for a moment think that perhaps your lord's tenant was telling you a story, so he could discharge a debt for next to nothing?'

Altman stuffed the pendant back under his tunic. 'He spoke quite sincerely.'

Jurg wiped tears from his right eye. 'And I am sure your master was also sincere, when he allowed you to take the relic off his hands, for a mere hundred.'

'He was most insistent, in fact.'

This statement sent Jurg pitching over at the waist, seized again by helpless laughter. Some of the others – the widow, the merchant, the lawyer – who'd been suppressing their amusement, now joined in explosively. Widow Kloster, overcome with laughter, pounded her nemesis, the sailor, on the back. He shifted, to put himself out of her range.

'Thank you, Jurg,' said the widow, 'this is nearly as good as music and beer!'

Angelika rose to join Franziskus.

'Remind me never to complain about your company again,' she told him.

'You're delirious,' Franziskus said.

'Outside of your young nun, and possibly the landowner,' Angelika said, 'there's not one of them I wouldn't love to drown in a good, cold creek.'

Franziskus turned to steal a pensive look at Devorah. As if detecting his gaze, she turned, blushed, and averted her eyes again. Franziskus flushed. He shook his head; his expression grew serious. 'They're frightened, Angelika. They find themselves a long way from home, in an undertaking that has turned out to be much more dangerous than any of them had reckoned on. They want to trust us to save them, but can you blame them for their apprehension?'

'Point taken,' said Angelika, heading toward the tent where they'd left poor Krieger.

'Rather than show their fear, they're sniping at one another. Be glad they're squabbling amongst themselves. They could be making us the targets of their blame.'

'I'd like to see them try.' Angelika slipped into Krieger's tent. He tossed his head, semi-awake. A fresh trail of drool, diluted with blood, dribbled down his chin. Angelika looked around for a cloth to wipe him with, but there was nothing at hand. She patted her sleeve against his wet lips and dabbed it on his forehead. His eyes flew open.

'I'm going,' he said. There was a certainty in his tone that Angelika found chilling. She saw that her sleeve had done nothing more than smear dirt across his forehead. It made him look like a congregant on the festival of Morr, after the ritual application of ashes.

'I'm sorry if I prolonged your suffering,' she said. A lump appeared in her throat. She got angry at it, but it stayed right where it was. She laid her cold fingers on the side of his face; he was icier than she was.

Krieger worked hard to smile for her. 'Death and pain await us all. I'm lucky to go in this…' His strength failed him. His eyelids dipped shut; Angelika thought he was about to slip again into his dying slumber. Then he opened them.

Angelika completed his sentence. 'You're lucky to go in service to Shallya.' She didn't believe it, but he did, it seemed.

'Please, if you get the chance, mention my name to Mother Elsbeth.'

'I'll do that.'

'I was not a good man, for most of my life,' he said, after a lengthy pause.

Angelika shushed him.

The dying officer would not be silenced. 'I was no worse and no better than the men around me, but is that truly enough? The preachers say no.'

'Should I go get one of them for you?' Angelika did not know who was worth bringing. Perhaps the prioress? The churchmen in the group seemed an especially ratty lot.

Krieger pitched his head laboriously from side to side and it took a moment for Angelika to recognise that he was answering her question. He was telling her not to go. 'It'll only distress them.'

'Aren't there last unctions, or some such, that could be performed?'

He grasped her wrist, his grip surprisingly strong. 'This is my unction: I want a promise from you.'

Angelika got a sinking feeling.

'You must guarantee their safety. Especially the ecclesiasts.'

Angelika returned the tightness of his grip, squeezing hard. She said nothing.

'Promise, please. Before I go.'

Angelika swallowed.

Franziskus stepped in closer. 'I'll guarantee it,' he said.

Krieger struggled to summon another tortured smile. He wanted it to seem fatherly and wise. 'Take no offence, boy,' he coughed. 'But it's her promise I want.'

Angelika leaned in close. 'I know you don't want a false promise.'

Krieger's eyes closed and stayed that way.

Angelika whispered in his ear, with a lover's softness. 'I've nothing against you, understand? It's sad you're dying, but I swore off sentimental gestures a long time ago. I'll do my best, but I won't martyr myself for those people – or anyone.'

Blood dribbled from his mouth. He tried to reply but died instead.

ANGELIKA AND FRANZISKUS walked back to the fire. Any burial would have to wait until later as there wasn't enough dirt here to sink him deep enough.

'He's gone,' she said, but her breath failed her, and her words were inaudible. The pilgrims were laughing, apparently at Ivo Kirchgeld's expense.

'I know,' said the miller. 'I have an idea. It'll pass the time and keep us all in good spirits.'

'What might that be, my dear?' asked the Widow Kloster, clamping an affectionate hand on his shoulder.

'We'll keep ourselves entertained with a spate of tale telling. Make a contest of it. Each of us will tell two stories in the course of our journey to the Holy Mountain, then two on the way back. How say you all?'

Angelika interrupted them. 'I'll smack anyone who even tries it.'

# CHAPTER FOUR

THERE WERE FOOTSTEPS.

They were his.

Mother Elsbeth had become skilled in the identification of footfalls, ever since Manfried Haupt's arrival at the Holy Mountain. His was a confident tread, though there was a pronounced scraping of the soles, as he moved along the abbey's stone flooring, like he was anxious to push the world behind him with every step. Elsbeth's frail heart ticked feebly in her rattling chest. The trembling of her bony, knotted hands accelerated. She rose from her wooden bed, with its thin, woollen pallet, to examine herself in a small round mirror she'd recently had nailed to a crossbeam in her tiny cell.

There, in the mirror, was that ghostly face. It looked back at her, its skin nearly translucent. All the veins and vessels were working sluggishly below the surface, backed up and brackish, like rivers clogged with silt. The whites of her eyes had turned parchment-yellow; the irises were the grey of an overcast sky.

Elsbeth tugged her top lip up, exposing the teeth and gum line. Although she knew that there was considerable rot and decomposition in the molar region, her slightly protruding front teeth retained their miraculous longevity: they were large, straight, strong, and had taken on the colouration of old ivory. She lowered her head to examine her scalp; she was losing hairs again, though those that remained were an increasingly coarse and determined crew. Under a bright light, these resolute survivors were not white, but clear. Elsbeth pointed the tip of her sagging jaw upwards, to expose her neck. She checked the red, blotchy blemish that had recently made itself known on the seam of her neck, just above the clavicle. Yes, it had expanded since she'd last looked for it. Now it resembled a crimson island marked out on a faded old map.

Elsbeth's cell had but one window: a small circle cut in the stone, about three feet above her head. She'd had it covered with oilskin, so that only a muted glow escaped through it. It was enough; there wasn't much to look at in her cloister, anyhow.

Until recently, she'd never much noticed how bare it was. She had always thought of it more as a retreat than a cell. Material things had never mattered to her before. Now, though, she thought she might ask for a small, painted icon of the goddess Shallya, to give her solace. Father Manfried could not deny her that. He would want to perform the gesture. He did not want to think of himself as her jailer. If she asked, he would go to one of the many travelling vendors among the flood of pilgrims and buy the fanciest, most expensive icon he could find for her. He would get her one of those ones with gold leaf pounded into the halo and semi-precious stones worked into the frame.

No, Mother Elsbeth decided, better not to rely on the young priest's taste. She'd have one of the novitiates hunt for something simpler.

She sniffed. The room smelled of mould and dust. Nearly eight decades ago, when she'd been a small girl, her scholar father had gleefully shared a terrible fact he'd picked up from one of his books: he'd explained to her that dust was mostly made up of bits and pieces of dead and fallen skin, too small to see.

At the time, when she was a little mouse-faced child with dull, credulous eyes, Elsbeth had not appreciated the full import of this. Now, surrounded always by the smell of this place, she found it perhaps the most salient fact of all: the journey from life to death, from ashes to ashes and from dust to dust, was not a sudden thing, an abrupt and shocking drop from the bright world of the living to the gloomy halls of the dead.

No, it was continual, a slow and inexorable slipping away. She'd been dying for nearly as long as she could remember. And now this man, this Manfried Haupt, this bright-eyed, bantam-sized, battering ram was here to make certain that she would linger in this state of near-expiration for as long as he could possibly prolong it. It made her want to renounce her vows, to take the stone bowl from which she ate her daily gruel, to feel its hard edge beneath the pads of her papery-skinned fingers, to dash it against his temple – and then what? To escape. To run down the mountain, Shallya's beloved peak, and let it take her.

But of course even if this were a sensible plan – and she had the strength to down such a vigorous young man in a single blow, without being intercepted by his underlings or the countless pilgrims streaming up the mountain like frantic rats – here was the greater point: it would be the grossest of sins against Shallya, the goddess to whom Elsbeth had absolutely dedicated her life, her thoughts and, ever since the gift came upon her, the very fibres of her body. This was not a test – Shallya was not so cruel as to continually tempt her most fervent followers – but Elsbeth would have to bear it as if it was.

The door opened. Manfried swept through it. Elsbeth did not flinch or jolt. She never flinched.

Diffused firelight filled the room. One of Manfried's stone-faced factotums stood behind him, setting a lantern down on the stony floor. Manfried came into the room without asking, and without knocking. No introductory pleasantries for him. They were a waste of valuable time.

He gestured to Mother Elsbeth, beckoning her to turn his way, for inspection.

'How are we today, your holiness?' he asked her.

Manfried Haupt was short and small of frame, but it was easy to tell that all of the flesh under his exquisitely maintained black cassock was muscle, ropy and well defined. A high, perfectly level hairline set off his rectangular face. Boxy ears hugged flat to the sides of his head, their inner structures as intricate and complex as any Mother Elsbeth had ever seen. Sharp, pointed eyebrows occupied the space above Manfried's eyes, perpetually signalling his many ambitions. But it was the eyes themselves that were Haupt's most memorable feature: they glittered, dark as coal, telling all but giving away nothing.

'I interrupted you at your meditations?' he asked. No matter how loudly he spoke, his voice always carried with it a harsh, whispery undertone, giving his simplest utterances the impetus of menace and emergency.

'If you learned to knock, you wouldn't have to fear interrupting me…' Elsbeth's voice still surprised her; she'd said little for many years, its thin, vibrating sound belonged to nearly forgotten memory.

Father Manfried dismissed her rebuke with a twitch of his razory eyebrows. 'I come to see to your health,' he said.

'I am tired.'

'Pilgrims continue to gather outside.'

Elsbeth said nothing. It was a good tactic: the one response that always seemed to flummox him was no response at all.

'More are arriving every day. They come by the dozens. Hundreds.'

'I told you this was a big mistake.'

'What was?'

'Telling the world I was once again ready to receive penitents. You shouldn't have done it.'

'Mistake? It shows the great need out there.'

'There will always be need.'

Manfried sat himself down on her pallet, testing it. He immediately stood up again. 'See there? This is what I've been talking about. The reversal. It's me, the servant of Sigmar, who always finds himself arguing for mercy, and you, the proselyte of Shallya, who wants to withhold it.' He was not looking at Elsbeth, but at his lantern-bearer, who made a more appreciative audience – he continually nodded at his superior.

Mother Elsbeth returned to her mirror. 'The world is sick and dying. There's never mercy enough to go around.'

'You make it sound as if you've lost your faith, your holiness.'

'Faith is not a well that can be constantly drawn upon. At least, mine isn't. I need rest.'

'That's what the powers of darkness would like you to say, isn't it?'

Elsbeth spotted a long and wayward hair corkscrewing its way out of her eyebrow. She plucked it, then held it close to her eyes to study it.

'I'll confess,' said Manfried, noting the confines of Elsbeth's cell, trying to work out how to pace in such a small space, 'that when I was denied my post at Averheim, I felt that my true calling had been stolen from under me. Now I see that Sigmar had a bigger task in mind for me. He sees the need for Shallya's mercy. As any general sees the need for medics in the field. And what is the general's greatest task?'

Elsbeth did not attempt a guess.

Manfried answered his own question: 'To attend to his troops' morale. That is my task here. To re-stoke the fires of your flagging determination. You must get out there and heal again.'

'I am not a soldier. And you are not my general.'

'We are all soldiers, in the fight against Chaos.'

The trembling of Elsbeth's hands stepped itself up even further. 'We didn't ask you here. The priests of Sigmar have no authority over the priestesses of Shallya.'

Manfried exchanged an almost smirking look with his lantern-bearer. 'Of course we don't. We've come merely to guard you from harm. A great wave of Chaos sweeps the lands of men. Haven't you heard?'

'So you say, but it still gives you no authority–'

'What lesson do you think it teaches the faithful, to come all this way, and be refused?'

'You've no right to enforce your will on us.' She turned to face the wall.

'My god's mission is the very survival of mankind,' hissed Manfried. He darted his head at her, so she couldn't help but meet his black-eyed gaze.

Elsbeth's knees wobbled.

The young priest continued, 'If we must protect you mercy priestesses from your own sloth and weakness, if we must seize authority in this time of tribulation, then I say: so be it.'

'No matter how eager I might be, I can never see everyone.'

As if nothing had happened, Manfried shifted back to his attitude of pretend concern. He shrugged. 'You can't serve everyone. So you insist on helping no one?'

Elsbeth sighed.

Father Manfried clapped his hands together, twice. On the back of his right hand, Elsbeth saw the crisscrossing slashes of an old war wound. 'In particular, there's a man and his daughter, who I want you to meet.'

Elsbeth lay back down on her wooden bed.

Manfried's brows spasmed in annoyance. 'He is an important man. A very pious man. He owns a good third of Averheim's best land. He's a copious contributor to the new cathedral there.'

'The cathedral your grandfather planned and your father built,' said Elsbeth, placing her sweat-stained, flattened pillow over the top half of her face.

Manfried smiled happily. He thought she was making his point for him. For such a calculating man, he had a wide streak of naiveté in him. 'Yes. And he is very influential in the church. He has sent his sole and precious daughter all this way. She is barren, you see.'

'Not crippled, or infected with some wasting disease, or suffering the creeping taint of Chaos?'

'No,' said Manfried, 'just barren. And it is very important to the father that she be marriageable.'

'If she's yet to be married, how do you know she's barren?'

'Her previous husband, when there was no issue, annulled the union, and sent her back. It was quite humiliating for the father. Now he has a chance to reverse his mortification and seal a great alliance – providing the girl can be made fruitful.'

'So now Sigmar is an arranger of marriages?'

'It is, in fact, crucial to the Empire that its wealthy nobles are bound together in this time of crisis. That they prosper, so that armies might be fielded and equipped.'

'And it wouldn't be that if you please this man, that he might use his influence to get back what was stolen from you? Make you prelate of the church at Averheim?'

Manfried's face constricted. 'You seem well enough. Or is it time for another treatment?'

Elsbeth felt the fear again. It shamed her, but she couldn't help it. Running a retreat full of sisters had never prepared her to deal with a man like this. She looked at her stone bowl. She imagined striking him with it. 'I don't need another treatment,' she said, her voice breaking.

# CHAPTER FIVE

A NIGHT SPENT sleeping on cold rock had dampened the pilgrims' spirits, rendering them dull-faced but compliant. They pulled down their tents quickly, hoping that vigorous effort would get some warmth back into their bones. The formation proved easier to set now that Krieger was dead; Angelika had Altman drag the stretcher, with the corpse strapped to it, down the side of the plateau.

After several hours worth of downward climb, they found a patch of forest where the earth was deep enough to make a shallow grave. The friar stepped up to speak words in aid of the slain. It would have been better to have a devotee of the death-god, Morr, do the honours, but Gerhold's prayers would have to suffice. He commended Thomas's soul to Sigmar, pointing out that he had died both a warrior and a pious man. Angelika

*Robin D Laws*

watched as Franziskus, Richart and Jurg spaded earth over Krieger's body, which was already shrunken and diminished. Under the handkerchief covering the poor man's face, Angelika knew that his expression still bore the shock of death.

Krieger's effects were not much, but Angelika had claimed them out of principle. She needed to assure herself that she had not taken leave of her senses altogether. In her pocket was the purse she'd removed from Krieger's belt. It contained a mere dozen crowns and a brass brooch of questionable value. His sword and hauberk would be worth more than these, so she'd added them to Franziskus's pack.

The group made good, quiet progress through the woods. They'd almost returned to the lowest level of the pass and were skirting a long stretch of impassable rock. The thick trees would screen them, Angelika hoped, from any marauders prowling the floor of the pass. They'd also give the miller more chances to whip branches in the summoner's face, but so far he hadn't availed himself of any.

Noon arrived along with the sound of a rushing stream, up ahead. Angelika declared an hour's stop for rest and water.

Franziskus volunteered to fill water skins for Devorah and the prioress. By the time he'd got back, Heilwig had gone off into the woods to attend to her bodily business, leaving him alone with the pretty sister. 'Here you go,' he said. She unscrewed the container's copper cap and lifted it to her lips, drinking greedily. The water glugged as it cascaded down her throat. Little streams of it escaped her lips and dripped down her skin. Her head was turned so that the sunlight illuminated the network of tiny, downy hairs on the side of her cheek.

'Aaah,' she said, as her thirst was quenched.

Franziskus tried to think of something to say. Over the course of an instant, a number of possibilities came to mind, all of which he rejected. He would not say 'Cold water, isn't it?' Or 'It's good to drink, after a long walk, is it not?' Or 'Whenever you need more water, just ask.' Or any of the dozen other variations of a similar theme.

'So are you a deserter?' she asked him, brightly.

He stammered.

'Why else would you be down here, a young man of such obvious qualities?'

'Ah,' Franziskus said, at length. He did not think she was teasing him, or criticising, but he could not be sure.

'I would think it would be very hard to serve in the army. It's a brutal life.'

Franziskus nodded. 'My troop was wiped out. If it weren't for Angelika, I'd have shared their fate.'

Devorah watched Angelika, who sat on the edge of the stream, trailing her small bare feet through the icy water. Her expression was masked. 'You two are...?' Devorah asked.

'No, no,' said Franziskus. 'Not in the slightest. We are travelling companions, that is all. I owe her my life, so I've sworn to protect her as best I can.'

Devorah gave Angelika a thorough squint. 'Though she, like me, is of the weaker sex, she doesn't look as if she needs much protecting.'

'She has made that point herself,' Franziskus said. 'And perhaps I made the wrong decision. But I decided it was to her I owed the higher debt, and so stayed at her side, instead of returning home to Averland and joining up with a new troop. Which is what the law would have me do.'

The sister cocked her head thoughtfully. 'I think fighting wars is right for only certain kinds of men. Others, with finer sensibilities, should do other things.'

'Perhaps you are right.'

'I had two brothers go off to the wars. One of them, the older brother, was the proper sort for it. He fought bravely and rose to quartermaster. My younger brother, was a frail sort, and melancholy. He didn't outlast his first engagement. In the end, though, my older brother wound up joining him. It's the way of this world of ours, or so I suppose.'

A pause ensued, during which Franziskus struggled for a way to navigate the conversation to more congenial waters. 'So what moved you to enter the cloister?' he heard himself asking. He cursed himself for being an idiot.

Devorah kicked absently at a small stone. 'My father was a free farmer. Our land got blighted by Chaos. We'd plant grain and vegetables and all we'd get for our labour was a field writhing with strange, rotting worms. In the end we were depending entirely on my brothers sending home part of their combat pay. When they both died…' She dipped her head down. Franziskus patted her on the arm. She snaked an arm around him and squeezed him tightly. Then, just as quickly, she disengaged from him. 'When they both died, my father pleaded with the prioress to take me in. If it weren't for her mercy – I wouldn't like to think how I'd be earning my living now.'

'Then you owe everything to Shallya's mercy,' Franziskus said.

Devorah nodded. 'I'm afraid that's so.'

'Are you still in contact with your father?'

She wiped at her eyes. 'Let's think of something cheerful to say to each other.'

Nothing came to mind. Franziskus saw Ivo Kirchgeld at the stream, bending low to fill his water container, his narrow buttocks wiggling up into the air. He caught Devorah's gaze and nodded toward the pardoner, letting her in on the joke. She covered her mouth, giggling like a wind chime.

'You've chosen some colourful travelling companions,' Franziskus said.

Devorah laughed. 'I didn't choose them. The group just formed itself, up in Grenzstadt. We were all ready to leave at about the same time, and–'

'So there you are!' a loud voice cooed. Franziskus turned to see the Widow Kloster bustling up toward them, thick feet tromping through the weeds and wet grasses. He sighed and clenched his teeth. He thought he saw an instant's worth of frustration on Devorah's face, too, but could not be sure. 'You now!' cried the widow. She tottered over to him, puffing from the effort, and steadied herself by grabbing onto his shoulder. He struggled to keep his balance.

'I've been meaning to talk to you, young man.' She'd added a new fillip of beet-purple makeup to her mask of rouge and powder; smudgy triangles ran from beneath her eyes up to each temple, in an apparent attempt to simulate cheekbones. In actual effect, it made her round head resemble a red cabbage. Though no expert on female self-decoration, it seemed to Franziskus that this new make-up colour did not go well with her orange hair.

'You're not going to just stand there like a post, are you?' she asked him. She brayed out a laugh and shot a practiced elbow into his ribcage. 'I know young men like you. All stiff and straight. It's the uncertainty of youth. You need a little breaking in. What was your name again?'

'Franziskus.'

'The exact name had slipped my mind but I knew it was a bold and handsome one.' The Widow Kloster fished into a little leather pouch that dangled from her belt. She withdrew a small silver box, enamelled with a pink and thorny rose, and popped it open. She held it under Franziskus's nose. 'Snuff?' she asked. Franziskus made a face. The widow packed a ball of snuff into her right nostril and inhaled mightily. Devorah and Franziskus watched as she coughed and sputtered. Finally she caught her breath again. 'They say the young are wild and profligate,' she went on, 'but my experience is the opposite. So many of them are like you two, nervous of your every desire and frightened of life.' She tamped a bigger wad of snuff into the other side of her nose.

'You wanted to speak to me about something?' Franziskus asked.

'I'm doing it right now.' She inhaled the snuff, shuddered as it did its work on her then placed her paws on Devorah's arm. 'He's a lovely one, isn't he?'

Devorah did not know what to say.

'See?' crowed the widow. 'That's what I'm speaking of. Clearly the two of you are moon-eyed for one another, yet you have no idea what do to about it. So you stand about like a couple of bewildered scarecrows. Young people must not waste themselves on one another. They don't know what they're appreciating. You, my dear' – she pointed at Devorah with the jagged fingernail of her little finger – 'must get yourself out of that wretched habit before you go all mouldy inside, like that stuck-up prioress of yours. Put that fine frame of yours to its proper use. Find a silver-templed old fellow with a codpiece full of coin. That's what I did when I was your age. Never regretted it.'

Devorah edged away from her. She ignored the girl, her attention now fixed on Franziskus. 'How many husbands do you think I've had, young Franziskus?'

'Only one at a time, I should hope.'

She caromed a jolly punch off his shoulder. 'A japester! How delightful! Five, Franziskus, I've had five husbands. Each one ideally suited, more or less, to my circumstances at the time. The first ones had money. And once I had their money, I made certain the later ones had... something else.'

She grabbed Franziskus's buttock, giving it a lingering, appreciative squeeze.

'Milady…' Franziskus protested.

Kinge Kloster chortled. 'I'm not a lady and I know you want to seem shocked but are secretly relieved by my forwardness. It was the same way with my previous husband, Baldwin. Muscular but shy. He was grateful that a woman of experience came along to take his reins in her teeth. Always said so.'

Devorah spoke up. 'What dreadful fate befell poor Baldwin?'

The widow's expression turned mournful – or as mournful as her painted smile allowed. 'He was taken in the night, by some ghost or daemon. I was awakened by our bedroom shutter banging in the wind, and my sad, beautiful boy was gone. The mattress was still warm where he had lain. A dreadful loss.'

'So you are going to the Holy Mountain to pray for Baldwin's return?' asked Devorah.

'I would not so impose on Shallya's powers. A replacement will do me fine.'

Franziskus saw movement on the fringes of his vision. He stepped back to peer into the woods. To shield the ladies from undue alarm, he kept his manner calm.

'As you say, Widow Kloster,' said Devorah, 'you are worldly and I am not. But is your attitude toward love not a little… mercenary?'

The widow's reply began with a laugh. Franziskus only half-heard it, his ears perked for untoward sounds from the trees. Then the smell hit him – the tell-tale sour vinegar of goblin sweat. He hauled his sabre from his scabbard. 'Angelika!' he shouted.

'Goblins!'

They came from the tops of the tallest pines, licking down the trees like green flames. There were at least a couple dozen of the hunched, human-shaped creatures, and they were coming at Franziskus and the ladies from all sides. They chittered and hissed, their tiny red eyes gleaming with violent malice. Their faces were pointed, oversized, and angular. They had big noses, sharp ears and spear-tip chins.

The goblins' greasy hides were a variety of forest colours, and their brownish warts and mottles lent them added camouflage. Some had clad themselves in furs, others in armour. Still others wore baggy, oversized clothing taken from waylaid travellers that were still stained with the blood of their original owners. A few were completely naked, save for a few splotches of war paint. They held crude, jagged daggers in their knotty little fists. They were four to five feet high, gobbets of muscle wired to their bony frames and they moved with an oddly riveting, crab-wise agility. Franziskus had fought goblins before. Although less frightening than their larger, braver cousins, the orcs, they were cunning hit-and-run fighters. He didn't see or smell any of the giant wolves that some goblins rode, and was thankful for that: the mounts were generally deadlier than their riders.

Goblins hit the flatland running and loped at Franziskus. They saw his big, swinging blade and altered their course to swerve around him, dashing at the sister and the widow. Kinge Kloster screamed,

'Franziskus! Save me!'

Franziskus lunged to Devorah's side, stabbing his blade downwards to impale a naked goblin. Pinned to the ground, it bucked and writhed. Franziskus kept his grip on its hilt and worked the sword back and forth inside the goblin's screaming body until he felt the blade get between vertebrae. Then he twisted it. Crunching ensued; the goblin stopped moving.

Another leapt at Franziskus's face. He smashed it with his elbow. As it went down on its behind, he planted his boot in its crotch. It caterwauled furiously until Franziskus brought his blade chopping down into its throat. Thick, gluey goblin blood, hot and sticky, squirted up onto Franziskus's face, matting his long blond locks to his tunic. He heard the widow screaming and turned her way. Then he saw that Devorah had a goblin clawing its way up her leg. He dived at it, bringing his sabre down like a cleaver, half-severing its left leg at the knee joint. It gargled, arterial blood firing into the air behind it, but it kept on clawing at Devorah, shredding her habit, exposing her pale, thin legs. Franziskus stabbed down with the tip of his sabre half a dozen times, not stopping until the thing went entirely limp.

Franziskus looked around for the widow. He saw her being dragged away by a quintet of armoured goblins, one of whom had shoved its fingers into her squealing mouth. Another goblin dashed from the bottom of a tree at Devorah. Franziskus stepped into its path, and used his blade like a bat to clobber it in the face, flattening its nose and sending a shower of malformed teeth raining down onto the forest floor. It fell back, stunned. Franziskus brought his blade back over his head, readying himself for a powerful slashing blow. The bleeding goblin turned tail and pelted for the trees, scrabbling on all fours like a wounded dog.

Franziskus called again for help from the camp but saw that they, too, were besieged. Angelika had rounded the able-bodied men into a circular formation around the less robust pilgrims; their weapons pointed outwards at the charging gobbos. Brother Lemoine smacked a goblin with his staff; it grabbed on tight, so he hefted it into the air like a massive fish and brought it crashing into a rock. It twitched, played dead for a moment then ran off, limping. One of its comrades took a dagger in the eye as Angelika broke from the formation to run Franziskus's way.

Franziskus heard a crashing beside him and wheeled just in time to incise a cut in another goblin's brow. Blood dripped into the creature's eyes. Franziskus kicked its blade from its hand and then swung again at its head, slicing off the tip of its cauliflower ear.

A trio of goblins rallied about twenty yards away and loped in together, brandishing daggers and yelling war cries in their discordant, throaty language. Franziskus backed into Devorah until he could feel the heat of her slim body against his. 'There's a dagger in my belt,' he told Devorah. 'Take it.'

'I don't–' said Devorah.

'Take it!'

'I don't–'

The goblins charged; Franziskus could tell that his dagger was still in its sheath.

Franziskus readied his next blow for the biggest of the goblins, which ran in the middle, its eyes locked on his. He would have to take it down in a single strike and then deal with the others who would start circling Devorah. The goblin carried a big wooden shield, haphazardly studded with nails and bits of melted lead, and had scraggly white mutton chops extruding from its cheeks. It opened its mouth and lolled out a long, veiny tongue.

It was within range and Franziskus sent his sword hammering down. The goblin deflected the blow with its shield then banged the edge of the shield up into Franziskus's armpit, throwing its weight onto him, knocking him off his feet. Franziskus's perceptions slowed for the ensuing moment of flight. He sailed backwards through the air, apparently for an eternity, his sword-arm helplessly splayed out at his side. The mutton-chopped goblin was lying on his chest, its eyes rolling crazily back in its skull. Then came the awareness of impact, followed by wracking, generalised pain–

Then time started up again.

The goblin slavered into Franziskus's face and raised its fist, which it had wrapped in a plate-mail glove studded with rusty spikes. At the same time it jammed its other forearm under Franziskus's jaw, holding him still to receive the blow. It gave itself a moment to chortle. A dagger sprouted from its neck, its point piercing its Adam's apple from the inside. The goblin slumped onto Franziskus's chest. Franziskus rolled it over onto the ground. He looked at Angelika's second dagger, shoved to the hilt in the back of his enemy's neck.

Her face, sweaty and scratched, loomed over his. She held out her hand for him. He took it and got to his feet. He saw Richart Pfeffer, the landowner, comforting Devorah, who trembled in his arms. 'I couldn't take–' she kept saying. 'I couldn't take–' Franziskus soon realised that she meant she couldn't take his dagger from his belt, and blamed herself for it.

'Your hide leaking?' Angelika asked, examining him.

'Not unduly,' replied Franziskus.

Richart's eyes met his, and the landholder stepped aside for him. Devorah rushed into his arms. 'I'm sorry; I couldn't take up your weapon. My faith forbids it.'

'Of course,' said Franziskus, placing his hand, gummy with goblin blood, on the back of her wimpled head. He pressed her face into his shoulder. 'Of course.'

She pushed away from him, struck by sudden realisation. 'The widow!' she exclaimed. 'You've got to go rescue the widow!'

A series of grim and knowing looks passed between Angelika, Franziskus and Richart.

Angelika patted the girl on the back. 'The prioress is back with the others,' she said. 'She was in the woods when the goblins came, and seems distressed. Go attend to her.'

Devorah nodded and slowly padded her way out of the trees back to the stream.

'You owe Richart your thanks,' said Angelika. 'I couldn't have dispatched all three goblins on my own. Not in time, leastways.'

Franziskus clasped Richart's hand. 'I didn't see you.'

'Melee can be confusing,' Richart said.

'How many of us are any good in a fight?' Angelika asked.

'The three of us,' said Richart, studying a sizeable slash across the back of his right hand. The young physic would have to part with more of his bandages.

Franziskus felt a pang of offence that the balding landowner had suddenly been admitted to the decision-making circle without his say-so, but decided that the feeling was envious and unworthy, so suppressed it.

Richart continued his list: 'The shipman. Altman and Lemoine, at a pinch. The doctor and the summoner, perhaps.'

'We all know what state the widow's in now – if she's lucky,' said Angelika. 'But for the morale of the others, we can't seem to callously abandon her.'

'On the other hand,' said Richart, 'you don't want to get anyone else killed for the sake of her corpse.'

'Indeed,' said Angelika. 'So we can't send the entire group crashing into the bush to find her. Nor can we leave them here undefended while we go off as a search party.'

The three of them spent a quarter hour reiterating the disagreeable choices they faced. Finally they decided that Richart would stay with the others while Angelika and Franziskus went out to track the goblins. They'd spend no more than half a day on the search, and would fall back at the merest whiff of another confrontation.

Angelika and Franziskus set off, leaving Richart to explain where they'd gone. Almost immediately they found a trail of flattened grass and followed it. A damp, dark substance spattered the grass.

'Blood,' said Franziskus.

Angelika nodded. She sniffed the air. No vinegar smell. She looked up into the tree-tops. No signs of goblins. They followed the trail as it wound around a rotten log. Behind it they found the widow's corpse, its torso opened up to expose the organs inside. Franziskus blanched. Angelika put the back of her hand across his chest, to stop him from going ahead.

Angelika crouched. She squinted, searching for snares or tripwires. She checked the ground beneath the body, in case the goblins had dragged her onto a deadfall. 'It's not trapped,' she said. 'I thought they might have taken her to lure us out here. But I don't see any sign of them.'

'Why did they take her, then?'

Angelika shrugged. 'Why do goblins prey on anyone? They thought she might be carrying some shiny things.' She squatted over the widow's feet and took a tentative tug at them. A gentle sloshing noise arose from her body cavity, as her innards shifted. Angelika's face wrinkled up in revulsion. 'This will be messy work. I wish we had a tarpaulin.'

'Perhaps we should bury her here. Spare the others the sight of her.'

'Then they'll just imagine ten times worse. Here, help me roll her. We'll let her drain out a bit before we try to move her.'

Franziskus paled but got on his knees to help roll the widow nonetheless. 'Once more I am proven the fool,' he said.

'How so?'

'I thought guarding a few pilgrims would prove less gruesome than our usual pursuits.'

They stood back as Kloster's juices soaked into the earth. Angelika tensed at a scrabbling sound. They whirled, but saw only a pair of squirrels chasing one another around the trunk of a beech tree. They waited. They hefted the corpse – Angelika taking the arms and Franziskus, the legs – and trudged warily back in the direction of the stream.

When they could see the stream through the trees, they set the body down. They approached the group, which Richart had gathered into a small knot along the stream-bed. Angelika beckoned him forward and told him what had happened.

'How fares your search?' asked Stefan, the advocate.

Angelika ignored him.

'We all have a right to know!' he called.

Angelika stared him down. 'Then go among her things and gather up some bedding. We need a shroud.'

Stefan appeared stricken. He stood rooted in place. Devorah got the widow's bedroll and went to Franziskus's side with it. He went to take it from her, but she kept it.

'I'll attend to her,' she said. 'It is nothing new to me. I have attended to sisters at the cloister, after their passing.'

'Very well,' said Angelika, leading Devorah to the corpse. As if tucking her in for the night, Devorah gently rolled Kinge Kloster's mortal remnants into the bedding. Angelika watched over her.

'I thought unmerciful thoughts about her, moments before she was taken,' Devorah confessed.

'She was an annoying person,' replied Angelika. 'The manner of her death doesn't change that.'

'It is my duty to rise above.'

Angelika did not have a reply. The prioress could give the girl whatever penance or counsel she required. For her part, Angelika was glad someone else was willing to do the dirty work, for once.

She helped the girl carry the body to the stream, where the group of pilgrims parted, eyes averted. Devorah unwrapped the widow, stripped her of her bloodied clothing, and washed her body with the rags. The pilgrims broke up. Normally, Angelika would have warned them to be careful and to stick together, but in this instance the point seemed obvious. The stream ran briefly red then was clear again.

Angelika took Franziskus and Richart aside as the young sister continued her ministrations. 'We'll need to get the widow quickly into the ground and get ourselves moving,' Angelika said. They spoke for a while about goblins, trading guesses on the odds of a return sally.

Devorah approached, the sleeves of her habit pushed up past her elbows, her hands and forearms damp. 'She's ready,' said the sister.

'Then let's get a hole dug,' said Angelika.

Richart cast his gaze around the camp. 'I have business to attend to,' he said, and marched off into the trees.

Franziskus grunted self-righteously. 'Herr Pfeffer turns out to be a shirker, when it comes to the spadework.'

'Why should that surprise you?' asked Angelika, as they went to find the shovels. 'The two of you come from the same stock, don't you?'

'I think not,' Franziskus said, working to keep the sniff of snobbery out of his tone. 'Nothing in his bearing suggests a noble education. He most likely came by his land holdings through a soldier's grant – or by trade, even.'

'Heaven forbid,' said Angelika, tossing him a shovel. He grabbed it and they walked over a small hump in the earth in search of an appropriately sheltered spot. 'You think she'd like it here?'

'I'm sure she'd prefer to be in some handsome young fellow's bed.'

'Wouldn't we all?'

They started digging.

A scream rang out.

Friar Gerhold came running at them, mouth open wide, snowy hair askew, his grimy rope belt flying out behind him. 'The goblins have been back!' he wailed. 'They've killed the bailiff!'

# CHAPTER IX

# CHAPTER SIX

'NO GOBLIN DID this,' said Angelika, kneeling over Altman's body. He was sprawled where the friar had found him, his eyes staring heavenwards. The bailiff's well-fattened features had settled into a frozen glare of fright and outrage.

The others gathered all around Angelika, hemming her in. She gestured for them to move back, and they did, only to creep up again almost immediately.

'But that's a goblin blade!' exclaimed Jurg. Indeed, a jagged goblin dagger, still slick with the bailiff's blood, lay in the pine needles, a few feet from the body.

'It certainly is,' said Angelika, picking it up. 'And that's why it can't have been a goblin who did this. To you or me, this dagger's trash – it hardly counts as a weapon. But to a wretched gobbo, a blade like this would be his most precious possession. You never see a goblin leave his weapon on the battle-field.'

'But it's quite evident that the dagger's covered in blood,' said Brother Lemoine.

Angelika held the blade up to the fatal wound – a jagged gash cut across Altman's throat. 'Oh, this is the weapon that did it, all right. The serrations match the wound. It's just that it was wielded by someone other than a goblin.'

Rausch was next to object. 'Who else but a goblin would use a goblin weapon?'

Angelika lay the weapon down in the grass and rose to her feet. 'Don't tell me you find this anything but obvious.'

The pilgrims indicated universal bafflement.

'One of you did it,' Angelika said. She kept her attention on the corpse, hoping that Franziskus would be clever enough to watch for telltale signs of guilt.

'Where would any of us have got our hands on a goblin blade?' Rausch asked.

Angelika beckoned to the site of the recent battle. 'Didn't we just slay a raft of the devils? They can't take their weapons with them when they get killed, can they?' She gestured to a fallen tree, behind which the greenskin corpses were heaped. 'Anyone here could have helped himself – or herself – to one of their weapons. Did any of you see anyone else skulking around the bodies?'

Ivo raised a trembling finger to point at Richart. 'He was the one who piled them all over there, while you were gone. He had ample chance to snatch up one of those stinking knives!'

Richart took a step at him; he hid behind the prioress. 'You wretch! After I stood up for you...'

'You were there...' Ivo burbled.

'Yes, I was,' said Richart, his olive skin turning rosy with anger. 'And I threw all of their weapons into a pile by the bodies, and left them. I was leery to even touch them, lest I give myself lockjaw.'

Devorah gulped, summoning the courage to speak. 'But Fraulein Angelika – how can you presume that one of us did it?'

'Indeed,' Waldemar said. 'Surely it could be that there's some human bandit shadowing us, hoping to throw us off the trail by posing as a goblin. We must depart in haste, and leave him far behind.'

'Or smoke him out as he tries to follow us,' suggested Udo, the merchant, idly running his fingers through his tawny fringe of beard.

Angelika threw up her hands. 'One of you did this. Those of you who pretend otherwise might be next.'

'What motive would any of us have?' asked Gerhold, in apparent sincerity.

'That's the question, isn't it?'

'We are penitents, on a holy pilgrimage,' said Ivo.

'I'm not sure what that has to do with anything. Whichever of you killed Altman might have done so out of some private grudge. Or you might be planning to slay more of us. I wish I could stop to figure out which of you did it, but with goblins all around us, we don't have that privilege. So gather up your gear. We've got to put some distance between ourselves and this place.'

'You mean you're just going to forget this ever happened?' asked Stefan, puffing his chest in preparation for an eloquent tirade.

'What do you think? I'll have to march and interrogate simultaneously.'

The advocate, his cap-feather bobbling in the breeze, faltered momentarily then recovered his dignity to embark on a new line of attack. 'I am an officer of the law. It should be I who conducts the interrogations.'

'You're a suspect,' said Angelika.

'Excuse me for asking this,' said Lemoine, 'but caution is the watchword, Fraulein Angelika.'

'Out with it.'

'How do we know it wasn't you?'

'Because it wasn't.'

'Angelika was with me, burying the widow,' said Franziskus.

'But – and I say this only because in my abbey, back in Bretonnia, we were taught to think in a highly methodical, critical manner, which I know is a mode of thought unaccustomed to you simpler folk of the Empire. It must be pointed out that the two of you are confederates, so to speak. Therefore, if you did intend a plan to systematically murder us and strip us of our goods, it would make logical sense that you would vouch for one another, ah, in the course of so doing.'

'Does anyone else here,' Angelika intoned, 'believe that Franziskus and I are here to murder you all and take your possessions?'

'Well, since you took over the task of looking after us, three of us are already dead,' Ivo muttered.

Ludwig swatted him on the back of the head.

'Ow,' he complained.

'You prize idiot,' said Ludwig. 'If it weren't for these two, the entire lot of us would be goblin food.'

Ivo had nothing to say to this.

Ludwig stepped from the crowd and pointed a gnarled forefinger around at his fellow pilgrims. 'And furthermore, I say anyone else who tries to stop Angelika here from finding out which of us did it, is probably the one, and we ought to string him from the highest tree branch. Is there any man to gainsay me?' His finger stopped on Brother Lemoine.

'I hasten to add,' Lemoine sputtered, 'that I was speaking not from my personal assessment of Fraulein Angelika and Herr Franziskus, which could not possibly be higher. I was merely making an academic point.'

Ludwig thrust his face into that of the other man. 'Well if you have any more academic points for us, you should know that you're in danger of me thrusting them up your monastical backside. Understand?'

Lemoine set his jaw. 'Perhaps it's just this sort of unbridled fury that Angelika should be examining as she–'

Richart stepped in to separate the two men, shoving Ludwig back. Ludwig shot his arm past Richart's head to jab his pointing finger once more at Lemoine's forehead. 'In my years at sea, I served with many a Bretonnian,' Ludwig spat, 'and none of them was worth a rancid dog's liver. And my opinion of monks ain't so high, either, come to think of it!'

'Does anyone else have any brilliant thoughts?' Angelika asked. They shut up. 'Then in that case do what I say and go get your things. And I'd like to get finished with this murder before the next one occurs, so no one is to wander away while we're breaking camp. Even if you're only ducking behind a tree to relieve yourself, take someone with you.'

'Preferably not the killer,' Jurg said.

'Go!' Angelika barked.

The pilgrims shuffled discontentedly away. Angelika could hear mutterings of mutiny as they went. Waving Franziskus over to her side, she crouched over the body once again.

Without enthusiasm, Franziskus approached. 'Do you really think you can tell anything by looking at the poor fellow's body?'

'I may have seen more battlefield deaths than ordinary murders, but I do know my way around a corpse. Look at this.' She held up Altman's limp right hand. 'Our culprit had some reason to break Altman's fingers.' The first three fingers were snapped completely back, broken at the knuckle. Holding it at the wrist, she offered the hand to Franziskus, but he declined to take it. He straightened himself back up and groaned, rubbing at the small of his back. The sudden exertion of the fight was catching up with him, and his muscles were cramping.

'Anything else of note?' he asked.

'Not that I've seen so far. But I'm going to stay kneeling here for a while, as if I'm learning all sorts of incriminating things. Then you can round them up and we'll get ourselves back on the trail.'

As SHE'D DONE during the first day of their journey, Angelika took the group up into the hills surrounding the floor of the pass. With goblins about, it would be supremely idiotic to stay down on the flatland, even though the well-forested slopes made it hard to keep a vigilant eye out for the killer.

Angelika told Franziskus to take the lead. She didn't entirely trust him with point position. Though he was steadily improving, the young Stirlander was not yet a seasoned woodsman. She could easily imagine him stepping into a viper's nest, or leading the group into an ambush. It couldn't be helped, though. If she was going to play the role of inquisitor, she'd have to devote her full attention to it. Perhaps she would be lucky, and Altman's murderer would turn out to be an inept liar. Most killings, Angelika knew, were impulsive or ill planned. With the exception of a few hardened professionals, most men found it easier to commit murder than to convincingly deny it afterwards.

The prioress was closest, so Angelika pulled her aside first. Heilwig huffed, and fussed agitatedly with a set of lacquered ebony prayer beads. 'Surely you need ask no questions of me,' she said.

'Of course not, but as an example to others I'm sure you'll play along.'

The prioress searched Angelika's face for the signs of condescension. 'Very well then.'

'You had no quarrel with the bailiff?'

'I have no quarrel with anyone. Murder is the very antithesis of Shallya's doctrines.'

'And Altman did not test your vows more strenuously than any other here?'

Heilwig shook her head. 'I would never stoop to harm any person, no matter what I thought of them. But if I was forced to name one among us who tests my forbearance, it would not be poor Altman.'

'What do you mean?'

'That silky-haired mooncalf you call your partner.'

'Franziskus?'

'He's leading my Devorah into gross and carnal temptation. With those dewy eyes of his. And those velvet cheeks. I request that you order him to cease all attempts at seduction. She has vowed her chastity to Shallya. By pursuing her, he imperils her soul.'

'But Shallya is the goddess of mercy, is she not?'

'You know that she is.'

'If Devorah were to take Franziskus to her bed, it would be a surpassing act of mercy. I'm sure Shallya would understand.'

'I should have expected my plea to fall on deaf ears. You've made your irreligion plain.'

'Don't worry about Franziskus. His finely attuned sense of guilt will stop him from doing anything more enjoyable than a little chaste pining.'

'I've seen his sort before. He cloaks himself in virtue, but when his lusts are aroused...'

'The preservation of Devorah's maidenhood seems of great importance to you. I don't suppose the bailiff laid his hands on her?'

'His eyes perhaps wandered where they should not, but I laid a righteous scolding upon him, and after that he comported himself acceptably.' Heilwig's speech slowed as she realised that she'd just assigned herself a motive for the crime. 'And even if I were inclined to callous slaughter, do you think I, a feeble old woman, could have overpowered that great hog of a man?'

Angelika shrugged. 'I merely ask questions. Tell me – is your abbey prosperous?'

'We are blessed with many benefactors. The funds I control are disbursed to the needy.'

'But they would be more than enough to pay one of these other rag-tags to send Altman prematurely to his maker, if you were so inclined?'

'I have said it already: I am not.' With a conclusive flap of her habit, she swept away. Angelika observed her as she fixed herself to Devorah's side. The canny old bat had certainly changed the subject quickly. Her concern for Devorah's chastity would seem a poor reason to kill – unless, Angelika mused, the prioress herself harboured a few untoward feelings for her pretty young charge. It wouldn't be the first convent romance. Angelika resolved to question Devorah closely.

But before doing that, she selected another pilgrim by whim, settling on the merchant, Udo Kramer, who had so far made little impression on her. He was perhaps on his way to fifty years old, with a vigorous manner, a trim frame, a healthy crop of curly chestnut hair sitting happily on top of his head. A matching fringe of beard highlighted his jaw-line. He wore sturdy, rugged clothing in forest tones: thick trousers of earthen brown and a pine-green tunic.

'We have not yet had much occasion to speak,' Angelika said.

'As you mostly speak to us in order to abuse us, I am pleased to have been excluded from your discourse,' the merchant replied, his tone light and bantering.

'You are a wit, I see.'

'In my profession, one must never let the customer know what one thinks of him. No matter how carefully honed my wit may be, I rarely get the chance to take it from its scabbard.'

The group reached a narrow trail bordered on the right by a steep drop down onto exposed rock. Angelika checked the front of the line; Franziskus seemed to be maintaining close attention to the pilgrims' safety.

'What is your profession, precisely?'

'I am an importer and reseller of goods. I bring in shipments from all over the Empire, to my shops in Averheim.'

'Shipments of what?'

'Grain and meal. Oil, and the lanterns to burn it in. Rugs, tapestries, fine brocades. If you can think of it, one of my enterprises most likely buys and sells it. Lately we've been doing a brisk trade in ornately decorated beer steins.'

'And you've come on this pilgrimage for what reason?'

'It is well known – at least, all the preachers say it – that trade stains the soul. Even one as successful as I am is little more than a wretched grubber after money, or so it is written. Yet without my efforts, they'd all starve: from the lowliest friar to the Grand Theogonist himself. But who am I to question the received wisdom of the ages? So here I trudge, seeking expiation for the sins of commerce I've already taken upon myself – and dispensation for those I'll commit in the future.'

'You seem to have the transaction all worked out.'

'A blessing from Mother Elsbeth will carry weight with Averheim's city fathers, with whom I must often negotiate.'

'And the bailiff – what was he to you?'

Udo thought a moment before answering. 'A fellow pilgrim, no more, no less. I had little call to speak with him.'

'A good merchant is a skilful judge of character. How would you assess him?'

'Not quite the jolly fool he made himself out to be. I am glad he fought against those orcs. He was brave.'

'Who would want to do him in?'

'The miller, as you know, mocked him in front of all of us.'

'Maybe Altman perhaps went after the miller, who then got the better of him?'

Udo shrugged. He sidestepped to avoid a cloud of gnats, but they shifted to follow him. Screwing his face up in revulsion, he spat one of the little insects out of his mouth then wiped his lips repeatedly, to rid himself of any residue. 'I don't know what happened,' he said.

'But it was Jurg who found him, correct?'

Udo parcelled out a noncommittal nod. 'I lack specific knowledge of his guilt.'

A shriek came from up ahead.

Angelika grabbed her knife and dashed past Udo, weaving between the other pilgrims. She saw Franziskus stooped on the tip of a granite outcrop, hands on the sides of his head. He was peering disconsolately down into empty space. She crept up beside him, first testing the rock to see that it would hold both of them.

Franziskus turned to her. 'Look what he's done now,' he said.

Ivo Kirchgeld had fallen down the slope, which was nearly so steep as to qualify as a cliff. Much of it was clad in a layer of earth and grass, but erosion had exposed a network of sharp-edged rocks and boulders. An intermittent brown streak of torn-up sod marked the path of the pardoner's jaunt down the hillside. Ivo stood on an expanse of naked rock, frantically struggling to free his foot from the roots of a dead and twisted pine. The pine enveloped the slab of stone, sending a dried-out, branchless trunk shooting up crookedly into the air. 'I'm stuck!' Ivo cried. His high-pitched voice reverberated up through the mountains above them. 'Stuck!' He was twenty feet or so down from the level of the trail.

Angelika hissed at him. 'Silence yourself, you nitwit, before you attract every predator in fifty miles!'

'But I'm stuck!' he cried, lowering only slightly the volume of his wails.

Angelika edged over for a better look at him. 'If you got your foot in there, you can get it out.'

'I'm stuck, I tell you!' His ridiculous ears paddled up and down.

'I need rope,' she told the others.

Franziskus, Richart and Ludwig went fumbling into their packs for it. Ivo's pine tree creaked alarmingly. Angelika shook her head and climbed down from the outcrop, carefully picking her way down the slope. The grass proved slippery; she found it easier to keep her footing by stepping from one protruding stone to the next.

'Don't fall!' Ivo shouted.

'I appreciate the advice.' She could hear the holding of breath above as the others watched her climb. The hillside became progressively more vertical the closer she got to Ivo. Angelika told herself that it was impossible for her to fall, because there was no earthly way she was going to die saving someone like Kirchgeld. She made her way down to him, holding onto the dead tree trunk, feeling gravity's pull.

'You're lucky your ankle got caught,' she said. 'Otherwise it'd be – how far down do you think that is? Fifty feet?'

Ivo followed her gaze to the floor of the pass below. 'It seems soft and grassy, however.'

'Then you won't mind if you slip.' Angelika incrementally tilted herself until she could jam a hand between the roots that held Kirchgeld's feet to the rock. 'You've just got to shift your foot a little,' she told him.

'I can't,' he said, trying to move his foot in the wrong direction.

'The other way,' she said.

Kirchgeld easily removed his foot from its trap. Holding tightly to the log, he moved his leg out over empty space, tentatively rotating his ankle, to see if it still worked.

'You hadn't tried the other way at all?' Angelika asked.

'I thought I was stuck,' he said.

'Start climbing. We're going to have to get moving quickly, thanks to your caterwauling.'

Kirchgeld directed an uncertain look up at Franziskus and the others, now a good twenty feet above them. 'We should wait for a rope, shouldn't we?' Roots tore from their tiny patch of dirt as Ivo scrambled up.

'I'll be right behind you,' Angelika lied. She would, in fact, be off to one side of him, ready to quickly sidestep and hug the cliff-side if it looked it looked like Ivo was about to plummet. But once he worked his way free of the tree trunk, the pardoner showed an unexpected agility, travelling easily from stone to stone.

'So would you have had any reason to murder Altman?' Angelika asked him.

'What? Why? Is there something I ought to know?'

'What do you mean?'

'You were asking if I had motive to kill Altman. I don't think I do. Have you discovered something? People are always plotting behind my back. Are they accusing me? I bet it's that summoner, Waldemar, saying I did it. Well, you should look at him. He has a streak of cruelty in him as wide as the River Reik.' A rock rolled out from under Ivo's foot, sailing past Angelika's shoulder. Ivo waved his arms, wobbled, and steadied himself. He chuckled in what seemed like disbelief. 'On the one hand, it's well known that I'm very clumsy. Except that I have a very good sense of balance. You'd think the two things wouldn't go together.' He continued on up the slope.

Angelika became aware of her heart, pounding intensely. 'Isn't there a saying, that Shallya has a soft spot for children, animals and idiots?'

'I think in the actual saying the word used is *fools*, and I resent–'

Up above, Rausch let loose a shout of recognition. He pointed at Jurg. 'Look! Look at his belt! He did it! He killed Altman!'

The miller reached wildly for an object swinging from his purse: it was Altman's relic, the supposed chunk of Sigmar's hammer.

'You lying swine!' he shouted. He grabbed the offending object and tried to rip it loose, but it was tied too tightly. Rausch lunged at Muller. Franziskus headed into the fray, but the pilgrims were gathered closely together. He tried to navigate around the prioress, but she turned the same way to avoid him, and they collided painfully.

Muller dashed along the lip of the slope, with Rausch on his heels. Richart Pfeffer followed.

'Murderer!' the prioress screamed.

The sailor joined the chase, but lost his footing on a skiff of dead leaves and slid along the ground, grunting in pain. Franziskus disengaged himself from the prioress. He smacked into Brother Lemoine, who'd been standing and vacillating, deciding whether or not to join the pursuit.

Muller ran until the slope smoothed itself out then dashed down a mound-like hill into a well-forested gully. Rausch leapt over a log to close the distance and come at his flank. Muller reached for the knife in his belt, but Rausch struck first, crashing into him shoulder to shoulder. Muller skidded on damp pine needles and slid into the trunk of a tree. He fell to his knees. Rausch stuck out an elbow, and fell on the gasping miller. It struck its target at the base of Muller's neck. Muller howled. He was crawling on hands and knees to Richart, who grabbed him and pulled him to his feet. Rausch grabbed Muller's legs.

'I've got him!' the young physic shouted. 'I've got him!' Muller twisted, wrenching himself from Richart's grasp, and launched himself at Rausch, pressing thumbs into his eyes. Richart threw himself onto Muller's back, knocking him off the doctor. Rausch staggered back, blinking furiously to confirm that his eyes were still safely in their sockets. His groping hands found a piece of branch as long and thick as a man's arm.

Angelika, stuck on the slope, clambered her way back up toward the trail. To get past Ivo, she angled herself to the right; Ivo compensated in the opposite direction, blocking her path. Angelika went left; Ivo went left. His boot heel knocked loose some dirt; the wind blew it onto a fuming Angelika.

Muller rolled on top of Rausch, punching furiously. Rausch raised the branch, readying his aim to club Muller down. Franziskus shouted for calm, as his boots slipped beneath him and he slid down into the gully. Rausch swung his branch, but it connected with Franziskus's temple, spinning him around, sending him to the forest floor. Rausch got his hands on Muller's throat and squeezed. Rausch looked at Franziskus, then at Muller, then at Franziskus, then at Muller, deciding who he should attend to. He chose the miller. He clubbed him in the back of the head with the big branch. Blood cascaded from Muller's mouth. His head hit the ground. Rausch brought the branch down on his head again. Muller's head bounced on the ground. Richart danced around the brawling men, and held up his hands as Rausch readied another blow.

'Enough!' he cried.

Muller's body spasmed; he coughed up more blood and reached an arm out to grab at Richart's trouser cuff. Richart stepped away from him.

Finally, Angelika made it into the gully. She pulled Rausch away from Muller who was lying on his back, his stare unfocused, his mouth working like a fish on a dock. Rausch circled him, moving into Angelika's blind spot. Muller lifted up a hand then dropped it at his side, next to his knife. Rausch smashed him in the face with the log. Muller twitched and was still.

'What the hell are you doing?' Angelika shrieked, seizing Rausch by the tunic and shaking him. The branch dropped at Angelika's feet. She picked it up and cocked it to swing at the physic. He flinched. She shook its blunt, dirty end in his face. 'Did you want to kill him?'

Franziskus stumbled over to Muller's side. He jabbed Jurg's throat in search of a pulse. He tested the miller's wrist. 'I think he did kill him,' Franziskus said.

Rausch sank, quaking, to his knees. Thick beads of sweat issued from his neck and forehead. 'He was the murderer,' said Rausch, his voice flat and distant. 'He was going to get us all.'

Without turning her back on the physic, Angelika bent to double-check Franziskus's diagnosis. Indeed, Jurg was dead, his skull deeply indented by Rausch's blows.

Rausch kept talking, his words gaining a childish speed and intensity. 'Bad enough we come out here and find that everything in the world wants to eat and kill us, when it's supposed to be a holy pilgrimage of love and mercy. Bad enough with orcs and goblins and wolves out to slay us. They're the enemies of mankind; that's how it is. But him. He was one of us. He was one of us.' Rausch stopped to twitch, and to take in short, shallow puffs of air. 'Traitorous swine. That's what he was. I didn't mean to kill him but I'm glad I did. He deserved it.' Rausch sat down in the dirt, sticking his head between his knees. 'Deserved it.'

'You don't even know for certain he did it,' Angelika said, more for the others' sake than for Rausch, who had clearly left rational thought behind him.

Richart tugged at the dead miller's purse, untying the bailiff's holy relic. 'He did have this,' he said, dangling it up for Angelika to see. Blood now slicked its chain. 'It is a motive for murder. Anyone who believed Altman's claims would think it worth a dozen fortunes.'

'But no one ridiculed those claims with greater fervour than Jurg.'

Richart clucked his tongue pensively. 'Maybe he thought it was clever, if he was planning on stealing it, to make a big show of how little he thought of it. Or he might have been overcome with sudden greed. He wouldn't be the first man to enviously disparage the thing he secretly covets.'

The rest of the pilgrims approached, led by Ludwig, his arms well scraped from his fall. Behind him came the summoner, the friar and the advocate. The others hung back. Devorah stood behind the prioress, who tightly held her hand.

'All of you come and look at this,' Angelika said. 'I want you to see the physic's handiwork.'

The hangers-back nudged infinitesimally ahead. Ludwig limped right up to look indifferently down into the dead miller's face. Waldemar frowned and did the same, though he quickly averted his gaze.

'From now on,' Angelika announced, 'the meting out of justice will be left to me. Do you all understand?'

'You are our guide, not our leader,' Waldemar sniffed.

'I agreed to get you to the mountain alive. All of you – not just those of you who remain after you start killing each another. Let me make it plainer. The next one of you to raise a hand to one of your fellows gets my dagger between their shoulder blades.'

'What difference does it make,' scoffed the sailor, 'that it was the doctor who dispatched him? You'd have done the same, once you were sure he killed Altman.'

'It's far from proved. Jurg was nettlesome but I saw no evidence he was stupid. Why would he murder a man for a relic, break his fingers to free it from his dying grip, then leave it dangling in plain sight, for all to see?'

The question provoked a chorus of shrugs and murmurs.

'The killer's still among us, alive and well,' announced Angelika, as she strode behind Rausch to wrap her fingers around his ear. He dryly swallowed. 'Clearly he slew Altman for some reason unrelated to the relic, then planted it on Muller to draw suspicion away from himself. Or perhaps he did kill for Altman's holy trinket, but then grew frightened and got rid of it. At any rate, you did his work for him, Physic Rausch.'

'What you say is merely speculation,' Rausch stammered. He seemed to have regained a portion of his composure.

Angelika shook her head. 'If I'm wrong, it makes little difference. If you're wrong, you rashly slew a man for no good reason.'

'But he ran away! Surely that implies guilt!'

'Or he might have thought he was in the sort of crowd who'd falsely accuse him and then beat him to death.' As she spoke, it occurred to her that maybe Rausch was the killer, and that he'd clubbed Muller's skull to cover his own guilt. Angelika resolved to keep an especially close watch on him.

As if reading her suspicions on her face, Rausch stood to address the others. 'Let us have a tribunal, then. If I am to be reproached, let's have the entire group reproach me. The rest of you would have done the same. I know it!'

Prioress Heilwig stepped forward. 'Indeed, Fraulein Fleischer. To elect you as our magistrate and executioner would be greatly imprudent. How do we know you'd hand down your sentences any more mercifully than the physic here? I've already petitioned you on a matter of justice, only to be rudely rebuffed!'

Devorah gave the prioress a puzzled look; Heilwig puckered her haughty brow.

Stefan Recht, the advocate, made it his turn to speak. 'The prioress is right. The entire group must decide what Rausch's punishment would be.'

'I don't warrant any punishment at all!' Rausch stood, exchanging his pitiable demeanour for one of anger. 'You all saw that things simply got out of hand! If he hadn't fought us, it'd be him on trial now!'

'Angelika's right,' said Ludwig. 'There's many a party of pilgrims who never made it to their destination, because they fell to fighting amongst themselves. I say we cease our squabbling, grant the physic proper naval justice, and string him up.'

The handsome doctor puffed in disbelief. 'You say that now, but just wait until one of you gets snake-bitten or needs a wound dressed. You need me – if you noose me up, you'll be dooming yourselves!'

Ivo snapped his fingers in thwarted recollection. 'Isn't there a test of guilt we could perform on muller's corpse? You know – as with witches, when you put them in water, to see if they drown?'

'No, no, no,' snapped Waldemar. He kicked a foot in the direction of Muller's body. A dark patch had formed in the dirt around the dead man's head. 'Again your doctrinal ignorance is conclusively exposed. Anyone with even the faintest awareness of the subject knows that such ordeals work only when the victim still breathes!'

'I was just making a suggestion,' said Kirchgeld.

The friar patted him on the shoulder. 'Your logical error is a simple one: the ordeal by water – or its cousin, the ordeal by fire – demonstrates the individual's innocence by killing him. Since Muller is already dead, he can't be so exonerated.'

Angelika crossed her arms. 'Now that we've finished hearing from the theologians, I'll tell you what will happen. Unless you count this tongue-lashing, no punishment will fall on Physic Rausch. He just got carried away by the madness of battle. I've seen it happen all too often. So the rest of you – do not start any more fights, because in the blink of an eye a body can end up dead. And that body could be yours.'

# CHAPTER SEVEN

A RUDDY-FACED ACOLYTE at his side, Father Manfried Haupt stood outside the abbey gates, impatiently shifting his weight from left to right and back again. He did not want to pace, not in front of his young inferior. Pacing was a sign of weakness. He had resolved to break himself of it, as well as the fidgeting, lip chewing, nail biting and his constant habit of clenching and unclenching his fists when his hands had no other duty to perform.

They stood near the edge of a lip of rock. A few determined patches of sod clung to it, along with the occasional woody, survival-minded weed. Their angle prevented them from seeing down the mountainside, so they looked out into an empty blue sky. Behind them squatted the dumpy abbey building. Around it brooded a trio of much higher peaks, draped in curtains of ice.

Manfried could not prevent himself from asking, 'Where is Father Eugen? You said he was on his way.'

'So the message said,' replied the acolyte, whose name was Gisbert, or Gismar, or Giselbrecht, or some such. He was a sharp-nosed, dark-haired fellow who concealed a glint of smirking intelligence behind an expression of bland obedience. Gisbert, or Gismar, was all of nineteen years old, thick of hew, sprung from a family of no great consequence. Manfried sensed that he was clever, and, since he distrusted the cleverness of others, particularly in the young and strong, he resolved to be rid of him as quickly as he could.

Caution would be necessary, however, as it was entirely possible that this Giselmar, or Gisbrecht, or whatever he called himself, had been installed in Manfried's retinue by his enemies within the church.

'Are you not cold?' Manfried inquired.

'We are exposed to the winds here, father.'

Manfried reached for the warhammer that swung at his belt. Its long handle was carved in oak and its blunt head had been cast in iron, moulded so that it bore the angry face and flowing beard of Sigmar, his warrior god. The acolyte had a hammer too, though not a fancy one. 'Perhaps we should spar, to pass the time, and keep us warm.'

The smirk fell from the acolyte's face. 'I am sure Father Eugen will be here any moment. The journey up is steep, and takes its toll on lungs unused to this thin mountain air.'

'To the true warrior, there is no such thing as a spare moment. There is always time to hone one's art.'

The acolyte looked up at the sun, which was making its slow and resentful progress up into the cloudy morning sky. 'It is still early, sir. I thought you promised the sisters there'd be no banging of hammer on shield until after morning prayers.'

Manfried placed his hammer's handle back in its loop on his belt and scowled back toward the abbey. The principles of ecclesiastical architecture were like mother's milk to him, and he despised this horrible brick pimple of a building with every iota of his being. The abbey at Heiligerberg was a modest affair: two storeys of crumbling stone rooms arranged in the shape of a box, with a meagre courtyard in the middle. A fat and cosy chapel grew like a goitre from the abbey's west side.

When Manfried had first heard of this fabled mountainside shrine, where a goddess herself had deigned to touch the stinking ground with her divine and perfect feet, he had envisioned a soaring, airy construction shooting delicate limestone spires up into the heavens, rooted to the side of a stormy, implacable peak by a network of regal buttresses. The real thing was nothing like this. Granted, the structure was very ancient and thus partook of the simplicity of earlier times. Manfried understood the impulse to mistake plainness for honesty, but in this case it was man's duty to make glorious, monumental church buildings that reflected the true and awesome power of the gods. To do otherwise was to disappoint the faithful, the simple worshippers who knew best about these things.

The countless pilgrims making their ant-like way to the Holy Mountain would have expectations like Manfried's. They would come all this way and have naught to behold but a dumpy assemblage of ancient, pitted, crumbling brick. There would be no decorations to catch the eye and provoke a sense of awe or wonder, as was fitting. Nor were there mouldings of unfurling leaves on the columns, or ornate traceries on the windows. Neither protective angel nor capering gargoyle stood above the archways to usher congregants from the profane outer world to the spiritual region of the abbey grounds.

To be sure, Manfried had to admire the effort of its long-dead builders – to make anything in such a distant and inhospitable place was an accomplishment to be reckoned with. He would not want to have had to haul so much brick up the side of a mountain, or to try to lure sufficient numbers of skilled and haughty craftsmen so far from civilisation's reach. Yes, he had drawn up several sets of plans for new, more suitable Heiligerberg abbeys during his brief time here. But he had done so merely as an exercise, to while away the slow, deadening hours. To undertake such a plan would be to admit defeat and to forfeit all of his ambitions. At any rate, it would be too difficult to marshal the fusty, resistant sisters to the cause. They liked the shrine in its present state, as dowdy and neglected as they were. Then there were the financial hurdles –

who would donate to the grandeur of a church few people would ever see?

Even the mountain itself had been a disappointment to him. By rights, it should have been the tallest peak the eye could see in any direction. Instead, Heiligerberg had mightier, sharper peaks looming all around it, like younger warrior brothers keeping their distance from a spinster half-sister. Its peak was not a thrusting spire, but a dome-like projection with a gigantic notch knocked out of it, as if it had been clubbed by some primordial titan. Granted, it was this very flaw that created the expanse of flat rock, about half a square mile of it, on which the abbey and its grounds rested. But it appeared naked and shabby, like an accident of nature.

The sister's ancient predecessors had carried mounds of earth up onto the flat rock, a legendary effort that Manfried could not help but admire. Every day the sisters toiled to keep alive a meagre expanse of green around their abbey. They tended to hardy weeds and scraggly bushes as if they comprised the private garden of the Grand Theogonist himself. There was even a patch of fresh soil, where the sisters constantly struggled to grow vegetables and the occasional, wizened rose.

Below this half-plateau, the mountainside sloped down at a forty-five degree angle for several hundred feet of bare, snow-swept rock. The slope became gradually gentler at the mountain's tree line, sweeping out and down for hundreds of feet. Hidden by the trees, Manfried knew, would be hundreds or even thousands of pilgrims, huddled up and shivering, but convinced that their ordeal was not only expected but worthwhile – if only they could gain audience with Mother Elsbeth. The angle of Heiligerberg's slopes was such that it was possible, though brutally trying, to hike all the way up to the abbey without the use of ropes. Once they reached the final stage of the ascent, the mountain took mercy on its climbers, as it devolved into a series of stepped rock terraces that were relatively easy to traverse. There were harder ways up – a sheet of glaciated rock on the south face, for example – but Manfried could not imagine why anyone would be foolhardy enough to take it. They would all use the simplest route, the one the sisters' servitors used for ferrying up their meagre supplies.

'I should have gone down for him,' Manfried said, referring to Father Eugen.

'Sigisbold and Volkert have gone down to receive him. They'll rope themselves to him and get him up fine.'

'We should spar,' Manfried said to his underling.

'Wait,' the acolyte replied. 'I think I hear them.'

Manfried walked quickly to the plateau's edge. Two more of his men stood at the top of the steps, ready to repel uninvited visitors. They had never been called on to do so: the real work of prevention was done by a team of men below. Manfried saw his men straighten their postures as he approached and was pleased. He treated them to a benevolent smile.

Looking down onto the precarious steps, he saw Eugen, roped between dark-eyed Sigisbold and blond-haired Volkert. Eugen's big bony face widened with pleasure. He waved up, huffing out a jolly greeting, rendered inaudible by his lack of breath. Sweat dotted his broad forehead, his wide, thick nose and his jutting chin. Further perspiration poured down from Eugen's dark mass of wiry curls. 'Ho, Manfried!' he said, pausing to refill his lungs and crack his knuckles. 'When our colleagues decide to exile a man, they don't do it in half measures, do they?'

Manfried frowned. Eugen sometimes spoke too freely in front of the rank and file. 'I see the climb has not dampened your humour,' he said, doing his best to seem unperturbed.

Sigisbold stepped up onto the lip of the plateau and turned to hold a hand out to Eugen, who grabbed it firmly and allowed himself to be hauled up onto level ground. He tottered dizzily over to Manfried, arms out. Manfried embraced him. He clapped Eugen on the back. Eugen returned the gesture with a weakened attempt at a bear hug.

'My head swims,' he said. 'It's like I am back at school, drunk on ale again.'

Manfried put his arm around Eugen, steadying him. 'Shallya is merciful, but at this shrine she parcels out air like a miser's gold.'

'I can see why one might have visions here. Me, I'm having a vision of a chair. Soft and well-stuffed.'

Manfried ushered him into the courtyard. 'A soft chair will have to remain a vision. The sisters' taste in furnishings ranges from austere to punishing.'

Eugen stopped in the middle of the courtyard to breathe and to take in the sight of the abbey. 'So this is the famous abbey at Heiligerberg,' he said, moving his eyebrows up as far as they would go. They resembled blackened caterpillars.

'Not so grand as one would imagine, is it?' Manfried said.

'It doesn't need to be. Look at those,' said the older man, gesturing around him to the mountain spires surrounding Heiligerberg. 'The wise architect never competes with nature.'

'You're quoting my grandfather to me, aren't you?' Eugen smiled.

Manfried looked back to confirm that his men had dropped out of earshot. 'So how did you fare?' he asked.

Eugen shook his head. 'It is difficult.'

Manfried clenched his fists. 'Those miserable sons of bastards. They know it is I who should preside over that cathedral.'

Father Eugen patted Manfried's shoulder. 'Your grandfather was my mentor, and your father, my dearest friend. Daily I pray for you to realise their great project.'

Manfried came to an iron bound wooden door. He paused with his fingers wrapped around the handle. 'But I must learn to conceal my sense of entitlement. I know, I know. I was foolish. Every day I spend in this frozen hole, I'm reminded of my folly. Acutely so.' Manfried wrenched the door open and ushered Eugen into the tiny cell he'd claimed as his working and living quarters. He left the door open, to let the light in. Mother Elsbeth and her grimy sisters might have preferred to creep about in the dark, but he wanted all the brightness he could get. He reached for a badly made wooden chair and set it out for Eugen to sit on. Eugen instead stepped to the tiny, mildew-spotted panel of a window and gazed out at the mountains. Manfried perched on the edge of his hard and narrow bed. 'I run through my litany of obvious mistakes and wonder how I could possibly have made them. I was arrogant. I failed to cultivate allies. I would not flatter, or bob my head, or humour their stupidities.'

'Careful. You don't want to sound like Luthor Huss.'

Huss! The very name set Manfried's chest to tightening. It was the name that had heralded his downfall. 'Don't tell me that contemptible insect remains uncrushed.'

'Afraid so. He's making worse trouble every day. His followers now openly proclaim their allegiance to him. They come to services and shout out catcalls during sermon. Go into the streets and you'll hear ordinary folk talk of the schism in the Sigmarite church.'

Luthor Huss was an apostate, a renegade priest who, after arriving at the sudden and startling conclusion that self-interest and money played a role in politics, had gone on to perpetrate an escalating series of outrages against the church of Sigmar, culminating in a symbolic attack on the new head of the church, the Grand Theogonist, Esmer. He'd smashed down the doors of the cathedral at Nuln and nailed an effigy of the holy father into their shattered remnants. Now he wandered the countryside, smiting the minions of Chaos, inveighing against the alleged corruption of the church fathers, and accruing to his side a raggedy band of followers, every one of them a frothy-mouthed flagellant or screaming heretic.

Manfried Haupt had never been within a hundred miles of Huss, but the man had laid him low just the same. The archlector of Averheim had demanded that his priests convene to draft a condemnation of Huss and all his Hussites, which each of them were to sign. Manfried had merely proposed that certain incendiary phrases in the document be reduced slightly in temperature. Let's not, he'd argued, cause hard feelings among those elements of the lay folk who ignorantly harboured sympathies for the apostate. Instead, let's win them back with openness and understanding.

Manfried could still hear the naïve words spilling from his mouth. Idiotically, he'd told those grey-faced men the truth: that Huss posed a greater threat than they realised. He'd even gone so far as to proclaim that certain grievances against the church, exploited so dangerously by the megalomaniac Huss, were real, and needed to be remedied.

The grim silence that followed his speech still haunted his nightmares. He might as well have pulled out a second effigy and nailed it to the archlector's forehead. All the priests he'd slighted over the years, all the envious seat-fillers who feared his ambition and hated his talent, saw their opportunity – and seized it. They went to the arch-lector. They whispered into his ear. They twisted Manfried's words. Before he knew it, he'd been tarred, if not as an outright supporter of Huss, as an appeaser. And when the Grand Theogonist issued a bill demanding that the leaders of the church search out and discipline potential schismatics within their ranks, the pointing finger fell on him. The lector sent him from Averheim to conduct a roving ministry in the outlands. Manfried would always remember the self-satisfied look on the lector's face as the new assignment was meted out to him.

Manfried stood and opened a tiny chest of drawers, out of which he plucked a bottle of fine Estalian brandy. 'One of my men went down among the pilgrims and acquired this. I saved it to drink with you, Eugen.' With a pocketknife, he sawed away the layer of hard wax that covered the cork.

Eugen rubbed his hands together in sublime anticipation. 'I wish I'd done more to deserve it. I spoke to Father Drechsler. He says some of those who spoke against you now regret the severity of your punishment.'

Manfried poured the brandy into a clay cup and handed it to Eugen. 'They're finding it hard to wring my donors' purses, I bet.'

'Yes, offerings are down. The pews aren't so full, either, now that you're no longer giving sermons.' Eugen sipped luxuriously from the cup, closing his eyes and breathing deep, to show his appreciation of the vintage. 'And with Chaos nibbling at the

Empire's edges, the city defenders have been complaining about your absence. They want you there to help lead the fight if hordes of beastmen come pouring into the city, lusting for blood. It doesn't help that you took all of the toughest young warrior priests with you when you went.'

'Then we have leverage.'

'You'd think so, but all anyone can think about is the schism. I was sure Drechsler would stand up for you, but even the suggestion of it terrified him. The archlector is looking for more scapegoats to present to the Grand Theogonist. They fear they'll end up here in exile, too, if they speak on your behalf. Or worse. There might be priest-burnings before this mess sorts itself out.'

Manfried put cup to lip and disinterestedly sampled the brandy. 'And what of these Chaos manifestations?'

'The city's abuzz with omens and rumours. The chapel at Friedendorf collapsed in a billow of choking green smoke; cultists are to blame, they say. A young girl, distantly related to the elector, vanished from her family's manor, and was found on the street a week later, bled dry.'

'I heard the story from a pilgrim but said it couldn't be true.'

Eugen bent close and spoke quietly. 'The worst part of it was – the girl was still alive. With not a drop of blood in her. She spoke in a terrible tongue, and thrashed and writhed for days before expiring. Oh, and beastmen were found inside the main grain warehouse. Forty tons of tainted grain had to be taken outside the city walls and set ablaze.'

'I should be back in the city, fighting this,' Manfried intoned. 'What of the war?'

'Chaos armies gather in the north. News is never reliable when it comes from so far away, but word is that they're on the verge of overrunning Kislev. Or perhaps they've taken Kislev already and are already on the Empire's northern borders.'

'Maybe I should take my men up there, to join the fight. If I came back to Averheim dripping with martial glory, the lector wouldn't dare deny me.'

'We're on the opposite end of the Empire. To get there would take months.'

Manfried slammed his cup on the side table. 'There must be something!' Eugen jumped back, startled. Manfried sat back on his bed, burying his head in his hands. 'I'm sorry,' he said. 'I think I'm losing my mind in this place.'

Eugen sat beside him. 'We'll find a way, Manfried.'

'Sigmar's testing my strength, isn't he?'

'That could be it,' he said.

Manfried stood. He grabbed his hammer. 'Let's go out and you can watch me spar with some of the boys.'

'If we're going back out in that cold, I need some more of this.' Eugen reached for the brandy, filling his cup to the brim.

'That's the thing of it,' said Manfried. 'Sigmar's testing me and I must be patient. He'll show me the way.' Leaving his cell, he smacked the door with his hammer. Eugen paused to look at the dent, took a careful sip of brandy and followed his protégé across the courtyard, holding the cup at arm's length, so as not to spill any.

# CHAPTER EIGHT

ANGELIKA LED THE group along a winding trail where two ridges of exposed grey rock met. The ground was uneven and hard on the feet, even Angelika had difficulty navigating it. The ridges caught the wind, squeezed it until it howled, before blasting it into the travellers' faces. Angelika turned her back to the wind and saw her charges struggling behind her, grit whipped down from the rocks and into their squinting eyes. They now struggled along with little complaint; Angelika reckoned that she'd finally broken their spirits. A day and a half had passed since they'd buried Jurg Muller. Altman's murderer had done nothing to reveal himself.

A laboured panting rose up just behind her. She turned to see Waldemar Silber, the summoner, picking his way through the rocks, an expression of pressing business on his elevated brow. She increased her pace just a little. He called out to her.

'Yes?' she said, her gaze still fixed on the treacherous pathway of rock before her.

'I would have a word with you!' Silber's tone had a peremptory note of command in it.

'Yes?' she repeated, easing back to her previous speed.

'Please wait up,' he said.

Satisfied that she'd shown him who was in charge, she stopped just long enough for him to come up alongside her. The rock sloped down wickedly, and she kept firm possession of the flattest portion of it. Waldemar had to walk on angled ankles as she pressed on.

'Yes?' said Angelika.

'Hurm,' said Waldemar. 'Yes.'

Angelika could have put him at his ease by giving him an opening to speak. She could have said, 'What is it, Waldemar?' Even a blunt, 'Out with it, Waldemar, I haven't got all day,' would have got him started. She did not, however, wish to encourage him.

'Hurm,' said Waldemar.

She skipped sideways to avoid a slick application of bright green moss on the stone beneath her feet.

'The point of the matter is this.' Waldemar paused. 'Or rather… because it is said with your best interests squarely at heart, you must agree not to be offended by anything I am about to say.'

'Now why on earth would I do that?'

'Hurm,' said the summoner. 'You are a wary creature, I'll say that.'

'How charmingly condescending of you, Waldemar.'

He sputtered and seemed to lick a bitter taste off his lips. 'The nub of the question is as follows. You are not the sort of woman I am accustomed to meeting.'

'Your social circle is not packed full with corpse robbers?'

'That statement encapsulates the issue in the shell of a nut. You clearly possess bravery, resourcefulness, and, indeed, physical magnetism, yet…'

Angelika blew a big disgusted breath of air through her teeth.

'Are you proposing to me, Waldemar Silber?'

His fine-soled shoes hit a patch of slippery moss; he jittered and nervously stopped himself from toppling headlong into the rocks. His face was still flushed deep crimson long after he'd recovered his balance. 'You mock me, fraulein,' he finally said.

'Yet you wonder what a creature of my obvious charms is doing, living on her own out in the wilderness, touching corpses, pawning jewellery, and performing all manner of other unwomanly acts?'

'You have cultivated a scathing wit, Angelika Fleischer, to protect yourself against the villains you meet. But I, Angelika Fleischer, am no villain. Far from it.' He reached out to clomp his hand onto her shoulder, but she evaded his gesture.

'You are proposing to me.'

'I would not impose on you that way, after so brief an acquaintance. But it is clear that you need protection. The shielding embrace of a respectable home. An income, so that you need never again… pollute yourself in this appalling way.'

Angelika laughed. 'You want me as your mistress?'

'Perhaps a more debonair man could express it more deftly. Negotiations of the heart have never progressed smoothly for me.'

'You don't say!'

'You repeat your mockery, but I will ignore it. Our journey together will be short – there is little time to squander on preliminaries. You want jewels? Jewels I can give you. Gold? It is but a petty thing. Safety? Any new situation would be safer than this.' He looked back at the others – Prioress Heilwig in particular. Her attention was devoted entirely to her struggle to remain upright on the uneven rocks. He inhaled deeply, filling his lungs to bursting.

'In your position,' he said, 'you'd be a fool to turn me away.' He leaned in close to her. 'Before I laid eyes on you, I thought there'd never be another woman to bring heat to my loins.' He snaked his arm out to snatch her wrist. She applied his momentum against him, taking his arm with both of her hands, thrusting it out to knock him off balance. At the same time she brought him to his knees with his elbow wrapped around his throat. She stood behind him, choking him with his own arm. Franziskus sprinted toward her, but she signalled him to stay. She had the situation well in hand.

She hissed into the summoner's ear. 'The only thing I might be planning to bring to your loins is the toe of my boot.' She let that one sink in for a while, then added, 'Is that ambiguous to you in any way?'

Waldemar did his best to shake his head. She let him go. He tumbled to the rocks; she kept on going. Silber waited until several pilgrims had passed him by – none of them looking him in the face – before getting up and slapping dirt from his trousers. He had deserved this. He had been his usual clumsy self – worse, in fact. He would have to improve his discourse immeasurably, if he wanted to tame this particular tigress.

The trail got tougher. Angelika checked on the pilgrims behind her. The prioress had slipped down the sloping trail, twisting her ankle again. Devorah caught her before she fell. The group stopped to gather around Heilwig. The physic pushed his way through them. Heilwig, held by Devorah and Gerhold the friar, stuck her foot out for Rausch to examine.

Franziskus left his position at the rear of the procession to confer with Angelika. She peered up into the mountains. She'd been hoping to speed the pilgrims to their destination by taking a hard but relatively direct route. Now she'd have to admit she was wrong. She felt a roiling in her gut.

Angelika suppressed the urge to argue and picked her way through the rocks to join the others. She gave them a choice – continue on through this difficult route, or to take a longer journey through less punishing terrain. The easier way won quick support.

'You understand that we're more likely to run into others if we do that,' she said.

'If we're presently on a path no other group would choose, perhaps we should ask ourselves why that would be,' deadpanned Udo, the merchant.

'Neither choice is lacking in danger,' said Angelika. 'The question is, which do you prefer – human or natural?'

She could not shake them from their preference for a more forgiving landscape, and so, after Rausch pronounced Heilwig's ankle no worse than the last time she'd wrenched it, they reversed course. The reversal alone would cost them half a day. Devorah slipped up beside her.

'We would like to thank you,' the young sister said.

'Who's we?'

'All of us. Most of us.'

'Thank me for what?'

'For asking us our opinion. Thank you, Angelika.' She dropped back to rejoin the prioress. Angelika did not know whether she ought to take her gratitude at face value, or to see it as a subtle knock against her previous behaviour. She tried to put the question out of her mind, but, as she jumped from stone to stone on their way back out of ridge lands, it preyed on her. It would be a terrible mistake to develop warm feelings for these hapless zealots. They were a business proposition and nothing more. At length she chose to be insulted and her sense of mental equilibrium was restored.

The rocky hills gave way to softer ground and soon they were once again surrounded by tall, thin pines. They had to walk crosswise down a fairly steep incline. Angelika now knew the general direction but could not be sure where exactly in the pass they'd come out. Also worrying her was the fact that it had been a while since they'd last been attacked. She sniffed the air.

'Smelling for goblins?'

It was Richart, walking just behind her, in her blind spot. Angelika did not let him see he'd surprised her. 'You should be careful, creeping up like that,' she said.

'You're right,' he said. 'I wouldn't want to get cut by that dagger of yours.'

'I might mistake you for the killer,' Angelika said.

'Still waiting for him to reveal himself?'

'I don't expect any confessions.'

They walked together. Behind him, the pilgrims were carrying on with their usual murmuring and chattering. Ivo and Gerhold shared a laugh. Gerhold's bassoon-like guffaws rang loudly through the woods. Angelika turned to shush them, but saw that Franziskus had already moved up to tactfully remind them of the need for quiet.

'Why can't they remember for ten minutes that we travel through hostile territory?' Angelika muttered.

'I've been thinking,' said Richart. 'The murder must have been connected with that relic Altman had.'

'If the killer wanted it so badly, why would he palm it off on poor Muller?'

'I think he got a good look at it and reckoned it wasn't so valuable after all.'

Angelika spotted glinting metal under a brown skiff of dead pine needles. She held up her hand to stop Richart in his tracks. 'Hand me your sword,' she said. He gave it to her. She swept its tip across the bit of concealed metal, revealing it as a mere pewter plate. She bent to examine it, then flung it aside. 'Worthless,' she said.

Richart continued, as if there'd been no interruption: 'To tell a good relic from a bad one, the killer would have to know a bit about the field.'

'Are you an expert?'

'Not remotely. I'm just an interested layman. But have you overheard anyone else going on about the subject?'

'About religious treasures?'

'Perhaps I'm wrong. But it seems a question worth asking.'

AN HOUR LATER, they proceeded as before, winding through the hills alongside the pass. Angelika took the lead; Richart, the rear. Franziskus, his head now throbbing, took a place in the middle of the procession. Devorah sidled his way, but was pulled back by Heilwig, a firm hand clutched around her wrist. The summoner sped his pace to catch up with Angelika.

'So,' he said. 'Ah. When you reach the abbey at Heiligerberg, do you intend to stay long?'

'No,' replied Angelika.

'Ah,' said Waldemar. Angelika increased her speed. Waldemar dropped back into the middle of the pack.

Half an hour or so into their trek, Angelika called a halt. She whistled for Franziskus and when he arrived, she pointed his attention down into the pass.

Nine or so bodies, plus the fresh-slain carcasses of five horses, lay spread out on the flatland below. Both men and women numbered among the dead; all were expensively clad and the horses had been fine, well-fed animals.

'You wait here and keep the others in line,' Angelika instructed.

'Should you take the physic?'

'No, I think they're all past his help.' Then she was off. Franziskus watched her as she found a spot where the hillside was not so steep and clambered down it, sideways. When she hit the bottom of the pass she crouched and looked in all directions. Then, still bent down, she scurried to the place of slaughter. Angelika moved cautiously from body to body, making a general survey before touching anything. Then she moved to the large packs strewn about the scene, moving methodically from one to the next. She started with one that was only a burlap bag, tied at the top with a noose. She dumped its contents on a bare patch of ground and laid the sack itself out flat, like a blanket. Minutely examining certain objects and quickly discarding others, Angelika sorted efficiently through the pile, then moved onto the next sack, her head swivelling regularly for any sign of approaching danger.

'What is she doing?' said a voice at Franziskus's ear. It was Stefan, the advocate, his mouth pursed up into a tiny, disapproving circle.

'Plying her trade,' said Franziskus.

The prioress came up on his other side. 'What do you mean?'

'She's searching for valuables,' Franziskus explained. 'Salvaging their gear.'

'She warned us she might do this,' Stefan told the prioress.

'She said something of the sort, but to actually behold it is another matter entirely.' The prioress snapped her head to face Franziskus. 'And you approve of this?'

'Do you see me down there with her?'

'I demand you stop her!'

Angelika had now sorted her way through a quarter of the packs. Franziskus braced himself, knowing that the worst was yet to come.

Rausch nosed his way into their little conclave, his handsome features running quickly from curiosity to outrage. 'What's this?' he asked.

The conversation repeated itself: Franziskus told him what Angelika was doing and Stefan pointed out that it was all part of the bargain they'd made.

'You must stop her,' Rausch told Franziskus. 'We are tainted by association! How can we expect to have miracles worked on our behalf, if we sanction such evil?'

The young Stirlander shrugged. 'Whatever argument you care to marshal, I can promise you I've already tried it.'

'But Shallya would never approve of this!'

Franziskus left them to their fuming and went looking for a good place to sit, knowing that

Angelika would take at least half an hour with the pilgrims' bodies. Rausch and Heilwig stayed hard at his heels.

Franziskus walked over to a mossy log. He bent down to feel its surface, concluding that it would stain the seat of his trousers if he sat down on it. He waited for further protests. He turned around. He saw the physic and the prioress marching down the slope toward Angelika. Franziskus sighed and hopped after them.

'It's best that you turn back,' he called.

He heard one of them respond with an affronted snort. He was not sure whether it was Rausch or the prioress.

'This can only lead to trouble!' he called. Behind him, others had noticed the fuss and now approached: Waldemar, Gerhold and Richart. Franziskus caught Richart's eye, telling him to go back and keep an eye on the others.

As Franziskus and the others followed after the prioress, Richart reluctantly turned back to obey.

DOWN IN THE pass, Rausch and Heilwig stormed at Angelika. 'Get back,' Angelika said, raising her head.

'We must have a word with you!' the prioress proclaimed.

'This is wrong and immoral!' Rausch cried.

Angelika ignored them, finishing up the last of the packs. The newcomers stopped, taking in the details of the carnage. Franziskus, at the head of the approaching group of pilgrims, had already perfected the art of looking away.

The prioress leapt back, realising that the dirty orb near her feet was a decapitated head. She let out a yelp as she trotted backwards, nearly stepping on a severed hand. She shrieked and covered her mouth with her hands.

Rausch's gaze was locked on the body of an old woman. She lay twisted on her side, her torso slashed open. Her attacker had taken hold of her intestines and strewn them about the field. Another of the slain pilgrims had been dismembered and stuffed inside the ribcage of a slaughtered horse. Rausch turned pale and dashed behind a boulder, where, loudly and at great length, he heaved up his most recent meal.

Angelika moved to the dead horse with the murdered pilgrim inside. Leaning to avoid the gore, she stretched out to unbuckle a pair of saddlebags.

'Shallya preserve us!' choked Friar Gerhold. 'Who could have done this monstrous thing?'

'Monsters, of course' said Angelika. Opening a saddlebag, she found a dinner fork with a cracked enamel handle. She tossed it onto her discard pile.

'It looks like the work of beastmen,' Franziskus told Gerhold. 'We've encountered them in the pass before.'

The very word sent a chill through the assembled pilgrims. They'd all heard of beastmen, the misshapen half-man, half-animal warriors of Chaos. But none had ever seen one, or hoped to. The mere sight of the things was said to be enough to drive a healthy mind to acts of madness.

'These ones were bold, to come right out into the open in broad daylight,' Angelika said. 'You should all get back up under cover. The things could be watching us right now.'

She's only saying that to scare them, Franziskus thought. If there really were beastmen about, they'd sense it. Their skins would be crawling. They'd feel light-headed. The edges of the world would seem unnoticeably wrong.

Gerhold rocked back on his heels, stunned. He'd noticed that all of the pilgrims had their tongues torn out. Then he saw the tongues, arranged in a neat row, on top of a log. 'Why,' he stammered, 'why do they do this?'

Angelika shrugged. 'Because they are Chaos?' She bent down over the remains of a burly pilgrim, rolling him from back to front. The prioress moaned at the sight of his pulped face and torn throat.

'What are you doing?' she asked.

'You're slowing me down. Go back.' Angelika's fingers darted in near the man's ruined neck. She had found a gold chain and was working around the back of his neck to find its clasp. Though her fingers were wet with his blood, she deftly got it loose. She held it up to the sunlight. A dark gem, set in filigreed gold, hung from the chain. 'Garnet,' she said to Franziskus, indifferently. She held it out for him, but he wouldn't take it. She dropped it into her keeper pile. Then she returned to her work, pulling the corpse's trousers down.

'This is outrageous!' the prioress said.

'Indecent!' the physic chorused.

'How can you allow this?' the friar demanded of Franziskus.

Angelika tugged at a leather belt strapped to the man's thigh like a phylactery. It came loose and she saw that it contained a dozen gold crowns, each neatly tucked into a slot of its own. She thumbed each coin from its hiding place, clanked them together in her cupped hand, then moved them into her open purse. The belt she threw onto the discard pile; it lay there like a fresh-killed snake.

Angelika arranged herself over the man's right leg. She clamped her hands around his ankle and pulled on the boot.

Rausch put his hand on her shoulder. 'We'll have no more of this. Stop that right now!'

Angelika whirled, knocking Rausch's legs out from under him. She was atop him in an instant, her knee in his chest, a dagger at his eye. She bared her teeth at him. 'Have you grown tired of living?' she asked.

Gerhold took a step in their direction. He looked to Franziskus, who shook his head, warning him off. The friar backed away.

'Answer my question!' hissed Angelika.

'No,' said the physic. 'No.'

Angelika moved the dagger an eighth of an inch closer to Rausch's eye. He whimpered. Angelika shifted more of her weight onto his chest. 'Then you'll never again interfere with me. Do you understand?'

'Very clearly,' Rausch said.

She rolled off him and up to her feet. She brandished the dagger at Heilwig and Gerhold. 'This is my profession,' she said.

Heilwig regarded her stonily. 'You even steal their boots?'

Angelika came at her. 'No – sometimes they hide items of value there. I would.'

Heilwig did not falter. 'It is grossly immoral. Eternal damnation awaits you if you do not immediately repent these vicious sins.'

Angelika turned her back on the pilgrims and went over to another body. It was that of a gaunt, dark-haired woman who appeared to be missing much of her brain. 'Get them out of here, Franziskus,' she said.

Franziskus took Heilwig by the arm and led her off. She pulled it away, but then meekly accompanied him as he took her back toward the hills. Rausch followed, walking with a peculiar gait. Franziskus saw why: the physic had stained his trousers.

AN HOUR LATER, Angelika returned to the temporary camp, weaving under the weight of a single heavy pack. This whole pilgrimage business presented a series of problems she had not properly considered. It had never occurred to her that pilgrimage could be more lucrative than war, but it was now clear that everyday citizens killed en route to a shrine carried goods that put all but the richest soldiers to shame. Just from this one windfall, she'd collected so much swag she'd have trouble carrying it all. She might have to detour off in search of a hiding place where she could safely cache her take. She would also have to beware of the others in her own party. No matter how self-righteous they made themselves out to be, there were surely one or two of them who might find an excuse to pilfer her newfound riches.

The pilgrims stood and surrounded her as she approached. She thunked her sack down near Franziskus's. Her stomach rumbled. Sitting cross-legged, she reached into her trail pack, groping around for a wedge of cheese. Paring knife in hand, she cut away its protective layer of mould and began to gnaw at it. The pilgrims milled around her, apparently waiting for Angelika to say something.

Finally Rausch spoke. 'We have taken a vote,' he said.

'Congratulations,' replied Angelika. She frowned; the cheese was leaving a nasty coating on her tongue. She spat it out. It landed at Brother Lemoine's feet.

'We can't be a party to your grave-robbing,' Rausch continued.

'Fair enough,' said Angelika, sorting through her pack in search of camping sausage. She was sure she had a good chunk of it left, but had trouble locating it. 'So what have you decided?'

'We present you with this ultimatum: unless you utterly renounce this vile activity, we will be forced to discharge you as our guide.'

'Must I renounce it for all eternity, or only while you employ me?'

Rausch appeared unprepared for this question. He leaned back to speak to Heilwig.

She pushed him aside. 'Each of us must see to our own souls. What you do after you've left our service is not our concern.'

'Not our direct concern,' amended Brother Lemoine. 'In the broader sense, it is every faithful man's responsibility to–'

'Shut up, Lemoine,' said the prioress.

Angelika found her piece of sausage and cut a disk of meat off the end. 'So I have to promise not to do any more scavenging until I get you to the shrine?' She popped the sausage bit into her mouth and chewed it appreciatively.

'Yes,' said the prioress.

'Forget it,' said Angelika. She stood and hefted her belongings. 'Goodbye.'

'Goodbye?' asked Ivo Kirchgeld.

'I dislike ultimatums,' Angelika said, buckling her pack on. 'And I don't like people who agree to arrangements and then want to change them. Are you coming, Franziskus?'

Franziskus addressed Rausch and the prioress. 'If you think she's bluffing, I can tell you she isn't.'

Rausch wavered. The prioress silenced him with a wrathful look.

Franziskus looked at Angelika, then at Devorah.

'You know your way around these parts,' Stefan Recht said to Franziskus. 'We'll hire you to take us to the mountain.'

Franziskus shook his head. 'I made a vow to stay at her side. I cannot break that oath.'

'Sure you can,' Angelika said.

Franziskus picked up his own pack. He looked back at the pilgrims. 'Your decision is a principled one, but still I beg you to relent. This place will not forgive mistakes.'

The prioress crossed her arms. 'It is not I who must relent.'

# CHAPTER NINE

FRANZISKUS FOLLOWED ANGELIKA down the slope and into the pass. Behind them, they heard a new procession of pilgrims, driving a half-dozen canvas-covered carts, protected by a phalanx of mercenaries, clad in varicoloured outfits and brandishing enormous halberds. The procession stopped briefly at the site of the beastman attack, then sped onwards. Their carts kicked up dust. It blew over Franziskus and Angelika.

He raised a hand to his face, shielding it from the cloud of dirt. 'We're heading to Heiligerberg on our own, I take it?'

Angelika clanked her bag of loot. 'There's more where this came from,' she said.

They walked. The day was growing warmer. Franziskus removed his hat and fanned himself with it.

'It's going to be like that, is it?' Angelika said.

'Like what?'

'The silent reproach.'

'I'm not reproaching you.'

'So you approve?'

Franziskus contemplated.

'Are you deciding what you think,' Angelika asked, 'or working out the best way to say it?'

'I will say this.' Franziskus said. 'They should have known what the result would be, when they confronted you.'

'But still you think I should go back with my tail between my legs and beg for the chance to protect them?'

'I think they need looking after. Maybe Richart can keep them safe. Though he doesn't know the pass, he seems to have a head on his shoulders. And he can fight.'

'I'm not so sure he doesn't know the pass.'

'What do you mean?'

'He was a more experienced woodsman than he let on.'

'Why would he pretend otherwise?'

Angelika shrugged. 'Doesn't matter now.'

A peculiar sound issued from the woods to their right. They froze. It sounded like painful, strained chirping. Then like singing. Then it was a voice.

'I love you,' croaked the voice.

'What is that?' Franziskus asked.

'I don't want to know,' replied Angelika.

'I need your help,' said the thing in the woods. Its timbre had changed; now it sounded like Angelika's voice.

Franziskus drew his sabre and headed toward the sound.

'Franziskus...' Angelika warned.

'I know,' said Franziskus.

She cursed and followed him.

'I'm so grateful to you,' said the voice.

'Sigmar's hammer!' blurted Franziskus. He stood over a patch of ground blanketed with puffy, pus-coloured toadstools. In its centre lay the half-digested body of a goblin, coated in translucent slime. Ropy, plant-like tendrils looped around it; thick bristles stuck into its flesh, as if drinking it dry. Portions of the goblin's skull had become visible through its skin. Its beady eyes fixed themselves on Franziskus. Its mouth moved. It spoke to him in Angelika's voice.

'Thank you for rescuing me,' it said.

'What are you?' Franziskus asked.

Angelika put a hand on his shoulder. 'Let's not engage it in conversation, shall we?'

'I am grateful for all you've done,' the creature said.

'What is this?' Franziskus asked the real Angelika.

She swatted him. 'What do you think it is? It's Chaos! Let's get out of here!'

'But how has it gained the mechanisms of speech?'

'Chaos, Franziskus, Chaos! Who cares?'

'A creature like this should be incapable of–'

'You can stay here and ponder if you want – I'm leaving.'

The goblin swivelled its head at Angelika. It spoke in a male voice that Franziskus recognised, but could not place. 'I really do care for you,' it said.

Angelika shuddered.

'Should I go in and kill it?' Franziskus said.

It spoke to Franziskus, in Devorah's voice. 'We can be together.'

'That's what it wants, for you to go in there.' Angelika yanked Franziskus's arm, turned, and ran. Franziskus ran after her. 'Come back!' the thing shrieked. They ran through the pass for a good half an hour, until Franziskus was out of breath. He stopped, hands on his knees.

'We should go back and kill that thing,' he gasped.

'I'm not going back there,' said Angelika.

'We've got to slay it, so it can't lure anyone else.'

'Let some warrior of Sigmar come along and give it a good smiting. I'm not going back.'

'What was that thing? It knew what was in our minds.'

Angelika twitched. She breathed deep. She put her arms over her head and stretched them, trying to work the fear out of her muscles. 'You heard the others going on about there being an eruption of Chaos up north?'

'That's why so many are anxious to go on this pilgrimage, to bless themselves against it.'

'When Chaos stirs, all sorts of weird and terrible things can happen. I heard a scholar go on about it once, in a tavern. Said that when Chaos gets strong, it can start to leak into this world. Bubble up through the cracks and start to devour nature itself, just like a Chaos mutation can infect a person. I thought he was full of it, but I guess he was right.'

'So what do we do?'

'Let's not even think about it. I don't want to give Chaos any further invitation to go rummaging in my thoughts. Do you?'

Franziskus thought she might mention the way it had used Devorah's voice on him, but she did not, and he was grateful to her. He started walking again.

Together, they rounded a bend in the pass. They saw the well-equipped pilgrims again; they'd stopped to roast a sheep over a fresh-dug fire pit. Delicious aromas of greasy meat wafted their way.

'I don't believe it. They'll have every greenskin in the pass swarming over them,' Angelika said. 'Let's get clear of here.'

Behind them, they heard their names shouted. Franziskus unsheathed his sword and spun around. He imagined he'd see the goblin creature, grown gigantic, tottering their way, translucent claws clacking at him. But it was Ivo and Richart, waving and panting.

'How did you find us?' Franziskus asked, when they got within earshot. He was still not sure they weren't a Chaos manifestation.

Richart hiked his shoulder at Ivo. 'Ivo thought you'd go follow the best chances for... salvage. That you'd stick to the pass.'

'I was right,' said Ivo, pleased with himself.

'What do you want?' asked Angelika.

'We need you back,' said Richart.

'No. There's trouble up that way,' said Angelika. 'There's a bunch of foolhardy pilgrims ringing the dinner bell for orcs and goblins.'

'I stopped and warned them,' Richart said. 'They put out their fire right away.'

'And there are Chaos things.'

Richart and Ivo exchanged weighty looks. 'There was a pit full of toadstools, devouring a goblin. It shouted some strange things at us. We kept moving.'

'I'm not going back north,' Angelika said. 'I'm freed from my promise.'

'We can head through the hills, skirt clear of the Chaos and those fool orc-attracting pilgrims.'

'No,' said Angelika.

'We need your help,' said Richart.

# CHAPTER TEN

THE TRIP BACK took half a day and the four of them arrived at camp as twilight crept up on the pass. The pilgrims wore sullen expressions, but brightened notably when they saw Angelika. Devorah bounded through the bush to Franziskus. She embraced him and sobbed. He could not make out her words.

Rausch sat propped against a tree, his arm in a sling, a dark bruise spreading from the centre of his face, the white of his left eye replaced by red. His once-regal nose was pushed to one side; it appeared broken. He acknowledged Angelika's arrival with a bleary nod.

'What happened to him?' Angelika asked.

'A scuffle broke out,' said Richart, looking away.

'He seems to have got the worst of it.'

She walked past Ludwig and Waldemar, their faces lacerated and etched with remorse.

'What was it about?' Angelika performed a quick head-count. The prioress was missing.

'The doctor's judgement was called into question.' Richart stepped around a large, waxy-leafed Emperor's Bush. Behind it were the two sections of Prioress Heilwig's corpse, cut raggedly in two, just above the waist. Set out beside her was the instrument of her demise: an ingenious, man-sized variation on the bear trap, made from logs and vines, with triangles of jagged scrap metal for teeth.

'She went over here, I assume to relieve herself and we all heard the snap and the crunch.' Richart explained.

'It was ghastly,' muttered Ivo.

Angelika bent over the device. She kept her fingers well clear of the jagged teeth.

'Goblins?' Richart asked.

'Most likely,' Angelika said. 'Could be skaven, I suppose, but you don't often see them around here. The trap's old; I'm surprised the vines had still enough tension in them to do this much damage.' She stood and addressed the group. 'This is why you must always be careful here. Act as if everything wants to kill you.'

'So you'll come back and lead us?' Waldemar said.

'Let's just see,' said Angelika. In a theatrical gesture, she placed a hand over her eyes and peered at each of the surviving pilgrims, in turn. 'Do I have everyone's attention?' Her gaze lingered on the resentful face of Victor Rausch. She turned and took the prioress by the arms, dragging her upper torso out of the trap. Devorah covered her face; the others stared dumbly at Angelika as she reached, with a flourish, down into the dead abbess's bosom. She withdrew Heilwig's silver dove pendant and held it out for all to see. She slipped it into a pocket. 'Is there anyone here who does not understand the nature of my arrangement with you?' she asked.

None spoke.

'Good,' she said, reaching down to take the abbess's purse.

TELLING THEM THAT the corpse-smell would attract predators, Angelika ordered the pilgrims to move out in darkness, as soon as they'd got the prioress into a soft spot in the ground. 'A humble burial for a humble woman,' the summoner had pronounced, over her improvised grave. Angelika restrained her laughter. After about an hour of struggle through thick brush across a steep hillside, Angelika stopped to listen to noises emanating up from the pass. She picked out laughter, the banging of tambourines, the scraping of cutlery against stoneware plates, the whicker of horses, and the whoops of young men drunk on lager. Angelika called a halt to the procession and motioned for the others to gather round. Through the trees, down in the pass, they beheld bobbing spots of orange-yellow torchlight.

'I'm changing the plan,' she told her charges, who now numbered only ten. There was Ivo, the pardoner; Friar Gerhold; Brother Lemoine; Advocate Recht; Ludwig, the sailor; Waldemar the summoner; the physic, Rausch; Udo, the merchant; Richart and

Devorah. 'Do you know why crows gather in flocks?' she asked them.

'The same reason men band together – for mutual defence,' said Rausch.

'It's safety in numbers, all right, but not for the reason you think. A crow in a flock plays a game of numbers. He's much less likely to be eaten by a fox than he would out on his own, because the fox has so many more other crows he can eat instead. Well, we're about to adopt the tactic of crows.' She parted the branches to reveal a pass swarming with pilgrims.

'We must be getting close,' marvelled Ludwig. 'There's enough wayfarers down there to fill a village.'

Rausch made a sour face. 'There's music. And merriment. Scarcely befitting a holy pilgrimage.'

Gerhold gravely bobbed his head. 'Yes, listen to them. They act as if they don't know the world's ending.'

'If I thought the world was truly ending,' said Angelika, 'I'd be drinking and listening to minstrels, too.' She gestured to Rausch's wounds. 'Let's contain our disapproval, shall we? The last thing we need is another fight.

'We'll be threading through the various parties of travellers, always keeping someone else between the hills and us on either side of the pass. So when greenskins or beastmen come crashing down from the woods, there'll be others to get killed first.'

'I feel that I must state the following,' Lemoine started.

'Let's all just pretend you said it already,' said Ludwig, tramping over to Angelika's side. 'I didn't trouble myself knocking sense into Rausch's head just so that you could take over as chief worry-wart.'

'It is my obligation to say it,' Lemoine continued. 'To do proper homage to Shallya, we should do as she would, and put ourselves selflessly between others and the dangers that threaten them.'

'Shut up, Lemoine,' said Physic Rausch, stepping around him and toward Angelika, adjusting his head-bandage.

As they walked down into the pass, Ivo sidled up to Angelika. He glanced back at his fellow pilgrims before clearing his voice to speak. 'Your momentary departure – it was all a ruse, wasn't it? To flush out the killer.'

Altman's murderer. Amid all the other matters concerning her, Angelika had allowed this crucial question to slip nearly completely from her mind. 'Yes,' she lied. 'I am deploying a clever ruse.'

Ivo made another furtive check to see that none of the others had got too close. 'I have a fact that might be of great importance. I think Richart Pfeffer's the killer.'

'How so?'

'I caught him going through my pack. He's nothing but a thief. He meant to rob me, just as he robbed Altman of that fake relic of his.'

Angelika called out to Richart, who was already heading toward them, angry red tones rising to colour his olive skin.

'What lies is that pusillanimous wretch telling now?' he demanded, as he reached Angelika's side. She positioned herself between the landowner and his accuser.

'He says he saw you going through his pack.'

'I did no such thing!' Angelika saw Richart's hand flit to the hilt of his scabbarded sword. 'He lies!'

'I saw it with my own two eyes!' Ivo exclaimed, his words taking on an absurd vibrato. 'I confronted him! He backed away! Guiltily!'

'Completely untrue!' Richart shouted.

Brother Lemoine, lifting his leg high to step over an exposed tree root, placed his finger in the air. 'Alas, I must bear witness,' he said.

Richart's head snapped around as the monk drew nearer. 'Witness to what?'

Lemoine shook his head mournfully. 'Honesty compels me to say it. I witnessed Monsieur Pfeffer yesterday, on a separate occasion, also fixing to open Ivo's pack. 'Twas I who warned Monsieur Kirchgeld to keep a close eye on his belongings.'

'Wait,' said Angelika. 'You're sure you saw Richart open the pardoner's bag?'

'Yes, we were encamped, and I was returning from the side of the trail, after performing necessary bodily elimination, and there was Monsieur Pfeffer, his fingers untying the clasp on Monsieur Kirchgeld's sack. He quickly darted them out again and made as if nothing was amiss, and I chose not to confront him directly – for I feel Shallya would frown on it – but instead issued a quiet warning to Monsieur Kirchgeld.'

Richart seethed. 'You saw no such thing.'

Lemoine pulled his shoulders up to his neck for a long, sad shrug. 'I place no interpretation on what I saw. Ivo says it proves you're the killer. Please note that I draw no such judgements, one way or the other.'

'It's obvious he's the killer!' Ivo declaimed.

'The killer is Richart?' said Waldemar. He and the others knotted around Ivo, Richart and Angelika.

Angelika looked up into the hills, waiting for orcs to appear and start lopping pilgrims' limbs off. 'The side of this hill is not the place for this discussion,' she said, and marched on.

Ivo darted down to stick by her right side. 'What are you going to do about this?' he demanded.

'There's nothing to do! I've done nothing wrong!' argued Richart.

'Silence yourselves – both of you!' Angelika commanded.

As they got closer to the bottom of the hill, a grunting sound rang out from the trees below. 'Who goes there?' Angelika shouted.

A corpulent, red-faced man wearing a breastplate came out from around a thick tree, hauling at his trousers and gesticulating at the approaching pilgrims with his sabre. 'More damned pilgrims!' he shouted. 'Can't you leave a man in peace for half a minute?'

Despite the fact that he'd drawn his weapon, Angelika judged that the mercenary – for this is what his motley garb made him out to be – planned to use it only for emphasis. The hill was too steep to allow her group to slow itself or change its course much, so she waved them onward. As she got closer to the man, her angle on the tree changed, and she saw a red-lipped woman behind it, reaching under her skirts to rearrange her undergarments. Angelika addressed the woman. 'Doing brisk business?'

The woman responded with a complicated obscene gesture. She took the mercenary by the arm and led him off to a more secluded tree, but he pulled himself away from her. 'The moment is ruined now,' Angelika heard him hiss at her. 'And I'm not payin', neither.'

Devorah watched them go, mouth agape. She saw Franziskus looking at her and flushed deep red. Franziskus turned a matching shade of crimson.

'A crowd this big attracts commerce,' said Angelika. 'There must be wagonloads of doxies trundling up from the domain of the Border Princes.'

'Will this ghastliness never cease?' exclaimed the young physic. He winced, holding his throbbing head, and steadied himself by grabbing Gerhold's shoulder. The friar patted his hand in a grandmotherly fashion.

'Let's go,' said Angelika, waving the others on 'Like I said, let's find the middle of this throng. And don't think the only dangers will come from the hills. Human beings can be just as dangerous as orcs and beastmen, even when they come wrapped in cassocks and collars.'

They meandered past shouting fruit-sellers, around wagons yawning with goods, and through a line of penitents lined up to receive sacrament from a mangy-looking priestess. She was chanting unintelligibly and holding up a chalice dripping with wine.

Devorah wrinkled her nose. 'False prophets and heretics,' she said, to Franziskus, who had given up his position at the rear of the group to walk by her side. 'If the prioress was here, she'd give them what for.'

'I'm sure she would,' said Franziskus. 'What'll you do now?'

Devorah's head turned as a halfling, wearing only a pair of black pantaloons, walked by, listlessly flogging his hirsute back with a knotted piece of wire. The little fellow, no more than three and a half feet tall, had shaved his head bald and tattooed it with a variety of holy signs, each significant to a different god. Blood rushed in rivulets between his shoulders and down to the waistband of his trousers. Dazed, he muttered something about the coming of Chaos and then bumped into Recht, the advocate, who shoved him away, before dabbing at his expensive outfit.

'Damned flagellants!' Recht cried. 'You can't get away from them, these days.'

'That is also heresy,' Devorah explained to Franziskus. 'To scourge yourself like that is to deny the primacy of mercy.'

'So,' said Franziskus. 'I was asking what you'd do.'

'What do you mean?'

'You were obligated to the prioress, but now she's gone. I imagine you'll continue to Heiligerberg, in her honour…'

'Yes, I owe her that.' Devorah's dull, dazed expression was not far from that of the halfling flagellant.

'And you…' Franziskus paused. 'I guess you haven't had time to contemplate, what might happen after that.'

'I'll let Shallya show me the way,' Devorah said.

Angelika halted the group. Oxen groaned to her right as a large party of travellers circled their wagons for the night. To her left, several dozen men and women, all garbed in identical off-white robes, bedded down in the open air, throwing down bedrolls. She spotted a recently abandoned fire pit that lay roughly between the two groups. Immediately she raced toward it, heading off a trio of stocky men in dark cloaks and high boots. They stood considering her for a moment. Angelika stamped her foot at them and they scattered, grumbling. She directed her group to circle around the fire pit and pitch their tents. Arms crossed, she watched over them, casting an evaluating look around the crowded pass.

Franziskus joined her. 'We'll have to set up watch, against robbers.'

'And now that Richart's suspect, we can't make use of our third-best swordsman.'

'I find it hard to believe that he's a thief, much less a killer,' Franziskus commented. 'But why would Lemoine lie?'

A voice rang out from amid the party with the carts and oxen. 'Waldemar!' it cried, jolly and surprised. Waldemar's head popped up. Angelika saw a pained look cross the summoner's face, which he quickly replaced with a mask of good humour.

Rising, he greeted a portly, harmless-looking fellow decked out in burlap robes, his puffy, indistinct face beaming out from under a wide-brimmed hat. The stranger halted for a blustering sneeze, wiped his nose on his sleeve and moved to embrace Waldemar, kissing him on both cheeks. Waldemar returned the gesture dispassionately.

Not satisfied with the kissing, the mush-faced man clapped Waldemar on the shoulders. 'Waldemar Silber, you old hound!' he happily exclaimed. 'You're the first decent sight I've seen in two weeks of arduous travel!'

'It is good to see you, also, Hildred Biber.' Waldemar watched a clear wet trail establish itself between the bottom of the man's nose and the top of his lip. 'You are not unwell, I hope.'

'No,' chortled Biber, chucking him on the shoulder, 'just my damnable hay fever acting up again. Shallya only knows what atrocious humours fill the air here. I reckon my left lung's glued shut with snot, and my right, with bitter black bile.'

'You have always imagined yourself in colourfully poor shape, Hildred.'

Hildred nodded happily at this observation. 'When I stand before Mother Elsbeth, I'll be well cured of all that ails me, for once and all. But I thought you weren't coming on the pilgrimage.'

Waldemar's hands drifted down to his belly; a queasy look came over him. 'I altered my plans,' he said.

Hildred gestured magnanimously to his party's massive carts. 'Well, it's fortunate we've come across each other. You can join us and travel in comfort the rest of the way.' He leaned into Waldemar's ear and spoke in a whisper that was louder than his regular speaking voice. 'Frankly, it looks like you joined into a party at the last minute and have fallen in with rather mangy company. It will be an utter scandal and outrage if you don't come right over and bunk in with us. Everyone's over there: Josef, Aldebrand, Ivan – even old Gobble-Guts!'

Waldemar shifted uncomfortably, stepping in front of his shabby tent, to hide it from his acquaintance. 'It would be an imposition, I'm sure.'

Without warning, Hildred sneezed heartily into Waldemar's face. Like a beagle, he shook his jowls. 'Nonsense!' he barked. 'There'll be some squeezing in to do, but we wouldn't hear of letting you stay with lice-ridden strangers.' He said this with a smile, apparently unconcerned that the lice-ridden strangers in question stood all around him. Angelika saw Ludwig reach for his gnarled club.

Hildred clapped hands over his porcine ears. 'You cannot still be angry at poor Aldebrand!'

'Naturally not.'

'He and that woman of which we shall not speak – they have parted company now, you know.'

'Is that so?'

'Yes, yes, she proved herself a most brazen strumpet – treating him as she did you. So now both of you are hoisted on the selfsame halberd. You should gather together and quaff a flagon or three of ale, commiserate, and drown your foolish conflict. I am quite sure Aldebrand is prepared to forgive you.'

Waldemar ground his teeth together. 'If I were still occupied by this affair, which I assure I am not, Hildred, I would say when a man beds another's wife, it is not he to whom forgiveness is owed.'

'Whatever, my fellow, whatever! A good friendship cannot be allowed to founder on the rocks of a woman's falseness. They are all harlots, Waldemar, to a one.'

Waldemar looked at Angelika. She did her best to seem as if she hadn't been listening, though the booming volume of Hildred's voice had given her, and the rest of the party, no choice but to hear.

'It is not true, Hildred.'

'Let us argue that over dark Tilean brandy.'

'We've all made a pact of mutual protection,' Waldemar said. 'I can't go breaking my oaths now.' He pointed heavenwards. 'Not with Shallya so close.'

Hildred dabbed his sleeve under his nose, then took a look at the dark spot. 'You always were a stickler for that sort of thing. Well, perhaps we'll meet up at the mountain. When I see her grace, I'll do my best to see she grants you audience.' He waddled back to his cart.

Waldemar squatted down beside his half-pitched tent, cold sweat beading on his pale and regal forehead. He caught Angelika's eye, as if inviting her to inquire into his affairs. It was a temptation she found eminently resistible.

A soft voice came up behind her. 'You've done it, Angelika.' It was Gerhold, the friar. The firelight from nearby camps played on his worn features.

Angelika squinted distrustfully at him. She had given him little thought over the course of the journey. Unlike almost every other member of the assemblage, Gerhold struck her as genuinely kind and pleasant. It had to be a trick. Maybe he was the murderer.

'Done what?' she asked.

Gerhold covered his surprise with an affable chuckle. 'Your responsibility weighs heavier on you than you like to admit,' he said.

'You know my rule about preaching. Now what are you telling me I've done?'

Unfazed, he smiled and pointed into the southern sky, where a low blanket of night clouds parted. Moonlight spilled onto the mountaintops, silvering their snowy reaches. 'Hold out your arm,' Gerhold instructed. She did, and he directed it toward a modest, truncated peak backed by a trio of more impressive brothers. 'That's it,' Gerhold said. 'The Holy Mountain. You've done it. You've brought us to Heiligerberg.'

# CHAPTER ELEVEN

ANGELIKA TOOK FIRST watch. She positioned herself on a makeshift bench made by draping her bedroll over her pack. Gradually the torches of the pilgrims around them were extinguished. She kept her ears alert. Every so often a stray traveller or two would come wandering past them, but none aroused Angelika's sense of threat. One, a beady-eyed young man with a half-witted grin, made to approach her, but she scared him away with a growl and a brandish of her dagger, which she'd been absent-mindedly sharpening with her whetstone.

Just as she was beginning to reconsider the wisdom of camping amid so many others, she heard a metallic commotion, followed by shouts of exertion and screams of pain. A fight had started to the north. It was hard to tell, with the din of struggle bouncing off rock faces to the west and the east, but

her experienced guess placed the scene of battle
about a quarter mile away. There were dozens of
encampments between them and the melee, but
Angelika woke her people anyway, so they'd be
ready to fight or flee, as required. Amid the shouts
rose harsh and guttural cries; Angelika recognised
these as the products of the orcish larynx. Her crow's
stratagem had proven wise.

The sound of clashing arms lasted for perhaps
ten minutes then subsided. Groans and curses
continued for a little while after that. But by then
the others in Angelika's party were already settling back into their tents and bedrolls. It was
time for Richart and Lemoine to take over watch,
but the clamour of the skirmish had set Angelika's
blood to racing and she decided to give them
more time to rest. Part of her wanted to creep off
and find the site of the battle, to glean its treasures. But if the humans had won – and it
sounded as if they had – there'd be nothing to
take anyway.

She stood and craned her neck, hoping to see
what had happened. She heard the sounds of parties breaking camp. Soon the pass shook with
tramping feet and creaking wheels, as pilgrims
moved away from the place of trouble. As they
began to tromp around her spot, she hailed them,
asking what had gone on. It was greenskins, an
angular sister called out, her face all straight nose
and high cheekbone. A dozen pilgrims were killed
before their bodyguards beat them back, she said.
No, corrected another woman, an ice-blonde

creature in noblewoman's attire, there'd been two dozen killed, perhaps three.

Richart stirred and came to join her. She told him what had gone on.

'I didn't kill Altman,' he said. 'You can trust me.'

'I don't even trust myself.' Angelika felt suddenly exhausted. She lifted herself up and dragged herself over to the snoring Lemoine. She delivered a swift, stern kick to his ribs. He jolted up, snorting and coughing.

She pulled her bedroll off of her pack and laid it out on the ground. She sank into it and soon was deeply asleep. Yet as Angelika slept, she maintained an awareness of the vast campsite around her, with its clanking of pots, its snapping, popping fires and the muted wails of the sick and dying.

She was propelled headlong into dream. Through a trackless forest she endlessly wandered, searching for an unspecified something. Franziskus was there, impossible to get rid of, as always. Her other companions melded into one another, changing identities like snakes bulging from their skins. She mistakenly joined a procession of the dead. Thomas Kreiger reproached her for not taking the oath he'd demanded of her. He told her he considered her bound to it regardless, and that her heart agreed with him. The prioress, her top half sliding around precariously on her severed hips, told her she was now obligated to marry Franziskus, so that Devorah's chastity would be protected. Muller, fluid leaking from an aching pit in his skull, demanded that she send his killer, Rausch, to keep him company in the afterlife.

Something is wrong with me, Angelika thought, as the dead circled around her, preventing her from moving forward. She saw the mountain – and in the dreams it was the tallest peak around – but every time she took a step toward it, the slain pilgrims grabbed hold of her and hauled her back. Altman climbed onto her, jutting his fat face down at her. At least Muller knows his killer, the bailiff accused. You forgot to look for mine, didn't you? You have no idea who it is, do you?

Angelika squirmed, trapped, wanting to tell him that yes, she did know who it was. And in her dream state, she did know. Angelika wanted to hear herself say it. She would remember it, she promised herself, carrying the knowledge into the waking state. But as she tried to speak, a stream of bloodied gold came from her choking mouth, blocking her words, and stopping her from naming Altman's killer. Now Altman was beside her, solicitous hands on her shoulders, popping the heel of his hand against her back, to no avail: she spewed up jewels, gems, stickpins, chains and a brace of tiny swords. You must tell us, dream-Altman demanded.

Wait, dream-Angelika thought. You're the one who was killed. You tell me who did it.

She woke up, chilled to the bone, her gorge still rising. She ached as if she'd been beaten. Through watery eyes, the darkened campsite swirled around her. On hands and knees she crawled past Franziskus, his features angelic in sleep. Devorah lay beside him, fully clothed and blanketed; her hand stretched his way. Angelika sneezed. She choked. She made her way to the camp's perimeter, to a muddy trail trampled by hundreds of pilgrim sandals. She opened her throat and sprayed their footprints with gelatinous pink vomit. For an instant, she was thankful that it was not gold and silver coming out of her. Then it felt like a fist had reached down into her innards and pulled them inside out and more vomit exploded from her guts.

By SUNRISE, IT was plain that nearly everyone had the sickness. Angelika stretched out on her side, passing in and out of consciousness. Franziskus could stand, but his head felt heavy and hot. Waldemar was on his knees, coughing and shaking. Gerhold and Devorah sat shoulder to shoulder, shivering.

Pinch-faced pilgrims passed their camp, turning up their noses at the stink of vomit. 'They've got the plague,' one muttered. 'Someone should have them burned, then,' said another.

Angelika fought to marshal a few drams of strength. She worked herself up to her hands and knees.

'It's Chaos plague,' said Stefan Recht.

'Don't be stupid,' said Ludwig. 'Bad things can happen without them being Chaos.'

Stefan had his shirt open and was checking his chest for any pustules or buboes that might be bursting from his skin. His search revealed nothing worse than a few speckly moles and some sweat-matted grey chest hair. 'The transformations will begin any moment now. Not even Mother Elsbeth can cure those.'

'Mother Elsbeth can cure anything,' Devorah insisted.

Angelika made it to her knees.

'Stefan's hypothesis, may not, I dread, be discounted out of hand,' said Lemoine, reaching under his monk's cassock to perform a self-examination of his own. 'The dread possibility of Chaos looms everywhere.'

'Nonsense,' snorted Ludwig. 'This is naught but a bad case of the croup.'

Ivo sat slowly up; the illness made him seem drunk. 'No point in talking sense to them. Little minds see Chaos everywhere.'

'Chaos is everywhere,' said Recht. 'Especially now.'

Ivo lay back down, pulling his road blanket closer around him. 'All right then, Chaos is everywhere. But we don't have to fear it, not as much as people think. It's fear that gives Chaos its power.'

'An arrogant doctrine,' Lemoine wheezed.

'A typically false and blasphemous doctrine,' amplified Waldemar, 'which is to be expected, from a shameless pardoner.'

Ivo threw off his blanket and capered over to Waldemar, holding his hands behind his head, mimicking the horns of a daemon. He wiggled his fingers and stuck out his tongue. 'Boo! Boo! I am a Chaos daemon! All must fear me!'

Waldemar shrank back. 'How dare you tempt fate so grievously?'

Lemoine stretched out to grab Ivo and pull him off his feet, but the effort exhausted him and he collapsed halfway to the pardoner's dancing feet. Ivo disgustedly tossed his blanket down on the ground. 'How many of you have actually met a Chaos worshipper?'

Ivo's question was greeted by a series of horrified stares.

'Well, I have, and I can tell you they're nothing to be afraid of. A pack of drooling, deluded cretins, that's all they are.' The pardoner arranged himself on his blanket, on his back, his fingers interlaced on his chest. 'And the likes of them are supposed to bring down the Empire? Later, when we're over this perfectly ordinary malady, and it no longer hurts to laugh, remind me to do just that.'

'And just how did you happen to keep company with the minions of Chaos?' Waldemar asked.

Lemoine protectively put his hands to the sides of his head. 'Let us hear no more! He might spill blasphemous secrets into our ears, leaving us with no choice but to scourge ourselves.'

'I don't know which of you is stupider,' muttered Ludwig.

'Flagellation is another false doctrine,' said Waldemar.

Ivo snorted derisively, but it came back on him and resolved into a wracking cough. He rolled on his side and pounded his breastbone for relief. 'Never fear, Lemoine,' he finally sputtered. 'There's no tale to tell. A covey of the gullible sots once approached me, wishing to purchase pardon for their misdeeds.'

'As if the taint of Chaos may be erased with gold!' Waldemar huffed.

'Gold? They weren't even willing to pay silver!' said Ivo. 'They thought they could cheat me and that the pardon would still be valid. Imbeciles, every last one of them, barely able to tie their own boot-laces. Ever since I realised that, I've given Chaos no hold over me.'

'Your logical error is thus:' pontificated Lemoine. 'Men who choose to worship the dark gods may, as you say, be nothing but fools. After all, their devotions guarantee their own eventual destruction. That, however, does not mean Chaos itself – its devouring gods and its slavering beastmen – lacks all capacity to harm us. You'll regret your loose words, when we begin to sprout black horns and ropy tendrils of corrupt, inhuman flesh.'

Angelika stood. She wavered. Franziskus tripped over to her side, to prop her up.

Ludwig picked up a stone and faked a throw at Lemoine. 'That's a steaming pile of fresh-laid twaddle! It ain't Chaos that's given us this little throat-rattle. It's Waldemar there.'

Waldemar closed his eyes, as if resigning himself to the downswing of the executioner's axe.

Ludwig kept at it: 'His rich friend, from last night. What was his name? Biber? He couldn't have been sneezing harder if he had been paid to do it. It was him who salted the air with ill humours.'

Lemoine bolted up from the waist, energised by this opportunity for academic argument. 'It is you who twaddles, Ludwig. All scholars agree that disease is communicated by malign configurations of the stars.'

'And Chaos leaking into the world,' added Stefan.

'Yes, yes,' Lemoine nodded. 'That goes without saying.'

Angelika opened her mouth to speak. Franziskus moved his lips too, as if this could coax the words from her. 'Got to get out of here,' she finally said.

'What did she say?' Ivo Kirchgeld asked.

'We're easy prey for others now,' Angelika managed. 'Find a secluded spot. To hole up.' She went limp in Franziskus's arms. With effort, he steeled himself and stayed upright himself. Devorah's face took on an unforgiving cast.

'Who feels well enough to find us a better spot?' Franziskus asked.

Richart sniffled. 'I'm hale enough, so far.'

'Once, aboard the *Entenmuschel*, I suffered simultaneously from scurvy and the shingles,' huffed Ludwig. 'This is nothing compared to that.'

'It's too dangerous to go off into those orc-infested woods when we're this weak,' Angelika said. 'But if you can find us a more sheltered spot, as close by as possible...'

'We'll do it,' said Richart.

Ludwig marched over to Rausch, who still slept soundly in his bedroll. 'He doesn't look sick. Not a drop of sweat on him. Let's wake him up and take him with us.' He bent to shake Rausch by the shoulders. Rausch's head lolled on his neck.

'There's something wrong with him,' Ivo said.

Ludwig shook him more vigorously. 'Claptrap! He's malingering!' Rausch did not respond.

Angelika lurched over to Ludwig, weakly shoving him aside. The old sailor yielded. She knelt down, put her fingers to Rausch's neck. She shook her head. Under her breath, she told Muller's spirit that he'd got the company he'd asked her for.

'He's dead?' Ivo gulped. 'Just when we need a physic most, he's gone and died on us?'

'He doesn't even look sick,' Ludwig said.

Angelika pulled at Rausch's bandage. She rolled him. His blood had stopped flowing; it was collecting in those parts of him that had been nearest to the ground. 'He died before the disease had a chance to get at him,' she said.

'From the head wound?' asked Waldemar, his complexion turning even paler than before.

'Had to have been.' Angelika felt another tide of nausea wash through her; she concealed it by sitting down beside the corpse.

'We slew him,' said Waldemar.

Ludwig protested. 'What we dealt to him weren't more than a series of taps!'

'Just go find us a new spot,' Angelika said. 'We can blame each other later.'

Ludwig peered down at the corpse. 'Worthless pansy,' he said. 'If you can't take a knock on the head, you've no business getting into tussles.' He stomped off to the west, followed by a dubious Richart.

They came back a few minutes later, reporting that there was a gully nearby, away from the main flow of travellers. Any enemies who wanted to come at them from the hills would have to climb down through a treacherous rock slope. Angelika lifted herself up to her feet; the others followed suit, the healthy aiding the sick. Tortuously hefting their packs and bags, they dragged themselves a distance of a few hundred yards, until they reached the gully. Angelika surveyed it through bleary eyes. It would not offer much protection. She checked the rock face: it might be hard going for human climbers, but neither orcs nor goblins would find it any great impediment. Still, she was too sick to go elsewhere, and some of the others were much worse off than she was. Waldemar dropped his pack and fell to his knees beside it. He propped himself up on all fours, dropping his head and opening his mouth, ready to retch.

Ludwig placed his boot on Waldemar's behind and shoved him with it. 'Go off to the side and do that!' he bellowed.

Waldemar meekly crawled on hands and knees to the hem of the rocky slope and then heaved extravagantly, his wretched groan echoing up the stony hillside. His companions cringed at the reverberant sound of his puke splashing into the rocks. Then a breeze caught hold of the smell and sent it drifting their way.

Richart gulped, paled, ran to the rocks and threw up. He was quickly followed by Gerhold, Ivo and Devorah. Their efforts sent another malodorous wave rippling through the polluted air. Lemoine clutched at his gut. Udo's hand clawed up to his throat. Ludwig inhaled deeply, to steady his rising sense of nausea. As one, the three of them stepped swiftly to the makeshift vomiting trough and began to disgorge.

Their exodus left only Franziskus, Angelika and Recht standing. The stink of stomach bile intensified. Angelika pressed a hand to her breastbone, expecting to join them at any moment. But the urge did not quite come; she'd already retched up all she had in her. She waved a hand in front of her face.

'Look on the bright side,' she choked.

'There's a bright side?' asked Franziskus.

'There's no creature that doesn't instinctively shy away from the smell of puke,' Angelika explained, wiping water from her eyes. 'Be you man, greenskin or skaven, you know it means sickness and misery, and you stay away.' She fumbled with the clasps on her pack. Franziskus took over for her, opening it up and laying out her bedroll.

'What about beastmen?' asked the advocate. 'Will it keep beastmen away?'

As she fell into sleep, Angelika's last thought was *probably not*.

SHE AWAKENED WITH morning light all around her and Franziskus sitting at her side, his long white fingers on his knees. 'You're awake,' he said.

She pushed herself off the ground, but he crouched over her, placing gentle hands on her shoulders to move her back down. She let her eyes close again.

'You're not sick,' Angelika said.

Franziskus laid his palm on her forehead. It felt like ice to her. 'My lineage is known for its ridiculously strong constitution,' he said. 'During the plague years, not a single one of my ancestors suffered so much as a single lesion.'

'I owe them my thanks then, for bequeathing you such a hardy bloodline.'

Franziskus arched a tawny eyebrow. 'Grateful for my presence? You have gone delirious.'

'Where's your Devorah?'

Franziskus's shoulder twitched. 'Over sleeping, with the others.'

'Have we lost anyone, yet?'

'Not so far, though Ivo Kirchgeld seems in a bad way. I'm worried about Waldemar, too.'

'Anyone other than you who hasn't fallen ill?'

'The advocate appears unaffected, so far. Gerhold is already recovered, it seems.'

'Maybe we're in luck, then, if the sickness is virulent but quick in passing.'

Waldemar crawled over on hands and knees.

'Go back to your bedroll,' Angelika told him.

'I heard my name spoken,' he croaked.

'We worried about your condition,' Franziskus said. 'So please don't make us fret any further.'

Waldemar clutched up at Franziskus's fine coat. 'If I am as ill as you fear, then the urgency of my purpose is increased,' he wheezed.

'Shut up and sleep,' said Angelika.

Franziskus crouched before the summoner, which seemed to calm him.

'You love her too, don't you?' Waldemar asked Franziskus.

'We are partners,' said Franziskus, quickly.

'See how she cannot even bear to look at me,' Waldemar moaned.

Angelika stood, hoping to escape. She felt woozy.

'I have offended her, Franziskus,' said Waldemar. 'I poured my heart out, which is always a rash and often unasked-for thing. I deserve her scorn. I am unlucky in love. Not just unlucky. Cursed, utterly. I tried to love your Angelika in a selfish, commanding way, to armour my heart, but I have failed at that too. Now listen to me. Shamefully burbling.'

'It is the illness speaking,' Franziskus said, crouching lower to shine his crystalline eyes into Waldemar's face. 'This is not you. You are a dignified, well-respected fellow. And you will go back to your bedroll now and rest, and all you have said will pass and be forgotten, along with the other poisons of this sickness.'

'Yes?' asked Waldemar.

'Yes,' Franziskus affirmed.

Waldemar did as instructed. He crept back to his musty field blanket, pulled it over his face and whimpered.

'Well handled,' said Angelika, as Franziskus helped her back down to the ground.

'Thank you.'

'I should have you field all of my marriage proposals.'

Now Franziskus looked a bit ill.

The friar padded over. From her prone vantage point, Angelika saw that his toenails were bleeding and caked with dirt. He ducked down to her, handing over her own water skin, full and heavy, its metal cap dotted with moisture.

'There's a stream down the ways a bit,' he said. 'I took everyone's vessels down to refill them.'

Angelika hesitated. 'You made certain the stream was clean?'

'I went past the muddy part.' He unscrewed the cap for her. 'Go on, drink. You all need your waters back.'

She drank tentatively at first, but then slurped it down with gusto. 'I know I said no more god talk,' she said, when she was finally finished, 'but answer me this, friar. We come all this way, reach the foot of your precious Holy Mountain, and now that it's right within our reach, we're all struck down, unable to so much as crawl toward it. If this isn't proof the gods are laughing at us, what is?'

'Despite your hard crust of scepticism, you hunger to believe, like everyone else.'

Angelika drew back in annoyance. 'Just like a priest. Never answering the question.'

Gerhold's mild features stiffened. 'The real answer, then, is this. One cannot blame the gods of virtue for—'

New boots strolled into the camp. Angelika looked up. Seven men strode in, cudgels in hand. All but one were blond and fair of skin, like Franziskus. The other, the bulkiest of the lot, had shaved his skull and sported a thick, black moustache. All wore the dove emblems of Shallya, embroidered on their quilted doublets. They walked to the sick, sleeping pilgrims.

'Ho there!' Franziskus called, stepping quickly at them. 'What purpose have you?'

The bald man spoke, pointing the tip of his cudgel at Franziskus. 'Hold now. We've no wish to hurt any of you.'

Franziskus gripped his sabre, but left it sheathed. 'Nor I, you.'

The bald man smiled tightly. A vein quivered at his temple. He looked at his companions. They smiled back at him, more amused than he was. 'That's a sharp sword, I'm sure, but you're outnumbered, boy. And as I said, we've no wish to bloody our hands.'

Angelika fought for the energy to raise her body up. She slumped down onto her bedroll.

Recht, who stood on the other side of the intruders, sidled around, warily seeking a good position. Two of the men turned to keep a watch on him.

Gerhold moved to Franziskus's side. 'You bear the emblems of Shallya. Surely you intend nothing wicked.'

The bald man bowed his head. 'No, friar, we do not. We mean only to take what we need, from those who need it no longer.'

'We have nothing to give you,' Franziskus said.

'Perhaps if you enumerated your needs,' Gerhold said, placing a hand on Franziskus's sword-arm, 'there are a few things we can spare.'

The bald man looked again to his companions; they kept their chins thrust resolutely forward. 'Shallya will understand,' he said. 'We were robbed by other pilgrims, while we slept. We've nothing to haul water in, and hardly any food. All our money is gone.'

One of the blond companions broke in. 'So we're doing to you what was done to us. If you stand back it won't be painful.'

Franziskus sneered. 'We're going to die of the croup anyway, so it's acceptable to rob us? Is that what you mean to say?'

'Restrain them,' the bald man told his men. Two advanced on Franziskus. Two marched at Stefan Recht.

'What are your names?' Gerhold demanded. 'Where do you hail from?'

An intruder unslung a length of cord from his belt and headed behind the friar, to tie his hands. 'If you want it to be easy on you, friar, you won't be getting our blood up, now, will you?'

Gerhold thrust his wrists behind him, ready to be tied. 'It's not my wrath you need worry about,' he said.

The man looped the cord around the friar's wrists and jerked on it viciously. 'Don't go threatening us with curses,' he threatened.

Franziskus unleashed his sabre and lunged at one of the intruders, who confidently evaded his blow. The other got behind Franziskus and grabbed hold of his sword-arm, wrenching it in his socket. Franziskus kicked back at his legs but the other man out-wrestled him. The target of Franziskus's blow danced from side to side, cudgel ready, waiting for a good chance to clonk his skull without hitting his partner.

Two intruders inched toward Recht, who had his rapier ready. Suddenly he ran at them, slashing wildly. He hit one on the arm, tearing open his sleeve but drawing no blood. The other brought his club down on Recht's back; it sent him stumbling to the ground. Recht flipped over and caught a cudgel blow on the edge of his chin. He stuck his rapier up at the intruder on his left, but the other got behind him and wrapped a beefy forearm around his throat. Recht dropped his weapon to claw with both hands at the choking arm.

Franziskus lurched forward, shifting his body weight to slip free of the man holding him. He spun and swung his sabre, but the man stepped back. His second opponent took a cautious step at him; he turned and cleaved his sword through the air. Then he turned to swipe it again in the other man's path.

By now the sick pilgrims had woken and were crawling out of their bedrolls. Two of the intruders circled around them, blocking their escape.

'This is absurd,' the bald man said. He drew a long straight knife from a sheath strapped across his chest and bent low over Angelika. She rolled over onto her stomach; he caught her by the hair and pulled on it until her throat was exposed. He held the knife to it. Angelika became still. Though the man hadn't bothered to disarm her, he could cut her throat long before she could get one of her own daggers out.

'Give up now, or she dies!' the bald man cried. Franziskus had already dropped his sabre. He held his arms up in the air. The intruder nearest him bent down to pick up the weapon. He moved to stash it in his own belt, then to unbuckle Franziskus's belt and sheath.

'What are you doing?' the bald man growled, his knife quivering at Angelika's throat.

'Taking his blade. And a belt to stick it in,' the intruder sullenly replied.

'What did we agree on?' the bald one prompted.

The sullen one threw the sabre down at Franziskus's feet. Its hilt hit Franziskus on the toe; he winced in pain. 'We only take the same things that was taken from us,' he said, like a scolded child repeating the household rules.

The intruders herded the healthy members of the entourage – Franziskus, Gerhold, Stefan – up against the trunk of a stripped and dying spruce. They left the others on the ground. They tied kerchiefs around their mouths to block the ill humours in the air and moved quickly, frisking each of the pilgrims and emptying their packs. They took purses and water skins and cheeses and sausages. When their own packs were full, they commandeered Stefan's, then Udo's. 'This is more than was taken from us,' one of the intruders said to the bald man, who looked anxiously back into the pass, as if fearing that some god-fearing sorts might come along to play havoc with their robbery.

'We don't have time to parcel out exact amounts,' the bald man said, letting his exasperation show.

'Just take what we said we'd take.' He reached over to open Angelika's pack. His hand darted in to grab at one of the leather purses inside. He clanked it. 'Shallya's teats, you're no ordinary pilgrim,' he said. 'What have you been up to?' He reached into her pocket and snatched out Heilwig's silver dove pendant. 'This wasn't come by honestly, was it?'

Angelika's hand itched for her dagger. She calculated: could she get it into her waylayer's neck before he could slice her throat open? No, she concluded. She could not.

The bald man ran his hands roughly along her body, taking a few moments to linger over her breasts and thighs. Angelika gritted her teeth. He reached down into her leggings, finding a thin leather purse strapped behind her knee. It was held only with a leather cord, which he cut with his blade. He took the purse and jammed it into his doublet.

'You've been robbing pilgrims long before we fell into it, haven't you?' he asked.

She wanted to spit into his face. 'Not like this,' she said.

The bald man rose and placed his heel over her throat. 'Time to go,' he called to his men. 'Let's depart carefully, yes? Don't want our backs sprouting any knives in them.' His men withdrew, taking cautious backwards steps, clubs ready. He stayed in place, looking down at Angelika, his boot held steady at her face. 'I understand now,' he said, his eyes darting up to the heavens. Angelika was not sure if he was addressing her, or merely speaking to himself. 'When I came here, when I first proposed this, I thought I had fallen into villainy. But now I see that Shallya herself has guided my hand. You're the villains and we are heroes still.' He had that far-away look on his face that came over religious fools when they got to talking their religious foolery. 'By stripping you of your ill-gotten gains, I do heaven's work. By letting you live, I show you Shallya's mercy, so you can have a chance to mend your ways. So it all does make sense, doesn't it?'

Angelika placed her tongue between her teeth and held it there.

The bald man waited until his men were well clear of the gully and then moved his boot from Angelika's throat. With his knife stuck out at her, he jogged back a few paces, then turned to run. Angelika saw that her own dagger was in her hand. She lacked the strength to throw it.

# CHAPTER TWELVE

MANFRIED HAUPT TURNED sideways, sticking his shoulder outwards, to guide himself through the multitude of pilgrims. They'd invaded the abbey grounds! Scarcely a square yard of the flat and barren ground around the abbey was now free of thronging penitents. With the press of their bodies, they'd snapped the branches from its few, pathetic trees. There had to be at least a hundred of them. Maybe twice that number. Moneyed burghers in fine, dyed clothing jostled elbows with rag-clad wretches. Men, women and children alike stamped impatiently, wailing and praying. Some carried tents in great bundles on their backs as Manfried's men stopped anyone who tried to pitch one. It was the same with fires; fires would have to be lit on the rocks below.

Manfried had underestimated these seekers of mercy. He had imagined them to be as ill prepared for this misbegotten wilderness as he had been. He should have known that their desperation would breed ingenuity. They'd found ways to bypass the ancient stairs, and with them, his gate keepers. They'd pounded metal rods into the very rock of the mountain and strung them together with filaments of dwarfish chain, making themselves a network of hand holds up the steep and naked slope.

Just yesterday, he had learned a fact so obvious in hindsight that he had literally been forced to slap himself in the forehead: the pilgrimage was now so famous that professional mountaineers had come to Heiligerberg, to make their fortunes ferrying petitioners along its slopes! Manfried could see a few of these ragged opportunists in the throng; they rang a bell and screamed out for customers who wanted help getting down the mountain, now that they were up it. A smirking halfling held the bell, as he sat on the shoulders of a swarthy bull of a man, his face a tangle of scars. Father Eugen had gone to talk to them. They styled themselves adventurers and said this was a much easier way of earning a living than plumbing monster-ridden old dwarfish ruins in search of antique gold.

These accursed adventurers – did not the very term scream out their blatant anarchy? – these accursed adventurers had found alternate routes that made a mockery of all Manfried's painstaking plans. One route stretched up the side of the taller mountain to the west, then required a thirty-foot vertical climb on ropes to the extant part of Heiligerberg's dome-shaped peak. The rest of the journey, though tricky, could be accomplished on foot, ending in the sisters' garden, which had now been trampled beyond recognition.

It also transpired that there was a passable route up along the side of the mountain, which the sisters knew about but had not thought to mention. Everyone just naturally took the terraces, they told him. The terraces were easier. The sisters were impossible. The thought that one might want to control the number of pilgrims on the peak was completely unnatural to them, and, despite many hours of trying, he had yet to instil it in their unworldly little heads. If they'd omitted these crucial details out of treachery, he might have understood it! They would be just like his fellow churchmen back home, those drooling curs! But to betray him out of sheer ignorance – frankly, he was astounded!

All around him the invading pilgrims coughed and chanted and wheezed and sweated and stank. He stuck out his elbows to part them, but they'd been pressed together long enough that gentle measures scarcely fazed them. He turned sideways to use his shoulder as a battering ram. The oval head of a skeletal young woman failed to bob out of his way in time. Manfried banged her in the face with his shoulder. She meekly stumbled backwards into the blobby arms of her pinch-faced nurse, who cursed loudly and variously while Manfried ploughed his way through the crowd.

He surged too close to an old woman who she bared her few remaining teeth at him until he barked at her to stand aside. After he had left her in his wake, he felt a sudden moistness at the back of his neck. He touched his fingers to it and saw that she'd hocked a great wad of foamy spittle onto him. Manfried resisted the urge to turn around and punch the last dangling teeth from the woman's rancid gums. He even restrained himself from ordering that she be ejected from the mountain. He would, however, point her out to the gatekeepers and instruct them never to admit her into her grace's presence. This was not petty vengeance, but prudence: it would not do if the crazed old harridan spat on Mother Elsbeth, would it?

He came finally to the gates, where four of his men nervously stood guard, halberds held aloft. Manfried looked at their faces, then at the heavy but deteriorating planks that made up the gate. He turned to take in the totality of the massing crowd and then exchanged grim glances with his men. The only force preventing the mob from trampling them, smashing flat the doors and stampeding as one into the abbey grounds was its collective desire to behave. In other words, the personal safety of himself and his men, and of all the sisters, now hung on a matter that could not remotely be depended on.

It was clear: Mother Elsbeth could not be allowed to slacken the pace of her audiences.

Because if she did, the mob would very likely fall into a frenzy and kill them all.

A distressed voice cried hoarsely from the other side of the gate. 'Father Manfried! I must find Father Manfried!'

'I'm right here,' Manfried boomed.

'You must come quick, sir!' said the voice on the other side of the door. It was Giselmar, or Giselbrecht, or whatever his name was.

Manfried gritted his teeth. 'Prepare to open the door,' he told his men. They kept agitated eyes fixed on the roiling crowd behind him. 'We must open the door,' he said.

The four guards turned, hammers in hand, seeking out the biggest, boldest pilgrims at the head of the crowd, staring them down. 'Ready!' one of them hollered.

Inside the gate, two other guards lifted the big, fresh-sawed plank that served as the door's bar. 'Ready!' they chorused. They pushed the doors open, on rusty, complaining hinges. They held their hammers, ready to strike.

Manfried stood facing the crowd, the gate on the periphery of his vision. He waited until the gap between the opening doors was large enough for a proper departure. He would not turn his back to them and slip through a mere tiny crack. These people did not know him, but he was their commander all the same. They could not be permitted to think he feared them.

The crowd surged at him. He stood his ground. A broad-shouldered fellow with a battle-scarred face was pushed from the mob, toward Manfried. Manfried stepped toward him. He trembled sheepishly and tried to force his way back into the mob. The crowd rippled as those in back pushed and shoved to get closer to the opening gate.

Manfried held his hammer aloft, as the Grand Theogonist would do with his dragon-headed sceptre. 'Halt!' he boomed at them. 'Halt now, lest you be forever cursed by Shallya!'

The shoving slowed then stopped.

'What unholy dogs are you,' Manfried bellowed, 'that you would try to rush these gates?'

He let a lengthy pause excruciatingly unfurl itself over the crowd. He breathed in deeply, to hide the pleasure it gave him, to exert mastery over this unruly throng.

'The patient – the deserving – will be healed!' he orated. 'But ye who make of yourselves an insensate mob, not only will audience be denied to you – your souls will be forever damned! So get back – and search yourselves for the strength to wait, as these trying circumstances demand!' With long backwards lopes, he swept backwards through the gap. The interior guards scrambled to bang the door shut. Pilgrim voices exploded once more, calling out prayers and panicked entreaties. Manfried's men grouped around him, bracing for the doors to come splintering in at them.

He turned smartly on his heels, beckoning Gismar, or Gisbert, or whoever he styled himself as, to lead him wherever he was supposed to go. He wished Eugen were here. With Eugen, he could let himself boast a little. He would have liked to see any of his fat-bottomed rivals back in Averheim handle a crowd like this. He pictured mutton-lipped Father Erwin in front of a horde like that, trying to worm his way out. Or his ultimate nemesis, boozy-eyed

Father Ragen. If it had been Ragen, the entire abbey would already be aflame.

'The exalted mother is faltering,' said Gisling, or Gasbert – whoever.

'Not again.'

The man nodded gravely.

Just what I need, thought Manfried, as he pushed his way past his vaguely-named inferior into the abbey's dank and coal-grey corridor. They passed together into the cloister and through its dull, unforgivably plain columns. Then he beheld the tent in which her grace met carefully selected members of her endless, bleating flock.

He stopped short. A dozen or so waiting pilgrims had somehow eked their way through the abbey gates and now milled aimlessly along a courtyard wall. Two more of his men poked at them with their hammers, trying to herd them back toward the big wooden doors.

'What is this?' Manfried asked.

'They slipped through earlier, sir, when the supplies were brought in. They refuse to rejoin the throng. They claim it's too dangerous out there, and–'

Manfried made a fist and shook it. 'Get them out of here, or club them down!' His words seemed to animate the heel-dragging penitents, who edged back toward the gates – and directly into the path between Manfried and the entrance to Elsbeth's tent.

'Make way!' Gibbrecht cried, taking the license to gleefully shove any pilgrims who moved too slowly

from his path. Manfried revised his estimation of
the fellow; perhaps he had potential after all.

'I keep forgetting your name,' Manfried confessed.

'It's–' the fellow said, but his next word was
drowned out by a sudden banging in Manfried's ear.
One of· the misplaced pilgrims, a gaunt, toothy
man, his face wreathed in an idiotic smile, banged
cruelly on an enormous drum, as his fellows began
an ululating chant that set Manfried's teeth to
clenching.

'You know what this experience has taught me?'
Manfried asked, frowning back at the cacophonous
worshippers.

'What, sir?'

'Religion should be left to the professionals.'

He pushed on as his still-nameless subaltern continued to part the way for him.

Father Eugen sat on a stool next to a crude
wooden bed, which someone had dragged into the
tent without Manfried's say-so. In the bed lay
Mother Elsbeth, her skin damp with sweat. Eugen
mumbled soothing words and mopped at her forehead with a cloth. Four of Elsbeth's fellow sisters
stood off to one side, their noses ostentatiously out
of joint. When they saw Manfried enter, they made
a point of sniffing at poor friendly-faced Eugen,
making it clear that their prerogatives had been
usurped. Among them stood a stooped old sister
with an emaciated figure that reminded Manfried of
the sticks and branches of a small tree. She wore a
soiled patch over her left eye; her chin wobbled in
the perpetual rhythm of palsy. Dema was her name,

and her disapproval offended Manfried; he had considered her one of his few allies here.

Manfried stood over Mother Elsbeth. 'You're certain you can't go on any longer?' he said.

She did not reply.

'She struggles just to remain conscious,' said Eugen.

'The supply of holy liquor is not infinite,' Manfried told him, repeating a fact the older priest already knew. 'We must receive the greatest possible number of pilgrims between each dosage.'

'She can't receive anyone in this condition,' said Eugen.

Manfried addressed Dema. 'How is it that we've got through so few visitations this time?'

'She has treated dozens since the last restorative,' Dema croaked.

'How many dozens?' Manfried demanded. 'Can it be that no one is keeping track?'

Eugen whispered at him. 'Manfried, she's awake and can hear you...'

Manfried bent over and took hold of Mother Elsbeth's limp and yielding arm. He felt the wrist for a pulse. Frowning, he forced open one of the holy woman's eyelids. 'Awake? She's barely alive!' Manfried rounded on the sisters. 'You're letting the life ebb out of her!'

Dema tilted her neck, in what might or might not have been a shrug. Another of the sisters, a trout-faced woman named Ursula, stepped forward to defy him. 'It is her stated desire that we should do so!' She drew herself close to Manfried; her breath smelled like cabbage. This Ursula had already impressed Manfried as truculent and uncooperative, but never before had she dared to openly challenge him.

He met her stare. 'You aim to replace her, do you?'

Ursula sputtered. 'How dare you!'

'You may have your naïve fellow sisters fooled, but I know ambition when I see it. You're putting yourself on record as having stood up to me – while at the same, ushering your predecessor into her grave.'

Ursula turned red. Her mouth gaped, as she groped for words. 'A shocking accusation!'

Seeing her response, Manfried revised his opinion of her. He concluded that she was sincere, as unsophisticated as the rest of them. Not that it mattered. 'Answer me this, Ursula. Are you a miracle worker? Certainly, you can take over temporal command of the abbey. You're a tough-minded woman and I dare say you'd do a better job of it. But I don't see you curing any plague, or knitting any twisted bone back into its proper shape, do I?'

Ursula crammed her pasty brows together.

Manfried almost felt sorry for her, but continued nonetheless. 'Nor do I see anyone else around here who can take on her mantle of healing power. If I'm wrong, show me her true successor and I'll regretfully stand aside as you hasten your dear Elsbeth's demise.' As this last comment left his lips, and he saw Ursula heave in a great gust of air, Manfried realised that he had overstepped himself. It was his favourite mistake – he could never resist that final twist of the knife.

'Don't pretend you care for Elsbeth's welfare!' Ursula cried, a fat finger in Manfried's face. 'We're the ones who care what she wants! And she has begged us to finally let her die a natural death!'

Manfried strolled nonchalantly to the mouth of the tent. 'And take all of those poor sick and dying people with her? Are you certain Shallya would forgive you for that?' He faced away from Eugen, avoiding his probable disapproval.

'Mother Elsbeth is my superior,' said Ursula, deflated. 'She must be the judge of Shallya's wishes.'

'Don't absolve yourself so easily, Sister Ursula. Your god and mine are very different, but both of them ask hard things of their followers. Shallya tests your faith, that much is plain, even to a blustering, bullish outsider like me. And to pass the test, you must help Elsbeth from her bed and down to the treatment chamber, so that Shallya may heal her, and she may resume the healing of others. Even though it makes you unhappy to do it.'

The argument would continue for several more minutes, but Manfried could tell from the defeated set of Ursula's shoulders that he had won it already.

Eugen stepped aside as Ursula moved to Elsbeth's bedside. Ursula pulled Mother Elsbeth's bony frame from her bedcovers and arranged herself under her arm. Dema's young, scar-pocked aide slipped in to hold her up from the other side. Manfried checked to see that the stray, milling pilgrims had been herded back out of the gates then gave the all clear. Ursula and the young sister carried Elsbeth out of the tent and into the courtyard. Manfried followed;

Dema came up alongside him. The profile she presented him was the one with the eye patch.

'This would be easier if we had the holy implements back,' she said.

Manfried mustered his most flavourless tone. 'There is no news on that front, since we last spoke about it.'

'You haven't heard back from your man?'

'I would not count on the implements' quick return,' Manfried said. 'As I believe I already explained to you, my man believes he has found the person who stole them. But he has not found the items. They've probably already been sold. He thinks the thief is coming back to get the rest of the set. When he has caught the culprit, I assure you he will be subjected to the most persuasive methods of interrogation available to the church of Sigmar.'

'If I had the full set of implements, we could double the time between treatments. We might even perfect the general serum.'

Manfried had nearly given up on the prospect of a general serum. His initial interest in Dema's project had made her his sole ally among the sisters. The treatment that revived Mother Elsbeth could safely be used only on the most holy devotees of Shallya. Dema hoped to use it as the basis for a restorative that would work its miracles on anyone, even those of merely ordinary faith.

At first, Manfried had seen this as his deliverance from Heiligerberg. Imagine if Elsbeth's healing power could be distilled into an easily transportable liquid form! He could return to Averheim with a barrel load of the stuff, dispense easy healing to the rich and powerful, and reclaim his patrimony as a matter of course. Unfortunately, it transpired that Dema's work was insufficiently advanced; she had yet to hit upon a formula that did not immediately and fatally poison those who quaffed it.

Just a fortnight ago Manfried had stood and watched, as the last subject's jaw had melted away, dribbling liquified flesh down his tunic and onto the hard stone floor. This most recent victim had been a self-important bellyacher named Vilmar, who styled himself a great friend of Manfried's rival, Father Ragen. He had importunately demanded access to this revolutionary new treatment as soon as Manfried let slip a hint of its existence, and although Manfried found it impossible to mourn his demise, he would admit, if pressed, to losing confidence in the one-eyed sister. She kept insisting that these stolen holy relics would make all the difference. It was beginning to sound like an excuse.

'You've made that clear, Dema. All we can do is wait for my man to do his work.'

'You said he'd be here by now.'

'He and his quarry are travelling with other pilgrims. I imagine they've found the journey more arduous than expected.'

Ursula and the scarred sister took Elsbeth across the courtyard. When they reached the cloister, the holy woman began to moan and weakly kick her heels. Ursula patted her on the head. Elsbeth attempted to wrench herself free but her protector kept a strong grip on her. Her cries resolved themselves into a single word, which she repeated, again and again.

'Please.'

A CHOKING ODOUR roiled up from below, cutting off her words. She reeled as the smell unfurled, by turns reminiscent of rancid butter, then honey, then dust, then wine, then rotting flesh. Manfried had withdrawn a cloth from his pocket to hold it over his mouth and nose.

Ursula and Dema hauled an increasingly resistant Elsbeth down thirteen stone steps to a round chamber, in the middle of which stood four copper vats. Each of the vats sat atop a grate, three of which were filled with liquid. Steam rose from them and billowed out toward Manfried; they were the source of the complex, awful stink. The vat closest to the stairs boiled and hissed. Just south of these a stone slab, about six feet long, rose up from the floor just past waist height. A man-sized washing tub was recessed into the uneven rock floor next to the far wall. A small dark archway could be seen opposite the stairs that led to a darkened chamber.

A pair of sisters slaved over the boiling vat, sweating in their heavy habits, perspiration slicking their faces. The first, young and plump, her face still round with baby fat, might have registered as comely, were it not for a dense cross-hatching of scars that marred both her cheeks. She brandished a wooden paddle, which she held over one of the vats, as she peered intently into it. The second had baleful, slate-grey eyes. She reminded Manfried of a dried apple jammed onto a stick.

The baleful sister interrupted her stirring. 'We are not ready,' she said.

'I told you to be ready at any time,' replied Dema.

'I did not expect it so soon.' She took an unhappy appraisal of Elsbeth's condition. Manfried could not be sure if her defiance arose from sympathy for the abbess, or a more basic truculence.

'Hop to it,' Dema said.

Baleful stood her ground. 'We have not harvested.'

'Then harvest,' Dema countered.

Baleful gestured to Elsbeth with her paddle. 'It upsets her.'

Elsbeth had slumped into Ursula's shoulder. Manfried hoped she'd gone unconscious, but she propped her head up and opened her eyes. 'That's right, Mechthild. You mustn't.'

Mechthild turned back to her vat.

'Am I not still the superior of this abbey?' Elsbeth asked, her tone more pleading than commanding.

Mechthild bowed her head. 'It's a sinful thing, you know, to want to die. You've no right to leave us, not until Shallya takes you.'

'It is unnatural!' Elsbeth nearly toppled off the stairs, but Ursula caught her in time. She wrapped thick arms around the abbess's frail midsection. Elsbeth sagged. Ursula cooed and petted her head, crackling off shards of desiccated hair.

'It is holy,' Ursula whispered. 'When you are better, you will see it correctly.'

'I will not be better for long.'

Mechthild and Dema bustled, along with the plump one, toward a darkened archway. Manfried, wishing to be spared Elsbeth's pitiful whimpering, followed. Mechthild turned to glower forbiddingly at him, but he ignored her and nonchalantly squeezed past the shoulder she stuck out to block him.

He entered a small chamber, its rough stone ceiling forcing him to duck his head. It snaked jaggedly into the rock for about fifteen feet or so, with less than two yards of clearance from one wall to the other. The chamber, lit only by spare light from the adjoining room, was the abbey catacomb. Weathered wooden shelves abutted each uneven wall, each holding up to five levels of linen-wrapped bodies. About half of the shelves were empty, so there were fifteen corpses in all, by Manfried's rough count. Dema's sisters had prevented him from making an exact inventory.

Manfried inhaled deeply. This room smelled sweeter and fresher than Dema's vat chamber. Manfried made out a tang of rose petals, overlain with traces of cinnamon, honey and nutmeg. The place settled his mood: he no longer cared about the threat posed by the mass of wheedling pilgrims above, or even his ultimate fate. The first time he'd stood here, he'd worried that it might steal from him all of his will and volition. The feeling had not lasted, thank Sigmar.

The sisters muttered to one another in muffled tones, but Manfried's ears were too keen for them and he heard them clear enough.

'Mother Kristen?' mumbled Mechthild.

Dema threw her head back, consulting a memo-rised registry of names and dates. 'Last harvested a fortnight ago. Unlikely.'

'Mother Emagunda?'

Dema briskly shook her head. 'Seventeen days.'

'Marien?'

'That was but ten days back!'

'But she's been producing well lately.'

Dema shrugged indulgently and moved to a body ensconced on the middle shelf of the stack directly ahead of Manfried. He edged up for a closer vantage point. Dema's rough hands took brusque hold of the shelf and yanked it out, along grooves filmed with sawdust. Mechthild and the plump girl swept in to unroll the corpse's milk-white shroud. Their movements were deft and confident, but also solic-itous, as if they thought their patient still lived.

Manfried never managed to completely suppress his surprise at the first sight of these beautiful corpses. Mother Marien's body showed no speck of corruption; her pink flesh retained all the spring and suppleness it would have had in life. Long brunette hair flowed extravagantly from the crown of her head. The nails of her fingers and toes had kept their sheen, and maintained a perfect trim. It was impossible to determine her age from mere examination; her face seemed old and wise, yet her elongated body had a willowy girlishness about it. If Dema had her facts right, Mother Marien was born in the year 2178 – well over three hundred years ago.

The young-old body lay unclothed beneath her shroud, a fact that Manfried found vaguely unsettling.

Mechthild backed up, crunching her heel deliberately on Manfried's foot. When he did not move, she croaked indignantly at him. He stepped back a little.

Dema reached out for the dead abbess's wrist. She manipulated it, twisting with both hands on the flesh of her freckled forearm. She bent down and aimed her single eye at the spot she was manipulating. 'No,' she said, straightening herself, 'she's dry.'

'Mother Adeline, then,' said Mechthild.

Dema ticked her tongue doubtfully. 'Perhaps. It's been a month, but last time she seemed brittle. We mustn't overtax her.'

They pushed back Marien's shelf and moved over to slide open a top shelf on the opposite wall. They unwrapped a squat, wide-hipped woman with short white hair and heavy, drooping breasts. A deathly grimace, exposing grey gums, pulled at the woman's lips. The three sisters recoiled.

'Oh, heavens,' said the plump one.

'She's corrupting,' said Mechthild.

They quickly rewrapped her. 'If we let her be for a year or so, she'll come back,' said Dema, but she sounded unconvinced by her own words.

Mechthild wheeled to face Manfried. 'You're burning them all up! They were never meant to be harvested at this continual rate!'

Dema's restraining hand settled on the baleful sister's shoulder. 'No, Mechthild. It is the terrible times that force this. Father Haupt is but their harbinger.'

'You must slow Elsbeth's audiences! Soon we won't have a single source of divine elixir!'

Not deigning to argue, Manfried returned to the vat chamber. Ursula had found a chair for Elsbeth, who swooned in it, her head held at a listless angle.

'No time to waste!' Manfried called, into the funerary chamber.

After a few more moments, the three sisters emerged, delicately hoisting yet another shrouded body. They carried it over to a stone slab that rose from the centre of the room, and laid her out on it. They unwrapped the shroud yet again, exposing a body barely escaped from puberty. Her hair was so blonde that it was nearly white; her eyes refused to close, their irises a penetrating, leafy green. Manfried had gotten to know her well – this was Dema's champion producer, the child prodigy Sister Friedhilda (2265 – 2250.)

Mechthild and the plump girl spread-eagled her on the slab as Dema crossed to a shuttered cabinet attached to the far wall. An old padlock hung from its rusted handles, a belated measure against thievery. It had been from this cabinet that an unknown thief had filched some of Dema's blessed instruments; he would have taken the rest if Dema hadn't removed some of the pieces for cleaning. The lock would not stop a determined bandit, but that was the job of Manfried and his warriors. Dema keyed the lock open and withdrew a bundle of strange gilded implements. Unpacking them on the slab next to the dead girl, Dema revealed a hook, several small paddles, a series of jars and a wedge-shaped scraper.

Dema moved close to Friedhilda's corpse and got to work dragging the golden scraper over the body's soft skin. She pressed firmly, running it along the grain of the dead girl's musculature. At first, her movements seemed to have little effect, but gradually, a strange, gummy substance the colour of beeswax began to eke from Friedhilda's pores. The air filled with the same sweetness that suffused the catacomb. Mechthild and the plump one beheld the process with open-mouthed awe, while Dema held herself to an efficient, dignified demeanour. After five minutes or so, she had finished work on Friedhilda's front parts and had scraped an ounce or so of saintly residue into the jars. Dema's assistants stepped up to roll the body over. Dema gave equal attention to the girl's back, harvesting another jar's worth of the substance.

Mechthild placed the open jars in a wire cage. The plump girl rewrapped Friedhilda's corpse, softly cooing to her as she would a child. Dema returned to the cabinet and withdrew various glass containers filled with salts and herbs. Taking up the stirring paddle, she poked it into the vat, sniffing to evaluate its vapours. She dropped in a handful of red salt from one container and a sprig of some dried plant from another. Mechthild handed her the cage; she lowered it into the liquid, hanging it on the vat's lid by its wire hooks. Old burn tissue covered the surface of her fingers. If contact with the vat's hot surface caused her pain, she did not show it. Glistening dots of golden grease appeared in the bubbling liquid. Dema threw in a few shavings of what looked like leather, stood back, then nodded in satisfaction.

Elsbeth stirred. 'No,' she said. 'I beg of you.'

Dema's two assistants hauled in buckets brimming with glacial water. They poured it into the tub then came back with more. Dema dipped smaller buckets into the boiling vat, tossing the liquid into the tub water. Steam billowed, obscuring vision.

When the tub was filled, Dema stooped to test its temperature. She nodded. Ursula and Mechthild flanked Elsbeth, drawing her unwillingly from her chair.

Mechthild fixed herself on Manfried, grinning. 'Are you sure you wouldn't like to dip your hand in, just as an experiment?'

'You've an odd sense of humour, for a follower of the mercy goddess,' Manfried remarked. He thought of Vilmar, the dupe on whom Dema had performed her most recent experiment. Manfried still had small scorches on the backs of his hands, where sizzling morsels of Vilmar's melting flesh had hit him.

Manfried turned away as the sisters stripped Elsbeth of her vestments.

'No!' she cried. 'Please!' Finding a hidden reserve of energy, she wiggled free of Ursula's grip and dashed for the stairs. A draft caught Elsbeth's grey hair and unfurled it into a mad, silvery halo. Manfried squinted in revulsion as her pale, naked body came at him. He saw the toll her healing audiences had taken on her, and gasped. She tried to run around him, but he was too big and fast for that. He caught her wrists. She turned her cloudy eyes on him. She opened her lips to soundlessly beg for freedom; her gums were coated and bloody; she had only a single jagged tooth left. Elsbeth kicked at Manfried with an unshod foot, her yellow toenails slashing at him. He jogged aside and her foot hit the stone-wall and turned. It snapped. She shrieked; Manfried winced. He ducked down to sweep her legs out from under her and carried her, one arm under her knees, the other holding her back. To see where he was going, he had to look at her, too. On the battlefield, he seen much worse things than the bare body of a dying old woman, but he was revolted just the same.

'Put her in the bath,' Dema said.

Elsbeth sobbed.

Manfried didn't know what would happen if any of the bath happened to get on him. It might do nothing. Or it might burn his flesh. Or fill his flesh with worms and tumours. Maybe Sigmar would protect him. He did not want to find out.

He dropped Elsbeth into the tub and stepped back so none of it would splash him. She thrashed, but, oddly, none of the liquid escaped. Instead, it adhered to her and soaked into her skin. Her frail, skeletal body shook. Dark streaks appeared in her wet, snowy hair. Morbid, flabby muscle firmed up and gathered around thickening bones. The cataracts melted from her eyes. As she screamed, her voice gained youth and renewed power from her lungs. New teeth jutted from her gums: they grew quickly and filled their sockets, before gleaming with a pearly, unnatural symmetry. Manfried could not help but watch as her flat, empty breasts swelled up and formed themselves into pink and perfect orbs like you'd see in a painting. Elsbeth rose from the tub, her strong and healthy fingers clutching its rim. The last droplets of restorative liquid found her pores and forced their way into her skin.

Manfried looked around for Eugen, but realised that he had not come down as far as Dema's chamber.

It was hard to say how old Elsbeth now looked. She was both newborn and ancient. Her skin shone youthfully, but her hair was still mostly grey and thinning, so the shape of the skull could still be seen beneath her glowing face.

She exposed her flawless teeth to him. The purity of her rage reminded Manfried of a mountain cat.

'You,' she said, 'must let me die.'

# CHAPTER THIRTEEN

ANGELIKA LAY IN the gully, aching. She stirred before taking stock of her condition. A throbbing sensation radiated out from the bridge of her nose and eventually filled her head with pain and dull stupidity. Acrid mucus poured down the back of her throat. She swallowed; another cascade of wretched slime slithered down to replace it. She coughed, rattling loose a chunk of phlegm. She spat it out, realising only belatedly that she'd hocked it Franziskus's way. He was crouched near her, inspecting her with that damned attentive look of his. That furrowed brow. The rosy bottom lip tucked just beneath those accursedly perfect front teeth. Franziskus moved his hand so that her airborne sputum would not hit it. He forced a shy smile, as if to deny that he'd been at her side for any length of time.

Angelika blinked wet and gummy eyes. 'You look healthy enough,' she said. 'How are the others?'

Franziskus did not need to answer. The pilgrims lay all around Angelika, wheezing, groaning, eyes half-open. 'Fate laughs at my folly,' she muttered. She imagined the warm tavern she might well be sitting in if she hadn't agreed to help these god-addled fools finish their suicidal mission. In her mind's eye, she saw herself raising a cup of brandy to her lips. She savoured the brandy's imaginary richness as she rolled it across her tongue. A hypothetical heap of logs burned in the tavern's fireplace; Angelika let its warmth seep through her, dispelling her chill.

She watched as a group of four heavily armoured pilgrims – or perhaps they were merely mercenaries – made a wide circle around their camp. They were sizing them up with sidelong looks, barely bothering to disguise their predatory intentions. Angelika cursed loudly, invoking the most intimate elements of the mercy goddess's anatomy. Her blasphemy sent a stir through the suffering pilgrims. She shot a hand out at Franziskus; with a gallant flourish, he grabbed onto it and hauled her stumbling to her feet.

The fever, or grippe, or whatever it was, had taxed her sense of balance. Beneath Angelika's feet, the traitorous ground whirled and shifted. She stumbled. Franziskus caught her, steadying her with a discreet hand on the small of her back.

She battled her congested lungs, gathering the air for an authoritative pronouncement. 'No matter how sick we are,' she hoarsely gasped, 'we have no choice… but to be on our way. Our robbers left us without slitting our throats… but we can't assume we'll be so lucky… the next time.'

'Yes,' grunted Ludwig Seeman, who'd propped himself up against a pine tree, his knobby-kneed legs splayed out on either side of him. 'It's time you lot of malingerers got up off your soft behinds and got moving.' Seized by a fit of coughing, he pounded himself on the breastbone until his balky respiratory apparatus submitted itself to his will.

'You don't exactly seem to be moving,' Recht said to him. Dark rings hung under the advocate's eyes. It took obvious effort for him to launch himself up onto his elbows.

Ludwig snorted. 'I was waiting for the lot of you, but you're right. This situation calls on a man to lead by example.' He remained in place. 'What we've got here, hardly qualifies as a disease at all. I've had so much worse I can hardly think which story to begin with. One time I–'

'Use your breath for standing up,' Angelika told him.

'This is nothing!' Ludwig scoffed, still firmly ensconced against the tree-trunk. 'It's certainly not Chaos.' He slapped the air dismissively with the back of his hand. 'I know, believe me. When I served aboard the *Stämmigkanonen*, the entire lot of us came down with something that shrivelled our limbs and dried up our bowels. But we kept working all the same and were the better for it. I promise you, what we've got here is hardly more than a throat-tickle compared to that.'

'Old sea stories aside,' said Angelika, 'who here feels well enough to actually be of assistance?' Richart, Gerhold and Franziskus raised their hands; Ludwig's remained conspicuous by its absence. Along with the volunteers, Angelika picked her way through the moaning pilgrims, helping – or pulling – them to their feet. Franziskus approached Ludwig and extended his hand. But the sailor stormed to his feet without aid, then held his hands in the air, like a man expecting applause. When none came, he grunted in displeasure.

Franziskus, Richart and Gerhold split up the packs of the weaker pilgrims, then added them to their own burdens. Franziskus made sure that he got hold of Devorah's pack. Everything was lighter, now that they'd been robbed of half their food.

Devorah trembled, transfixed, as a chill wind came down at them from the mountains. Her skin had taken on a pale, papery quality and her lips were dry and chapped. She swung her willowy frame listlessly from side to side as Franziskus and Angelika approached. Angelika frowned. Devorah seemed the least able to move, but she also had the most to lose if they remained as targets in the gully. No matter how bad she looked now, she was still a fetching young woman.

Franziskus stooped beside Devorah. Angelika turned, to keep a watch on the armoured men. They appeared to be heading off south, toward the base of the mountain, but it could easily be a ruse.

She saw movement behind her and turned to see that Ludwig had sunk back down to a seated position, his back up against the tree. So many fine and cutting remarks occurred to Angelika that it was impossible for her to choose between them. So she settled for a derisive snort and moved his way.

Ludwig's face turned grey. His eyes became pin-points of appalled realisation. His Adam's apple bobbled in his throat. He threw his head back and his mouth popped open. A shower of bright orange liquid blew past his lips and washed down his tunic and leggings. Angelika rocked back on her heels, covering her nostrils, as the combined odours of decaying food, bile and blood rolled over her. The acid stench made her eyes water.

When she was able to open them again, she saw that Ludwig had pitched forward, and orange muck was still issuing from his mouth and nose. His head hit the ground. He lay there, convulsing. The smell stopped Angelika from approaching him. As it wafted onto the rest of the party, Recht stooped over to vomit, followed by Waldemar, then Devorah and Udo. Ludwig's body ceased writhing. Trickles of blood escaped from his ears and the corners of his eyes. Angelika did not need to touch him to know he was dead.

She turned her back on the corpse. There'd be gold in his purse. Angelika suspected there was more, sewn inside his shirt: she'd heard Ludwig clanking as he walked. She hesitated. If he'd merely been covered in gore and viscera, she'd already be sorting him out, relieving the body of every last groat. She sniffed tentatively at the air and shook her head. No, this was too much, even for her. Maybe for thirty crowns she'd do it, but she was sure Ludwig didn't have half that much on him. She plodded on, ordering the others to follow, leaving Ludwig in a pool of his own rotten juices.

She waited for someone – Franziskus, if no one else – to complain, to tell her she ought to stop for a decent burial. No one did. She thought Gerhold, at least, or Lemoine maybe, would offer a few pieties, or find a few words of praise to speak in the dead sailor's memory. Silence prevailed.

Finally Angelika spoke. 'I never saw a man kill an orc like Ludwig did on the day we first met.' She listened to the trudge of her boots as she worked her way up the slope. 'To shove a cudgel down a green-skin's throat, handle first. That was a new one on me.' Richart indicated his agreement with an appreciative nod. Angelika turned back to see if she could see a hint of sorrow on any of the faces behind her. She hadn't cared for him particularly, but someone ought to. Someone ought to at least pretend, for a moment or two.

Other pilgrims, already labouring their way up the hillsides, filled the air with chatter and the grunts of bitter exertion. Tinny bells clamoured from higher up in the hills. A round of chanting began, but it was abruptly silenced. Somebody laughed, somewhere.

The group moved out of the gully toward the base of the mountain, which was swaddled with layered foothills, like the rolls of fat on a glutton's belly. Not long before, these would probably have been covered with tall grasses or even overgrown with shrubs, like the other hills around them. Now, the skirts of the Holy Mountain were bare and brown – they had been reduced to mud and rock by the teeming, crawling masses. Angelika stopped. She reckoned that a healthy party could make it up the hills in just under a day. How long it would take her group remained an open question.

She craned her neck to survey the rest of the mountain. The hills eventually gave way to a flat expanse of dark, scraped rock. Rising from this plateau was the final rock summit, draped with carpets of glacial ice. It would be these, Angelika realised, that the party would have to climb before they reached the summit, which was now hidden in a mass of charcoal-coloured clouds.

What Angelika could not determine was the effect that the sheer number of travellers might have on their progress up the mountain. Several hundred travellers, at the very least, were scrabbling up the soiled hills. She watched as an oversized woman slid backwards, spilling loose earth and soil beneath her heels. She was roped to about a dozen other climbers, so her weight pulled them downwards with her, until all of them were somersaulting down the hillside together. They screamed, their limbs thrown helplessly outwards. Pilgrims below them scattered to escape the line of tethered, falling climbers. The less agile among them were caught up in the growing tangle of bouncing, rag-doll bodies. Finally the mass of tangled bodies hit a small shelf of relatively flat, exposed rock and came to a scraping, collective halt. They lay groaning and wailing, but it was not long before they clasped their hands together and began to chant out a wounded, weeping prayer to Shallya. A couple of the fallen seemed to be dead; their companions wailed and lifted their arms heavenwards, in either supplication or reproach. The fallen party reconstituted itself with surprising efficiency; the strays caught up in their dragline dusted themselves off and hauled themselves up to rejoin their own groups. Angelika watched as the slain were laid out on the rock and left behind with nothing more than a few hasty prayers. From here on, the dead could expect neither burial nor ceremony. They might – if they were exceedingly lucky – be retrieved by loved ones on their return.

Angelika plodded up the hill, no longer caring who kept up with her, or what formation they maintained. Soon they would merge with this rippling human mass and it would no longer much matter who kept beside who. No half-sensible orc or bandit would bother to attack the mob on its way up the hill; they would have to expend breath climbing. If there were marauders about, they'd be hiding in the woods, waiting to pick off travellers as they returned and broke off into small, vulnerable groups.

'I feel better, having purged myself of unclean humours,' Udo announced. Then he stopped abruptly before rushing a few paces away to throw up. Angelika kept the others moving and not long afterwards a pale and chastened Udo caught up with them.

'I thought myself empty,' Udo said to Franziskus, who had taken a position at the back of the straggling procession. He held up Devorah, who leaned against him. He turned her head away from the merchant.

'Please,' said Franziskus. 'No more vivid descriptions.'

Devorah's lips brushed the lobe of Franziskus's ear. He straightened his spine. He angled his shoulder a bit, so as to put a more discreet distance between himself and the soft-voiced young sister.

Udo, not too bleary to lift a knowing eyebrow at Franziskus, moved on to join Ivo and Lemoine, who were the next nearest travellers in the ragged column.

Devorah wormed her way past Franziskus's defences, cuddling into him again. Franziskus felt a tingling of arousal. He tried to smother it with a quickly mumbled prayer, but the feeling remained.

'Muh,' Devorah said.

'Ssssh,' Franziskus shushed.

'Muh-Mother H-Heilwig.'

Franziskus patted the back of her wimpled head. 'Yes,' he said. 'She is gone, and that is a source of great sorrow. But you haven't the strength to mourn her now. So ssshh. Lean against me and I'll get you to the mountain.' He pulled her close to him. He couldn't tell whether his words had helped the girl, but they'd quelled his own shameful urges. Franziskus made a silent promise to Shallya, that he would find some worthy sacrifice to make on her behalf, when they reached the top of the mountain, in atonement for this unseemly moment of carnal awareness.

'Mother Heilwig,' Devorah mumbled.

'Don't talk. Conserve your strength.'

'Mother Heilwig, you will forgive me, won't you?' Devorah turned glazed and imploring eyes on Franziskus.

Realisation dawned on him – she wasn't speaking to him *about* Heilwig. In her delirium, she'd confused him with the prioress. 'It is not Heilwig,' he said to her. 'I'm Franziskus.'

Devorah touched his face with blind and groping fingers. 'Heilwig,' she said.

Franziskus saw that he and Devorah were falling further and further behind the other members of the party. Ivo and Udo, the nearest of the bunch, walked at a meandering pace, about three yards ahead. He wondered if he should call out for help, to find someone to take the girl off his hands. He dismissed the thought; there was no one else in the group he'd trust to take better care of her.

'Delirium clouds your mind,' he said. 'Heilwig is dead, Devorah. Remember?'

A giddy smirk appeared on her parched lips. 'Yes, mother. I know that you are dead. I can tell because you are surrounded in... radiant light.' Widening awestruck eyes, grinning ecstatically, Devorah went limp in Franziskus's arms. She lolled her head back, basking in some unseen energy. Franziskus, unprepared for her entire weight, tottered backwards, and nearly twisted his ankle in a narrow depression forged by the wheels of a heavy cart. Devorah thrust her arms out before her in a gesture of supplication. 'Oh, thank you, Mother Heilwig,' she said. 'Bless you. You already know what is in my heart. I do not have to ask you.'

Franziskus knew it would be wrong to ask what this meant. It would be like listening in on a confession.

'You know, and you already forgive me,' Devorah said, to her vision of the dead prioress, who once again seemed superimposed over Franziskus.

He blurted the question out. 'Forgive you for what?'

'Now I can be with him.'

'With who?'

'You know,' she said, firmly, as if it was a silly question. 'Now I can renounce my vows.'

'No, no,' said Franziskus. 'You can't do that.'

Devorah was unperturbed. 'You saved me, Mother Heilwig, from a life of wretchedness and iniquity. My debt was always to you. Now that you have transcended to Shallya's realm of perfect love, that debt is discharged.'

'When you recover from this state,' Franziskus said, 'you will realise that your vows were made not to the prioress, but to the goddess. Surely these vows remain in force...' Franziskus disentangled himself from her. Then he set her on her feet and began to march ahead. Now a good ten yards separated them from Ivo and Udo. Angelika, who was at the head of the column, was at least twenty yards away.

'Shallya is merciful,' Devorah muttered, stumbling reluctantly along beside him.

'Yes,' he said, 'Shallya has mercy.'

'She takes mercy on those who follow her. If they see true happiness on another path, she permits them to take it.'

Franziskus put the back of his hand on Devorah's forehead. It burned. 'How can you be sure you're right?' he asked. 'The goddess may have other plans...' Realising that he was arguing with a fever dream, Franziskus cut himself short.

'I know,' said Devorah, her face glowing with perspiration and beatific certitude. 'I see it just as plain as I see you, Mother Heilwig. He and I, in a clay-shingled cottage, smoke curling up from the chimney. Already I feel the hearth-fire's warmth. Children play at our feet. Laughing, squealing. I hold him tight' – she tightened her grip around Franziskus's waist – 'and it is through him that I feel Shallya's grace.'

Franziskus pictured the things she spoke of. His breath caught in his throat. 'No,' he said.

Devorah's eyes were shut. 'I am so happy, mother, that you and Shallya understand.'

'No,' said Franziskus.

'I love Franziskus.'

'It is temptation.'

'And Franziskus loves me.'

'It is blasphemy.'

'Goodbye, Mother Heilwig.'

'These thoughts, Devorah – they are the sending of some foul imp or daemon.'

Devorah pitched abruptly forward. Franziskus grabbed at her, but could not catch her. She fell flat into well-trodden mud and grass. She lay there, unmoving.

She's dead, Franziskus thought. She's dropped dead, just like Ludwig did and Rausch before him. I rejected her, and it killed her. If I hadn't rejected her, it would have been a gross sin against the gods. I did, so she died.

He crouched over her. He felt hot tears spill down his cheeks. He heard himself burbling and sobbing. He heard the others, running back toward him.

He rolled her over. Her porcelain face was muddied and still.

I murdered her.

Her mouth opened. She spat out a mouthful of damp grass. Her eyes opened.

'Franziskus!' she said.

She reached up to wrap her arms around him and pulled him down onto her. She lapsed once more into unconsciousness.

Another pair of hands gripped Franziskus by the collar and yanked. It was Angelika. Franziskus fought his way free of Devorah's grip and let himself fall backwards into Angelika's. She let him drop, then stalked off to the side of the trail, as the other pilgrims, led by Brother Lemoine, tended to Devorah. Franziskus heard someone say, 'I think her fever has broken.' He stumbled over to Angelika.

'I've been keeping an eye out for our interests,' she said. 'While you've been busy trying to get your paws under that girl's habit.'

'I assure you the opposite is true,' Franziskus said.

Angelika watched as the others helped Devorah to her feet. 'I don't doubt that for a moment, sad to say. If you did give her a nice, solid groping, you'd both be better off for it.'

Angelika turned back toward the mountaintop and resumed her ascent.

An enervated, gasping voice spoke ino her ear. 'We'll all die on these hills, won't we?' Angelika turned to see that it was Waldemar. She bared her teeth at him. She shoved her hands on his chest and grabbed up handfuls of his tunic. She shouted huskily at him, shaking him, and she kept doing it until the others had gathered all around her with sorry, querying looks on their faces.

'No!' she shouted, finally letting go of the summoner's shirt. 'All of you are going to hear me, understand, and believe what I say! Am I making myself clear?'

They nodded haplessly, frightened of her again. Even Franziskus stepped back from her. Part of Angelika was caught up in her anger; the other part wanted to laugh. She wondered which part of her was crazier.

'You're all going to stop dying now. How about that? Is that fact clear to you?' She darted among them, bobbing her head like a crow, poking her face into each of theirs in turn. Ivo gulped, his moony ears twitching. Richart stuck his chin out in a gesture of defiantly maintained dignity. She snapped at him. He weaved back from her. 'You won't be dying on me, will you?'

Richart shook his head, solemnly promising that he wouldn't.

Angelika noticed that pilgrims from other parties were beginning to gather around, drawn to her fury like moths to a lantern. She told herself that they did not exist.

Brother Lemoine poked a crooked finger into the air, ready to ask a question. To get at him, Angelika let go of Devorah and elbowed Recht aside. She clasped Lemoine's wrist, the one with the question-asking finger on it, and twisted it around to face him. Lemoine feebly moaned.

'Yes?' she growled. Lemoine quivered. 'Did you mean to ask if this shows some kind of change of heart on my part? That I now somehow care about your fates?'

Lemoine's trembling seemed to suggest that no, he was not under this impression.

'Because that is not the case,' Angelika said, letting the monk's arm flop down to his side. 'If anything, your collective inability to survive this situation, into which all of you raced headlong, makes me angrier every time I stop to contemplate it. You idiots. You damn holy fools.' She raised her voice to encompass everyone on the despoiled hillside. 'Is this worth it? No'

'I assure you,' she hissed, still bearing down on Lemoine, 'that I am still as selfish as ever. I want you to live merely because your dying disturbs the sublime tranquillity of my thoughts. And I do not intend to let you do that any longer. Understand?'

Lemoine, belatedly realising that he had again been called upon to react, nodded mechanically.

She turned to survey the entire group, or what was left of it: Ivo, Gerhold, Waldemar, Udo, Stefan, Richart, Lemoine and Devorah. Gerhold earned himself a second look, as he was the only one who had kept his composure. Beneath his reserved demeanour Angelika detected a distinct whiff of pious condescension.

'Go ahead – tell me I'm talking nonsense!' she spat.

Gerhold raised a white, caterpillar eyebrow. 'I would never dream of it.'

'You're thinking my threats are idle, aren't you? Because if you're dead, what more can I do about it? Well, I promise you, one day, when my long life ends and I wake up in hell, the first thing I'll do is seek out each and every one of you who let me down by getting himself killed. And you have my direst vow that no matter what torments you're suffering, whatever daemon is gnawing on your innards, whatever spit you're being roasted on, those punishments will utterly pale compared to what I'll do to you! Need I elaborate?'

No one answered her.

'Good,' she said, stomping upwards, a new energy coursing through her. Overhead, the clouds lightened and finally parted, revealing a sky of shining blue. Cold air swept down from the mountain; Angelika let it roll over her; it was refreshing. Her words had worked, she decided. From now on, they would all be too frightened to die.

Hours passed. When Angelika grew tired, the group rested. When she felt ready to go on, they went on. No one grumbled. No one tugged at her sleeve. She told herself that she felt free and confident.

She stumbled. She looked to see what had tripped her. It was a dead hand, barely visible in the freshly disordered soil. She called another halt. With her bare hands, she dug the body up. It turned out to be the remains of a fat, moustachioed man. He had been dead no more than a few hours. His belt had no purse on it; neither did he wear boots or jewellery. But he looked like he'd been a wealthy, well-fed individual, so Angelika opened his mouth and found what she was looking for: a quartet of gold teeth, one at the front and three around the back. Yes, her haul to date had been stolen from her, but that didn't matter. Now that she was on the mountain, she would replace what she'd lost, and more. Whistling contentedly, she plucked her dagger from its sheath and started harvesting.

# CHAPTER FOURTEEN

ANGELIKA BOUNDED UP the slope, relying on the others to keep up with her. It was as if she'd never been ill at all. Corpses littered the hillside, many abandoned as they had fallen: some were lying face down in the gravel or with limbs pinioned under their torsos. Others had been left under blankets, carefully arranged on their backs, with hands clasped together over their chests. Up ahead of her, Angelika saw one such blanket being taken by the wind and blown across the slope to land on a troop of struggling sisters. Angelika whistled happily. She had already found a pair of golden earrings dangling from the dead lobes of a sunken-eyed maiden; their green stones were jade, from the distant Cathay. From the wrist of a wire-haired old woman, she'd helped herself to a silver bangle, bristling with dwarfish-cut diamonds.

Seven pendants, each bearing Shallya's dove emblem, tangled together their chains of gold and silver in Angelika's pocket. Then there were the purses – four in all so far, just left there in the open, for anyone to take. One of them had given up nearly a hundred crowns! Her total now stood at one hundred and forty-two, bringing her nearly to where she'd been before the robbers came. She bent to roll over the bloating remains of a fat-bellied burgher. Though he lacked a purse, his cloak-clasp was exquisitely enamelled and would earn her five or six crowns. None of the dozens of pilgrims around them, who were heaving themselves up the slope, puffing and dull-eyed, shook so much as an impotent fist at her. If it weren't for Gerhold's dismayed clucks and Waldemar's showily averted eyes, she would have felt no judgement upon her at all. Angelika's pack of feckless pilgrims had led her to a grave-looter's paradise.

She had also found a surprising quantity of food, and so many containers of water that she had to leave some behind. Angelika parcelled out figs, salted fish, slices of dry sausage and misshapen lumps of hardtack. Intertwined in the deceased fingers of one emaciated traveller, she found a jug of bitter brown ale. She poured most of it out before handing it over to the others. As much as they deserved a good drink, it would not help their progress any.

Devorah sank to her knees. Franziskus caught her.

Angelika bounded down to his side. 'I thought she was recovering.'

'The disease has relapsed.' The sister drew tortured, shallow breaths. Angelika felt her forehead. It was hotter than it had been during her first bout of fever.

'I think she's dying,' Franziskus whispered.

'No, I won't let her do that,' said Angelika. 'I've already explained this.'

'We need to find a sheltered place, where she can rest.'

'Over there,' it was Ivo, pointing off to the north where big buttresses of raw stone burst out of the earthen hills. 'Behind those rock formations. I think,' – he stopped for breath – 'I think there are some ledges there, where we can stop safely for a while.'

Richart came up behind the pardoner and clapped a hand on his shoulder. 'You've never been in these hills before,' he said.

Ivo stepped deftly away from him, slapping at the landowner's unwelcome paw. His eyes worked from side to side. 'No, I haven't.'

'It just seems curious.' Richart turned to face the formation he'd pointed at. 'That you should know what's behind there, without having seen it.'

Ivo was quick to answer. 'I said I think there's probably ledges there. Based on my observations of similar formations that we've seen before throughout this journey.'

Devorah stirred in Franziskus's arms, then fell back into unconsciousness. 'We've no time to debate the principles of geology,' he snapped. 'If we don't get some food into her...' There was no need for him to complete the sentence.

Angelika's attention flew to a couple of figures on the ridge above them. 'Yes,' she said. She drew her knife. She addressed Franziskus without looking at him. 'You take her around to see if Ivo's right about the sheltered spot. Anyone who feels like a tussle, come with me.' She pointed at the men in the distance with the tip of her blade. 'I thought I saw them earlier, and there they are. Our robbers.'

Her targets stopped for a moment, as if to consider why their ears were burning. The bright sunlight clearly highlighted the features of the lead bandit. Another of them was by his side. There were only the two of them.

'I'll go,' said Waldemar, grim and eager.

'Me too,' said Gerhold.

'We'll get above them before we go at them,' said Angelika.

Angelika crept up the hillside, heading for a point about a hundred feet to the north of the robbers' position. Waldemar and Gerhold kept close by her. Ivo stood in contemplation and then took off after them. Richart followed him.

This left Lemoine, Stefan and Udo to help Franziskus with the girl. Lemoine bent to help pick her up, gently lifting her by the legs. Franziskus held her under her arms. Stefan took the lead, picking his careful way along the slope toward the rock formation Ivo had shown them. Udo followed the procession, watching their war party scramble cautiously up the hill. 'If they get themselves killed, we're all done for,' he said, but no one was listening.

Angelika, nodding meek apologies, threaded her way through a group of unlikely-looking, bearded penitents cloaked in heavy furs. Waldemar and Gerhold did the same. The furry men grumbled and closed ranks, staunchly blocking Ivo's path.

'What are we,' one of them said. 'A herd of sheep, to be walked through willy-nilly?'

Ivo turned to check on Richart's progress. There was a boulder beneath his foot. He kicked it loose. It rolled down at Richart, then bounced. Ivo spun on his heels and ran crabwise up the hill, away from Angelika, and away from the robbers. Richart hugged flat to the hillside; the rock flew well past him. He cursed and bolted up to chase the pardoner.

Angelika stopped, holding a halting hand up to Gerhold and Waldemar. They'd moved quicker than the robbers, who seemed not to have spotted them among the swarm of climbing pilgrims. They were now about twenty feet higher than the two bandits, who'd stopped to lie and catch their breath with their backs flat against the steep hillside. Waldemar stole a backward glance and saw that Ivo and Richart had gone missing.

'Weren't they–'

Angelika ssshhed him. He reached for the hilt of his rapier. She shook her head. They moved diagonally to close the lateral distance between themselves and their prey. The robbers had chosen to rest under an especially steep spot, and it was all Angelika and her companions could do to remain upright.

'Now,' said Angelika. Waldemar hauled his sword loudly from its scabbard. Gerhold brandished a thick oak branch, which he'd been using as a walking stick. They had to skid to prevent themselves from overrunning the men and rolling down the slope. The bandits beheld them with weary faces and held their hands up. The leader coughed; vomit caked the other's tunic. They reached slowly for their belts and undid them, tossing aside their still-sheathed blades.

'The vengeance of the gods is complete, then,' the leader choked.

'Where are your friends?' Angelika demanded, her dagger jabbing their way.

'Claimed by the plague you gave us,' said the robber-pilgrim.

Angelika gestured to a pack by the man's side that bulged like a sausage. Gerhold slipped over to it and hefted it.

'Is our food in there?' Angelika asked.

The leader tried a laugh; it came out as a croak. 'Except for one meal, we haven't had much of an appetite.'

The second robber groaned and shifted in discomfort.

'Don't drag it out,' the first man said, addressing Angelika. 'Do what the deities command.' His dry tongue came out to brush his whitened lips.

'I don't work for them,' said Angelika.

With a gesture, she got Waldemar and Gerhold moving. She waited until it was clear that the sickened robbers wouldn't try anything, then turned and followed them.

* * *

Ivo RAN, CURVING around a knot of barrel-chested, naked-backed men, who were making resolute progress up the hill, whilst simultaneously flaying themselves with long, delicate lengths of spiky chain. Richart scrabbled up the slope behind him and leapt, hurling himself at the pardoner. He hit Ivo in the midsection, bringing him down. He grabbed a fistful of hair and pushed Ivo's face into the dirt. Ivo's hand shot down to his scabbard. Richart seized him by the wrist. Ivo wormed his way onto his back and out from under the smaller man. Richart smacked his free elbow into Ivo's teeth.

One of the flagellants shambled over. Blood dripped down from his shoulders onto Ivo's face. 'Do not strike each other,' he intoned. 'To gain salvation, you must strike yourselves.' He placed his hand on Richart's shoulder. Richart shrugged him off; Ivo took advantage of the distraction and jumped to his feet. He kicked Richart in the throat. Richart fell to the ground, saw-horsed. The flagellant gulped and scurried off to rejoin his fellows.

'Why are you doing this to me?' Ivo petulantly demanded. He directed several kicks, one of them well aimed, at Richart's ribcage. Richart groaned. 'You're working for them, aren't you?' Ivo howled, his absurd voice fluting upwards to its highest pitch. He wiped his mouth with the side of his hand. 'You've cracked open my lip!'. Seeing that Richart's hand was near his foot, he brought his heel down on it, twisting. 'You're with the damn priests, aren't you?'

Richart hung his head and caught his breath. 'And what quarrel have you with priests?'

'If you're so cleverly ignorant of what we're speaking of, then why did you chase me?' Ivo kicked at him.

Richart spun around and wrapped both hands around Ivo's flailing calf. He pulled on it, bringing the pardoner down on his backside. Ivo grunted. Richart reached for his sword. Ivo struck out with his legs, wrapping them around the scabbarded blade, and bending it, so that it could not be drawn. 'I bet you wish you weren't posing as a landsman now,' he triumphantly yowled. 'Then you could carry something stronger than an effete nobleman's blade.'

'And when I'm done with you, you'll wish you were truly a mere stinking pardoner, not a purloiner of holy relics!' Richart tugged fruitlessly again at his weapon hilt, then threw himself on Ivo, punching furiously at his face and chest. He took hold of his enemy's oversized ear and twisted. Ivo shrieked childishly, then found his knife. He swooped it past Richart's throat, with scarcely an inch between his enemy's jugular and the edge of the blade. He brought it stabbing down at Richart's face. Richart clawed his hands onto Ivo's arm and wrenched the muscle until he dropped the knife. Ivo brought his knee smashing into the side of Richart's face. Richart fell back, stunned, and Ivo turned to run.

With blurred vision, Richart sat and watched as Ivo fled, bounding around wary climbers. Richart stood, shook off the pain, and followed him. Ivo's movements were a paradoxical mixture of the nimble and the clumsy: he slipped often as he skittered along the hillside, but deftly incorporated these mistakes into his stride, somehow using them to propel himself onwards. Richart pounded ahead; Ivo was faster now, with his longer legs, but he also had less muscle on his bones, and his sprint would likely falter before long.

Richart ran straight at a nobleman's palanquin, borne by six breathless, purple-faced strongmen. He ducked under it, regained his full height, and saw Ivo standing stupidly on the edge of a precipice. He took his scabbard in hand, unbent his measly rapier, and drew it. He advanced on Ivo, swishing it experimentally through the thin, cold air. A plume of steam escaped from Ivo's worried lips.

'Well, thief,' said Richart. 'It appears you've run out of mountain.'

'There must be an arrangement we can make, you and I.' Kirchgeld said, holding his palms pleadingly before him.

Richart halted. 'You still have the stolen implements?'

'Not on me.'

Richart advanced. 'Do you still have them somewhere, or have you already sold them?'

'Yes.'

An aggravated scowl twisted across Richart's round, brown face. 'Don't play games with me, worm. Which is it?'

Ivo formed his mouth into a small, open circle of hurt and outrage. 'There's no need to insult me.'

Richart lunged at him, grabbing around, trying to get a good bunch of Ivo's hair into his fist. Ivo smiled and slipped aside. He seized Richart by the shoulder and heaved him off the precipice. He spun to watch Pfeffer fall, but by the time he was safely around, his pursuer had already dropped out of sight.

Ivo rubbed his hands together and treated himself to a heaving, blissful breath. People thought Ivo was stupid. But it was in fact they who were stupid.

ANGELIKA HUGGED THE robber's pack to her chest and made her way down and around to the rock shelf Ivo had shown them. Gerhold and Waldemar trailed behind her. Sure enough, it was sheltered from the view of other climbers, and offered a large, flat surface for the entire group to rest on. Franziskus stood beside a prone Devorah, who slept, wrapped in a blanket. Franziskus's cloak lay under her head, bunched up into a pillow. Angelika performed a count: Udo, Stefan and Lemoine sat ringed around Franziskus and Devorah, staring dully into the middle distance. So with Gerhold and Waldemar, they now had six pilgrims and two guides.

'Where are Ivo and Richart?' she asked.

Franziskus's face was drawn and mournful. 'They left with you.'

'We got split up. I thought they'd come back here. Ivo knew where it was.' She sat cross-legged and opened the robber's pack. She found her accumulated treasure and threw it aside. She dug out sacks and emptied them: she located the trail sausages, the sacks of nuts, the crusts of cheese and the desiccated fruits that had been stolen from them. They were still wrapped in brown paper. At the bottom of the sack were skins full of water, cold to the touch. She drank heartily herself and passed the skins around.

'Gulp down all you want,' said Angelika. 'There is no need to ration: we'll soon be up on the glacier, and we can scrape the containers full of ice.' All but Franziskus pounced on the food, stuffing their mouths with more than they could chew or swallow. The young deserter took a handkerchief from his pocket, wetted it with the mouth of a water skin, and then dabbed it carefully onto Devorah's lips.

'How long do we wait for them?' said Udo, taking a fastidious pull on his recovered water skin.

Angelika cast a doubtful glance up at the mountain. 'With or without them, I think we should spend the night here. I'm spent, and I look better than the lot of you.'

'Is it safe?' Udo inquired.

'It's a little late to be asking that.'

Waldemar shifted himself closer to Angelika. 'What could have happened to Richart and Ivo? One moment they were behind us, and…'

Angelika shifted away from Waldemar. She shrugged.

'Should we go look for them?'

She got up and wandered over to Franziskus. 'How is she?'

Franziskus shook his head.

Stefan came up behind them. He spoke quietly. 'Our only hope is to get her up to Mother Elsbeth for healing. Otherwise we've lost her.'

Angelika stood back. 'But we're likely to finish her off trying to get her up that mountain.'

'Nonetheless we must try,' Stefan said.

The three of them stared for a while at Devorah's peaceful, dying face. 'Maybe,' Angelika said, 'the true mercy would be in letting her slip away from this rotten charnel house of a world.'

'You can't think that way,' Franziskus said.

Stefan deftly performed the sign of Shallya. 'If you had asked me, even a few days ago, why I embarked on this pilgrimage, I could not give you a good reason for it.'

'That's because–' began Angelika. Franziskus silenced her with a forbidding look. For some reason, she obeyed him, and let the advocate go on.

'It was just a feeling I had,' Stefan said, fixed unwaveringly on Devorah's features. He touched his chest. 'In here. I have always been a man of the mind, not the heart. Of argument, debate, precedent. Law. For once, though, I felt impelled to follow the dictates of my heart, so I joined this group of fellow fools and sinners, without knowing why. Only now do I understand. It is Shallya's mercy that has placed me here, to ensure that this one innocent girl is carried into her arms, to gain intercession through Mother Elsbeth. I do not need healing. I am already healed. It does not matter what the rest of you say: I will do my best to get her to Heiligerberg, and if I die, I shall do so in a state of divine grace.'

Gerhold's eyes glistened. Lemoine tottered over to fold his arms around Stefan. Udo joined the scrum from behind: 'I know of what you speak, good Stefan! I, too, came here insincerely! I was even more insincere than you! And, although I do not feel it yet,' he said, his voice breaking, 'if I act like I feel it, I know I surely will!'

THE MOON HUNG low and bright in the black sky over Heiligerberg. Winded, Ivo fruitlessly choked in ragged breaths of thin mountain air. He paused to pound on his sunken chest, in a desperate attempt to pummel his lungs into greater efficiency. His head spun; the last bit of the climb had been punishing, even more so than the last time he'd done it. He bent; hands clasped onto his thighs and pointed his head earthwards. He waited. Gradually his body quieted its protests. Ivo straightened up, hummed merrily, and pushed his way through the pilgrims who thronged the gate.

# CHAPTER FIFTEEN

THEY CLIMBED. ANGELIKA looked up. The sun hid its position behind a canopy of thick, dark clouds, but she knew it was the middle of the afternoon, or thereabouts. Or maybe it wasn't. Perhaps the ache in her muscles was fooling her. Another possibility: it merely seemed as if a long time had passed, because the struggle had been so hard. Because they had gone so far. Because there was so far to go.

Angelika turned and looked behind her. They were all on their hands and knees: Gerhold, Stefan, Udo, Waldemar. They appeared to her as shambling, amorphous dots on a vast and angry field of ice. Behind them, Franziskus and Lemoine fought to pull a sled, to which Devorah was lashed. They'd found the sled with a dead noblewoman and a large guard dog that was also dead stuck fast to its wooden slats. It had taken some chipping and kicking to get them off it, to make a transport for their sick young sister. Devorah was unconscious, and had been that way since the marrow-chilling morning hours. Now she sweated feverishly, and her face was flushed. Her head jerked tortuously from left to right. Stefan and Waldemar had been told to keep themselves below the sled, but they'd abandoned their rear guard positions to scramble on the glaciated slope along with everyone else.

Angelika calculated the slope's angle: thirty degrees, perhaps. Thirty-five? Her lungs burned. She could not see the top of the mountain. Somewhere up there, it terminated in some sort of ledge or plateau, but all she could see before her was filthy, trampled snow, gouged and pitted by the efforts of hundreds of scrabbling pilgrims. Nor was it possible to turn and look back to see where they'd come from, there was just more ice, receding into a curtain of fog. They were nowhere, hurting, and eking their way up into more nowhere.

She could see no other pilgrims but her own. Past the boundaries of the fog, there were voices and shouts. Grunts of pain, perhaps, or of defeat. But no one else to see.

Blood, half-coagulated, half-frozen, coated the tips of each of her fingers; she could no longer see her nails. Angelika punched them into the glacier's outer crust, a layer of crystalline snow like dead and sloughed-off skin. After making a handhold in the crust, she hoisted herself upwards. Then she did the same again. And again. Her fingers had enough feeling in them for a new jolt of dull pain to throb up through her arms each time she made a new handhold. The others would follow her path, using her handholds, so their hands would not suffer as much as hers. She paused to pant and wheeze. Many other pilgrims had already made this trek, she reminded herself. Surely they could not all have perished and slid down the mountainside. Yes, she had found many bodies, some of them lucratively kitted out – but not that many. Someone had to be surviving this trip. She would survive, too. It was true that the others were impelled forward by faith, by their moronic belief in the importance of this mountain and the woman who lived atop it. That was not true of Angelika. She had something better. Her own faith. Faith in herself.

And as soon as she got down from this stinking mountain she would promise herself never to go up another one ever again.

Abruptly she realised that she'd dropped down onto the ice. She pushed herself up, brushing frozen crystals from her cheek. She stretched her arms out. She dug her fingers into the crust. She made another handhold. She pulled her body upwards. Her thin chest heaved, exchanging one lungful of chill, unsatisfactory air for another. She pulled herself up. She thrust her arms out. She stuck her fingers into the ice. Made another handhold. Hauled her body up.

What am I doing this for, she asked herself.

For money, she answered.

For little bags of gold I don't even spend, squirreled away in dozens of tiny holes, dug all across this misbegotten wilderness.

Angelika questioned the validity of her goals.

Then she pushed.

Stretched. Dug. Pulled. Heaved. Pulled. Pushed. Gasped. Pain. Hauled.

Pushed.

Stretched.

Dug.

Pulled.

Hurt.

Heaved.

Fought.

Pushed.

Gasped.

Pain.

Wheezed.

She'd rested her face in the ice again. She jolted up. She wrenched around. She sat on her behind. Let it freeze for a while, she thought. Let it match the rest of her.

'How is everyone down there?' she called.

She wasn't sure whether she'd really said it. Yes, her lips were working up and down, and she was vocalising the thought, but was there enough air to make the actual sound?

Apparently so.

The others stopped. They waved. They pulled, pushed, hauled, hurt, wheezed, gasped.

Franziskus called. His mouth moved. She heard the sounds he made, but she had to furrow her brow hard to understand what they were.

'She is fading,' he appeared to be saying.

She. The sister. Devorah. She was fading.

Well, good for her.

Miracle she made it this far.

Isn't that what they all want, when all is said and done? To die on this holy slope?

Angelika turned back to the unending carpet of ice. Dug in another handhold. Grimaced.

She hurt, hauled, wheezed. The handhold was icy and her bloody lungs were rasping.

Angelika realised she was hallucinating.

All the whiteness had become warm and good, and she no longer strained. Her muscles no longer felt strain and pain; the snow had become a balm.

And she was floating somewhere, somewhere good. Space and her relation to the physical world no longer mattered. It was just whiteness, and that's all there was to it. There was no need to trouble her mind any more than that. Just whiteness.

And there beside her, glowing, clean, swaddled in robes of purest white linen, and radiant from the inside, was the old officer, Thomas Krieger. There was no sign of his wounds.

'You're angry with me,' she said.

'No I'm not,' he replied softly.

'You have good reason to be. I didn't swear to protect the others, as you wished.'

Krieger shrugged. It was beautiful, the way he did it. 'You made no promise, so you broke no promise.'

'I've let so many die,' she said. She ticked off the list on perfect, bloodless fingers. 'The prioress. Jurg. Rausch. The widow Kloster. Ludwig.'

'You promised nothing.'

'And now Richart and Ivo – they're both dead, aren't they?'

'If you say so.'

'And Altman – murdered. And yet I am no closer to naming his killer.'

'What does it matter?'

'What does it matter?' she repeated, suspicion seeping into her tone. This was not what the real Krieger would say, if he sent his shade to visit her.

The false Krieger chattered blithely on. 'Chances are, whoever killed Altman was among those who have themselves since died. Ludwig, let us say. Or Rausch.'

'I'm in a delirium, aren't I?' Angelika said, accusingly. 'Brought on by thin air and exertion.'

'You were right to make me no promises, Angelika. Promises lead only to disappointment.'

'You're just my own starved mind, telling itself what it wishes to hear.'

'When next you get the chance to make a foolish promise, do exactly what you did with me. Refuse. Give away nothing.'

She treated the imaginary Krieger to a series of her favourite obscenities. He blurred, became indistinct, then there was nothing at all. Not even the whiteness.

It's me who's dying now, Angelika realised.

She shook herself.

She found she could not move.

She shook herself harder. Shook her head. Shook her hands. Put them in front of her weary eyes. The tips of the fingers were bloody again. That was a good sign at least. She shuddered.

Whiteness faded, gave way to greyness.

She came to. Franziskus loomed over her. He was jostling her up and down, commanding her to awaken. She lay on her back in the snow. She bolted up – so quickly that her forehead smacked right into his. The dreary sky and the dirty white mountain swam and buckled hazily before her, until her vision sharpened and resolved itself. Franziskus took her by the shoulders. Tiny diamond beads of frozen water had taken up housekeeping amid the feathery white hairs of his invisible, boyish moustache.

'You collapsed,' he said.

'I did no such thing,' she replied, brushing snow from the arms of her jacket. He pushed his face, made florid by the frosty wind, so close to hers that it entirely occupied her field of vision. A bump was already rising on his forehead, where she had smacked him.

'The sister,' she said. 'Is she–?'

Franziskus gestured to the sled. Devorah's chest moved in time to her shallow breathing.

A frozen spike of dark hair dangled down to tickle Angelika's forehead. Franziskus brushed it out of the way for her. She rewarded him with the slightest of smiles.

'You know we'll get off this frozen rock alive, don't you?' she asked him.

He nodded.

'The two of us, I mean,' she said.

He stole a glance at Devorah. 'More than just us,' he said.

A bellow arose from below. Angelika did not know whom it was coming from, until she saw him charging up the glacier: Waldemar, face crimson, eyes screaming back in his head. 'Get away from her!' the summoner cried. 'Get away!'

Franziskus, still crouching, spun, hand ready on his sabre hilt. Flecks of froth fell from Waldemar's howling mouth. 'It's the sister you love!' Waldemar shrieked, making startlingly quick progress up the slope, grasping hands held out before his face. 'Angelika is mine! Move away from her, or I'll–'

He tripped on a large, buried object and flipped face-first into the ice. He rose up, snow caking his beard, making him seem even wilder and madder than before. He stepped over the obstacle, then fell – backwards this time – as it gave way beneath him, rolling down, taking him with it. Waldemar frantically whirled his arms, but he could not regain his balance. He slid, yowling, then disappeared from view in a cloud of displaced snow particles.

Angelika stood and moved carefully down the slope, until she could again see the summoner. He lay flat on his back, a widening nimbus of deep red blood suffusing the snow and ice around the back of his head. Dizzily at first, Angelika ventured toward him. He'd slid about ten yards, until a sharp jut of rock had stopped him short, piercing his skull. Angelika knew he was dead before she reached his side. She shouted up to the others: 'He went mad and now he's dead. Keep going. I'll catch up.' She stooped over him. 'So you loved me, did you?' she asked him. With dully aching fingers, she reached into his pockets, relieved him of his purse, and teased fat gold rings from his swollen hands.

SHE FOLLOWED HIS tracks up the slope. As she had suspected: the object that had tripped him up was a corpse, frozen to the side of the mountain. It was a young woman, younger than Devorah, though with coarser features. She brushed snow crystals aside. The corpse's eyes were open and frozen to the core; it occurred to Angelika that if she were to tap them with the tip of her dagger, they would make a chinking sound. Between stone-solid fingers, the young dead girl clutched a string of silver prayer beads, complete with a jewelled dove. Angelika cracked the hand with the pommel of her dagger, breaking the fingers off. She teased the beads from the shattered hand, dropped it into her purse and then hustled to catch up with the others.

Soon she was ahead of them. A peculiar energy, from a source she could not name, suffused her. But it did not last. And the ice went on for hours.

The putrid green of a distant Chaos-storm tinged the clouds as ice gave way to a patch of rock. The angle of the slope flattened out. Other pilgrims huddled before a fire, sheltered by a shallow natural alcove. They waved and called out in praise to Shallya. There were half a dozen of them, men and women, wrapped in furs. They warmed uninjured hands at a fire. Leather gloves hung from their belts. Coiled ropes lay at their feet, along with chains and spikes and hammers – all the proper equipment for a long climb on ice.

Angelika stumbled alongside Recht and hissed. 'Why didn't we have this?'

Recht shook his head. 'Clearly they were better informed than we. We knew the journey would be difficult, but we scarcely imagined…'

'Idiots,' Angelika muttered.

Seeing Devorah's condition, the climbers rushed to her sled and dragged it, scraping on the rock, towards the fire. They poured a hot cup for her from a steel teapot, but she remained unconscious, even when Franziskus laid his warming hands directly on her soft, pale cheeks.

'She's not long for this world,' said one of the fur-clad pilgrims, a tall man with pinched eyes and a long, leathery face.

'No time to waste,' said another, a round-faced, flat-nosed fellow with a reedy voice. Their accents marked them out as northerners. 'We must get her up the rest of the way, so Mother Elsbeth can cure her.'

Without further discussion, they doused their fire with their fresh-brewed tea then efficiently assembled their climbing gear. 'You've done the hard part already,' said the leather-faced man, thrusting a hearty hand to Stefan. He introduced himself as Primus Lichtman. He did not bother to name his companions. 'Coming up the ice without suitable clothing and no gear whatsoever. The lot of you are quite insane,' he cheerfully observed.

'I wish I could disagree,' said Angelika.

He pressed his squinty eyes even further shut, clasped his hands together, and addressed the sky.

'Bless you, oh goddess Shallya, that you have brought these unfortunates to us, that we may extend the benefits of our superior planning to others needier than ourselves, and thereby prove our love to you, that our prayers of mercy toward all may be strengthened, and the rancid hosts of Chaos be thus turned back and dashed upon the shoals of all-encompassing love.'

This place, Angelika thought, is blessed with more than its share of entirely mad persons.

But the happy, healthy pilgrims did as they promised, wrapping Devorah's skid in a cocoon of ropes, as the others jaunted ahead up the rock, happily pounding in spikes and laying in a preparatory network of ropes and chains. 'This last expanse won't be difficult at all,' Primus Lichtman reassured them. 'There is a great hustle-bustle of importuning persons up around the shrine, and we have been waiting for a pressing cause to join it.'

'Yes,' said Angelika, still wondering what trick these well-fed pilgrims meant to play. Would they dash her and her charges down the side of the mountain and then venture down to collect their valuables? She kept her hand as near her knife as decorum allowed. 'I reckon there's no greater cesspool of contagion and disease within a thousand leagues of here. All those sufferers of the mange and shingles, and Chaos plague no doubt, all packed together around the gates of a tiny abbey…' The leathery face of Primus Lichtman lost some of its deep-brown colour. Angelika's mood improved immensely.

Like a swarm of eager, helpful rodents, the pilgrims clambered back down the rocks, having fashioned a makeshift pulley system to ferry Devorah's pallet up the rocky summit. Contentedly brushing both Franziskus and Lemoine out of the way, they moved to the young sister's side. They attached her to their rope system and heaved her up, harmonising their rhythm with a breathy chant. Using their rope-and-chain handholds to drag herself up the stony slope, Angelika followed the blissful pilgrims, and was followed in turn by Franziskus, Lemoine, Stefan Recht, Friar Gerhold and the merchant, Udo Kramer. She braced herself, waiting for Primus's men to slash the ropes, and send Devorah's sled crashing down on them, but they did no such thing. Instead, they disappeared over a lip of rock, taking the girl with them. Angelika tensed, imagining any number of cruel scenes. But Primus and the double-chinned man quickly returned, standing on the ledge, their uncallused hands beckoning her on. They reached out for her and pulled her up.

# CHAPTER SIXTEEN

ANGELIKA STOOD BEFORE a throng of pilgrims that
crowded the worn, pitted walls of an old, drab
abbey. She couldn't see a front gate and asked
Primus to explain. He pointed to her left, where the
sound of shouting and chanting suggested an even
greater mob of penitents around the corner.

'We came up the side way,' he said. 'There are natural
terraces around the front,' he said, proud of himself.

'There are terraces?'

Primus nodded.

'On the mountain? Stairs on the mountain?'

'Indeed, yes.'

'And we came up the side?'

Primus became grave. 'We scouted those terraces
and found them suspiciously hospitable. In the scal-
ing of mountains, there is no killer more ruthless
than simple complacency.'

A familiar voice fluted ominously in the distance. 'That's them! That's her!'

Angelika clenched her teeth.

It was Ivo Kirchgeld, flanked by two guardsmen, who clanked towards her in the full armour and martial regalia of Sigmarite warrior priests. Ivo pointed his forefinger at her face. 'I knew it was fruitless waiting for them at the front. If there was a sneaky way to come, they'd find it!'

Franziskus placed a restraining hand on her knife-arm. The gesture was redundant; Angelika had already figured the odds. Two large, fully-armoured, doubtlessly well-trained men against one slim woman. Even if she weren't exhausted, she'd never be fool enough to start a tangle with fighters like these.

'Hands above your heads!' the older of the two guards commanded, addressing both her and Franziskus.

Ivo Kirchgeld rocked back on his heels. 'Yes, that's it. The two of them. Don't mind the others, they're harmless dupes. I was the only one to see these two for the impious villains they are.'

'Hands above your heads!' the elder Sigmarite repeated, animating a complex network of wrinkles and creases. Angelika slowly moved her hands out from her sides, crooking them slightly above her head. Franziskus did the same.

'It is true that there are dupes present, but they have been misidentified,' said Angelika, meeting the lead soldier's glare. 'I don't know what tale this jack-anapes has peddled to you, or what he hopes to gain by it, but you can be sure that it and the truth are only coincidentally acquainted.'

A series of tics cascaded across Kirchgeld's face. 'The hag's tongue is as sharp as I said it would be.'

The older guard took a step away from Ivo as his younger companion, an open-faced man with deep-set blue eyes, advanced on Franziskus.

'No, her first,' said Ivo, tapping the elder Sigmarite's armoured shoulder. 'She's the dangerous one.' The guardsman jerked away from Kirchgeld, silencing him with a scowl. The young Sigmarite bared his teeth and took hold of Franziskus's belt, working the buckle open. He seized Franziskus's scabbard as the belt loosened, handing it back to his superior.

'At least tell us what we stand accused of,' said Angelika.

'You know full well,' Ivo sing-songed.

The young guard moved to Angelika and reached for her belt. She put her hands in front of her. 'I'll do it myself, thank you,' she said. The guard pulled a baton from his belt and slapped it into his glove. Angelika unhooked her belt and tossed it at her feet.

'The boot, too,' Ivo said. 'She's got another in her left boot.'

Angelika's face tightened. She placed her foot in front of the young guard. His cheek twitched. 'You want the knife, don't you?' she asked him.

He stared down at her boot.

'You don't want me to reach down for it, do you?' Angelika asked.

'Listen to her!' Ivo fluted. 'Even under threat of arms, she mocks you!'

'Quiet yourself,' the elder Sigmarite told him. Then, to his subordinate: 'Get the knife!'

With his blue eyes trained guardedly on her, the young guard knelt before Angelika, patted the side of her boot, found the dagger, and teased it out. Angelika smiled hatefully at him. He stood, walked around her, and seized her by the back of her neck.

'Recht, you're an arguer of law,' she said, her tone only slightly strained. 'Aren't you going to ask them what crime we've committed?'

'The girl,' Recht said, stepping forward. His fancy hat, with its lordly feather, had gone missing – another casualty of the climb, no doubt. Its abscence left his balding pate exposed. Recht caught the senior guardsman's attention and pointed over to Devorah's sled. The sister faintly moaned. 'This girl,' Recht said, 'is desperately ill. We must get her to Mother Elsbeth without delay.'

The guardsman wiped at his nose. 'That's not my responsibility.'

'I tell you, she is dying,' replied Recht.

The young Sigmarite removed his hand from the back of Angelika's neck and took a cord from his belt. 'Hands behind your back,' he said.

'I'll do as you ask,' Angelika said, 'but tend to the girl.'

The guardsman slapped Angelika on the back of the head. 'You'll do as we tell you, whether we help the girl or not.'

Primus Lichtman stepped up to clamp his hand around the young guardsman's wrist. 'Now look here, you mannerless whelp!'

The guard planted his free hand in Lichtman's gut. The fur-clad pilgrim doubled over, jowls puffing out, veins dancing on his temples.

Lichtman gasped up at him. 'You bloodstained Sigmarites have no place here.'

'No,' said Angelika.

'Stop,' said Stefan Recht.

Lichtman continued, even as the guard grabbed him by the throat: 'You are usurpers. Get us a priestess. We demand to speak to a priestess.'

'Stop it,' said Stefan.

Ivo slipped away.

'I'm sick of you spotty useless pilgrims!' the guard cried, tightening his grip on Lichtman's throat. 'And your constant screaming and whining!'

He'd turned his back to Angelika, but the cord had not completely tied her hands. If she wanted to, she could wrap it around his neck, like a garrotte. She decided she didn't want to. She checked the position of the other guard. He was wading toward her. Brother Lemoine rushed in from the side to importune him.

'The girl,' Lemoine said, his pontificating finger crooked into the air before him. 'Let the girl be saved.'

The older guard shoved Lemoine aside. Angelika took the opportunity to reach for her dagger, which the young Sigmarite had stashed in his own belt, at the small of his back. As he struggled with Lichtman, she plucked it loose.

'All of you, stop it!' the senior guardsman cried. 'Stop what you're doing!'

Quickly, Angelika took the tip of her dagger and cut a notch in the cord.

Lichtman made to free himself from his enemy's grip on his throat by falling backwards, but merely brought the young guard sprawling down on top of him. The guard kneed him between the legs before laying down a flurry of slaps on his face and neck.

Angelika dropped her dagger in the mud, a few feet from the fray.

The old Sigmarite charged toward his junior. One of Lichtman's fellows rushed in to intercept. The helmeted warrior downed him with a single head-butt and then stepped neatly over his body as it folded to the dirt. He grabbed his own man by the cloak, hauling him to his feet. Lichtman flailed his limbs, working to right himself. Both guards joined forces to kick him in the side until he curled into a quivering ball and begged for mercy.

'You dropped that,' said Angelika, pointing to her knife.

Grimacing, the young guardsman stooped to pick it up. Angelika turned, the cord still looped around her arms. She thrust her wrists out at him. 'Go ahead,' she said. 'Finish your work.' Panting, the young guard did so. Angelika had arranged the cord to conceal the cut from him.

One of Lichtman's companions knelt at the man's side, examining him for injuries. He hissed at the guardsmen: 'You'll pay for this, when we finally speak to the priestesses.'

Recht's features puckered in chagrin. He turned on the young fellow. 'Dolt! Do you seek to doom the girl with your damnable insolence?'

Primus's man stammered. Recht shook his fist at him, before turning to the senior warrior priest. 'These men are recent acquaintances. I disavow their rude and violent behaviour.'

The old guardsman sniffed at him.

'I am Stefan Recht, an advocate of Averheim. You are…?'

'Bernolt Steinhauer, hammer-brother of Sigmar. Also of Averheim.' He over-enunciated, to make his impatience clear.

The junior finished tying Angelika and moved on to restrain Franziskus.

'Then perhaps I know your commander.'

'It is not impossible. Father Manfried is known to many.'

'That would be Father Manfried Haupt, whose father built the cathedral in Averheim, soon to be consecrated without him?'

'He is that Manfried Haupt, yes.'

Recht patted the damp hair on top of his head. 'I won't tell you that he and I are intimates, but… Let us say that I know of his dilemma, and also that I know certain intriguing facts about those responsible for it.'

'We have orders to take these two thieves into custody. Those orders are not flexible.'

Recht swiped an arm in Angelika's general direction. 'What of it? They merely served as our guides on the way here. I disavow them and whatever they have done. But the girl...'

The tip of the guardsman's tongue ventured thoughtfully out between his pursed lips.

Recht leaned in to softly press his case. 'Father Haupt will have instructed you to grant special attention to persons of influence. I am sure those orders, too, are lacking in flexibility.'

The man nodded.

'Then you will see to it that this girl is taken directly to Mother Elsbeth, that she bypasses all other penitents, and that she is given all possible care. You will do it now, for both our sakes.'

'Take her then!' the guardsman cried. Lemoine, Udo and Gerhold scurried to pick up her sled. 'You deal with these two,' he instructed his junior, as he placed himself in front of Devorah's bearers. He withdrew his baton from his belt and held it out, as a crowd-parter, leading the way around the corner of the abbey wall. Recht followed without looking back.

'I never thought I'd see the day,' Angelika said.

'When Recht would betray us?' whispered Franziskus.

'When an advocate would prove himself useful.'

'Shut your holes,' the junior guardsman sulkily demanded. 'I suppose now I have to decide where to put you.'

Angelika smiled sweetly. 'There's no jail here? What kind of holy place is this?'

The guardsman clenched his fist but chose not to hit a woman. He saw that Primus Lichtman still lay on the ground, a few feet away, clutching his gut, and went over to feint at him, as if prepared to kick him a few more times.

Bernolt Steinhauer led the pallet-bearers, including Stefan, past the queue of penitents gathered inside the abbey courtyard. He marched toward the large tent in which Mother Elsbeth's healings were staged. Its front flap was down, but that would not deter him. A leprous old woman, her expression dazed, wandered out of the line and into his path. He barked at her and her companions skittered out to reel her back in before the guardsman could push at her with his out-thrust baton.

Bernolt disliked this place. The tent he disliked especially. He would never question the judgments of his blessed commander to commit the sin of pride, but the tent seemed to him a sign of the entire place stinking and not being worth a rounded ball of frozen horse dung. Surely an abbey worth defending would already possess a decent-sized indoor receiving hall? It would not require them to press one of their field tents into service.

Bernolt bit down on his grumbles and forged on to the entrance. A figure muddled its way through the flap — Father Eugen. Eugen did not, at first, notice Bernolt; he was intent on making an announcement to the muttering, snaking queue. He cupped his hands around his mouth, bushy brows accenting his eyes like a pair of uneasy circumflexes.

'Pardon me, my friends,' he said, his voice failing to rise above a conversational volume. 'Many pardons!' Then he turned and saw Bernolt, then the sled, then its carriers, then the pale and feverish girl strapped to it. 'Goodness,' he said. 'Bernolt?'

'This one must be taken to the healer right away,' Bernolt said.

Eugen peered dolorously into the girl's dying face. 'No, I don't think that will work.'

'Tell me how it can be made to work, father.'

Eugen scanned past the makeshift procession to the wall behind them. 'The others here have been waiting a long time... Mother Elsbeth's last audience was severely taxing...'

With a precise jerk of his shoulder, Bernolt indicated Stefan Recht. 'This one's a fancy advocate. Says he can be of help to the cause. But only if we help the girl.'

Stefan gave Father Eugen a curt wave, suggestive not only of respect, but knowledge and influence too.

Eugen bit his lip. 'I don't know if she has another healing in her, just now.'

A hoarse voice grated out from the middle of the queue: 'You're not taking her ahead of us, are you?'

Steinhauer twisted back to brandish his baton. 'This one's dying, you mewling idiot! Can you say the same for yourself?'

The crowd groaned an inarticulate protest.

Stefan thrust himself in front of Eugen. 'We beg you, my friend. If you can't take her now, she'll get no other chance.'

'Yes, yes, of course,' Eugen muttered, clumsily parting the canvas flap. Steinhauer stepped up to open it wider and the four pilgrims carried in the sled.

The tent was spackled with mildew and stank of urine and lamp oil. Near its far wall lay a bed, linen sheets draped messily from its elevated wooden pallet. Stains from various fluids blotched the sheets; a pile of even more greatly soiled bedding sat bunched in a corner. A circle of lanterns surrounded the bed, leaking smoke.

A stringy old man, naked except for a precariously dangling loincloth, danced a tiny-stepped, exultant jig on the well-trampled mud floor. 'They're gone,' he delightedly cried, looking down at his slack and wrinkled flesh. 'The tumours! The lesions! Gone! Gone! I am whole again!'

A weary sister sidled up to the cured man, mindful of his recklessly swinging elbows. 'You must go now,' she whispered.

'Whole!' he cried.

'Put on your robes and go,' she commanded.

He stopped dancing and huffed peevishly. 'I am grateful that my life is saved, but you still must accord me the respect my position demands.'

She stalked over to the cured man's attendants, took hold of the robes they held out for him, and thrust them into his arms. 'Go,' she said. The man grumbled but quickly wrapped himself up.

Then the priestess turned her attention to Bernolt and Eugen.

'No,' she said.

'You must,' said Bernolt.

'No more until her next treatment.'

'She's dying,' said Eugen.

The sister wiped at her eyes. 'So is Mother Elsbeth!'

No one spoke. Udo suppressed a cough. Stefan bent to lower Devorah's pallet to the ground; the others followed suit.

'No,' said the priestess.

A frail voice came from the bed. 'I will take her.'

The priestess bowed her head. 'Do not do it,' she said.

'Bring her to me,' said the woman on the bed, raising herself tremblingly onto her elbows.

Stefan Recht jerked backwards, recoiling into Udo Kramer, who stood behind him. Lemoine gasped.

The woman could barely support the weight of her head; as she rested it on one sharp, bony shoulder, then on the other. It appeared oversized in comparison to her shrunken body. Rheumy eyes blinked dimly from dark pits beneath her brow. She opened her mouth in a tortured smile, showing jagged, decomposing teeth. An incisor dropped from her top gum and fell into the rancid bed sheets. 'Please,' she hissed, 'bring her quickly.'

'Mother Elsbeth!' Lemoine gasped.

Father Eugen took Bernolt Steinhauer by the shoulder. 'Get Manfried,' he whispered. 'Quickly.'

Steinhauer loped from the tent.

'Bring her here, I tell you,' croaked Mother Elsbeth. She picked at the back of her head, then examined what she'd caught between her fingers: a sheaf of brittle, colourless hair. She crackled it in her palm, turning it into dust.

Recht twisted back, to see that Udo, Lemoine and Gerhold all stood frozen, the only difference between them the degrees to which their mouths swung agape. Mumbling disgustedly, he bent down to unlash Devorah from the sled, then folded her carefully in his arms. On unsteady feet he dragged her over to Mother Elsbeth's bed. The healthiest-looking of the sisters moved to block his progress, but seeing Devorah's face, relented. Sighing desolately, she helped to roll the unconscious girl closer to the dying high priestess. The death's-head of Elsbeth's features transfigured itself into a rictus of maternal anxiety. She coughed and another rotten, yellow tooth detached itself from her mouth, tumbling over her lips and into the linens. The holy woman opened her arms, pulling Devorah closer to her.

Devorah's eyelids fluttered.

'My daughter,' croaked Elsbeth. 'Don't fret. You're home now.' She enveloped the girl in twig-thin arms, rocking her as if she were an infant. 'You are a special young one; I can feel that.'

Devorah murmured and rolled onto her side, hugging herself tighter to the old woman's feeble body.

Recht stepped back from the bed, hands clasped in prayer.

'You will need all I can give,' said Elsbeth, laying her palms on Devorah's forehead. She pulled the front of her robe open.

Recht meant to avert his eyes but could not.

Open, puckering lesions broke the skin of the healer's naked torso. The tell tale discolorations of leprosy spotted her body. Purple bruises mottled the flesh of her distended belly. Tumours, greyish and fist-sized, hung from her ribcage like extra teats.

Recht put hand over mouth as understanding came. This was how Mother Elsbeth healed wounds and ailments of her suffering flock – by taking them on herself.

Elsbeth tightened her embrace on the girl. She shuddered. The healer's already sallow skin grew paler. Her pupils dilated. Her pores opened, leaking turbid sweat. She and the girl convulsed together.

# CHAPTER SEVENTEEN

GREY LIGHT SNUCK through the weathered planks of the tiny shed, which, before being hastily pressed into service as a prison cell, had held only tools for the abbey's meagre garden. Franziskus sat glumly, his back resting against a wall, the edges of his cloak protecting his posterior from the floorless shack's cold ground. Angelika paced, the cord still around her wrists.

'It's been, what? Six hours now, at least? How long are you going to pretend that rope still binds you?' sighed Franziskus.

'What?'

'I know you cut it. I saw you.'

'Well, yes.'

'So?'

Angelika squatted beside him. 'I'm still deciding,' she said. 'If I untie myself and you, I'm fairly certain we can break through the walls of this shed.'

'They are in poor repair,' Franziskus agreed.

'But what then? There's at least one brawny Sigmarite on the other side of that door.'

'I think I heard two.'

'Without weapons, we're no use against even one guard,' calculated Angelika. 'But let's say we do get past them. What are our odds of getting down the mountain before they catch up with us?'

'Unpleasant at best.'

'Whatever it is they think we've done, we're in the unusual position of not having done it. So, before trying the hard way, why not at least try to talk our way out?'

Franziskus made a grumping noise.

'Why so sceptical? I thought these Sigmarites would be just your sort. They're the forces of good, aren't they? The smiters of Chaos?'

'Yes, but they are large men with warhammers. And I am a deserter, and you are… you do what you do. So let us not delude ourselves. Ivo may seem a heretic to some, but he's still a churchman.'

'Or claims to be.'

'At any rate, they believed him over us.'

'Another reason to stay. I'd like a few minutes alone with him.'

'If the place doesn't erupt first.'

'What do you mean?'

'The mood is palpable. There are too many penitents here. We know how desperate the journey has made them. You saw how quick Primus Lichtman and his fervent friends were to lunge at the Sigmarites, when a dispute arose. And how eager the

Sigmarites were to smack them down. How long will it be before they shove the pilgrims one step too far, and the abbey winds up in flames?'

The door opened. 'An intriguing scenario,' said a new, rich voice. A Sigmarite in well-polished armour stepped through. His eyes were intense; his face, long; his ears, wide. He squatted beside Franziskus, like a comrade.

'I am Father Manfried Haupt,' he said. 'I command these... large men with warhammers.'

'How long have you been listening?' Franziskus asked.

Manfried reached forward to snatch the bindings at Angelika's wrists. He yanked on them, finding the notch, snapping the cord. He smiled malignly. 'Long enough,' he said.

He stood before Franziskus, leaving him bound. 'So you think I'm an incompetent, do you?'

Franziskus kept his head down. 'I said no such thing.'

'Not directly. But you implied it, didn't you? You think me incapable of controlling one paltry little abbey in the middle of nowhere?'

'If we knew we were being spied on, we would have spoken more diplomatically,' said Angelika.

Manfried whipped round to Angelika, a razor grin slicing across his face. 'So, from now on your words will be perfumed?'

In a gesture both ironic and precise, Angelika held out her hand for Manfried. He bared his teeth and played along, heaving her to her feet. She recovered her balance and deftly concluded her move in a pose of mock daintiness. 'It seems you believe something told to you by Ivo Kirchgeld. And he is a jackass of the highest order. What does that make you?'

He grabbed her by the hair on the back of her head. 'I won't be spoken to that way.'

She grimaced but did not cry out. 'Ah yes, you're in control, aren't you?'

He pushed her down to her knees. 'Do you always antagonise those who hold your destiny in their hands, wench?'

She kept her face serene, despite a tear of pain traitorously welling in her right eye. 'It is my strictest rule,' she said, with voice unbroken. 'What's yours?'

'I serve Sigmar!' he shouted. 'I have no time for this – Chaos eats the fabric of the world!' He slapped her. Franziskus lunged for him. He whirled and punched the blond Stirlander in the throat. Franziskus wheezed, clutching at his jaw-line, and sank to his knees. As he battled his way back up to his feet, Manfried smashed him on the side of the face. Franziskus hit the wall and slumped to the floor. Manfried strode over to him, picked him up by the front of his tunic, and shook him. 'The implements – where are they? They're no mere curios, to be flogged off for a few pieces of gold! They're weapons against Chaos – they can get us out off this misbegotten mountain and back into the fray!'

Blood dribbled out from a crack in Franziskus's lip. 'Neither of us has the faintest notion of what you're talking about,' he said.

Manfried threw him to the ground. 'Richart Pfeffer! Don't tell me you don't know that name!'

'Of course,' said Angelika, drawing his attention away from Franziskus. 'He was one of the pilgrims we shepherded up here.'

'He was my man,' Manfried said. 'I hired him to find the person who, posing as a pilgrim, came here and stole a set of blessed thaumaturgical instruments from the abbey's reliquary. He suspected you, and so joined your pilgrimage in the hope of finding proof – or perhaps the implements themselves. You led him to his death, but not before he confided in this good pilgrim, this Ivo Kirchgeld.'

Angelika laughed. 'That's absurd. We met Richart and the others completely by chance, in the middle of the Blackfire Pass, long after they'd assembled themselves into a party. If he joined the pilgrimage to track a thief, it would have to be one of the others – I'd say Ivo, wouldn't you, Franziskus?'

'Indubitably,' Franziskus groaned, lying on his back in the cold dirt.

Angelika knelt at his side. 'It's a surprisingly common thing, for people to seize on the very first version of a story they hear. And they cling to it tenaciously, despite all contrary evidence.'

Manfried twitched.

'I understand,' said Angelika, dabbing at Franziskus's lip with a corner of her sleeve, 'it is especially prevalent among those of a religious cast of mind, who are accustomed to taking things on faith.'

'Quiet yourself and let me think,' Manfried growled.

'If I were you, my thinking would be as follows: is there anything else in this place worth stealing, and, if so, is Ivo Kirchgeld currently stealing it?'

He made a fist for her. 'Shut up!'

A rap echoed through the shed's flimsy door. 'Sir?'

'What is it?'

The door opened. It was Bernolt, with Devorah behind him. Franziskus lifted himself up. His eyes widened. The girl was not only upright, but she was apparently strong and healthy. She wore a fresh new sister's habit. Her skin glowed; her eyes had regained their piercing clarity.

Devorah saw Franziskus and cried his name. She rushed through the door, but Manfried interposed himself so she couldn't get to him.

'What is it?' he barked.

'Mother Elsbeth. sent her,' faltered Bernolt. 'To fetch this... this Angelika Fleischer and bring her to a private audience.'

Manfried spoke through gritted teeth. 'Quite impossible. Her holiness requires another treatment.'

Devorah raised her chin up and pointed her stunning face at Manfried. 'She has had another treatment. I watched as it was administered to her. I was healed by her, so I saw her condition before she was bathed in the healing mixture, as well.'

'Just who is this?' he demanded of Bernolt.

Devorah straightened her spine. 'I am Sister Devorah. I am a devotee of Shallya. You are here at the pleasure of our most merciful goddess. And I am here to tell you that Mother Elsbeth, abbess of Heiligerberg, desires to speak with this woman, Angelika Fleischer.'

Manfried shook his head like a spaniel flecking water off its muzzle. The girl had somehow transfixed him. He looked to Bernolt, then to his two captives.

'Very well,' he said, 'the situation is at any rate ambiguous. The blond-hair stays captive, as a surety. And find me that Ivo Kirchgeld!'

He stormed from the shack, angrily gesticulating. After a moment of indecision, Bernolt stalked off, too, in another direction, then reversed course to take Angelika by the arm, leading her toward the abbey gate.

His departure left Devorah inside the shack, under the questioning gaze of the Sigmarite warriors stationed to guard it. 'I must speak to my friend here,' she told them. 'Then I'll return to her grace's side.'

They shrugged and retook their positions outside the shack. Devorah swung it gently shut. She took Franziskus's cloak, rolled it up into a pillow, and slid it under his head. She gripped his hand in hers and looked down into his battered face.

'Oh Franziskus,' she said.

'You're alive,' he managed.

'Yes.'

'You've recovered.'

'Mother Elsbeth healed me. But, oh, the terrible price she pays for it…'

'What's going on here? Are the sisters Manfried's prisoners?'

'In all but name. But Manfried is sure he acts right-eously.'

Franziskus sat up. He looked at her perfect hand, resting in his. He brought it to his lips, ready to kiss it.

She pulled it away from him. She averted her eyes. 'Franziskus,' she said.

'Yes?' He put his arm around her. She patted it. The gesture was a touch too sisterly for Franziskus's taste.

'There is something I must tell you,' she said.

In matters of wooing, and in fact of the entire female sex, Franziskus considered himself far from expert. But even he had enough experience to know, with absolute certainty, what those seven words foretold.

'Go on,' he said. He had never really loved her anyway, he decided.

'I am transformed, Franziskus. Although I love you with a passion that words cannot express, and will always love you until the day I die, I cannot be with you. Shallya has reclaimed me for her own!' She threw her arms around him and held crushingly onto him, pushing her tearful face into his shoulder. Her hug put pressure on the contusions Manfried had just given him.

'I feel the holiness in me, reverberating,' she wept. 'Growing. I do have a calling. And the fact that I must sacrifice our love on the altar of Shallya's mercy – why, that is the spiritual fuel that makes it all the more powerful!'

'You're hurting me,' Franziskus whispered.

She let him go, then sobbed all the harder. He put his arm reluctantly around her.

'You do understand, do you not?'

'It is a matter of the gods, and they are an ineffable, eternal mystery.' Franziskus did not know what this meant, and in fact suspected that it meant nothing at all, but also was reasonably sure that it would make Devorah happy if he said it.

Her face brightened. The tears ceased. 'You *do* understand!'

ANGELIKA STOOD JUST inside the threshold of Mother Elsbeth's cramped cell. Bernolt stepped past her and closed the door behind him.

'No,' said the thin, elderly woman perched on the edge of the pallet, her features lost in shadow. Though elderly, she seemed quite hale. Her teeth were particularly striking: each one straight, firmly in place, as perfectly white as a young baby's. Angelika could only presume that this was the vaunted Mother Elsbeth. Her voice and carriage suggested a certain authority, but even so, Angelika could not see what it was about her that would inspire hundreds of people to risk death, journeying dozens of leagues into this malign, unforgiving wilderness, just for a chance to stand in her presence.

'No,' Elsbeth repeated.

Bernolt realised that she was addressing him. 'Pardon me, your holiness?'

'You will leave the two of us to speak privately.'

'But–'

'Go.'

Bernolt addressed Angelika. 'I'll be just outside the door, waiting,' he said, sounding a softly threatening note.

The old woman watched the guard leave. 'He thinks you'll do me harm,' said the old woman. A dusty beam of light escaped from a narrow window; she tilted her head slightly and it fell across her face long enough to illumine an odd, ironic smile.

'Why would I want to do that?' said Angelika.

'Devorah told me all about you.' Elsbeth patted the bedding next to her, bidding Angelika to sit. Her touch freed a cloud of dust and sent it spinning up into the air.

Angelika remained in place.

The old woman shifted to face her better. A cough rattled around her voice box. 'You are wary,' she said.

'It is a prudent stance to take, when summoned to the side of an influential person who has yet to make her purpose clear.'

Elsbeth shook her head ruefully. 'Influential? Me?'

'Your word was good enough to get me out of a cell. Maybe my perspective is limited, but that seems like power to me.'

Elsbeth bowed her head. 'I am a prisoner too.'

'Then why do they fear you?'

'Fear?' She rubbed at her eyes. 'They do not fear me – only my departure. This Manfried, the poor tortured soul – he thinks my poor tired bones will end his exile.'

Angelika stuck out a hand to lean against the sloped roof of the abbess's cramped quarters. 'How so?'

Elsbeth told her about Father Manfried Haupt – his expectations of presiding over the family cathedral, his expulsion from Averheim, his arrival in Heiligerberg, and his decision to put himself in charge of its miracles.

Angelika fidgeted impatiently while she spoke. She waited until she was sure the old woman was done. 'I don't know what fit of babbling nonsense Devorah succumbed to, but if you think I'm capable of ridding you of this enemy, you've been seriously misinformed.'

Elsbeth stood and shuffled to her, placing a dry hand on her cheek. 'I am a high priestess of Shallya. I would never ask you to harm another person.'

'Even your captor?' Angelika tried not to flinch from the old woman's touch. Up close, she smelled like a sneeze that hangs in the air.

'Shallya forbid! My only hope for the poor boy is that he learn the difference between the greater good and his own desires.'

'So if you don't want me to strike against Haupt on your behalf, what do you want?'

She shuddered and lost her balance, tipping toward Angelika. Angelika caught her. She righted the abbess quickly before stepping back. The old woman had backed her into a corner. She felt its cobwebs brushing into her hair. 'I want you to speak to Devorah. She has seen the toll it takes on me, to heal this endless throng Manfried has so capriciously attracted here.'

'If you want something from me, you'll have to come out and tell me yourself.'

'I can scarcely describe it. Perhaps I will let you attend to me, as I endure another round of healings. Then you will see the suffering.'

'I thought you priestess types enjoyed suffering.'

'If you enjoy it, it isn't suffering, is it?' Elsbeth spasmed as a series of coughs wracked her body. She gasped. Angelika sat hesitantly beside her and applied a few gentle thumps to her back. Elsbeth took Angelika's hand in hers. 'Do you think me some faith-crazed flagellant, mistaking agony for epiphany: Suffering is suffering, and over the years I've done more than most. More than my share. And I wish it to stop. Again, I implore you to ask Devorah what she has seen. I cannot share the gruesome specifics; I am too ashamed.'

Elsbeth told her of the nature of her healing gift. Of the healing baths Manfried forced her to take.

'No,' said Angelika.

'Beg pardon?'

Angelika stood. 'I finally see what you want.' She tried to look out the smudgy window. 'I won't do it.'

The holy woman bolted up and moved in close. 'But Devorah says you are a robber of graves. She has seen you paw through the bloodiest of corpses for a few mere coins!'

Angelika spun to face her, staring down into her milky little eyes. 'Yes, I earn my living in a way that all fine people despise. That doesn't mean I'll do anything. Specifically, I will not kill you.'

Elsbeth's knotted hands grabbed up big folds of Angelika's tunic. 'You must.'

'I will not.'

'I beg you.'

'No.'

'It would be an act of sheerest mercy.'

'I reject all faiths and theologies, old woman. My rules are my own. Chief among them is a rule against murder.'

'You have never killed?'

'I do make an exception for people who try to kill me, but somehow I doubt you're up to it.'

'How can I convince you?'

'There is nothing you can offer me that will make me murder you.'

Mother Elsbeth tottered back from her, recovering her composure. 'You will not waver?'

'If you're so anxious to die, why not order one of your fellow priestesses to do the job?'

'They'd refuse.'

'Then don't tell them. Have them brew a poison for you; tell them it's medicine.'

'They'd never be deceived; they know their herbs better than I.'

'Have Devorah do the deed.'

'I cannot stain that innocent soul.'

'But mine is already soiled enough, so one more little slaying won't matter?'

'It's a costly favour I ask of you, I know. If there was another I could turn to, I would not trouble a stranger.' Elsbeth moved to the foot of her bed and pulled out a wooden trunk. She bumped it along the stone floor. She lifted the lid and reached inside, withdrawing an armload of cotton robes, each as plain and unadorned as the one she wore. She held them out for Angelika to take. Angelika twitched her nose in annoyance but accepted the mound of clothing. Elsbeth again stooped into the trunk, this time taking out a bundled blue scarf, dripping with tassels. She dropped it onto her bed and unrolled it, flipping loose a dagger with a six-inch blade of gleaming steel. It was an expensive display piece, its hilt gilded, its pommel cast in the shape of a wolf's head, with gleaming ruby chips for eyes. The materials were valuable, but it was the craftsmanship that would make the piece eminently saleable. Angelika guessed that she could get seventy-five crowns for it – a hundred, if she dickered well.

'That's a fine piece.'

Elsbeth turned it over in her hand. 'It was given to me decades ago, by a warrior I healed. I wanted it but could not explain why. It is beautiful, isn't it, in its own terrible way? I told myself I was keeping it so that it could shed no more blood. I'd offer it to you, but I suppose you'd be offended.'

'Good thing you're not offering it, then.'

She handed the knife to Angelika, hilt-first. 'It would be helpful, when you want to escape…'

'We've done nothing wrong.'

'When Manfried has his mind fixed, he is hard to budge.'

Angelika weighed the dagger in her hand. 'I doubt this blade ever shed much blood. It's an art piece, not balanced properly for fighting.'

'But in a tough spot it would be better to have it than not.'

Angelika shrugged. 'Yes, but what of it? I won't do as you ask. Not for a knife, not for any price.'

Elsbeth curled her fingers around the hilt and took back the knife. 'I wish to trade this weapon for a different favour.'

'You buy and sell jewels and other items of value, yes?'

'I retrieve and sell them.'

'You have heard of holy relics?'

'Of course.'

'And that sometimes these items are the very bones of famous priests and priestesses? Finger bones, cross-sections of arms and legs, even bits of skull...'

'I have seen such things. They are hard to properly value.'

'Even after I die, these weary bones of mine will know no rest. If I am lucky, my body will be hauled down to the mausoleum, where eventually it will be unwrapped and laved for bits of holy grease. But I know Manfried. He has been waiting for a gift from heaven, to free him from his exile here. He will haul my corpse onto a cart and take it back to Averheim. He'll lay it out before his rivals as the greatest of treasures, and say, "Give me my cathedral back and I will give you an unending stream of miracles." And then I'll be installed there, on display, under glass, for the pleasure of every gaping curiosity seeker. Every year, perhaps, I'll be taken out and put on display. My miraculous state of preservation will be remarked upon. From these few moments together, Angelika, I can see there's nothing you hold dearer than your dignity. Would you want such a thing to happen to you?'

'A grim fate, to be sure. But you'll manoeuvre me into no foolish promises.'

'This is what I want you to do: make sure I am buried in my home village. It is a place called Ruhgsdorf, about a league south-east from Averheim. Bury me with no marker, no special ceremony – I want no one to guess who I was, and dig up my bones. If anyone's to get the benefit from them, it should be the people I abandoned, years ago, to come to this place. Ruhgsdorf. You'll remember that name?'

Angelika shrugged. 'Remembering it doesn't mean I ever have to go there. Especially not with the mouldering body of a presumptuous old woman bundled over my shoulder.'

Elsbeth held the tip of the wolf's-head dagger close to her face. 'Is this a sharp blade?' she asked.

'Yes,' said Angelika.

'Devorah said there was another whose promise you refused. What was the name?'

'Don't say it.'

'Thomas Krieger. That was the name.'

DEVORAH PUSHED UP close to Franziskus. He felt the warmth of her body through the thin fabric of her habit. His back was pressed against the shed wall; its splinters tried to prick him.

Devorah opened her mouth but struggled to find her words. Finally she said, 'But if I am to sacrifice all chance at ordinary, human love, in favour of a pure, disembodied love for the goddess, should I not acquaint myself with its nature, a little first? Otherwise, what does the sacrifice mean, if I give up a thing I have never known, except from songs and poems?'

'I am no expert in theology,' hesitated Franziskus.

She touched his face, the tips of her fingers lingering over his bottom lip. 'Kiss me,' she breathed.

The shed door banged open. A short man hunched in the doorway, backlit by the grey sky behind him. He grabbed the doorframe for balance, paused for a moment and then lurched into the shed, drawing a sword from his belt.

Franziskus shoved Devorah away from him guiltily. She whirled, checking her wimple to hide any escaped locks of hair.

The man stopped. He frowned. 'You're not Ivo,' he said.

Franziskus altered his angle for a better look at the man's face. It was bruised purple and pitted with superficial, pinprick scabs. 'Richart?'

Richart Pfeffer wrinkled his brow and winced from the effort. 'They told me they'd caught my relic thief. What are you doing here, Franziskus?'

'We thought you were dead,' said Franziskus.

'Ivo did his best to see to that. He threw me off the side of the mountain – but I fell only a dozen yards or so before I hit a green patch and bounced. I lay hurt for a good long while. Still, here I am.'

'You can clear our names then. Among other charges, Kirchgeld has us accused of murdering you.

He said you were working for the Sigmarites. The two of you found evidence to prove Angelika and me guilty of stealing sacred relics from the abbey – or so his story went.'

Richart groaned and propped himself against a wall. 'I was hired by Father Manfried to find out who had stolen holy implements from the sisters here.'

'You're not a landowner at all then?' asked Devorah.

Richart shook his head. 'Just a lowly man at arms,' he grinned, painfully. 'I traced the pilfered items to a dealer in Grenzstadt. He purchased them through an intermediary, without ever meeting the thief face to face. Though he couldn't describe him to me, I made him tell me what he did know: he planned a second expedition to the Holy Mountain, to steal what he couldn't the first time. Supposedly he'd just joined a group of pilgrims led by an old cavalry officer. When I found Krieger's party, I reckoned his was the group I was looking for. When Altman was slain for his holy relic, I knew I was right.'

'But if Kirchgeld's a stealer of relics, why didn't he keep the one he took from Altman?'

'He looked at it long enough to decide it was a fake, then planted it on Muller to throw me off his trail.'

'And I'd judged Kirchgeld a mere fool.'

'From the beginning, there was a wrong smell about him,' Richart said. 'He's no more a pardoner than I am a landsman. But it wasn't until he showed detailed knowledge of the mountain landscape that

I knew he'd been here before, and so he was my man.'

'So you went to confront him?'

'And he got the better of me. His clownishness led me to underestimate him. He can handle a weapon. So you have no clue where he might be?'

'No, but he must be planning to rob the abbey again, mustn't he?'

'Doubtless. He was clever to have someone else arrested for his crimes – he's put Manfried's men off their guards.'

'Take Angelika and me to this Father Manfried, and see to the clearing of our names. Then I am sure there's nothing she'd sooner do than help you catch up with Ivo Kirchgeld.'

# CHAPTER EIGHTEEN

MOTHER ELSBETH HELD the knife. She'd rolled up the sleeves of her habit, uncovering sallow forearms traversed by a marching legion of scars and discolorations. She saw that Angelika was looking at them. 'The healing bath is powerful, but the worst of the wounds still leave permanent marks.' She held the edge of the blade against her skin. 'You won't try to stop me?'

'What you do is your business. But I don't see why I have to watch.'

'It is not my intent to distress you, but I am rarely left alone these days. This may be my only chance for quite some time.'

'There's a guard outside the door. If you do it, I'll be blamed.'

'You are a resourceful woman. And Shallya shall unfold you in her mercy, and protect you from harm.'

Angelika faced the door, uneasily figuring her chances of getting away from Bernolt. He was older than she was, so she might be faster, if she could just get past him and into the hall… 'Surely if you tell Bernolt to return me to my prison, you'll have enough time then to–'

'I can wait no longer.' Angelika heard a faint but telltale squish of flesh parting on either side of a blade, and turned to see that Mother Elsbeth had pierced her forearm with the knife. Gouts of dark blood, sluggish as molasses, dropped reluctantly from the wound and onto the floor. Elsbeth shuffled backwards, regarding the dripping knife. A whimper slipped free of her barely parted lips. The blood made a suppressed slapping sound on the stone floor as it fell around her feet.

'That's not enough,' said Angelika, her voice hushed. 'If you want to die quickly, you have to keep going.'

'I can't.'

'You've got to widen the cut.'

'Please…'

'Then do the same with the other wrist.'

'I can't.' She held out her arms, the wounded one still speared through by the dagger blade, in a gesture of pleading and supplication. 'Please.'

'No.'

'Please.'

'Damn it,' Angelika said.

She wrapped her left hand around the blade's decorative hilt and yanked it out of Elsbeth's arm. The old woman lost her balance and fell into Angelika, who held her up. With the blade still in her hand, Angelika embraced Elsbeth, pulling her into her own body and holding her tightly. Angelika could feel the wetness of the old woman's blood as it soaked through the sleeve of her own tunic. She cradled Elsbeth's head. 'You want this fast,' she said.

'Yes,' Elsbeth managed.

Angelika placed one hand on the holy woman's shoulder and another on the back of her head. Then she jerked Elsbeth's head, snapping her neck. The old woman gasped once and then went limp in Angelika's arms, dead.

The door opened. Angelika turned, her hands and face sticky with Elsbeth's blood.

Richart Pfeffer stood there. Behind him was Franziskus. Bernolt Steinhauer peered in, too.

Richart shouted: 'Murderer!' He rushed into the room, drawing his sword. He took it out too soon, so it clanged against the doorframe as he bolted in. Angelika fumbled for the ornamental dagger, which had fallen into Elsbeth's bed sheets. Richart charged into her sideways, his shoulder pointed at Angelika like a battering ram. She leapt up on the bed, but its rickety frame gave way under her weight, sending her crashing into Richart, who swung wildly back at her with his sword. She pushed his arm aside, adjusting her position, wrapping her long legs around his chest and neck.

Pitching forward at the waist, Richart tried first to throw her off, then to smash her head into the sloping stone ceiling over Elsbeth's ruined bed. Her hands flat against it, her knees now firmly pressing against Richart's temples, Angelika twisted herself around. Richart wrenched himself out of her grip and then collapsed. Angelika fell on top of him. She groped for the dagger but came up only with a handful of bloodied bed sheet. Richart rolled back and up to his feet. He charged at her with a swinging sword. It banged against the low, inclined ceiling. He tossed it aside and leapt on her, fists clenched tight. She threw the blanket over his head and then proceeded to punch his injured face. He cried out in muffled pain.

Franziskus and Bernolt stood shocked and gaping. As Franziskus jerked abruptly into the room, Bernolt seized him by the shoulders and dashed his head into the doorframe. His vision blurring, Franziskus reached down to yank Bernolt's baton from his belt. Bernolt grabbed his arm and twisted, but Franziskus stomped his boot, forcing him to let go. He wrapped a hand around each end of the baton and jammed it into Bernolt's throat, pressing him against the doorframe. Bernolt shot a muscular knee into Franziskus's groin. Franziskus groaned but maintained his choking grip on the baton. Bernolt's face went slowly blue.

Angelika manoeuvred her way behind Richart, twisting the bed sheet to tighten its grip on the nut-brown man's head and neck. He clawed at it.

'Relent,' Angelika commanded. 'Don't make me hurt you.'

The sheet over his mouth smothered Richart's response. 'You murdered our saint!'

'I'll explain if you relent,' Angelika told him.

He drove an elbow into her ribs. She held the sheet snug around his head and smacked it into the wall. 'Relent!' she cried. He struggled. Again she dashed him into the wall. 'Relent!' He sank to his knees, trying to force her down. He choked. She kicked him; he fell flat against the floor. She kicked at his ribs until he stopped moving.

Bernolt Steinhauer passed out. Franziskus supported the man's weight as his legs gave way beneath him, then laid him gently out on the floor. He fished two fingers around his mouth to make sure he did not swallow his tongue.

Angelika surveyed the wreckage of the room. 'Help me get her onto the sheet,' she told Franziskus.

'What? We have to run!'

She picked up the sheet and unfurled it, laying it out on the floor. 'Roll her onto it,' she said.

'Are you mad?'

'Yes, undoubtedly, because we're taking her with us.'

Franziskus heard shouts and rushing footsteps. 'Someone's heard the fight! We must go!'

Angelika took a final look at the holy woman's body and then followed him out of the door and into the corridor. They checked right and left for oncoming guards.

'What's the best route down the mountain?' Franziskus asked.

'We have to stay and hide,' said Angelika.

'Pardon me?'

'We can't let them take her body.'

* * *

DEVORAH POKED HER head outside the shed. A dry,
cold wind buffeted her face, yanking back her wimple and tugging at her lush chestnut locks. She was
sure that there was a place she ought to report to,
but did not know where that might be, or even
how she might find out. Elsbeth had made her a
sister of the Heiligerberg Abbey, but had not
thought to tell her where her quarters might be, or
which priestess or senior sister would supervise her
devotions. Devorah's spirits sank. She was as lost
as ever. She put her hands on her forearms, to
warm them, and set off back toward the abbey
gate. It would be a terrible struggle to get through
all of those poor wailing pilgrims again. Perhaps
she would find Lemoine, or the others, and could
tell them of her new status. Say final farewells. She
would not tarry with them, however, as the twin
voices of regret and doubt were already whispering
in her ear, telling her to cast off her habit, flee this
place, and never again set her slippered foot inside
a cloister.

She stepped through the trampled garden and
hugged the abbey wall as best she could, ducking
and dodging her way through the mass of pilgrims.
Some of them, seeing her habit, grabbed at her,
implored her, and wheezed into her face. She was
one of the sisters, they told her. She could help
them. She could get them in to see the holy woman.
Devorah wanted to scream and tear herself away
from them. She wanted to kick at their spindly,
weakened legs, with their sores and their bandages.
'No,' she told them, she could not help. She had

only just started here. 'Let me through,' she told them. 'Please let me through.'

It took her half an hour to push through the crowd. Just as she was thinking she should have waited at the shed for an escort to take her back through the throng, one of the guards stationed at the gate saw her and pointed. 'That's her, isn't it?' he asked his fellow. They both plunged into the crowd. They took her by the shoulders and pulled her through the last few layers of mobbing, crowding penitents. Two guards opened the gate, as another four stood ready with warhammers, to repel a surge at the gates. 'Order!' one of them screamed. A liver-spotted hand shot up above the level of the crowd to hurl a rain of pebbles and stones at him. A chant swelled through the throng. 'Let us see her! Let us see her!'

When Devorah was on the other side of the gates, a new pair of guards took her, each taking a firm grip on one of her upper arms. 'You can't touch me like this,' she said.

'Father Manfried wants you,' they replied, slightly off unison.

# CHAPTER NINETEEN

DEVORAH STOOD WAITING in the middle of Elsbeth's abandoned healing tent, alone, fighting back a wave of nausea. About a quarter of an hour had passed. The place still smelled of burnt oil, blood and pus. Every so often she heard a distant, muffled eruption of hoarse male shouts, or the rattling footfalls of running, armoured men.

The tent door parted as Father Manfried entered, striding directly at her. He wore a breast-plate and armour on his arms and legs, but had no helmet and carried no weapon. Black leather gloves encased his wide hands; he flexed them, and the leather creaked. 'You were bold with me earlier,' he said.

Devorah could not think how to reply. When she'd demanded that Angelika be taken to see Elsbeth, she'd spoken not with her own authority, but with the holy woman's. As she hesitated, Manfried studied her voraciously. She shrank back from him. He moved nearer. He stooped to pick up an oil lamp, then he held it close to her face. Her mouth and throat dried out.

'What?' she stammered. 'What is it in my face you search for, father?'

'Evidence of guilt,' he replied, calmly.

'Guilt?'

'I am curious how knowing a confederate you were.'

'Confederate?'

Manfried smiled. He brought the lamp closer; Devorah could feel its heat on her cheeks. 'That is true innocence I see, isn't it?' Manfried said, more to himself than to her.

'Innocence of what?'

'Yes, yes, yes,' he said, turning his back on her, setting down the lamp. 'She sullied herself, but left you pure.'

'Sir, I am just a poor sister, unschooled in sophisticated discourse. You must speak more clearly, if I am to understand you.'

He spun gracefully on his heels, plucking up a small wooden stool and moving it over beside her. He gestured grandly to the stool. 'You should sit yourself down, my poor little fawn. I have news that will break your heart.'

Devorah sat. 'It is a heartbreaking world,' she said.

'Wise words.' He knelt beside her and spoke with the gentleness of a country priest. 'Mother Elsbeth is dead.' Devorah quivered and Manfried caught her hand in his, steadying it. She had not noticed him doing it, but at some point he had slipped his hands free of his dark leather gloves. His hand was callused but warm.

'Dead?'

'Yes, dear Devorah. And worse, it was not a natural death. Richart – you know Richart Pfeffer, though not as one of my men – came upon Angelika smeared in Elsbeth's blood. She was standing over her freshly killed body, a knife nearby. Naturally, he thought it a case of murder.'

'Murder?'

Manfried let go of Devorah's hand. He gave it a paternal pat. 'Yes, you are quite innocent. Richart was mistaken – it was suicide. Certainly, Elsbeth was feeble and used your guide, Angelika, to bring about her own death. But self-slaughter it was. A terrible thing, don't you agree, to deprive all those people out there of her blessed touch?'

'Suicide?'

Manfried gravely nodded.

'Why did she do it?'

'Shallya's power became a burden to her. It weighed her down, and finally broke her. At first I thought it selfish, her decision to end her life. But then I came to wonder.' He paced, deftly circumnavigating the various piles of soiled linen. 'I've been studying the chronicles of this abbey,' he continued. 'Never once has there been a time when more than one woman was gifted with Shallya's healing touch. Sometimes – always when the forces of Chaos slumber – there is no one at all to act as conduit for the goddess's miracles. Yet in troubled times, like those

we live in now, there is always one. As near as I can
tell, a new recipient's powers manifest shortly after
the death of her predecessor. Do you see what I
mean?'

'No.'

He had reached the other side of the tent. He
turned and moved toward her in slow, perfectly
measured strides. 'The chronicles never vary. The gift
is always given to the youngest, fairest, most innocent among the sisters of Heiligerberg.' He put his
hand gallantly out to her; she took it and rose, as if
mesmerised, from the stool.

'Who could that be, do you think?' he asked her.

'I could not say. I do not know the sisters of
Heiligerberg.'

Abruptly he took Devorah's face in his meaty
hands and adjusted its angle, so that she peered up
at him. She trembled. 'Your soul already knows
what your mind does not. It is you, sweet girl. You,
Mother Devorah, are Shallya's gift to me.'


BERNOLT STEINHAUER GINGERLY patted his bruised
throat. He leaned uneasily against a slab in the sub-
terranean chamber that housed Sister Dema's
reeking alchemical vats. Bernolt did not like this
place. It was dank. Inky mould grew in its corners.

He'd been assigned here, he was sure, as penalty
for his failure against Elsbeth's killers. He wanted to
be out with his comrades, scouring the mountainside for the evildoers – especially the one who'd
choked him, that deceptively lank Franziskus.
Instead he'd been sent down to take orders from the

eerie, one-eyed Dema. Yes, his throat still hurt a bit, but a contusion or two did not turn a hammer-brother of Sigmar into an invalid. Bernolt leaned over a vat to peer in, but as an acrid stink penetrated his nostrils, he immediately regretted his curiosity.

His instructions were to protect the cabinet full of Dema's tools – not from Angelika and Franziskus, but from yet a third, unconnected miscreant – a man named Ivo with a comical voice and oversized ears. It was ridiculous. For the ninth time, Bernolt strode to the cabinet in question and tested the lock.

One of the old sisters came stooping into the room, shaking and bobbing her head. Her wimple disguised her features. The sisters, with their stale old woman smell, were all the same to Bernolt. He wished he were nowhere near them. Bernolt wanted to be back in the Empire, fighting Chaos, risking all in service to his warrior god.

The sister shuffled up behind him. With a thin, sharp blade, she stuck him in the side, between his armour plates. She stabbed repeatedly, twisting the blade to rend tissue and mince organs. Bernolt gurgled; the sister clamped a long-fingered but masculine hand over his lips. She cut Bernolt's throat for good measure, then swept back to let his body topple. Bernolt fell against a vat; his hand dropped into the flames beneath it, to blacken and scorch.

Ivo Kirchgeld pulled off his wimple for a better view of the cabinet. It had been difficult, hiding among the wrapped corpses in the mausoleum. He was sure that the sisters would be smart enough to check. But they hadn't. It must have been reverence for the dead – or perhaps they simply lacked imagination. He scanned the room for something heavy enough to break the lock. Of course – Bernolt's hammer! He ducked down to pick it up.

THE SKY WAS clear but starless. Franziskus and Angelika shivered, crouching behind an old and crumbling wall they'd found on the sheltering mountain slope that abutted Heiligerberg's flattened summit. The stand of mortared blocks belonged to some long-ruined outlying building; Angelika did not care to expend her attention guessing what it had been used for.

They pressed against each other for warmth. They had their hands under each other's tunics.

'You'd better not be enjoying this,' said Angelika.

'There's no need to say that every single time,' said Franziskus. It was too dark for either to see the expression on the other's face.

'Hrmp,' said Angelika.

'It's far from the first time we've been caught out in the cold, and not been able to light a fire.'

She growled.

'If you're going to make a belittling, threatening joke every time, you could at least make it a new joke.'

'Objection noted,' said Angelika.

'I still think we should just start climbing down the mountain.'

'You're still free to do so.'

'All this risk — out of loyalty to a dead woman?'

'I made a promise.'

'Krieger asked you to make a much nobler promise, and you refused him.'

'What does one fact have to do with the other?'

'And let me ask you this. Let us say the mere presence of her earthly husk can now work miracles. Shouldn't it be taken to the place where it can do the most good?'

'Those weren't her wishes.'

'But if she's withholding balm from the people in a time of terrible trouble, her wishes are wrong, are they not?'

'I won't let them chop her up and make her into trinkets. I won't let them put her on display.'

'Of all people, to suddenly care about the dignity of the dead...'

'Let me ask you this.'

'What?'

'Do I sound as if you're going to convince me?'

'Hrmp,' said Franziskus.

'Go to sleep,' said Angelika.

He put his head on her shoulders. 'Before Richart came in, I had the strangest encounter with Sister Devorah…'

'I'll wake you when the night's half done.'

As PROMISED, ANGELIKA woke Franziskus in the middle of the night.

Franziskus, in turn, woke Angelika at the first shudder of pre-dawn. 'There's a commotion up above,' he said.

Angelika ventured out from the alcove and peered up. Sure enough, the pilgrims at the summit were stirring as a mass, buzzing in collective dismay.

'They're learning the news,' Angelika said.

The buzz became a groan.

'They know Elsbeth's dead.'

# CHAPTER TWENTY

UDO KRAMER SHOOK Stefan Recht awake. They'd spent the night under blankets, beside a now-dead fire, a few yards from the abbey wall. Gerhold snoozed beside them. Lemoine, who'd been with them when they fell asleep, was gone.

'I'm not sure what, but something is happening,' Udo said, taking Gerhold by the shoulder and giving him a careful shake.

The white-haired friar snuffled into consciousness. He blinked and wetted his lips. 'What?' he asked.

Lemoine ran at them, pushing his way through a gauntlet of pilgrims that surged the other way. 'Come quick!' he called, his sandaled feet flying beneath him. His three companions fought the cold from their bones and shuddered to their feet.

Lemoine tugged on Gerhold's collar. 'She's dead! Mother Elsbeth is dead!'

'Shallya be merciful!' cried Gerhold.

'How did she die?' Stefan inquired.

'She's dead,' chorused the roiling throng.

'What happened to her?' Stefan demanded. He fumbled in his pockets for his splendid cap, but remembered that he'd lost it for good.

'To come all this way for nothing,' Udo muttered.

Lemoine hauled on his collar, too. 'But there's still chance for a blessing! They bring the divine remnants out now!'

The monk's momentum pulled Udo into the crowd. A beefy elbow, swung high, smacked him in his curly-haired temple. He called out in protest, only to have his foot soundly tromped on by a bovine young woman to his left. Udo retaliated with a two-handed push, sending the offender bowling into a rough-looking fellow beside her. The rough man shoved the woman into a third pilgrim. A fist, emanating from an unrelated scuffle, flew at Udo from the opposite direction; he ducked. The blow hit Lemoine in the shoulder. Udo looked back for Gerhold and Stefan, and saw the silver-tongued advocate stumbling to pick up the friar, who had fallen and was in danger of being trampled by a new cascade of pilgrims coming in behind them.

Udo and Lemoine reached a clearing in the crowd. They both flailed their hands and elbows with abandon, battling for a forward position. Before them stood a high-wheeled wooden cart, covered with a long white sheet. The obvious shape of a slim human form stood out beneath the sheet.

'Mother Elsbeth!' a man shrieked, in Udo's ear.

'It is her!' came a cry from the crowd, as it converged on the cart's other side. A dozen Sigmarite warriors ringed the cart, their backs against it, alarm dawning on their helmeted faces. One close to Udo deftly drew his axe and whirled it through the air in a parade-ground display. 'Get back!' he grunted. His fellows all pulled out their axes too, though they brandished them with less aplomb. 'All of you get back!'

Udo reeled as a sudden fury welled up in his chest. Each of his fists formed itself into a tight, hard ball. He dug his ragged fingernails into the soft flesh of his palms. 'We've come all this way!' an angry voice proclaimed. Udo was about to call out in agreement when he realised the voice was actually his. It had been him, shouting down the hammer-wielding men. He, Udo Kramer, was drunk with rage. Never had he felt so free, so invincible. 'It would be a great injustice to deprive us of her final blessing!' he crowed, flushed with confidence. He widened his eyes into an expression he hoped would seem mad and intimidating, and stomped a slippered foot in the direction of the nearest guard.

The Sigmarite shrank back and shook his weapon. 'None come near us!' he rasped.

'Injustice!' cried the crowd, echoing Udo's words.

Something hit Udo behind the shoulder blades. He looked back and saw that it was Gerhold, propelled forward by pushing hands behind him. Udo

executed a counter-shove to maintain his footing
then turned sideways, giving the old friar a spot in
his wake.

The throng howled. 'We've come all this way!'
Their disparate protests sorted themselves into a
single, unified chant. 'Give us our blessing! Give us
our blessing!'

Another shove pushed Gerhold forward a pace. A
Sigmarite feinted the haft of his weapon at him.
Udo grabbed out to take the friar by the collar. He
turned back to issue commands to the pilgrims
behind him. 'Stop pushing!' he ordered.

They kept pushing. Udo held his ground. Gerhold
slipped and was thrown out into the no-man's-land
between crowd and guards. Tripping, the friar
landed at the feet of the axe-flourishing Sigmarite.
The man scowled, baring yellow teeth, and brought
the steel pommel of his weapon down on Gerhold's
head. The blow scraped open Gerhold's scalp, spray-
ing his blood across the guard's leggings. Udo
screamed the friar's name and lunged toward the
cart, tearing a short sword from the scabbard at his
belt. The crowd surged with him, wailing and grunting. A blow caught him in the ear – whether from
the front or back he could not tell – and soon he
was awash in a sea of squirming, shoving bodies.
'Give us our blessing!' the penitents roared. Udo
tasted blood in his mouth, and was not sure that it
was his.

ANGELIKA LEANED OUT from the rocks to see what
was happening above. She heard screams. She

watched as the mob engulfed the cart, rocking it. Then there were so many pilgrims around it that the cart could no longer be seen at all. The mob surged closer to the slope. A man jogged back to extricate himself from the roil of flying limbs, slipped, and fell backwards, falling down onto the rocks directly above Angelika's head. She winced as he bounced her way. The falling man's head impacted on a sharp jutting piece of dark limestone. Angelika ducked back as his corpse dropped past her. Above her, the crowd's caterwauling reached a new crescendo.

'What's happening?' Franziskus asked.

'The next time I ask you why I live in a godforsaken wilderness, far from contact with the great mass of humankind,' said Angelika, 'please remind me of this moment.'

'The riots have begun?'

Angelika nodded. 'I think that's Elsbeth's body they're clawing at.'

Franziskus leaned out for his own peek. He saw a woman slide slowly down the mountainside, weeping a prayer to Shallya. 'What can we do?'

'From here?' Angelika pulled the decorative dagger from her belt, looking for something to stab. 'Nothing!'

'What of our friends?' Franziskus hefted himself up, as if preparing to scale the rock face. 'What if they're in the middle of it?'

'Friends?' Angelika sank back into the stone alcove. 'We don't have any.'

\* \* \*

UDO'S SWORD-ARM MET resistance as his blade sank into a torso. A man in a helmet groaned, so he was reasonably sure that it was a Sigmarite he'd stabbed. There was a pilgrim mashed up on either side of him. At least two men pressed against his back, pushing him forward. A woman was lying on the ground, in front of him, her helpless hands held up in a defensive posture. Udo tried to move back, but there was another body on the ground behind him. Viciously elbowing the pilgrim next to him, he forced himself to one side, avoiding the toppling body of the guard he'd run through. Evidently, he'd killed the man. It surprised Udo, that all signs of inner life had so quickly left the man's face. The Sigmarite landed face-up, right beside his foot. Udo could not resist. He placed the sole of his slipper on the man's face, his toe on the forehead, his heel on the chin, and pressed down. He felt gratified, and, at the same time, more furious.

The mob bayed exultantly and Udo saw why: they were tipping the cart over. Its wheels rose into the air, shattered and spinning. The press of pilgrims broke as  the crowd ran frantically around the tipped cart to get at the body. Udo whipped his sword backwards so that the rushing penitents would give him a wide berth. He saw that Gerhold lay in the mud, his robe in disarray, his bare legs exposed and dirtied. With his off-hand, he pulled the friar to his feet.

'Are you hurt?' he asked.

'Where's Stefan?' replied Gerhold, his face scraped raw, his scalp still bleeding freely from where he'd been hit with the axe pommel.

Together, their heads turned, and they saw Stefan, in his dark finery, running around the cart with the rest of the pack. Udo grabbed Gerhold by the arm and pulled him along, in the same direction.

'We must–' panted Gerhold, as Udo belaboured his fellow pilgrims with the flat of his sword, smacking rumps, shoulders, arms and skulls, parting the mob like a curtain. Dazed, Gerhold allowed himself to be pulled into the fray, muttering. 'We must touch the sacred body,' he said. 'Merely touch. To be blessed…'

They cleared the corner of the cart and Gerhold, shocked out of his stunned reverie, drew back in horror. The pilgrims had set upon Elsbeth's body, unrolling it from its snow-white shroud. At least a dozen of them pawed her naked flesh with their filthy hands. Most held their heads back, their eyes fluttering skywards in ecstatic transport. Others readied knives and swords, or merely pulled and twisted at her toes and fingers. And there, amid the blaspheming horde, crouched Stefan Recht, his face puffed and sweaty, his eyes wide. He held the dead abbess by the wrist, drawing his knife.

'No!' Gerhold shouted, hurling himself at the advocate. He hit Recht in the side, bowling him over, knocking the blade away. His thumbs flew to Recht's throat. 'Blasphemous rogue!' he shouted, grinding them into Stefan's thyroid cartilage.

Stefan seized the friar's hands and pulled himself free of them, gasping. Gerhold leapt on him, punching wildly. Stefan's groped at the friar's face, and pushed him away, eventually manoeuvring him into a headlock. 'What are you doing, you old fool?'

'Stopping you from committing the basest act of–'

Stefan caught him with a sudden blow to the chest, knocking the air from his lungs. Gerhold let his weight drop onto the advocate, pinning him against the frosty ground. Stefan kicked and struggled to be free. 'Dunderhead!' he sputtered. 'She's no ordinary corpse, to be respected with flowers and pieties! She's a veritable mine of precious relics!'

'Sacrilege!'

Stefan grabbed a hank of his hair and pulled. 'You know it to be true! We must get our share before they do! Look!'

Gerhold turned his head and saw that a massive, bosomy matron standing over the body with a captured axe raised above her head. She was ready to strike, presumably to lop the abbess's lolling head from her shoulders.

'Stop her!' the friar cried, catching Udo's eye. Udo nodded and bulled his way in. Gerhold cried, 'Not like that!' as Udo caromed his sword into the woman's neck, opening an artery. The shocked woman clamped a fat hand to her neck then her legs gave way beneath her. Udo stooped to disentangle the axe-haft from her dead fingers.

'Yes, Udo!' exhorted a smiling Gerhold. 'Heel the rest of these slavering curs till the guards return!'

Udo took the axe and chopped off Elsbeth's right hand, severing it just below her already-mutilated wrist.

'No!' wailed Gerhold.

Two other pilgrims, one ruddy-faced and balding, the other young and muscular, dived simultaneously to fight for possession of the lopped-off hand.

Udo sank the axe deep into the young pilgrim's back. Stefan leapt into the melee, taking the balding man from behind and wrapping an elbow around his throat.

'You mustn't!' Gerhold called.

'We've earned our claim to it!' Recht grunted.

Udo reached down to snatch up the hand. A stout stick of severed bone protruded slightly from its torn flesh. 'I hold here the holiest of relics! Do you have any concept of its worth, old friar? Ten thousand crowns, at least!'

'A hundred thousand!' said Stefan, as he scrambled backwards in the dirt, pushed by the ruddy-faced man, who tried to free himself of the lawyer's grip by rolling to one side.

Hungry-eyed pilgrims surrounded Udo, grabbing for the hand. He swung the axe in a wide arc, driving them back.

'Let go of it,' Gerhold begged, on hands and knees.

Stefan's pilgrim flipped the advocate onto his back and climbed up on him. He planted his knees on his brocaded chest and flailed laboriously at his face with heavy fists. Stefan slipped his arms between his chin and the rain of incoming blows.

Udo feinted at his encircling pilgrims; others dropped away to saw at the corpse with swords and pocket-knives.

A familiar voice cried at them from the direction of the abbey. 'Scatter! Scatter! They're readying their crossbows!' Ivo Kirchgeld ran, stork-like, into the tangle of pilgrims, headed for Udo.

Udo exclaimed in surprise. 'Kirchgeld?' Then he saw the line of regrouped Sigmarites, raising sleek, well-polished crossbows to firing position.

Ivo kept to his course, running.

Gerhold, palms out, staggered at the Sigmarite crossbowmen. 'Peace, brothers!' he coughed.

'Out of the way, old man,' growled their sergeant.

Stefan writhed under the weight of the red-faced pilgrim as the man found a brick-sized rock and held it up above his head, ready for the downstroke.

Ivo bounded past Udo, snatching Elsbeth's hand away from him. 'This way!' he called, beckoning Udo to follow him. A large sack, slung over his shoulder, bobbled and clanked as he ran. Udo hesitated, then bolted after him. They disappeared past the lip of a ledge.

Gerhold took another step toward the sergeant. 'Let reason prevail!'

'Now!' called the Sigmarite sergeant, to his men.

The thwangs of released bowstrings reverberated through the crisp mountain air. The line of crossbowmen let loose a rain of metal-tipped bolts.

Gerhold jolted. He looked down at his chest. It was penetrated in three places. Blood leaked from the impact points on his shattered breastbone. He plunged to the ground.

All around him, pilgrims fell, crossbow bolts protruding from limbs and torsos.

The red-faced pilgrim still crouched on Stefan's chest. A bolt thunked through the back of his neck and exited out the front. The rock tumbled from his fingers. It hit Stefan between the eyes, caving in his forehead, robbing him instantly of his senses.

It took Gerhold a minute to die; he spent it praying for mercy. Recht would linger for nearly half a day, never regaining consciousness.

Lemoine stood a hundred yards away, against the abbey wall. He could not bring himself either to approach, or to look away. He crooked his finger into the air, as if petitioning Shallya to take mercy on his fragile senses, and reverse everything he'd just seen, or at least to remove his recollections of it.

# CHAPTER TWENTY-ONE

'ARE THEY SHOOTING the pilgrims?' Franziskus asked.

Angelika did not budge. She spoke quietly, her jaw held tight. 'Only as many as they need to, I reckon.'

They waited for a second volley, but none came.

'Should we move from here?'

'Not until it's safe,' Angelika said.

MANFRIED FROWNED AS Elsbeth's body, now missing a hand, was gently rewrapped and placed on a sledge. Father Eugen stood at his side, worriedly flexing his heavy brow.

'What was she doing on a cart in the first place?' Manfried asked his sergeant-at-arms.

The sergeant cast a doubtful look at the mountain slope.

'Carts do not go up and down mountains,' Manfried enunciated elaborately. 'This cart has been here for generations; it was used for the sisters to move items about. But it would not help us get our holy cargo down the mountain, would it?'

'I accept your censure, father,' the sergeant agreed. 'But I respectfully submit the pilgrims would have swarmed any conveyance whether it was suited to the task or not.'

'Which brings me to my next query — why was it so ill-guarded?'

'Th-these–' The sergeant was reduced to inarticulate stammering. 'These were penitents on a holy pilgrimage – how was I to dream they'd stoop to such blasphemous depths?'

Eugen cut off the impatient response he could see brewing on his protégé's face. 'You have a point there,' he told the sergeant.

Manfried picked at his teeth with a well-lacquered fingernail. 'We need a sledge of some sort. Possibly guided by a system of ropes or pulleys. Find some mountaineers among these pilgrims, who can arrange such a thing.'

The sergeant nodded. Manfried turned; Richart and Devorah stood several paces away from him. Lemoine hung even further back. Manfried frowned and strode at Richart, pulling him aside.

'I told you to keep her away from this.'

Devorah ran to the pile of pilgrim bodies, dropping to her knees beside Gerhold's lifeless frame. Richart kept close behind her. Manfried shadowed him, clearing his throat unhappily.

'They were our travelling companions,' Richart said.

'Some companions, to treat her grace as loot to be pillaged,' said Manfried Haupt.

A comment came to Richart's mind, but he declined to enunciate it.

Devorah cradled Gerhold's head in her lap. 'Gerhold would never have done so,' she said. Manfried shrugged as she spotted Stefan's body and crawled to kneel beside it. Her breath caught in her throat as she saw that the advocate still breathed, though shallowly. Her healing knowledge was that of a mere novice, but even to her it was clear that Recht was dying. She intertwined her fingers in his. She thought about what Manfried had said, that she might be the inheritor of Elsbeth's gift. Might she use it, to revive poor Herr Recht? The very concept froze her insides. She shifted to keep Manfried in the corner of her eye. He would catch her at it, if she even tried. She let go of Stefan's hand.

Manfried took advantage of the girl's distraction to speak in a low tone to Richart. 'I don't expect that the loss of the hand will mar our plans completely. Nonetheless, I want it returned.'

'I've already spoken to witnesses,' said Richart, 'and I have a very good guess whose stinking little clutches it's in right now.'

It was Father Eugen who located the mountaineering pilgrim, Primus Lichtman. After a round of apologies for earlier rough treatment and general indignities, the latter created a system to convey Elsbeth's body down the mountainside. Lichtman's companions banged pitons back into their holes in the rock. They set up their pulleys. They taught the other members of the procession how to safely navigate their way down.

The pallet on which Mother Elsbeth's body lay passed directly over the alcove where Angelika and Franziskus hid. Franziskus stood as far back from it as he could. Angelika stayed in place. She could have reached up and marked its underside with a piece of chalk. If she'd had a piece of chalk.

ANGELIKA WAITED FOR about three hours before emerging from the alcove. It was a good enough interval of time, she decided – not so long that she couldn't follow Manfried and his procession, but also not so short that his men could turn back and catch her.

'Are you certain Manfried still has reason to wish us ill?' asked Franziskus, as he crouched precariously to slow his slide down the glacial slope. 'Surely he's realised by now that it was Elsbeth who sought her own death, and that you helped her under protest.'

'That could be true, but somehow I don't feel like confirming it.'

The mountaineers had left a trail of piton holes behind them, clearly marking the procession's path across the ice. Franziskus fell on the ice and rose up, rubbing his backside and cursing euphemistically. He resumed his backwards crouch and continued to ease his way down. Below him and off to the side, Angelika moved in the same diagonal, tentative manner.

Franziskus paused to dolefully examine his frost-damaged fingers. 'I thought going down would be easier,' he complained.

'It would be,' said Angelika, 'if you went down extremely quickly.'

Pilgrim corpses lay neatly stacked beside the path of piton marks. Lichtman's mountaineers must have moved them there, out of the way as they laid their trail. The fallen pilgrims stared up at Angelika with frozen eyes, their pockets gaping tantalisingly open. She scowled and passed them by.

Four hours and three falls onto the ice later (one for Angelika, two for Franziskus), the mountain deposited them at the glacier's hem, on the flat, rock-strewn expanse where they'd rested before the final ascent. They heard voices; Manfried's procession had paused there too, in a milling assemblage of priests, warriors, mountaineers and hangers-on. They were at least fifty strong.

The nearest of them were twenty-five yards to Angelika's right. She ducked down and scouted for cover. About a dozen yards to her left loomed a menhir-shaped rock, its fat base tapering up to a spiking point. Angelika dashed for it; Franziskus joined her. If they squeezed tightly together, they could both hide from Manfried's crew. After a minute's pause, Angelika peered around the rock for a better look at the evacuation party. Watchful Sigmarite guards, perhaps two dozen of them, formed an outer orbit around the rest of the group. Mountaineers and favoured pilgrims gasped and puffed, leaning on pick-axes, or against boxes, or simply sitting on the ground. In the centre of the crowd rested the sledge, a rough coffin of old boards was securely lashed to it. The coffin's planks, Angelika guessed, had been pillaged from the walls of the shed where she and Franziskus had been imprisoned.

An angry female voice rang out from the other side of the sledge. It was Devorah's. The young sister came rushing into view, pursued by a solicitous Brother Lemoine and a worried Richart Pfeffer. Richart caught up to her, taking her by the arm. She pulled away from him, but he danced around to block her path. Manfried, in full black armour, also appeared from behind the sledge. He marched over to Devorah to settle a gloved hand on her shoulder. She drew back from him, treating him to a bitter vituperation that Angelika could not quite make out.

Angelika ducked back behind the menhir. She leaned into Franziskus's ear: 'Let's say I told you that they've got your Devorah and are keeping her against her will. You'd so something foolish, wouldn't you?'

'For the moment,' Franziskus whispered, 'I'm prepared to be sensible.'

They leaned against the big stone, listening as Primus Lichtman strode among the procession, ordering pilgrims and soldiers alike to rest fully and efficiently, to prime themselves for the long downward climb they were about to face. 'More injuries occur on descent than ascent!' he warned. 'Maximum care must be taken!' Angelika saw two of the soldiers make a throttling gesture behind Lichtman's back.

A hubbub arose from the glacier above. Within moments, the soldiers had their weapons out and were pointing up at it. A wave of pilgrims slipped and slid down the glacier's face, surging toward Manfried's rest stop. There were about a hundred pilgrims, Angelika guessed, slipping and bouncing down the unforgiving ice-face. Many fell, bowling over others; soon, a cascade effect took hold and a mass of screaming penitents crashed uncontrollably toward the sledge and the travellers gathered around it. The Sigmarites bolted into action, forming a barrier between the sledge and the onrushing agglomeration of shrieking pilgrims. A few readied their firearms but most stood ready merely with their enormous hammers. Brother Lemoine rushed at a guard, trying to push aside the man's blunderbuss. His altruism earned him a sharp kick in the leg that sent him down to the rocky ground.

'Overwhelm them!' exclaimed a man perched well out of shot-range, on a small, level shelf of ice about a hundred feet up. 'Claim what is ours!' Angelika did not have to look to know who it was, but she did anyway: it was Ivo, goading the pilgrims on. Udo Kramer stood at his side, his posture apprehensive.

The first wave of sliding pilgrims crashed into the Sigmarites, who roamed among them, punching with gloved fists or crunching down with the butts of their weapons. Manfried had joined them, vigorously kicking and punching and ordering the attacking pilgrims to stand down, in the name of Sigmar and Shallya alike. One scrawny, half-naked old man in an unfurling robe leapt from the ice onto Manfried's chest. Manfried scrambled back, allowing his assailant to land face-first in the rocks. Then he bent down to seize the man by the neck and by one of his thighs. He raised the skeletal, squalling old penitent up over his head. Red-faced, Manfried heaved the man down, collapsing him into a heap of twisted limbs.

'How dare you?' he bellowed, reaching for a blunderbuss, which one of his guardsmen held ready for the firing of a warning shot. 'You style yourselves true pilgrims, yet you defy the manifest will of Sigmar?' Gun in hand, he pointed the barrel down into the writhing mass of oncoming penitents and pulled the trigger. A mist of blood wafted up, but Angelika could not see who he'd hit or how fatally he'd aimed.

Franziskus shook her by the shoulder. He'd abandoned their cover and now stood in full view of Manfried's men. Thankfully they were occupied with the cascade of pilgrims.

'Look!' he exclaimed, pointing at Devorah, who had broken from the party and was running at full bore across the rock flat and toward the yawning down-slope. There was no one to stop her: Lemoine lay moaning on hands and knees in the rocks, and Richart had joined with Manfried's other followers to hold off the invasion from the glacier.

Franziskus ran after Devorah. Angelika shrugged and did the same. Devorah leapt from the rocky shelf, disappearing to the incline below. Angelika and Franziskus reached her point of take-off moments later. They paused to see that she'd selected a spot where the grade was more forgiving, so they jumped down after her. Long-legged Franziskus soon caught up to Devorah and they ran together, half-tumbling down the slope. Angelika chased them. Hearts in throats, the three ran until the path became too steep to safely negotiate. They broke their fall by crashing into a stand of young pine trees. Gravity pulling on them, Angelika, Franziskus and Devorah held onto branches, their chests heaving. At first they could hear only the blood rushing in their own ears, but eventually it gave way to the grunts, shots and screeches of the clash above. Angelika rolled onto her stomach and found a safe, stable position. Devorah copied her and then Franziskus did the same.

'You're going to complicate our lives, aren't you?' Angelika asked the young sister.

'Father Manfried wants to keep me for his own,' Devorah gasped. 'As he did Mother Elsbeth. He thinks I might have inherited her gift. He wants both a dead and a live healer, for his cathedral in Averheim.'

'Shallya's teats,' Angelika cursed. 'So now he'll be hunting us…'

Devorah sobbed. 'I'll go anywhere with you. I don't care where. I won't be his prisoner.'

'Unfortunately,' said Angelika, 'we're bound for Averheim too. Not the best hiding place if you're running from Manfried Haupt.'

'She's decided to liberate Mother Elsbeth's remains,' Franziskus explained, as moans of pain chorused above.

Devorah widened her features in shock. 'As one of your ghastly treasures?'

'No, you tedious little–' Angelika took a deep breath. Then she started again. 'To fulfil her last presumptuous wish – to be buried in a peaceful, anonymous grave.'

'Don't ask her why,' Franziskus said. 'She hates that.'

Angelika made her favourite rude gesture and wrenched herself up into a sitting position. She studied the steep curtain of stone below them. 'There are better places on this mountain to climb down from,' she muttered. 'But we'd better get at it. I don't imagine Ivo's gang of suicidal cretins will last much longer against Manfried's guns. And after that – how many days to Averheim, do you figure?'

# CHAPTER TWENTY-TWO

IT WAS EIGHTEEN days to Averheim, they decided, give or take. The return trip would be faster, with only one defenceless pilgrim to shepherd. The descent took them the better part of a day; they made their way circuitously down and spent the night in a gully concealed by ground-hugging shrubs.

The next day, Angelika kept herself, Franziskus and Devorah hidden in the gully. Manfried's men would be looking for the girl. The three of them would be too easy to spot if they moved up the pass right away. Better to let the procession get a head start and trail after them. Angelika went off, attracted by the sounds of a nearby stream and came back with six fat, silvery fish impaled on a sharpened stick. She permitted them a fire, but for only the time it took to cook their meal. Then they

342       *Robin D Laws*

lay with full bellies on the gully floor and slept in shifts.

On the second day, they ventured northwards, past Heiligerberg's footprint and into the Blackfire Pass. Word of Elsbeth's passing had travelled, reversing the flow of pilgrims, so they now streamed back toward the Imperial border. Angelika found seven freshly fallen corpses and with them a handful of coins (bringing her total to one hundred and fifty-seven crowns), some good sausages and a wheel of barely-mouldy cheese. There was even a hooded cloak in which to conceal Devorah's face. Even so, a hatchet-faced young man, travelling alone, fell in with them.

He pointed at Devorah, exclaiming, 'You're the one they're looking for! There's a reward for you, you know!'

Angelika caught him in a chokehold from behind and held him until his limbs stopped twitching. She dragged him off the trail into a thick stand of trees. Then she stripped him to his well-bleached loincloth and tied him to a spindly young oak with his own shirt and leggings. A dozen crowns jangled in his purse but, as he was not dead, Angelika left it at his feet. She rubbed at a shoulder muscle, which she'd pulled during the struggle, before turning to Devorah, 'If I have to do that too often, I may just leave you to your own devices,' and tramped back to the trail.

On the third day, rain poured down from a light grey sky, as a stiff wind twisted low-hanging clouds into troubling shapes. Most pilgrims sought shelter in the trees, and the three made good progress padding steadily on through the downpour.

On the fourth day, Franziskus said to Devorah: 'If you don't mind my asking – do you have the gift?' Devorah said nothing.

On the fifth day, Angelika came upon a quartet of dead pilgrims, propped against the grey-barked base of a copiously branching hornbeam tree. She had opened the first one's purse when the second pilgrim, his chest peppered with shot, opened a weary eye. 'Take it,' the man said, revealing himself to be not quite as dead as he initially appeared.

'You were shot by the Sigmarites, up on the glacier,' Angelika said, half-recognising him.

'Go ahead and take it,' the man nodded, 'and finish me while you're at it.'

'I've had quite enough of that,' said Angelika, leaving another purse behind.

On the sixth day, exhaustion caught up with them and they spent an afternoon's good travelling time huddled against a rotting log, watching a colony of small black snakes catch and swallow an unending succession of mice.

On the morning of the seventh day, the sky turned the colour of blood and its surface rippled like water on the verge of a boil. 'Chaos,' Angelika whispered. They backtracked to the rotting log and made themselves small, while the black silhouettes of flapping, leather-winged lizard things glided calmly through the corrupted sky. 'Is this the end?' Franziskus asked. The manifestations continued past twilight. They stayed awake all night, afraid to dream.

But the next day all seemed normal again. They slept a bit, then set off, not saying a word until the chill of evening came. Then Devorah killed the silence by saying to Franziskus, 'I do not have the gift. And even if I did, I would commit sins of the flesh until I drove it out of me.' Later she added, in a smaller voice, 'Not so terrible sins of the flesh you understand.' Franziskus kept his face turned away from Angelika, to avoid the wiseacre look he knew she'd be wearing.

On the eleventh day, they had just woken up from a sleep amid dead leaves when they heard a stream of urine steadily splashing against a tree. They looked up and saw one of Manfried's men. They became still; Angelika slipped the decorative dagger from her belt. But the man finished his business and wandered off, unawares, to join a comrade. Eavesdropping, Angelika learned that the two were deserters and that Manfried's procession was at least two days ahead of them by now.

On the thirteenth day, Devorah fainted. They took her to a stream, dashed water on her face, and waited for her to come around before plodding on.

Two days later, they entered the Empire, passing through the ruined gates of the border town of Grenzstadt, where Devorah and the other pilgrims had met up. Angelika and Franziskus knew the town too: they'd been present just before its recent sacking by orcs. Franziskus suggested that Angelika pay for an inn, but she reckoned that certain of Grenzstadt's authorities might still have a low opinion of them. They staggered past the town and along a dusty road through the farmland to its north. They slept in a hayloft, leaving before dawn.

They walked for half a day, but then bought three mules – named Daemon, Horror and Patches – from a farmer called Hostler. They rode off the main road for most of a day. They lodged above a tavern named the Sickly Friar. Its sign reminded Devorah of Gerhold and made her throat bobble up and down when she first saw it.

Another day of mule travel brought them over a rise, from which they could finally see, off in the distance, the mighty walls of Averheim.

Just below the rise, a crew of frightened men, kerchiefs over their mouths and noses to protect them from the smoke, dragged the corpses of men, women and children onto a raging pyre. Some of the dead had additional eyes blinking blindly out from their foreheads. Others had tentacles in place of hands, or strange fissures on their bodies, lined with tiny teeth.

'Chaos,' Franziskus said.

# CHAPTER TWENTY-THREE

THE THREE OF them walked through deserted streets.
A stiff wind moaned across the city's cobble-stoned
alleys and walkways, whirling around the corner-
stones of its leaning, stuccoed buildings, tossing a
dust of dry, fine sand against the shuttered windows
of its close-huddled taverns and workshops.

Angelika kept her head down. Even at the best of
times, she hated this city and the grit it was throwing in her eyes provided a splendid reason not to
have to look at it. Devorah took it all in by shielding her eyes with her hands. She marvelled at the
worn, creaking old buildings as if she had never
seen a city before, which she hadn't. Most of its
structures were tall, thin wooden houses three or
four storeys high, covered in plaster and framed by
blocky, blackened oaken timbers. The few that

boasted any ornamentation bore linen-fold mouldings cut into the timbers, or perhaps the odd imp or
cherub carved in wood, clinging insouciantly to a
steeple or roof-point. Flags and pennants, in the yellow and gold of the province of Averland, hung
from poles. They flapped suicidally, tearing themselves apart in the violent wind.

Devorah's childish amazement aroused doting
feelings in Franziskus. He opened his mouth to discourse knowledgeably on the architecture, to
explain that these buildings were in an old style, but
one that Averheimers considered fine and proper.
That the black timbers suited their famous melancholy. But then he got a mouthful of dirt and halted
his lecture before it had begun.

The trio drew back as a man in a butcher's smock
came cantering out of an alleyway, twirling a cleaver
over his head and screaming about encroaching
Chaos. The raving man even mentioned several of
the Chaos gods by name. Angelika reached for her
dagger, but when the butcher saw them, his ham-
hock features convulsed in alarm, and he turned
and ran back the way he had come.

Above Averheim's low-slung buildings soared a
few monstrous structures, clustered in the centre of
town, about a league away. Franziskus pointed
them out to Devorah: one would be the old town
fortress, another, the elector's palace. The tallest was
a vaulting structure, surrounded by flying buttresses, bristling with turrets, in lustrous grey
limestone, fresh-quarried and sharp-edged. A multitude of writhing gargoyles and hammer-wielding

holy warriors, chiselled from unyielding stone, framed its stained-glass windows and stood guard around its vast and haughty arches. Angelika squinted at it. 'Manfried's cathedral,' she said. 'But before we scout it out, I need food and sleep.'

With the wind pushing at her, Angelika strode up to the stoop of a tavern. Overhead, its sign, a large iron ball painted cobalt blue, swung threateningly on squeaky hinges. Angelika knocked, waited, knocked and waited, knocked harder and waited, banged and yelled, waited and banged some more. Finally she leaned back as the door swung open in front of her. A middle-aged woman with haggard rings under her bulging eyes ushered them quickly inside. Her body, wrapped in folds of linen, was a comforting collection of curves; her bodice offered up a generous helping of cleavage.

'You're mad to be out there,' the tavern keep said.

'Good thing you let us in then,' replied Angelika.

A room full of unhappy faces regarded the new arrivals. Angelika challenged their suspicions by straightening her posture and marching determinedly to one of the few empty tables. 'We've come a long way. We're hungry, thirsty, and well-funded,' she announced, plunking a gold coin into the taverner's wrinkled palm.

Tall flagons of ale appeared before them; Devorah pushed hers gently aside, but then relented and sipped from it apprehensively. Plates of food followed soon after: red cabbage, white sausage, dumplings and pork steaks glistening with beads of fat. As the tavern keep delivered the last of the grub,

Angelika took her by the forearm and urged her to sit with them for a moment. 'We need news,' Angelika said. 'Tell me what goes on here and why the streets are so empty.'

Bosom jiggling, the taverner leaned in close, casting a nervous glance around the room, as if afraid unseen beings might overhear her. 'Chaos is on the loose. There's a plague of it. No one's safe from the foul winds. My own cousin, sprouted tiny, crippled wings, greasy and black, only last week.' She shuddered. 'Naturally her parents had to turn her in to the city guards, to be bludgeoned and then burnt on a pyre.'

A full-bearded oldster at a nearby table chimed in. 'Where've you been? Word travels fast in times of woe. The whole Empire's suffering in the grip of Chaos, from top to bottom. There's armies of beastmen marching from the north. The crops are blighted in Stirland. Burghers of Nuln have been caught coupling with curs and swine.'

'That's nothin' new for Nuln!' cried a joker behind him. His jape netted only a smattering of weary chuckles and he took to murmuring bitterly, something about a little gallows humour never hurting nobody.

The taverner put her hand on Angelika's wrist. 'Here it's the Chaos plague. The city authorities have put in a curfew, but there's no need. No one wants to venture out and get infected by Chaos humours. They come in on the wind, near as we can figure. We keep praying that it'll die down, after the Theogonist comes and performs the ceremony.

It has imprisoned us here. We are no longer ourselves – now we're no better than rats, scurrying in the dark.'

'Theogonist?' asked Angelika. The Grand Theogonist was the highest-ranking Sigmarite in the entire Empire – the whole Old World, for that matter. The earthly representative of the Chaos-smiting hammer god himself. Even she, who did not give half a fig for priests and their religions, could not help but draw back in her chair, impressed.

'The new Theogonist, Esmer, will be consecrating the great cathedral. I forget exactly when it's supposed to happen, but he should be coming into town any day now. When that happens, surely the tide of Chaos will be turned back, held at bay by Sigmar's almighty power.'

The bearded man again interjected. 'And they've got an awesome relic now, to install in its crypt – the beatified body of the holy woman, Mother Elsbeth. That's sure to turn the Chaos back.'

Angelika gripped her fork so tightly that its handle began to bend. 'Let me guess. The one who fetched it has been put back in charge of the new cathedral...'

'So runs the scuttlebutt,' said the tavernkeeper, standing to acknowledge a signal for more ale. 'Though the workings of churchly politics is beyond me...'

'Don't listen to her!' joked the jokester. 'She's always got a priest or two beneath her bedcovers!'

She flicked her wiping rag at the man and bustled off into the kitchen.

Angelika's throbbing head demanded a pillow to lie itself on. Her task was already difficult enough, but now that there was a Theogonist on the way...

EVEN THOUGH THE world was seemingly on the brink of annihilation, Franziskus could only think of only one thing. He was alone, in a room all his own, in an inn, with an actual bed to lie in. It had been over a month since he'd slept in a real, genuine bed. This one looked scruffy and he was sure the straw mattress was full of biting insects, but he didn't care. There were linen sheets. They even seemed clean, more or less. He stripped off his clothing and flung himself into the bed. The pillowcase was cool against his face. He felt himself drifting immediately to the realm of sleep.

A tap came at his door, jolting him. It would be Angelika, no doubt, determined to discuss plans of attack. He scrambled back into his breeches.

'Please, let me in, quickly,' a voice said, on the other side of his door. It was not Angelika's. His toes tangled in the cuffs of his trousers. Franziskus tripped over to the door and lifted up its bar.

Devorah rushed at him, taking hold of the door handle and gently shutting it. She had a sheet wrapped around her.

'Devorah,' said Franziskus. 'What is it?'

She dropped the sheet. The only light in the room slipped in through the door-jamb, but even so, Franziskus could not help but see. She surged into him, wrapping her slender arms around his back, pressing her bare chest against his. She kissed his breastbone, his throat, his lips. He turned his head from hers. She took his face in her hands and pulled it down to hers, and kept kissing him.

Again he pulled back. 'Devorah,' he said. 'I cannot be the one to sully your purity.'

'Sully me,' she breathed. 'Franziskus, I beg it of you.' She climbed on top of him. 'Sully me.'

BEFORE DAWN, ANGELIKA crept along creaky corridor floorboards to Franziskus's room. She passed Devorah's door and saw that it was ajar. Smirking, she departed the inn on her own and ducked through gusty, winding streets until she reached the city's central square and stood before the cathedral. Across from it stood a smaller, more modest Sigmarite temple; a few priests and penitents scurried up its worn steps. It would, no doubt, go out of use after its replacement was consecrated. Beside it, an even humbler temple to Shallya nestled, its roof bowed in, its shingles shaking as each gust rushed over it. But it was the cathedral where Angelika's business lay. She sidled across the square and hid herself behind a marble fountain depicting a covey of cavorting nymphs. Its waterworks sprayed her with mist droplets.

A grand set of steps led to the cathedral's massive, iron-shod doors, bounded on each side by a stone rail decorated with axes, hammers, and the fierce heads of divine, Chaos-eating wolves. Living guardsmen, alert and fully armoured, lined the cathedral steps, ready to repel any onslaught of mutants or beastmen that might suddenly decide to fall upon Manfried's mighty church tower.

She would need to know where the hidden entrances were. She required a floor plan.

The wind blew harder; the spray from the fountain became a drenching torrent.

It occurred to her that there was a person who would be almost guaranteed to have a full set of architectural plans already in his possession, with secret entrances clearly marked. And, though she did not know where to look for him, there was a second person who could surely point her in the correct direction.

WITH THE STREETS empty, and those few who ventured out driven witless by the fear of Chaos, it was difficult to get passers-by to stop and answer questions. Those willing to speak to her were mostly of the male persuasion; circumstances forced her to stoop to eyelash batting. Each time, she halfway expected the man she was interrogating to throw off his robes and reveal a hideously mutated body, festering with the tendrils, suckers and sores of Chaos, ready to engulf and devour her. But if the minions of the dark gods were about, they were also keeping to themselves.

She knew that Udo Kramer had business interests in Averheim, but she hadn't guessed how extensive they would be. Half of those she spoke to had heard of him. Each named a different store, warehouse, or workshop. Each time she found one, she was directed to another. Angelika leaned wearily against a storefront wall, then trudged on to her next destination: a rug shop that Udo had apparently bought, or was thinking of buying, or perhaps had recently sold. It would be found without sign or symbol, at the end of a snaking, dead-end laneway, distinguished only by its bright yellow door and a stone carving of a jester's head above its archway.

She found the place after a series of wrong turns. Her ankles ached from walking on uneven paving stones; she'd grown too used to soft forest floors. Angelika ventured down the alleyway, looking for hiding spots. She heard a groan, nearly drowned out by the keening wind. Plastering herself against a wall, she inched cautiously along it and turned a corner. The groan came from a basement window, no more than six inches high, covered by a wrought-iron grate.

She bent down and peered inside. A man in monkish robes sat tied to a broken-down wooden chair. His head was slumped down, his chin resting on his chest. Angelika recognised him from his abundant curls of caramel-coloured hair: it was Brother Lemoine.

Through bloodied lips, he addressed a figure Angelika could not see: 'No matter how many times you strike me, I can't tell you what I do not know.' He braced himself for another hit.

Udo Kramer stepped from the shadows and obliged him, smacking him in the side of his face with a chainmail glove. Red droplets sprayed the basement's limestone wall. 'No matter how many times you deny it, you pontificating prig, I won't believe you. You know when he's coming. You have to know.'

Lemoine vainly struggled to loosen his bindings. 'What makes you think that? I'm not one of them. I'm not a Sigmarite warrior priest, just a monk – and a foreigner, at that!'

Udo took hold of Lemoine's left ear and squeezed it as if he was wringing out a dishrag. Lemoine winced. 'I refuse to believe that it's such a damn secret!'

'It is! It is! The Theogonist faces many threats to his person! Chaos minions... the rag-tags of that heretic, Luthor Huss... Esmer will arrive with fanfare, but no advance notice!'

Angelika moved to the yellow door and pounded on it with her off-hand. Her fighting arm already held her blade.

'Who is it?' called Udo, his voice muffled.

'Hrmmm hrmm!' replied Angelika. 'Hrrmm!'

'What?'

'Kirchgeld sent me!'

'What?'

'Kirchgeld!'

The door opened. Udo stood dumbfounded. 'Angelika?'

She kneed Udo in the groin. His eyes bulged. He stumbled at her, grabbing at her legs. She brought her dagger hilt down on the base of his skull. The sharp edges of the decorative handle sliced into his flesh. He slumped at her feet. She stepped over him, moving through a small foyer into a storeroom stacked high with eastern-style rugs, stacked flat. She shouted Lemoine's name. He shouted back, his voice coming from behind a curtain. She pushed it aside, finding stone steps on its other side. Running nimbly down them, she stopped short in front of Lemoine, tied to his chair. As Angelika moved behind him to untie the knots that bound him, she made a quick survey of the cold basement. It was expansive, its walls mortared with rough chunks of limestone, its floors flat and tiled in stone. Raw timber support posts appeared in twin rows. Stacks of rugs, some piled to shoulder height, occupied most of the room's floor space.

'You've come to rescue me!' Lemoine cried.

'You were not in my plan, I assure you,' Angelika said, giving up on the knots, which were too well-tied. She began to saw her way through the rope with her knife.

'They're planning to steal holy Elsbeth's body!'

'So am I, and I was hoping to trick them into helping me. But you ruined that, didn't you? Sitting here looking pathetic and getting yourself mutilated.'

Udo staggered down the basement steps, an ungainly matchlock pistol in each hand. 'So — you meant to trick us?'

He straightened his arm to aim at Angelika. She dived behind a pile of carpets. 'Now what kind of argument for mercy is that?' she said, ducking her head down. 'I could've slit your throat, just now, you know.'

'Point taken,' said Udo, edging across the basement floor, his bowlegged stance showing the toll of Angelika's groin-kick. 'Remind me to send flowers to your grave.' Snarling, he approached Lemoine, then saw that the monk's bindings had been cut.

Lemoine let loose with a garbled cry and leapt on the merchant, who cudgelled him neatly in the temple with the butt of his gun. The monk folded, toppling from the chair, onto his knees. Udo kicked him in the buttocks; Lemoine went prone. Udo bent down, placing a pistol barrel at the base of the Bretonnian's skull. 'Don't give me cause to waste a valuable shot on you,' he said.

Lemoine whimpered his obeisance; Udo straightened.

Angelika popped up from behind a stack of rugs to hurl her dagger at Udo's head. But the intricately decorated piece was not balanced for throwing, and it spiralled wide, missing the merchant by a good two feet. It clattered into the stone wall behind him. A grin unfolded like the bellows of a squeeze-box across Udo's bearded face. Angelika ducked back behind the rugs, looking around for something else to throw.

'I misjudged you,' she said.

Udo inched cautiously toward the rug pile. 'Is that so?'

Angelika deepened her crouch. By her estimate, Udo would now be standing on the other side of the rectangular stack of rugs. If he went to the left, she could keep covered by going right, and vice versa. She wanted him to talk as he moved, so she could tell which way he was headed without peeking up and exposing herself to the barrel of his gun. 'During the journey, Udo, you struck me as cynical, self-satisfied perhaps... but to learn you're a torturer and killer – I admit, you had me fooled.'

For a moment, the only noise was Lemoine's low, injured wheezing.

Then Udo obliged her: 'I haven't murdered anyone. Though that last leap is but one squeeze of the trigger away, isn't it?'

Yes, he was moving to the left. She scrambled to the right.

'You were in league with Ivo all along?'

'Not remotely. To be frank, I was never completely certain why I risked life and limb to go on that pilgrimage. It was not until the incident with the cart, when I beheld Mother Elsbeth's body, that I finally knew why destiny had impelled me there.'

'Destiny?' she prompted. She checked the flooring around her feet. There was nothing to throw at him, not so much as a stray pebble.

Udo had turned a corner, and was standing at one of the rug pile's narrow ends, facing roughly east. Angelika hunched down at the other end, her back near a wall, pointed west. The door out of the basement would be about twenty paces away, if she ran diagonally. Kramer could easily get off a shot, probably both of his shots, in the time it would take her to cross that distance.

'Throughout my life,' Udo began, 'I have dedicated myself to a single goal, the only one I consider important in an otherwise brutal and meaningless existence. That goal is the accumulation of wealth.' He paused to listen to her movements; Angelika stayed still and made no noise. 'The hypocrisies of society being what they are, I would normally be loath to reveal this. But with you, Fraulein Fleischer, I feel free to say so, as you so clearly believe the same.'

'I agree; gold is the only thing worth struggling for,' she said, a plan forming in her mind. 'But Mother Elsbeth's corpse isn't composed of it.'

'Ah,' said Udo, warming to his subject. 'Gold is a mere representation of a higher goal, the achievement of superiority over others. A man may be the most influential of priests, or born with the bluest blood in his veins, but when he must come crawling to me for a loan, he is the basest of beggars, and I – I am the man with the gold. But do you know what, Angelika?'

'No. What?'

'Believe it or not, I came to a juncture where I had as much gold as I could possibly use. All around me acknowledged my brilliance and acumen. Then I reached that most sorrowful of days, when the most recent bag of gold to cross my threshold seemed, for all intents and purposes, identical to the last.'

'Surely you were deluded.'

She jumped up to lob an imaginary object at him. And by the time he had fired his matchlock, she was already back down again. Curls of grey smoke wafted past her and her ears rang. Now Udo was down to one shot. Even in the hands of an experienced gunner, pistols like these took nearly a minute to reload.

'Did I hit you?' he asked, his voice raised to compensate for the damage he'd done to his own hearing.

'Sorry to disappoint,' she called.

She heard his shoes scraping her way. He turned a corner and now stood along the rug pile's southern edge. She in turn moved to its opposite side. They had exchanged positions. Lemoine lay directly behind her and if she dared to risk it, the door was back there too. She reconsidered her position. Udo did not seem especially proficient with his expensive weapons. It was possible, even likely, that she could make a break for it without getting herself shot. That, however, would leave the injured Lemoine behind, and herself no closer to her original objective.

'You were saying,' she said, 'that you lost your faith in money.'

'A man unanchored by eternal verity is lost. I did not undertake the trip to Heiligerberg merely to impress pious business acquaintances. I sought a new system of meaning, to replace what I'd lost.' He aimed his gun at a spot just above Angelika's head. 'I admit now that I felt utterly alone among the other pilgrims. I aspired to all their fine feelings. Yet, try as I might, I could not summon them. I pretended, Angelika, to be just like that quaking buffoon on the floor behind you, but could not do it.'

'Then you saw Mother Elsbeth's body.' Her fingers crept up, sliding surreptitiously beneath the top carpets on the pile, brushing under its fringed, silky hem. 'And you knew why you were there.'

'Yes,' said Udo.

Angelika moved her legs beneath her torso, coiling them. 'You were looking at a treasure infinitely more important than mere gold.'

'Yes,' Udo breathed.

'And your alliance with Ivo Kirchgeld – a momentary convenience?'

'Naturally. I'll dispose of him once I've got the relic safely stashed away. I think I'll have a secret crypt dug for her. I'll top it with a tower, perhaps. A pity no one else will know what's in it, but I will, and that's what truly counts, isn't it?'

'To be the one who has what everyone else desires.'

'Yes. Yes...' Udo intoned. 'You do understand me, Angelika.'

She nodded to Lemoine, who by crawling on all fours, had finally come within an arm's-length of her. He set the dagger, which he'd retrieved, on the floor beside her boot. 'And now,' she said, 'you're going to tell me what a pity it is you have to kill me.'

'I apologise for my predictability,' he replied.

She sprang up, taking the rug in both hands and flipping it out like a washerwoman folding a sheet. She swiftly brought it up into the air and then dropped it over Udo's head, blinding him. He fired his pistol, blasting a hole through the rug. It filled the air with a dust of atomised threads. Angelika swept back, took up the dagger, jumped onto the rug pile, dived on Udo, and stabbed. She stabbed and stabbed. Udo, still thrashing under the rug, sank down, his throat guggling, crimson quickly spreading through the pricey carpet.

Angelika kicked the rug aside to be sure he was dead. He was. She released it back over his surprised, frightened face. Backing up, she bumped into Lemoine.

'To think, we treated him like one of us,' said the monk, 'when, all along, his heart was a nest of churning vipers.'

'He gave greed a bad name,' shrugged Angelika. Her body quivered, as it sometimes did in the wake of sudden violence. She gripped the stack of rugs, trying to hide this embarrassing show of weakness. 'Where's Ivo?' she asked.

Lemoine touched his forehead, bloodying his fingertips. 'Gone to an abattoir near the piers. Ivo stopped here first, to get some guns Udo'd stored here. They were illegal, I gather.'

'Not to mention phenomenally rare and expensive. The Emperor prefers to keep powder weapons out of the hands of all but state forces.'

Lemoine retrieved his chair, threw the ropes aside, and sat, dropping his head between his knees. 'When they started speaking openly in front of me I knew they'd slay me, no matter what I told them.'

'What did they say?'

'The Chaos winds plaguing the city – Kirchgeld reckoned he knew who was responsible for them. The abattoir – it's a meeting place for Chaos cultists, he said. Followers of Tzeentch, the god of dark manipulations, he said. Though it seems to me that the creation of a pestilence is more the modus operandi of a different dread deity, Nurgle, the lord of decay–'

'Stifle the tangents, Lemoine.'

'Whichever god these cultists follow, whatever their ultimate allegiance, Ivo knew them from a transaction several months ago, when he tried to sell them a set of consecrated implements.'

'The alchemical equipment he stole from Heiligerberg the first time around.'

'These items, if desecrated, could then be used to great effect in certain dread rituals. But the cultists would not pay Ivo's price. As the negotiations dragged on, he came to suspect that they meant to kill him and take his goods. So he sold them elsewhere and thought little of it – until he got back to Averheim and found it gripped by this plague. Then he remembered his dealings with them and seemed quite delighted. He was hopping up and down, testing the firing mechanism of Udo's blunderbuss, practising his reloading. He also borrowed a hand-axe and chuckled as he swiped it through the air. I knew not what to make of it, except to shudder.'

'I know what to make of it,' said Angelika. 'Udo wouldn't have any other weapons stashed here, by any chance?'

Lemoine fell to his knees, clasping his fingers, shaking them beseechingly. 'I beg of you, Mademoiselle Angelika, there must be no more weapons! No more bloodshed!'

'I agree with the general sentiment, but there are particular persons who'll have to bleed copiously before this is over.'

'No, mademoiselle! Violence begets only violence!' His Bretonnian accent seemed thicker now that he was burbling and crying.

'If he had guns hidden here, I bet he had other weapons too. Where do I look for them?'

Lemoine wrapped his arms around Angelika's legs and held on tight. 'The world's gone mad! All thought, all reason, all analysis – pointless, utterly pointless!'

It suddenly dawned on Angelika that Lemoine was not staring blankly off into some religious haze, but that he had his eyes fixed on a real, concrete point behind her. Still clamped in his blubbering embrace, she turned to see a rumpled, disarrayed carpet on the stone flooring in a corner, about twenty paces distant. Extricating herself from Lemoine's scraped and clutching hands, she swept over to the carpet and yanked it out of place.

Lemoine wailed. 'Humanity is left with but one hope – utter prostration before the gods!'

Below the rug was a board. Angelika heaved it out of the way.

Lemoine's wounded face contorted. 'We must be scourged!' He pulled at his monk's shift, hauling it up over his head. 'The only blood we may shed must be our own!'

Beneath the board was a hidden recess in the floor. In the recess sat a large, wooden chest, its exquisite surface gleaming with thick layers of lacquer. Angelika hopped down into the recess, flipped up the chest's filigreed silver latches, and opened the chest.

Except for a linen wrap precariously twisted around his waist, Lemoine had stripped himself bare. 'Our only salvation,' he danced, 'is self-flagellation!'

The chest was full of guns, placed haphazardly, like pick-up sticks. Angelika whistled. Udo truly did have more gold than he knew what do with. On another day, she might have carted these prize pieces off for resale, but now she needed armaments she knew how to use. She dug through the rifles and pistols, tossing them aside without regard to their value.

Lemoine lurched to Udo's body, freed the dagger from the dead man's chest and, gritting his teeth, used it to dig a narrow slice across the length of his own pectoral muscles. Gobbets of sweat gushed from his pores, mingling with his blood. 'Sigmar! Shallya!' he screamed. 'Hear a sinner's humble plea!'

Angelika found a sabre for Franziskus, its scabbard dripped with silk tassels. She tore them off, set the sword carefully aside and then resumed her digging.

Lemoine dug another line in his chest, marking himself with an X. 'I suffer for you! I suffer for you!' He ran at a black-timber support beam, smacking his face into it. He fell back and flopped on the floor like an eel.

Angelika unrolled a supple sheet of leather the size of a washcloth, on which four thin, silvery daggers hung. She slipped a dagger from its leather slats, wrapping her fingers tightly around its blued, swept hilt. Immediately she could tell that it was a good, sharp blade. It seemed the right design for throwing, too. To test this hypothesis, she whipped it at the support beam Lemoine had just head-butted, using as a target the irregular blot of a bloodstain he'd left on it. The dagger hit the beam and vibrated proudly.

It had hit the spot precisely. Angelika crossed to the beam, circumnavigating Lemoine's wriggling limbs, and tugged the dagger out.

She stuffed it into the empty sheath on her belt and made to exit. But she hesitated. Something in the bottom of Udo's gun chest had caught her eye. She darted back over to the chest and took a careful look at an irregular bundle of raw tapestry fabric, which was loosely wrapped around an object a few inches in diameter, tied off with a strip of blackened leather. With the tip of her finger she gave it a cautious prod. Her head bowed down as queasy realisation dawned. She tore loose the leather strip, unwrapping the bundle. As she'd feared, it contained Mother Elsbeth's severed hand. An impulse made her touch it; its flesh was at least as fresh and pliable as it had been when she'd last seen it, attached to a living owner. In fact, a pleasant burnt sugar smell wafted from it. The touch of Elsbeth's hand suffused Angelika with a feeling of peace. She hastily got it bundled again, to block its influence over her.

Devorah had told her all about the hand incident, but Angelika hadn't expected to recover this particular bit of the abbess. She wondered what to do with it. She looked to Lemoine; could he be trusted with it?

Lemoine stood, unsteadily, and touched the welt rising in the middle of his brow. If he'd seen the hand, or understood its significance, he made no show of it. 'You must scourge yourself as well,' he told Angelika. 'All must scourge themselves.'

'I need you to do something for me,' Angelika said.

He held out clawed, palsied hands. 'The knife. Take the knife. Cut yourself. Cut me.'

'This is for Mother Elsbeth.'

He covered his face. 'She's dead. Dead. Our impiety killed her. Mankind's grossness and corruption and changeability–'

'Lemoine, concentrate.'

He lunged. She tripped him. He went ludicrously sprawling onto the floor. No, he was in no condition be a custodian of anything. Angelika moved to the stairs and headed up them.

'All must scourge themselves,' said Lemoine. He rose to take a second run at the beam, but collapsed before reaching it, and lay on the floor, weeping impotently.

THOUGH TIME WAS in short supply, Angelika had no intention of poking into a den of Chaos by herself. She ran back to the Blue Ball and found Franziskus sitting glumly on his own in a corner of the tavern. A dish of pork hocks had grown cold on a plate in front of him.

'The girl's upstairs?' she asked.

'Sleeping,' he said, turning his head listlessly toward her.

She tossed a sabre, liberated from Udo's weapon collection, onto the table. 'I need you,' she said.

He stood and took the sword. She detoured up to her room, where she hid the hand inside the straw of her pillow. It was not the best hiding place history had ever known, but at least there was no risk of the proprietors cleaning the bed-clothes.

A few minutes later, Angelika and Franziskus strode together through deserted midday streets. As they traveled, she told him where they were going, and why. He unsheathed the sword and tested its weight. 'A quality weapon,' he said.

'I'm sure Udo would be pleased by the compliment, if he were still around to hear it.'

They walked through the centre of town without further words. They reached its docklands district, which smelled of river and wet, rotting wood. Long, single-storey warehouses sullenly sat along dark, bowed piers, doors and windows shuttered tight. Indignant gulls patrolled flat storehouse rooftops, hoping that the workers would reappear to spill scraps of food for them. They screeched at Angelika and Franziskus, bobbing their heads in outrage when their plaints were ignored.

'You'd think a fellow would be cheerier,' said Angelika, 'after having had his first tumble since... how long have we known each other?'

Franziskus ground his teeth. 'If you're trying to make me angry, so I fight better, keep on going.'

'Oh, I understand,' said Angelika. 'She lacked accomplishment, between the sheets.'

Franziskus stopped, his expression hot. 'Not everything in this world is a joke.'

She softened her tone. 'I know that.'

He strode onward. 'A man can feel used, you know.'

'Forget I spoke.'

'Not everything is a joke.'

Angelika held up her hands, relenting.

Franziskus kept on. 'It was not me she wanted. Not specifically. I just happened to be at hand.'

'Couplings of convenience are not to be underestimated. Some of my most satisfying times have been–'

He clapped his hands over his ears. 'I will not hear this!'

Angelika shrugged. 'If you don't want cheering up...'

'I shouldn't have given in. I wronged her, and I wronged myself.'

'You can't expect me to hold my tongue, if you persist in saying things like that.'

'I had a duty to Shallya to refuse her.'

Angelika paused to adjust the dagger in her right boot. It was a little sleeker than the ones she was used to, and kept slipping out of place.

'And also,' said Franziskus, 'I think she may be manipulative. And of a changeable nature. I'm not sure I even like her.'

'Some of my most satisfying times have been with men I didn't even–'

'Maybe, when I have been at this life as long as you have, I'll have succeeded in making myself heartless, too.'

Angelika laughed. Franziskus's expression darkened.

They found two ordinary, working slaughterhouses before they located the one they sought, at the end of a street of decaying buildings. It was a low-slung structure with a bowed roof, plaster falling from its walls in pancake-sized chips.

'Notice something different?' asked Angelika.

'What?'

'To be specific, the lack of something? Listen.'

Franziskus listened. 'The winds have died down.'

'Right. The howling has stopped. And if there was any truth to Lemoine's story, and these cultists of Ivo's brought them into being...'

They circumnavigated the building, squeezing through a tiny space between it and the decaying tenement next door. Behind it they found a back door, unpainted and scored by woodworms.

'Do we talk our way in, or fight?' Franziskus whispered.

'A moot question, I think.' Angelika put an ear to the door. 'I hear no one.'

Franziskus kicked the door in; it fell satisfyingly to pieces beneath his boot.

Sun streamed into a large stone chamber, stacked high with sheets of quarried granite. The fallen door displaced clouds of fine, sandy dust that rose to fill Franziskus lungs. He doubled over, coughing and shielding his eyes. Angelika waited for the dust to die down and stepped into the room, moving to a workbench loosely strewn with stone-cutting tools. She picked up a mason's chisel.

'Not the equipment you expect to find in an abattoir,' she said.

Franziskus tried vainly to lift one of the stone slabs stacked near the doorway. 'You recognise these stones, don't you?'

'They are identical to those on Manfried's cathedral.' Angelika crossed the room, to a wooden shelf structured like a wine rack, with half a dozen long, narrow openings on each of a dozen shelves. Inside about a third of the openings sat either scroll cases, or large, rolled-up sheets of parchment. She pulled out one of the sheets, untying a small piece of dirty twine. When unfurled, the parchment contained a crude sketch of an architectural plan.

'A section of the cathedral?' Franziskus asked.

'I'm no builder, but I'd lay a hundred crowns on it.' Angelika squinted at the parchment, turning it sideways.

'So Manfried had a nest of Chaos worshippers helping to finish his family's cathedral?'

'Not knowingly, I'm sure. These maggots live by trickery.'

'What do the cultists mean to accomplish?'

'What do they ever mean to accomplish?' Angelika tossed aside the parchment she had in her hand and popped open the nearest scroll case. 'Think like a slavering, slack-jawed minion of Chaos. What prize would be so important that you'd get off your robe-wearing posterior and give up all your chanting and blood sacrificing in order to undertake genuine, backbreaking labour?'

'A chance to sabotage the cathedral. A secret entrance, perhaps?'

'My money's on a secret tunnel into the basement.' Angelika pitched another plan over her shoulder. 'Curse it, this one's just a staircase.'

Franziskus joined in the search, plucking another tube of parchment from the rack.

Flies, buzzing and iridescent, zigzagged in through the open doorway.

Angelika took hold of the most striking scroll case: an ivory tusk carved with orgiastic figures. She unscrewed its cap. It was empty. 'And I'll bet you a second hundred crowns that this case used to hold the plan we're looking for – the one that shows their secret entrance.'

'Why would they leave an empty case?'

A small swarm of flies had materialised, each member butting its mindless insect head incessantly against a small wooden door in thr room's furthest corner. Angelika nodded once; Franziskus stepped over to it and shoved it open.

It opened into a small, shadow-strewn chamber. Murdered bodies lay strewn about it. Other flies, already inside the room, were hard at work, flitting from corpse to corpse, laying their eggs. Their colleagues hummed in to join them.

The dead numbered seven in all, five men and two women, all robed in coarse burlap decorated with strange sigils, which Franziskus and Angelika both took to be occult signs. Many had been torn apart by gunshots but most had been finished with sword blows to the head and neck. Under their bodies, Angelika could see a pentagram incised in the floorboards.

A pile of skulls – mostly of cattle, but with a few humans, and even that of a man-sized rodents, thrown in for good measure – sat atop a crude wooden altar. Franziskus made the sign of Sigmar and hesitantly approached it. Angelika marched right up.

A length of thin copper chain dangled from the altar, fastened to its surface with an eye hook. Angelika examined its last link, which was broken. She took a close look at the darkened oak panel that served as the altar's top. She pointed, showing Franziskus the dark brown dots that spattered its surface. 'Dried blood,' she said.

Franziskus's complexion betrayed his nausea. 'I shudder to imagine how many sacrifices have taken place here.'

'But look at this spot in the middle – there is not a speck on it.' Angelika indicated a rectangular shape, about three feet wide by one foot high. 'Something used to sit here, while the blood sprayed.'

'The space is shaped like a book,' said Franziskus.

'Ivo Kirchgeld did this. He knew about the cultists and their secret entrance. He came here and dispatched them, stole the map to their tunnel and a book from their unholy altar.'

They contemplated the implications of this. Flies feasted.

'Franziskus,' she said, 'I think this bodes ill.'

As THEY RUSHED from the abattoir, Devorah stood, a good mile away from them, in the cathedral square. She wore a simple shift she'd borrowed from the tavern keeper. Devorah nervously patted it down, straightening a line of fabric that bulged across her curving hips. She looked up at the line of Sigmarite warriors arrayed on the temple's great staircase. She pulled her fists tight and swallowed her fear. Stepping quickly, she glided over uneven cobblestones to shudder open the heavy wrought-iron gate leading to the cathedral grounds. Its creaks brought her the immediate attention of the soldiers above.

# CHAPTER TWENTY-FOUR

FATHER EUGEN'S EYEBROWS knitted themselves together. He rubbed his hands as if he were cold. He shifted his head from side to side. Then he patted the top of his head, pushing down a thick mat of dark, wire-brush hair. 'Well truly,' he said. 'Truly indeed.'

He stood before Devorah, inside the cathedral, on the lacquered wooden tiles of a private chapel built for a wealthy family: the Abendroths. They would take possession of it after the consecration ceremony. The pater- and materfamilias of the Abendroth family would get to meet the Grand Theogonist, when he arrived. But for now the chapel was empty and it was as good a place as any for Eugen to speak to the young girl. She sat on an oaken pew, gazing up at a colossal marble statue of a grimacing Sigmar, his crushing hammer held aloft. A wretched minion of Chaos was planted beneath the tread of his relentless boot. Stained glass in the tall windows above placed diffuse patches of coloured light on the girl's white garment.

'Well truly,' Eugen repeated. The girl's eyes glittered at him. They made him wonder what it might have been like, to have trodden a different path, to have had a daughter.

She'd started talking again, he realised. 'So you will act to help me – Mother Elsbeth, I mean.'

Eugen had left too long a pause. 'Ah,' he said. 'Ah. You do make a number of persuasive points.'

She leaned close to him. 'It is not the usual thing, is it, for temples to Sigmar to contain the bodies of devotees to Shallya?'

Eugen swayed back a step. 'No, indeed, it is not usual. Though I can see the justification for it. All the gods of life and virtue are on the same side, after all, arrayed against Chaos. And if Elsbeth's weary bones can act as a bulwark–'

Devorah took hold of his oversized hands. Her porcelain skin was too soft and delicate for Eugen's liking. He could see why poor young Manfried had been stricken by the girl's beauty and purity. His protégé was a young man, his veins charged with warrior blood. A creature like this could easily, without even trying, wrench him from duty's path.

'But it is not usual,' she pressed, 'and moreover, Mother Elsbeth herself forbade this. By installing her in this temple, against her will, might you not turn her blessing into a curse?'

Eugen backed into an exquisitely carved rail of gleaming rosewood. 'Yes, yes, that point struck me as telling, when you made it before,' he said. 'I will argue it with all possible vehemence when next I speak to Manfried.'

She clutched his forearms, backing him completely into the railing. 'You mustn't!' she wailed. 'You must do this on your own, without telling him!'

Eugen's spine stiffened. 'Young woman,' he said, 'I may have trained Manfried, and I am lucky to say I still have his ear. But he is my commander; not I, his.'

Devorah inched closer. 'Your care for your student reverberates in every word you say about him. You must know he's headed for perdition! Madness and pride eat at him, as a flame slowly licks a log of wood into ash and charcoal. You must do your best to steer him straight again!' Finally she backed away from him; Eugen sat on the front pew and sank his head into his hands.

'You speak with insight,' he glumly moaned. 'You have indeed inherited her grace's voice.'

'Don't say that,' she whispered. She wiped her eyes. Then her chin jutted out, as she recaptured her composure. 'You know, it isn't safe for me to be here. And the two guides who brought my party to Heiligerberg – Angelika and Franziskus.'

'The ones who helped Elsbeth to die.'

Devorah let the tears pour down. She took to her knees before the curly-haired priest. 'I was with them for weeks. They are unpredictable, resourceful, ruthless. And they intend to take her grace – by violence if need be. You must avert this and have her smuggled out peacefully.' She swept an arm to indicate the cavernous nave of the great cathedral, its elephantine columns, its gilded archways. 'Otherwise blood will be spilled here, I am sure of it. And even a warrior like Sigmar cannot want this, not in his own holy house, just as it is to be consecrated!'

She waited to see the effect of her speech on Eugen, but he seemed stunned by it, which was not the precise result she'd hoped for. Then she realised that he was gazing behind her. She turned, but not in time.

Manfried seized her from behind, gripping each of her wrists in a big, bony hand. He bent down, touching his weathered cheekbone against the side of her face.

'I thought you'd come here to plead for your predecessor,' he said, 'though I never imagined you'd show the perfidy to try to set my truest friend against me.'

Eugen rose, his face flushed.

Manfried turned, minutely examining Devorah's face, as if searching for imperfections. 'Nothing worth taking comes without struggle,' he said, 'but you will be brought to heel. And made to *heal*.' He paused to savour his own wordplay.

Eugen became intensely interested in the condition of his shoes.

'Whether or not either of you likes it, you and Mother Elsbeth are indispensable assets in our war against Chaos,' Manfried said. 'You will fight that battle here, in my spiritual fortress, under my command. Do you comprehend me, girl?'

Still on her knees, she grinned up at him, with a smile twisted at the corners. 'I have quit,' she told him.

'What?'

'I have sullied myself.'

Manfried seized her by the elbow and hauled her up to face him. 'What do you mean?'

'High priestesses of Shallya must love only the goddess,' she said. 'Need I spell it out?'

Manfried raised a hand to smack her, but he caught Eugen giving him a reproachful look. He turned away from her. 'With the blond mercenary?' he asked. He held up a hand to forestall her answer. 'No. I am better off not knowing.' He whistled up his guards. 'Find a place to store this one,' he said. 'We'll see later if we can't return her to her original, useful condition.'

FROM THE NORTH of the city came the lowing of distant horns. On the streets of Averheim, the people looked up. For the first time since the arrival of the Chaos winds, ordinary citizens had found it safe to venture past the thresholds of their homes and hovels. Housemaids scuttled through the streets on errands for their masters. Merchants took the shutters off storefronts. Farmers drove pigs and sheep through cobbled streets, to meet their butchers. Drunkards found their way to jugs of ale. Now all were stilled as the horns grew slowly closer, soon to be joined by the rattling of

382          *Robin D Laws*

martial drums. Averheimers traded questioning
glances; what did this portend, exactly? Mothers
pulled children nearer. Men checked their belts,
taking comfort in the nearness of their weapons.

Barefooted children came pounding through the
street, calling out the news. 'The Theogonist is here!'
The shout went up, travelling from balcony to balcony, from window to window. 'The Theogonist has
come!'

'Our prayers are answered,' some breathed.

'Finally,' other tongues wagged. 'He should have
got here sooner, when there was still a Chaos plague
to banish.'

The procession lumbered carefully across the
main bridge over the River Aver, and into town,
where it trundled majestically down the city's central thoroughfare. It was a messy column of men,
beasts and conveyances. At its head rode a lector on
a mule, holding aloft the pieces of a mended shield,
as Sigmar's bearer, Tobias the Humble, had done
nearly twenty-five hundred years before, at the Battle of Unberogen Hill. In the lector's wake hovered
an agitated young squire, equipped with a long-
handled silver shovel for the immediate scooping of
any mule droppings that should happen to fall at
his pointy-shoed feet. Then followed a full company of Sigmarite warrior priests, three hundred
men in all, their armour polished, their hammers
proudly poised above their heads, ready to smite
any Chaos creatures that might lurch their way.
Behind the priests came the banner-bearers, waving
flags commemorating the great victories of divine

Sigmar, and of the most famous inheritors of his mantle. Then the trumpeters marched, bow-legged, blowing into their serpentine instruments, each a monstrosity of brass modelled after the famed and magical horn of Sigismund. Then the drummers, then a covey of older priests, too feeble to fight, swinging censers, wafting blessed smoke to billow down Averheim's streets. Behind them came the squires and altar boys, young men in training to become tomorrow's warrior priests, if there was to be a tomorrow. They wore white tunics and dark red stoles; they scattered rose-petals on the paving stones. Some chanted in eerie countertenor voices.

Giant wooden wheels, bound in ancient lead, rolled forth, crushing the rose petals laid out before them. Now came the most awesome component of the procession: the Imperial war altar. Pulled by a pair of barded, caparisoned warhorses, thick of haunch and wild of eye, it creaked and rolled, axles groaning to support its four crunching wheels. At the back of the cart loomed a bronze statue of a screaming griffin; it held a mammoth warhammer clutched in its inhuman claws, and a spectacular cape of feathered wings rose up behind it. In the centre of the cart sat the stone altar where Sigmar, when still a mortal, was pronounced king, and later crowned Emperor. It stood but a few feet high, solid and grey, sculpted with arches and relief figures, marked out in fresh red paint.

The people of Averheim lined the edges of its great central laneway, pushing and jostling for a glimpse of the ineffable artefact. Fathers told sons that they

would never again see an object so important. Sons
squinted to understand why the altar mattered; then
gazed upon it, and understood.

'Hmp,' said Angelika, as she watched the procession enter the square and circle around to the
cathedral gates. 'It's not even made of gold.'

Franziskus elbowed her in the ribs. They were part
of a quickly assembled throng. 'Easy on the blasphemy,' he whispered into her ear.

'That's the Grand Theogonist?' She sounded
unimpressed.

On the lip of the cart, shoulders staunchly level,
jaw grimly set, glowered a man of average height,
weighed down by a solid seventy pounds of ceremonial garb. A crescent collar rose like a halo
behind his round, white-haired head. A phoenix
breastplate spread its wings across his chest, the tips
of its jade wings obscuring the lower reaches of his
face. Emerald robes, their hems burning with brocaded flames, flowed all around him, shaping his
form into a cone. With a quivering arm, he thrust
skyward a titanic sceptre, its pale wooden haft bearing the blessed name of Sigmar.

Angelika sidestepped a young, dirty-faced girl
who intended to push her way between her legs. A
fat burgher shoved her back. A hand appeared on
her shoulder.

She looked back, then down a bit. It was Richart
Pfeffer. 'Someone wants a word with you,' he said.


MANFRIED HAUPT STOOD on the cathedral steps.
Arrayed around him were his erstwhile rivals, the

men who'd engineered his banishment. Fat-jowled
Father Erwin had informed on him to the Theogonist, when he had been foolish enough to waver on
the issue of heresy. Father Varl, thin-lipped and
petty, who had never tired of drawing unfavourable
comparisons between Manfried and his father and
grandfather. Dear old Father Wechsler, his mouth
wide as a toad's, had not acted against Manfried, but
then again, he hadn't been of much positive use,
either. And, at his very right hand, Manfried's chief
rival, the corpulent, brandy-breathed Father Ragen,
suffered and grumped. Ragen had been behind all
of it. He had very nearly had himself installed as lector of this cathedral. But then he had not brought a
relic so fresh and potent as the body of Mother Elsbeth. He had not secured any relics at all. And now
he was doomed to a career of submission to Manfried's boot. Manfried smiled at him: Ragen blinked
blearily in return. Manfried had a detailed list of
humiliating tasks prepared for Ragen and his
cronies.

As his loyal warriors drew back the iron gates to
admit the Theogonist's procession onto the temple
grounds, Manfried's heart thudded, in delirious joy.
He looked for Father Eugen, then remembered he
was occupied elsewhere, preparing the Theogonist's
quarters. Poor planning, really: no one had more
right to gaze upon him in his triumph than good
old Eugen. Manfried would make it up to him – he
would assign him the lavish apartments Ragen now
tenanted. Manfried chuckled. He bounded down
the steps to shake the mailed hand of Esmer, Grand

Theogonist of the Empire, prince of the church, the earthly avatar of divine Sigmar himself.

A WORKER HAD left a pickaxe in the hollowed catacomb beneath the cathedral; Angelika picked it up and whacked its haft against the stone, searching for the hollow reverberation that would signal a hidden tunnel on the other side.

'I'm very sorry to rush you, but there's no time for that,' said Eugen, who fretted at the foot of a narrow stone staircase. It led up two dozen-feet to a small door of newly painted pine. 'I'm supposed to be seeing to the Theogonist's living arrangements.'

'You have a right to fret,' said Angelika. 'I understand the risk you took, sneaking us in here.' She moved a few steps along the wall, and again whacked it with her pick handle. Tiny chips of rock flew from the point of impact, but the wall sounded good and solid. 'But the Theogonist might not be in need of living arrangements of any sort if Ivo Kirchgeld bursts through his hidden entranceway and does what I think he's going to do.'

They were gathered in a largish chamber beneath the cathedral's nave, hewn from rock and lined with marble shelves, on which the caskets of wealthy donors would some day lie. The shelves lined three of four walls, stacked six high. Manfried had made provision for a great many benefactors. Angelika leaned in across a shelf to tap at the wall behind it. Nothing.

Franziskus slipped the tool from Angelika's hand. 'Heed him, Angelika. As vile as he may be, Ivo

Kirchgeld is no more than a distraction to your true aim.'

Richart who stood a few paces behind Franziskus, stoutly crossed his arms. 'I'll take care of Kirchgeld.'

Angelika cocked her head at Father Eugen. 'And Manfried – you consider him your protégé, you say?'

Eugen could not meet her eyes. 'As a son, since his father passed away.'

'Explain to me again why you're betraying him.'

Eugen's gaze returned to the door, as trumpets blared above. 'I am saving him, just as you intend to save Mother Elsbeth. Perhaps it would not be such an odd thing, to inter a Shallyan holy woman in a Sigmarite temple – if it were done for righteous reasons. Manfried, though, has given into his pride and his vengefulness. This place of worship would be forever blighted if such motives were consecrated along with its altars and fonts. That's why you must take the body far from here – so that this church may be a true beacon, and that Manfried may return to the path of selflessness and sacrifice.' He cleared his throat. 'It was the girl's words – no, her eyes – that convinced me.'

'Where is she?' blurted Franziskus.

Eugen tugged uneasily at the phoenix clasp that held fast the collar of his ceremonial cassock. 'Manfried will be introducing her to his holiness.'

'And when he does, you should act,' said Eugen. 'Young Devorah has a... mesmerising effect. She will rivet the attention of all. She is your distraction.'

'I don't care for this,' said Franziskus.

'He's coming in now,' said Eugen, ears perked. He mounted the first of the stairs. 'I must go to join the ranks. Wait until the line's fully formed for his holiness's inspection. We'll be facing toward the altar and away from Elsbeth's crypt. The only one who might spot you is Esmer himself – and it's my understanding that the great vicar is... somewhat short of stature. It's my hope that those of us in the inspection line will block his view–'

'We know the plan, Eugen,' Angelika said. 'The key.'

'Oh yes,' said Eugen, nodding like a pigeon, as he fumbled in the front pocket of his blindingly decorated cassock. He found a small shiny black skeleton key and tossed it to Angelika. His throw fell short, causing the key to bounce off a step and onto the floor near Franziskus's feet. He stooped to take it. The thick-browed priest rushed up the steps, the heavy fabric of his robes fluttering like a flock of winging birds. Eugen heaved open the door at the top of the steps, leaving it slightly open.

Silence descended. Angelika regarded Richart. 'Don't you have to be up with the others?'

The short man snorted out a laugh. 'I'm no priest, let alone a grandee of the church.'

'You aren't going to be a problem to me, later?' she said, claiming the key from Franziskus. 'You were unhappy with us, when last we met.'

Richart's shoulder twitched dismissively. 'My hands have an appointment with Ivo Kirchgeld's throat.'

'Manfried pays your hire. He'll feel you ought to stop us from making off with his prize.'

'It's been a problem all my life – only being able to think of one thing at a time.'

Angelika crept up the stairs with Franziskus close behind her. Richart grabbed the pick handle and took up where she'd left off, tapping the walls.

Tensing her shoulders, Angelika pushed gently on the door, widening by an inch or so the space between it and the doorway. She exhaled, silently, thanking its hinges for staying quiet. Peeking out, she saw a line of priestly backs pointed at her, some clad in plated armour, others in colourful cassocks like Eugen's. There must have been three or four dozen of them, more than a hundred paces to her right. About eighty paces to her left, a raised dais displayed a sarcophagus of lead and crystal, in which Elsbeth's body stretched out in deathly repose. It was draped in a rich blue silk she'd never have worn in life.

Angelika watched the backs of their heads, which moved almost imperceptibly, in unison, following the approach of a figure that remained unseen to Angelika, except for the top of the staff he carried. The Theogonist. Now was the time.

Franziskus clutched her shoulder. A young woman in a sister's habit stood in the middle of the line. The priest beside her – the confidence of his carriage identifying him as Manfried – stepped from the formation, pulling her reluctantly with him.

'Devorah!' Franziskus said.

Ignoring him, Angelika embarked on a crouching sprint, heading away from the array of priests and lectors, toward Elsbeth.

Franziskus stood frozen in the doorway. His head turned to Angelika, then to Devorah, then to Angelika.

THE UNHAPPINESS OF Esmer, the Grand Theogonist, always manifested itself in the form of phlegm that clogged the back of his windpipe. This, he supposed, was why some of his erstwhile colleagues, now inferiors, referred to him, behind his back, as phlegmatic. And as this Manfried fellow, the ambitious man who he, Esmer, sight unseen, had elevated to this important lectoric, broke from the line of inspection, to present an unexpected thing to him – an unexpected thing in the shapely shape of a young woman in a sister's habit – the ball of phlegm increased suddenly in size, so as nearly to choke him. Esmer hocked to dislodge it. But his attempt gave rise to a rasping, guttural crack that was magnified to a humiliating degree by the cathedral's merciless acoustic.

In short, the Grand Theogonist was displeased.

Esmer – a wrinkly, stubble-headed man cursed with pudding-soft features that he laboured mightily to harden, practising daily before a shining mirror – advanced on Manfried and the unknown girl. The fabled robes and accoutrements of his office fought to impede him, but Esmer charged on all the same. He paused to clear this throat again, and in this brief moment, Manfried, obliviously smiling, inserted his words of introduction.

'Your divine grace,' Manfried began, 'I beg the indulgence of a small surprise. This is–'

'Haacccck,' interrupted Esmer, completing the clearing of his throat.

'This is–' Manfried continued, slightly discomfited by the sounds emerging from his pontiff's larynx. 'Permit me to introduce to you a puissante new ally in the battle against Chaos, the heir to the legendary healing gifts of–'

'I am here against my will!' Devorah cried.

The Grand Theogonist reared back, unbalanced by the weight of his jade phoenix breastplate. His throat-blockage expanded exponentially.

Manfried grabbed Devorah by the wrist. 'Graceless wretch!' he spat.

Devorah jerked on his offending hand, pulling it to her face. She bit him, drawing blood.

The line of priests and warriors broke. Some rushed to pull the girl from Manfried; others, to place themselves between this strange new threat and their Theogonist. Eugen edged to block Manfried's view. But Manfried spun and saw a figure hunkered at the foot of Elsbeth's sepulchre, working away at the lock that secured its crystal lid.

'Angelika Fleischer!' he screamed.

Franziskus ran three strides from the doorway then halted. He looked to Devorah, then to Angelika.

Behind him came a crash of collapsing rock. He heard Richart Pfeffer's piteous screams. Franziskus turned, into a billowing cloud of granite dust. An inhuman shriek emanated up from below, so piercing that he felt it in his marrow.

He swallowed and rushed into the dust, toward the terrifying cries.

Manfried ran at Angelika but Devorah jabbed a delicate leg between his, tripping him, sprawling him headlong across the cathedral floor. She fell, too, landing on his back.

Angelika's head darted back, to take in the commotion behind her. She twisted the key in the lock. It snapped. Cursing, she withdrew its twisted, broken end from the lock mechanism.

Franziskus bolted back down the narrow steps into the catacombs, stopping himself desperately short, almost toppling. The flooring of the catacomb level had collapsed. It gave way to an open maw of a hole, dozens of yards in diameter, revealing an entire second basement below it.

The new chamber was hard to see, amid the dust that filled the air, but it seemed roughly hewn, with a dirt floor and walls shorn up with bending timbers. A carpet had been rolled out in its centre, and on this plain white rug was marked a pentagram limned in a brownish dried-blood hue. On the edge of the carpet, Ivo Kirchgeld howled and gesticulated, reading from a hefty, yellowed tome bound in cracked and mottled leather.

Richart Pfeffer dangled from the bottom of the stairs, his fingers scrambling for purchase, his legs kicking directly above the sweeping claws of a horrible apparition that rose from the pentagram's borders.

The creature was ten feet tall and growing. Its screams emerged from a flattened, wide-jawed head that combined elements of bear and lizard. With a trio of long, multi-jointed arms, each of its seven fingers tipped with a dripping, dagger-like nail, it reached for Richart's frantic legs. A fat, warty belly jiggled over wide hips, from which flared stubby, toad-like legs. A tail lashed furiously. Ivo, still chanting from the text he held in his wildly trembling hands, ducked each of its swipes nimbly but nervously.

Franziskus covered his mouth, choking, as the beast's stench assailed him. Bulging warts covered the creature's hide. As it expanded, fissures parted on its flesh, exposing a layer of fungal black flesh, which then bubbled and fizzed until it hardened into leathery scar tissue. The thing was still gaining mass. It became eleven feet tall, then twelve, thirteen…

Finally swollen large enough to grab Richart, it did so, wrapping slimy fingers around one of his legs, and dashed him into the stone wall. It held Pfeffer's limp form in front of its face. It bit off his right foot, spat it out, then tossed him over its shoulder. Richart's body landed behind Ivo, who concluded his chanting, snapped the book shut, and dropped it unceremoniously at his feet. He grabbed Richart's head by the hair and bobbled it up and down like a puppet. 'You thought I couldn't, didn't you?' he yowled. 'Who's the fool now, hah? Hah? Who's the fool now?'

Franziskus ran down to the last extant stair, drew his sword, prayed to Shallya for protection, and leapt down into the hole, on a trajectory he hoped would bypass the creature's swinging arms and gnashing mouth.

Up on the cathedral floor, Angelika had her dagger out, using its pommel to smash the lock open. So far she had only bent its thick loop of metal shackle.

Manfried fought his way out of Devorah's restraining grip and up to his feet. He kicked her in the face, stunning her, he tore his warhammer from his belt and ran bellowing toward Angelika.

A knot of war-priests bunched themselves around the protesting Theogonist.

'Haacccckkk!' Esmer's phlegmy throat rattled.

Others, mostly Manfried's loyalists from his months of banishment, bolted after their commander.

In the basement, Franziskus bounced off the creature's back. It swam through the dusty air past him. He landed in the sub-basement beside Ivo, who still maintained his grip on Richart's head.

He raved: 'Finally, I'll be rich! Unimaginably rich! And can you stop me? You can't!'

'I can,' said Franziskus, slashing down at Ivo with his sabre. Ivo rolled under the blow, staggered back, ducked under a second sabre-swipe, and snicked his rapier from its scabbard. 'You've no cause to be butting in!' he protested. 'I don't even have a grudge against you!' He thrust at Franziskus with his sword tip. Surprised by the move, the young Stirlander barely managed to deflect it.

'Then why did you accuse me of your crimes?'

'I had to accuse someone, didn't I? To take personal offence is unjust!' He lunged forward with a
new vicious thrust. 'Besides, your partner – she kept
making sport of me!'

'I'll make more than sport of you, Ivo Kirchgeld!'
Franziskus exclaimed, pressing on with a new flurry
of wild swipes.

'Again,' fluted Ivo, 'what business is this of yours?'

Their swords smashed together, forming an X.
They pushed against each other, muscles straining.

'You're a minion of Chaos!' sputtered Franziskus.

'No, no, no!' rebutted Ivo, aggrieved. 'I just need
the diversion!' He kicked the legs out from under
Franziskus and whipped his sword down at him.

ABOVE, MANFRIED REACHED Angelika. She stood with
her back to the sarcophagus. She was crouching,
ready, with a dagger in each hand. Manfried was
bigger and stronger than she was, and he swung a
formidable weapon. One good hit could kill her.
She was faster than him – perhaps. It would be her
only advantage.

Oh, but wait. There was one other: taunting.

'You don't want to swing that now,' she said. 'And
risk smashing up your prize.'

He swung his hammer. She ducked. It banged
against the thick crystal dome shielding the holy
woman's body. A tiny crack appeared in the crystal.
Manfried swung the hammer again. Angelika rolled
acrobatically away from him. Springing back up,
she tossed a dagger. He intercepted its trajectory
with the haft of his weapon and then stomped after

her. She leapt up onto a pew, where she balanced, cat-like.

'These benches are expensive, aren't they?' she cooed. He charged her. She stepped onto the back of the pew behind her. He raised his hammer to smash through it, but reconsidered. Instead he rushed down to the end of the row. He looked back to see where his men had got to.

They engaged the Chaos daemon that had burst through the doorway to the catacombs, leaving a huge hole in the wall behind it. They thumped at it with their hammers, but it grabbed them in its arms and picked them up in its claws. It dashed heads against walls and lashed throats open with its razor tail. It stomped torsos until they squished.

Eugen joined a covey of lectors hustling the Theogonist behind the high altar. They cowered behind the rooster-like foot of a towering bronze griffon. Devorah hid behind them, at a remove.

'Truly, this is the end!' quailed a stalwart of Esmer's entourage. 'A daemon in a high temple of Sigmar!'

Esmer bristled and hacked. 'Idiot. It isn't a temple until I consecrate it!'

The offending functionary blushed and submissively bowed his head. 'I profusely apologise for any offence my ignorance has–'

Esmer smacked his sceptre on the floor. 'And if it was anything more than a lesser daemon, you'd be bleeding from the ears by now!'

'Of course, your holiness! A lesser daemon!'

'And I may have only recently been installed as Theogonist, but I'm still the living legate of Sigmar on earth and a lesser daemon is something I am fully capable of exorcising!' He aimed a stubby finger at a book, which rested on a stand about twenty feet away, on the cathedral pulpit. 'Get me that text, one of you!'

The assembled pontiffs of the church looked at one another, to see which of them would rush from hiding to seize the book.

ANGELIKA RAN FROM pew to pew, as Manfried raced along the rows.

'Don't you want to join your men, in battle with that thing?' she taunted.

'And leave you to steal the holy Elsbeth?' With his hammer, Manfried broke apart the pew she stood on. It sent her tumbling back and smacked her head on the pew behind her. He lumbered at her as she sat dazed on the floor. She recovered as he reached her; she lifted up her knees and caught him just the right way, using his momentum to hurl him over and past her. He crashed into the side of a pew. She dragged herself clear of the seating. To her left was Elsbeth's coffin. To the right was an exit onto the cathedral grounds. Ahead of her was the opening to the basement, where she presumed Franziskus was trapped. She ran that way.

THE WARRIORS BACKED the creature up against one of the cathedral's great columns, where it hissed and lashed at them. Some held it at bay with their hammers while others ran for crossbows and blunderbusses. The creature mewled and backhanded the column, shattering it. Stones fell, crushing warriors. The cathedral's domed roof groaned and shifted.

Eugen was the one to skitter up to the pulpit to get the Theogonist his book. He tripped back to his holiness and proffered the hefty volume. Esmer snatched it from his hands, wetted the tips of his fingers with his tongue, and flipped to the relevant page.

Manfried tackled Angelika, halfway to the catacomb door. She broke her fall with outstretched hands and rolled from the path of an onrushing fist. She kicked herself free, slashed her dagger across Manfried's forehead, and ran through the nearest doorway. She saw that she'd retreated into the entrance to a cathedral tower. She tried to duck out again – fleeing upwards was always pointless – but Manfried kept on her. She ducked a hammer blow. It loosened stones from the tower archway. He backed her up the stairs.

'Why thwart me in this way?' he cried, smashing down at the steps in front of her, forcing her to leap back and up. 'How do you profit from this, gutter wretch?'

That's it, she thought. Keep talking. Use up your breath.

'You think you are free to do what you want?' His wayward blow brought a banner down from the staircase wall and it fell onto him, giving her the time to turn and bound up several sets of stairs, increasing the distance between them. She turned and was ready by the time he'd untangled himself.

He panted. 'You are an outlaw. Perhaps your kind is, unlike the rest of us, truly free.'

She backed up the stairs. He paced her.

'But you cannot free Mother Elsbeth.'

Five stairs. She breathed. He breathed.

'She has a destiny.'

Six stairs.

'A responsibility, even in death.'

More stairs. Her backing up, him coming inexorably forward.

'She will meet it here.'

More stairs. More.

'Even if I must smack open your skull, to prevent you from troubling her any further.' Manfried roared and surged up at her. Twisting lengths of railing bounded the staircase as it spiralled up the tower. Angelica put a hand on each and tried to push herself up over him as he came at her, so she could get back on the other side of him. But he reached out to butt her with his hammer, knocking her against a wall. She fell against a stair. She felt a heavy blow land on her – a punch or kick, but not a hammer strike. He lifted her into the air.

BELOW, ESMER READ from the book, chanting the rites of abjuration. Stricken by Sigmar's power, the creature lurched across the cathedral floor, gripping another column, tearing it from its moorings. A ripple traversed the arched ceiling above it. A dozen Sigmarite gunners dropped to one knee and fired; a dozen shots hit the creature's generous target of a belly.

Further below, Ivo attacked and wheedled. 'Just surrender and get out of my way!' he told Franziskus, who had a leg bent behind him. He was struggling to bash aside Ivo's raining slashes. 'Hear that? I'm losing my diversion!'

Ivo's head turned a bit, to indicate the action on the cathedral floor above him. Franziskus took advantage: he directed a snapping blow to the wrist of Kirchgeld's sword-arm, then whisked the rapier from the false pardoner's twitching fingers. Ivo dashed to grab it up, but Franziskus leapt into his path and got the tip of his sabre under his enemy's throat.

'No,' Ivo pouted.

'Yes,' said Franziskus.

'But Franziskus, old comrade.' Ivo held out his palms, placating. 'I know you. You're too sweet and honourable to injure an unarmed man. Aren't you?'

Franziskus paused, relaxing his arm just slightly. Above him, the monster rallied, and the cathedral chorused with the final shrieks of dying men. Ivo attempted a mollifying smile.

Franziskus speared his sabre through Ivo Kirchgeld's throat, steadying it with both hands while he convulsed and died.

MANFRIED, ON THE tower steps, pressed Angelika against a stained-glass depiction of Sigmar's coronation day. Angelika kicked and writhed, but Manfried was too strong. He had one hand around her throat and the other firmly clamped on the top of her head. 'I'm going to snap your neck,' he told her. 'But first, you godless, interfering slut, you will acknowledge the supremacy of Sigmar!' His spittle sprayed across her upper lip. One of his eyes, injured by her slash to his face, had clamshelled closed.

Through one of the window's few fully translucent panes, Angelika saw Ivo's creature, leaking inky blood. It made one last lurch across the cathedral floor, bashing through the pews as if they were toothpicks. Esmer, sceptre raised, advanced on it, completing his holy imprecation.

Angelika pointed a hand around her throat, indicating her readiness to speak the surrendering words Manfried demanded of her. He moved his hand down to her tunic, which he grabbed up in a great bunch.

She spat in his face. 'I scrape to neither god nor man!'

He reached back for his warhammer.

The creature smashed into the base of the tower, tearing it from its foundations. As the tower buckled beneath them, Manfried was thrown into Angelika, pressing her into the window. Its frame twisted, exploding the stained glass portrait of Sigmar behind them to a thousand shards. Both Angelika and Manfried were cast out into the empty air above the cathedral floor. They fell, a wave of stone and mortar cresting behind them.

Manfried landed on the floor amid his slaughtered men. He hit shoulder-first, pulverising bone and pulping muscle. He had time to glimpse the decapitated head of Gisbert, or Giselbrecht, or Gismar, or whatever his name was, beside him. A shadow appeared over him; it was the rain of stone. Tons of granite hit the flooring, pummelling Manfried Haupt. They flattened his helmeted skull, and mixed his gore and tissue to those of his subordinates.

Angelika hit Mother Elsbeth's coffin with sufficient velocity to crack open its crystal casing, dislodging its lid. Her body struck it, then rolled to the other side, and fell onto its back. Her neck was broken, her organs ruptured, her lungs and oesophagus pierced by sharpened stakes of shattered rib bone. A spring of arterial blood welled up through her mouth. Angelika felt no pain; she only knew that she could not move, even to close her eyes.

Franziskus, climbed up through the wreckage of the basement, howling her name. He ran heedlessly past the jaws of the expiring Chaos beast, which was already desolving into a black, foetid dew.

ANGELIKA COULD TELL she was dying; she saw the shades of those she'd disappointed around her. All the pilgrims were there, crouching, peering down curiously into her ruined face. Waldemar, the summoner, blinked away tears of thwarted passion. Rausch, the physic, reached into his spectral bag of medicines and bone-saws. A mournful Friar Gerhold shook his head and closed its clasp. The Widow Kloster shoved both aside to get a better look. Prioress Heilwig took her by the collar and dragged her back, where the gnarled salt, Ludwig

Seeman, held her grudgingly by the shoulders. Jurg Muller's ghost, with an unwelcome arm slung around Stefan Recht, leered sardonically down at her, as if this was all a big joke, and an expected result, besides. Udo Kramer, still clutching his neck-wound, hovered at an abashed distance. The bailiff, Altman, had also separated from the others. His fatty face stiffening, he headed for the doorway to the catacombs, some urgent business on his mind.

Closest to Angelika, the old campaigner, Thomas Krieger, crouched.

'I forgive you,' he said.

'I don't need your forgiveness,' she said, through ghostly lips.

Krieger's ghost shook its head indulgently.

A light sprang up, blinding and white. The dead pilgrims parted. Mother Elsbeth shuffled toward her; it was she who radiated the light. Angelika squinted, but still she could see the holy woman, now looking young and fresh, all her wounds washed away, coming at her.

'Come with us now,' Elsbeth said. 'We'll take you to Shallya.'

'I scrape to neither god nor man,' Angelika said.

Elsbeth reached out her perfect hand for Angelika's broken one.

Franziskus skidded through blood and ichor, leaping over fallen stones, to get to Angelika.

Mother Elsbeth's corpse had been pushed over onto its side by the force of Angelika's fall. A wrinkled, deeply gashed hand dangled from the sarcophagus, over Angelika. She reached up to touch it.

Angelika's body shook. She died.

Franziskus reached her side. He took her up in his arms. He rocked her and bawled unashamedly. Franziskus felt a compulsion to let her go so he set her down gently on the floor, in her pooling blood, and wept.

Devorah, hidden behind the altar, peered out, features rigid. Her lips became a hard, horizontal line.

A SECOND SPASM bucked Angelika's corpse. Her ribs withdrew from her lungs and guts, and moved back to their designated places. They knitted back together; the punctures they'd left behind sealed up. Her torn heart rethreaded itself; her liver and spleen ceased their haemorrhaging. Blood reversed its flow, pulling muscles back to their previous tautness. A convulsive fist of breath unfolded itself inside her. Angelika coughed, shook, shuddered and lived.

Eugen tentatively approached the holy woman's coffin. While the corpse was busy healing Angelika, an inner light had shone from its chest. Now the body blackened, and wisps of sweet-smelling smoke curled from the sarcophagus.

Franziskus wrapped his arms around Angelika, but she squirmed her way loose. Pain descended. Before she passed out, she looked for the ghosts; they had all gone.

# CHAPTER TWENTY-FIVE

IT WAS A crisp early summer morning in the hamlet of Ruhgsdorf when, in the absence of a priest of Morr, Lemoine performed the final rites of memoriam over an unmarked hummock of grass, where Mother Elsbeth's body, its severed hand included, had just been interred. Ruhgsdorf was nothing more than a small cluster of buildings around an old mill. But its hills rolled, its birds chirped, and its grass was green. There were worse places for one's bones to moulder, Angelika thought.

She stood uneasily by the graveside. The last thing she wanted to hear was more praying and god talk, but without a good look at the final resting spot, she could not be sure that she'd won.

Franziskus was glued to her side, ready for her to succumb to a fainting spell and heave herself, helpless, into his arms. This had been a danger during the first few months of her recuperation, but no longer. She now felt whole again, or reasonably so. Her lodgings and nursing had been underwritten by the Sigmarite lectoric of Averheim; it was her opinion that the irony inherent in the arrangement had greatly hastened her recovery.

Lemoine concluded his prayers and stepped away from the grave. He carefully folded the liturgical stole he'd worn around his neck. He was clad in the simple muslin tunic and cotton leggings of an ordinary peasant. He had given up the cloth; this would be his last act as an ecclesiast.

He put his arm around Devorah. She had likewise given up her robes and wimple. Her peasant garb clung tightly to her, scooping flatteringly at the bodice. Lemoine kissed her temple. She hugged him tight. They walked in silence to a small farmhouse.

Richart lingered by the graveside, propped up by his crutch. His right boot concealed a false foot of oak, but he had yet to grow proficient in its use. He caught Franziskus's eye and gestured to the departing lovers.

'You can't win every battle,' Richart told him.

'Better him than me,' Franziskus replied.

'I've some brandy in the house.' Richart had been granted use of a small plot of nearby land owned by the temple, so he could keep an eye on Elsbeth's grave and see that no one pillaged it. Eugen, the new lector, had deemed this a wise course of action. He and the Theogonist had been in staunch agreement – to keep the body in a Sigmarite temple would be profoundly ill-fated, whether or not Manfried's cathedral was ever rebuilt. Since he was crippled, Richart would be unable to work the land, so he'd extended an offer to the former monk and former sister, to join him.

'I've an itch to keep moving,' said Angelika. Franziskus and Richart embraced. Her forbidding posture warded off any similar maudlin gestures.

A quarter of an hour later, Angelika and Franziskus walked by themselves, along a road.

'So,' said Angelika, breaking a silence. 'During the pilgrimage, did you see any hint at all that Devorah lusted for Lemoine?'

'Not one,' replied Franziskus, his tone carefully neutral. 'But then much of the time we were looking for a murderer. One can't notice everything.'

'She changed horses quickly, didn't she?' Angelika got no answer. 'It was funny, wasn't it? When he reappeared, claiming to be back to his rightful senses and retreated from the dread error of flagellation. I told him he'd never shown much in the way of rightful senses before and ought not to bother now.'

Franziskus seemed cheerless.

'And no sign of any miraculous healing powers,' Angelika continued, her tone unusually buoyant. 'That's a great relief to her, I'm sure.'

'Gifts from the mercy goddess ought not to be refused. Perhaps, though, there is some young novice at Heiligerberg who has become the new vessel of Shallya's compassion.'

'If there is, you can bet they'll keep it secret. They'll be glad to be rid of all those pilgrims.'

'You'll go on saying impious things all day long, if I continue to engage you.'

A russet-coloured cow regarded them blandly from a pasture, then returned to its chewing.

'She could have been yours, you know,' said Angelika. 'If you'd pressed your case, during my convalescence.'

'A man who must press his case is not truly wanted.'

'And her leap into Lemoine's bed – that just confirms that you were right all along?'

'I wish them well.'

'I think she was just trying to make you jealous, and is too proud to back down.'

'You have, I see, completely recovered your jaundiced view of humankind.'

'I bet, even now, if you went back and bent your knee, and spoke fine aristocratic couplets into her ticklish little ear…'

Franziskus shrugged. 'I have a new topic for us to discuss as we travel. Where are we headed, incidentally?'

'Where do you think the next battlefield will be?'

'My new topic is this: as someone would sooner be spat on than receive divine blessing, how did it feel to–'

'It's still you she wants, Franziskus.'

'How does it feel to be the recipient of a miracle?'

Angelika paused. She reached for her purse and clanked it. It was heavy. 'This is the miracle. That I get to finish one of our little enterprises with more gold than when I started.'

'You reached out for her hand, Angelika.'

'My vision was clouded. I thought the hand I reached for was yours.'

'Mine?'

'So next time, don't be so blurry.' She sped up. 'In my final moments, I don't want to be grabbing any old stranger.'

He moved in front of her, jogging backwards. 'Jesting aside, Angelika. What was it like? What did you see?'

'Nothing,' she said, marching smartly. 'Our senses were all addled by that creature's presence.'

They came to a bigger road; it gave them the choice of going either north, or south. She picked a direction at whim. Franziskus followed.

'It never happened,' Angelika concluded. 'None of it.'

## ABOUT THE AUTHOR

*Robin D Laws* is an acclaimed designer of games, perhaps best known for the roleplaying games *Feng Shui*, *Dying Earth* and *Rune*. He has also worked on computer and collectible card games and is currently a columnist for *Dragon* magazine. Just recently, Robin began working as a writer for Marvel Comics, including an *Iron Man* story arc and the upcoming miniseries *Hulk: Nightmerica*. *Sacred Flesh* is Robin's fourth fantasy novel.

# The first explosive Angelika Fleischer novel!

**WARHAMMER**

# HONOUR OF THE GRAVE

- ROBIN D. LAWS -

As the Empire's mighty armies clash against the rampaging hordes of evil, they leave in their wake the detritus of war, including the dead and the dying. Resourceful Angelika Fleischer ekes a living by looting the bloody battlefields, searching for the trinkets and gold carried by soldiers of all sides.

The bloody and gruesome Warhammer world is seen in its brutal glory!

**Available now from www.blacklibrary.com**

LET THE GALAXY BURN!

More Warhammer from the Black Library

# The Gotrek & Felix novels
## by William King

*THE DWARF TROLLSLAYER Gotrek Gurnisson and his long-suffering human companion Felix Jaeger are arguably the most infamous heroes of the Warhammer World. Follow their exploits in these novels from the Black Library.*

### TROLLSLAYER

TROLLSLAYER IS THE first part of the death saga of Gotrek Gurnisson, as retold by his travelling companion Felix Jaeger. Set in the darkly gothic world of Warhammer, this episodic novel features some of the most extraordinary adventures of this deadly pair of heroes. Monsters, daemons, sorcerers, mutants, orcs, beastmen and worse are to be found as Gotrek strives to achieve a noble death in battle. Felix, of course, only has to survive to tell the tale.

### SKAVENSLAYER

SEEKING TO UNDERMINE the very fabric of the Empire with their arcane warp-sorcery, the skaven, twisted Chaos rat-men, are at large in the reeking sewers beneath the ancient city of Nuln. Led by Grey Seer Thanquol, the servants of the Horned Rat are determined to overthrow this bastion of humanity. Against such forces, what possible threat can just two hard-bitten adventurers pose?